THE
WHITE
CROW

The Death of Colonel Mann

Murder at Bertram's Bower

THE
WHITE
CROW

A BEACON HILL MYSTERY

CYNTHIA PEALE

DOUBLEDAY

NEW YORK   LONDON   TORONTO   SYDNEY   AUCKLAND

PUBLISHED BY DOUBLEDAY
a division of Random House, Inc.
1540 Broadway, New York, New York 10036

DOUBLEDAY and the portrayal of an anchor with a dolphin
are trademarks of Doubleday, a division of
Random House, Inc.

Library of Congress Cataloging-in-Publication Data
Peale, Cynthia.
The white crow / by Cynthia Peale.— 1st ed.
p. cm.
1. Beacon Hill (Boston, Mass.)—Fiction. 2. Brothers and sisters—Fiction.
3. Boston (Mass.)—Fiction. I. Title.
PS3576.A74 W48 2002
813'.54—dc21
2001047359

ISBN 0-385-49638-9

PRINTED IN THE UNITED STATES OF AMERICA

March 2002

First Edition

1 3 5 7 9 10 8 6 4 2

FOR

ALEXANDRA

THE
WHITE
CROW

CHAPTER
1

IN A DARKENED ROOM IN A HOUSE ON LIME STREET, ON THE flat of Beacon Hill, Caroline Ames sat at a table clasping the hand of her friend, Dr. John Alexander MacKenzie, and tried to speak to her mother, who had been dead for a year and a half.

There were six other querants in the room. The medium, Mrs. Evangeline Sidgwick, was in deep trance. Her control, a temperamental entity named Roland, had spoken some minutes before in answer to a question—not Caroline's—but since then he had been silent for what seemed a very long time.

Caroline shifted in her chair. Her back itched just below her waistline, but her corset made the place impossible to scratch. The room was very warm—too warm, the windows closed and the curtains drawn against the bright May afternoon—and filled with a scent she could not identify: some heavy, musky odor that smelled the way she imagined incense might smell.

As if in answer to her movement, Dr. MacKenzie squeezed her hand. Impulsively she squeezed back. Improper, she knew, but she didn't care. Dr. MacKenzie, over these last months, had proved to be the best friend she'd ever had, and she realized she had grown perhaps too fond of him. What would she do if he decided to move on, to return to his position as a surgeon with the army in the West? Well, she would worry about that when it happened. For now—and particularly now, at this moment—he was here with her, and that was all that mattered.

It had been a daring thing to come here this afternoon. She'd had to swear Dr. MacKenzie to silence, make him promise not to tell Addington where they were going. Addington—her older brother, the guardian of her life—disapproved of mediums. Very probably he would have forbidden her to attend this séance today. In which case, she'd have had to engage in a deception even more blatant than the one she'd devised. We are going to walk in the Public Garden, she'd told him, such a lovely day, the first really good spring day we've had. He'd accepted it and gone about his business.

And now here she was, and after all her maneuvering, she'd failed. Her mother hadn't come through.

Dear Mama. Where was she? Was she happy? Busy about her work, up there in the ether or heaven or wherever she lived, now that she had passed over? Surely she'd gone to heaven, Caroline thought, where all good souls went.

She blinked back her sudden tears. Her mother's death had left a terrible emptiness in Caroline's life that hadn't eased until Dr. MacKenzie had come to board. She hadn't missed her mother so much these last months, and she knew that the doctor's presence in the Ames household was largely responsible for that.

But still, when the opportunity had presented itself to attend one of Mrs. Sidgwick's séances, she had been unable to resist. Mrs. Sidgwick was reputed to be the best medium in Boston, and Caroline had heard intriguing, even astonishing reports of her abilities to contact loved ones who had left the earthly plane.

Meeting her for the first time today, she'd been surprised, for the medium was a small, modestly dressed woman, soft-spoken, even seeming rather shy, nothing about her to make one suspect she had such extraordinary powers.

But despite her powers, she—or, rather, her control, that irascible "Roland"—hadn't managed to reach the late Mrs. Ames.

Other spirits, yes. Many of the people there today had had the satisfaction of speaking to their loved ones. Before the séance had begun, they'd gathered in this room and gotten to know each other a bit. That nice Mrs. Ellis, for instance, an elderly widow who said she'd been trying for years to reach her son, killed at Gettysburg. He'd come through for her loud and clear, with fulsome assurances that he was doing splendidly, no pain, no sorrow, living in harmony with the hundreds—thousands— of other spirits like himself, no bodily ills, choirs of angels . . .

And Miss Price, a fortyish spinster here to contact her brother, who had died years ago when they were children. Miss Price was still weeping now—weeping from happiness, they all understood—a full half hour after Roland had relayed her brother's message. Essentially it had been the same message as that of Mrs. Ellis's son: a happy existence on that ethereal plane, no troubles.

And Mr. Theophilus Clay, poor man, here with his daughter, both of them trying to reach the late Mrs. Clay, who had died, Caroline knew, a very painful death.

Although "poor man" was hardly the way to describe Theophilus Clay, Caroline thought, since he was not only one of the wealthiest men in Boston but also one of the most generous and therefore loved, a liberal philanthropist widely known for his good works. So he was rich in friendship as well as money, and not to be pitied.

Still. All the money and all the friends in the world couldn't bring his wife back to him, could they?

He sat on Caroline's left. He'd clenched her hand tightly as he'd asked his questions and Mrs. Clay had answered them through Roland She'd told him her agony had ceased and she was happier now than she'd ever been.

The late Mrs. Clay's sister was there as well, but her questions had not been answered. Caroline had heard the woman's voice choked with tears as she put her queries to Roland, but for some reason Mrs. Clay's spirit had chosen not to respond.

Despite that disappointment as well as her own, Caroline had to admit that it had been a successful—amazingly successful—afternoon. Whoever Roland was, he was very knowledgeable. He transmitted information that Mrs. Sidgwick herself could not possibly have known. She could never have studied up on the family histories of everyone there today to prepare herself, as some mediums, fraudulent ones, were reputed to do.

That Mr. Jones, for instance, sitting on Mr. Clay's other side. He was a small, nondescript-looking man who had mumbled his queries as if he had a speech impediment. But Roland had understood him well enough and had answered him promptly. Perhaps Roland had mind-reading capabilities and didn't even need to hear the questions spoken out loud.

No, thought Caroline, despite Addington's scoffing at mediums and séances and making contact with the "other side," this exhibition today was genuine enough to make a believer out of anyone.

She tensed. Mr. Clay's daughter was asking another question.

"Is Grandmama with you in heaven, Mother?"

"Yes." Roland's voice, coming through Mrs. Sidgwick, was deep and rasping, very different from the medium's own.

"Is Grandmama there with you now?"

"Yes."

"Might I speak with her?"

"I am here." A different voice, higher. The voice of an older woman? A grandmama, in fact?

"Oh, Grandmama, I am so glad to speak to you!" cried Clay's daughter.

"Good works."

"You mean—what Papa does?"

"Laying up his treasures for heaven."

Caroline heard Mr. Clay clear his throat as if he were embarrassed at this praise. Was "Grandmama" his mother or his late wife's?

"Oh, Grandmama! How we miss you!"

Clay's daughter had married a young man-about-town, dashing and handsome—a bit of a rake, some people thought. She and her husband were among the young fashionables, with a magnificent new mansion on upper Commonwealth Avenue and a lavish lifestyle that was looked down on, Caroline knew, by some of the older, less affluent Boston families. But the girl was Clay's only child, and he had always indulged her freely. Her coming-out had been the most extravagant that Boston had ever seen, and now she and her husband entertained regularly and expensively and traveled widely, with apparently none of Clay's concern for doing good.

"Grandmama! Are you there?"

No answer.

"Mama! Mama! Don't go yet!"

Caroline heard the girl's voice break. For a moment there was silence in the room as they all strained to hear, but Roland apparently had nothing more to transmit.

Then she heard a new sound, like a pencil scribbling and scratching, papers shuffling. She looked in the direction of the sound, toward the medium, but in the darkness she couldn't see anything. Amazing, how on a bright, sunshiny afternoon this room was as black as a moonless midnight.

They make the room dark so as to deceive their credulous clients, Addington had said, his long, lean face drawn down into an expression of disdain. If you go there, you can expect to see a glowing phantom appear. It will be the medium's accomplice, shrouded in a sheet covered in luminescent paint. You can expect to hear weird music coming from afar. It will be another accomplice, hidden away in the medium's cabinet, playing a harmonica. It is all a cheap carnival trick, Caroline.

Well, he didn't need to know she'd come. This would be her secret—hers and Dr. MacKenzie's, whom she knew she could trust. And in any case, none of those things Addington predicted had happened. There had been no glowing phantom, no music. Too bad she wouldn't have the satisfaction of telling Addington that.

The scratching stopped. Her neighbor on her left, Theophilus Clay, started and made a sound like a grunt, as if something had bumped into him. He kept hold of her hand, however, so she assumed he was all right.

From the place where Mrs. Sidgwick sat, Caroline heard a low moan, as if the medium were in pain. And perhaps she was, Caroline thought; who knew how these mental voyages into the beyond strained the physical body?

Another moan, louder. Then the door opened and the maid appeared, as if that sound had been a signal. Moving briskly around the room, she turned up the gas and twitched back the heavy draperies. Caroline blinked as her eyes became accustomed to the light. All around the table people were shaking their heads, unclasping each other's hands.

With a small final pressure, Dr. MacKenzie removed his hand from hers.

"Are you all right?" he said in a low voice, smiling at her. She'd been disappointed not to contact her mother, he knew; he hoped she wouldn't take it too hard.

"Yes. I'm fine."

As she spoke, turning toward him, she flexed her left hand to release it from Mr. Clay's grasp.

Mr. Clay's hand didn't move.

She turned to look at him as she pulled hers away, shaking it a little. Mr. Clay's arm dropped and fell straight at his side.

And then, to her horror, he began to tilt toward her, his rather heavy torso threatening to fall onto her, and it would have done so if Dr. MacKenzie hadn't quickly risen and stepped around to straighten him.

"What is it, Doctor?" said Caroline, not caring if anyone overheard her. "Is he—what's wrong?"

MacKenzie was grappling with Mr. Clay, fumbling with his cuff to get at his pulse, with his shirt studs to reach his heart.

Across the table, Clay's daughter sprang to her feet.

"Papa!" she cried. "What is it? What is wrong?"

Dashing to her father's side, she pushed MacKenzie away as she slapped at Clay's face and squeezed his hands. The other people in the room, not realizing what had happened, stared at her in amazement.

"Papa!" She was screaming now, shrieking and sobbing. "Speak to me! Papa! Papa!"

But she was too late. Theophilus Clay, who had apparently been too greatly excited at contacting the spirit of his late wife, had gone over to the other side to join her.

CHAPTER 2

"HE WAS DEAD, ADDINGTON! AND I—I WAS HOLDING HIS hand, and I never knew!"

It was evening, after a dinner Caroline had been unable to eat. She hadn't minded not eating; she was too plump as it was, and if she'd had the willpower, she would have fasted often. She reclined now in the parlor at No. 16½ Louisburg Square, her sweet, pretty face, ordinarily rosy with good health, still pale and drawn, her fair, curly hair escaping a little from its Psyche knot. Her feet were propped on the cricket before the fire. Ordinarily the Ameses stopped their hearth fires on the first of May every year, not starting them again until the end of September, but on this chilly night Ames had ordered that sea coal be brought and the parlor fire lit, as well as one in Caroline's bedroom.

Caroline had told him what happened at Mrs. Sidgwick's séance. She couldn't seem to stop telling it. Dr. MacKenzie hovered by her side, his broad, honest face a study in worry and concern. He was twisting the ends of his mustache—always, for him, a sign of distress. He longed to help her, but he didn't know how. Although he was a medical man, his entire experience had been with the army on the western plains; he knew very little about women, and nothing at all about their often mysterious vapors and swoons. And so now he could only stay by her, ready to offer brandy or *sal volatile* in case she fainted.

But to her credit she had not fainted—not here at home, nor at Mrs. Sidgwick's either. What a to-do that had been! In the immediate aftermath of the discovery that Theophilus Clay had died, old Mrs. Ellis had uttered a loud cry and had toppled from her chair, causing a little sideshow. Clay's daughter had carried on with her hysterics, shrieking and sobbing like a madwoman. But Caroline had been cool and clear-headed. She had gone at once to Mrs. Sidgwick, who, still weak from her exertions, had not at first understood what was happening. An ambulance, Caroline had said; we must send at once to the hospital.

Dr. MacKenzie had gently reminded her that the unfortunate Clay was beyond medical help; the police, he said, were surely the ones needed now?

Mrs. Sidgwick had a telephone. MacKenzie himself had placed the call; Caroline had heard him shouting in the front hall below. Clay's daughter had collapsed at her father's side while her aunt, Mrs. Briggs, tried to calm her. Mrs. Ellis had been cared for by Miss Price. Jones, the small, quiet man who mumbled, had moved from the table to sit by himself in a corner, his lips moving as if he were caught up in prayer.

Mrs. Sidgwick, after her first horrified reaction, had sat quite still, allowing Caroline to hold her hand but uttering no word. The maid who came in to open the curtains had retreated to the hall, where they could hear her sobbing.

"And then the police came?" Ames said now. He spoke gently, prompting her to go on because he understood that talking about it was helpful to her.

"Yes."

"But not Crippen?"

They were well acquainted with Deputy Chief Inspector El-wood Crippen, a fussy, officious little personage who got some things right but many wrong.

"No. Thank heaven."

Ames tolerated Crippen; Caroline disliked him; MacKenzie loathed him.

"And they went through some kind of pro forma interrogation?"

"Yes. Well, there wasn't much they could ask, after all. I mean, what could we tell them?"

"Heart attack, Doctor?" Ames asked MacKenzie.

"As far as I could tell, yes. I thought when I met him, before the séance, that he looked unhealthy."

"Poor fellow," Ames replied. "I hope he had his affairs in order."

"Did you know him, Addington?" Caroline asked.

"Not well. I've seen him occasionally at the Somerset."

That was one of Ames's clubs, a handsome granite neoclassical building on the rise of Beacon Street across from the Common.

"He didn't strike me as the kind of man who would go in for séances," Ames added. He gave his sister a look.

"I know you don't approve, Addington." She bit her lip; she was not in the habit of apologizing to him, and doing so came hard to her now. "And perhaps I was wrong to deceive you, but I so wanted to see if I could contact Mama." Her voice broke, and she turned away.

"I understand what you wanted, my dear." He didn't wish to bully her; she'd had a scare, and perhaps it had taught her a rough lesson. "And I was perhaps too harsh in my judgment of

Mrs. Sidgwick," he added kindly. "If it gives you some comfort to—but you didn't, did you?"

"Make contact with Mama? No." Suddenly she was very tired. "I tried, but she didn't—couldn't—come through. Although—"

"What, Caro?"

"That's odd. I'd forgotten all about it. Dr. MacKenzie, do you remember, just at the end, Mrs. Sidgwick seemed to be doing some kind of writing. And in fact I saw it afterward, when the lights came on—sheets of paper on the table."

"Writing?" Ames asked. "About what?"

"I don't know. I didn't examine it. Just scrawls. It looked illegible."

"Perhaps she was taking dictation from her control," MacKenzie offered.

"Yes. I'm sure that's exactly what she was doing. What are you smiling at, Addington?"

"I was thinking of the Oracle at Delphi. It is a wondrous place, Delphi, high in the mountains—a fitting place, near the gods, to receive a message from the beyond."

Ames was an amateur of archaeology, among other things. Several times he'd accompanied expeditions led by his former professors at Harvard. He'd traveled to Italy, to Greece, to Persia.

"The Oracle was always a poor girl from the village," Ames went on. "The priests would give her laurel leaves to chew, to intoxicate her. Then they would take down her babblings and transmit them, always suitably ambiguous, in perfect dactylic hexameter—Homer's meter."

"Are you saying that Mrs. Sidgwick may have been intoxicated, Addington? I can assure you—"

"No, my dear, I am not saying that. I am saying that like the

Oracle at Delphi, Mrs. Sidgwick may—wittingly or not—have been transmitting nonsense. Although not, I imagine, in dactylic hexameter. And if people want to deceive themselves by patronizing her, it is none of my affair. Poor old Clay got his money's worth, though, didn't he? He reached the other side with a vengeance." He just managed to keep from smiling; sometimes he had a rather mordant sense of humor, which he knew his sister did not appreciate.

"She is a private medium, Addington. She does not advertise, nor does she charge a fee."

"Hmmm. Then I wonder where she gets her living?"

"I so wanted you to be with us," Caroline added plaintively. "Not for the séance—of course not—but afterward, when the—when we found him. If I could have telephoned to you—"

She broke off. They had occasionally discussed—had argued about it, even—subscribing to the telephone, and although Caroline thought it a splendid idea, her brother had always said no. This was not the moment to take up the issue once more.

"I could have done nothing," he said. In an unaccustomed gesture of sympathy, he patted her hand. "You know that. And now—" The grandmother clock in the hall had begun to strike the hour: ten o'clock. "I suggest that you retire. You have had a shock, and you need a good night's rest. In the morning, all this will seem nothing more than a bad dream."

CHAPTER
3

HE WAS RIGHT. IN THE MORNING THE TREES IN THE SUNNY square bursting with greening spring, the birds in those trees singing loudly, the events of yesterday afternoon did seem far away, something like a dream that had—almost—not really happened.

To Caroline's surprise she had slept soundly, and now, standing before her dressing table, she smiled at her reflection. She'd just finished vigorously brushing her curly, light brown hair—her daily regimen, twenty minutes in the morning, ten at night. But when she sat down to complete her toilette, her smile vanished as something caught her eye.

Oh, dear. A white—no, a shining silver—hair, just above her right temple. Deftly, almost angrily, she plucked it out. Never mind about it, she thought. If too many white hairs appeared, she could always discreetly apply a little walnut water to disguise them, and no one would ever know.

In two days she would turn thirty-six. For some years now,

she'd let her birthdays pass without comment or celebration. She was an old maid—a spinster; she would be a spinster until she died. Once, years ago, she'd had a hope of marrying—had in fact fallen painfully, desperately, in love—but the young man in question had gone away without warning, without explanation, and she knew now that she would never see him again. She had taken back her heart, which she had given to him and which he had broken, and carefully she'd mended it to the point where she could live her life with some tranquillity and even happiness, but she had been careful ever since not to risk having it broken again.

Not that there was much danger of that, she thought as she began to dress her hair. Deftly she twisted it into a Psyche knot at the crown, secured the knot with three large tortoiseshell hairpins, and combed her fashionably frizzy bangs down over her wide, smooth forehead. No danger at all, in fact. Eligible young men looked mostly for young ladies with a fortune, or at least with some amount of money, and while the Ameses had been comfortable enough in Caroline's girlhood, they hadn't been really rich since their grandfather, a noted China trader who had built this house, had made his last voyage.

And then, ten years ago, she'd never known exactly how or why, they'd lost a good deal of what money they'd had. A confidence man named Chester Snell, who had had some connection to their father, had been tried for fraud and had gone to prison. Their father died shortly afterward, and finances were tight ever since. Dr. MacKenzie's seven dollars and fifty cents a week board money made a tremendous difference in the household accounts; over the past few months, she'd even been able to save a little nest egg in the porcelain box on her mantelpiece.

Dr. MacKenzie. She'd been dusting her face with rice powder—just a little, hardly noticeable—but now she stopped, her powder puff still clutched in her hand.

Dear Dr. MacKenzie. What would she have done without him yesterday afternoon? How calm he'd been, how reassuring. Of course, as a doctor he'd probably been trained to be calm and reassuring, but still. He'd been a brick. Had been a brick, in fact, ever since he'd first come to them to recuperate after an operation on his knee, and how grateful she was to Dr. Warren across the square for suggesting that she and her brother might be willing to take in a boarder.

Thirty-six in a few days. Well, and what of it? Thirty-six wasn't the end of the world. And certainly Dr. MacKenzie didn't seem to mind her age, if, indeed, he knew what it was. She looked younger than that, didn't she? She leaned forward, peering at herself. Yes. Definitely she looked younger than almost-thirty-six. Thanks to her daily applications of Balm of Iberia, she hadn't a wrinkle on her face, her complexion hadn't begun to roughen and redden, and her neck was still as smooth and firm as when she'd made her debut. Some women, she knew, used Laird's Bloom of Youth to preserve their complexions, but the chemist at Bright's Apothecary had warned her that Bloom of Youth contained a large amount of white lead, which was poison.

Nevertheless, this morning, in light of what had happened yesterday afternoon, perhaps she would allow herself just the faintest, lightest caress of one of the French rouge papers that she kept secreted at the bottom of her jewelry box. Just one dusting on each cheek, she thought, so she wouldn't look too pale in the harsh morning light at the breakfast table. She was sure Addington didn't know about her rouge papers, and because she didn't want him to find out, she always kept them hidden and used them sparingly. This morning, however, she wanted to look her best—yes, she admitted it—for Dr. MacKenzie. He mustn't think she was a weak, hysterical female. With practiced skill, she dusted the rosy paper once across each cheek. There.

She looked perfectly natural and, more important, perfectly healthy.

She sat back and folded her lips into a severe line and frowned at herself. Stop it, Caroline Ames. Men—even the best men, even the kindest, most dependable men—are not dependable when it comes to matters of the heart. Not unless they are chasing a fortune that you don't have, and in any case, Dr. MacKenzie isn't the fortune-hunting type. He lives on his army pension, and very possibly he is going to return to the army when his convalescence is over.

So keep your promise to yourself and don't put your heart at risk ever again. Enjoy his company for what it is while he is here, and prepare yourself for the day when he will leave.

Ten minutes later she found MacKenzie and her brother waiting for her at the breakfast table.

"Feeling better?" Ames asked, smiling at her as he looked up from the morning *Globe*.

"Much. You were right, Addington. It seems like a bad dream." She shuddered slightly. "What does the newspaper say?"

He arched an eyebrow. "What it does *not* say, I am happy to report, is that a certain lady from Louisburg Square was present at Mrs. Sidgwick's séance yesterday afternoon. They do give old Clay a good write-up, though. 'Philanthropist will be widely missed' and so forth."

Caroline was just giving MacKenzie his coffee when they heard the door knocker. What now? she wondered.

They heard Margaret, the maid, hurrying down the hall to answer, and after a moment, she announced their visitor.

MacKenzie's heart sank. Encountering Deputy Chief Inspector Elwood Crippen of the Boston police was unpleasant enough at any time, but encountering him before breakfast was well-nigh unbearable.

"Sorry, my dear," Ames murmured to Caroline. "I don't see how I can refuse him."

MacKenzie thought she'd gone a little pale. He didn't wonder; he felt pale himself. Before she could reply, however, Crippen was upon them.

" 'Morning!" he said brightly, nodding at Ames as he advanced to shake his hand, smiling at Caroline, and ignoring MacKenzie altogether.

Crippen was a small, graying man, his plump corpus nattily attired—too nattily—in a brown checked suit, bright yellow waistcoat, and loud green cravat. In one hand he clutched his brown bowler; in the other, a folded newspaper. It was not the *Globe*, Ames saw, but the rather more sensationalist *Post*.

"Sit down, Inspector," Ames said. "Coffee? Have you breakfasted?"

Crippen accepted the invitation to sit but waved aside any refreshment. "I'm an early bird, I've already eaten," he said, smiling more broadly and exposing a gap where his right incisor should have been. "And I don't mind telling you, I'm here to catch my worm, so to speak."

Since he was so obviously brimming with news, they waited for him to continue. MacKenzie thought about helping himself to oatmeal—the sole item, most days, on the breakfast menu—and decided not to.

"In fact," Crippen went on, "I'm here about a murder." Suddenly his ugly little face was no longer smiling, but stern—forbidding, even.

"Murder, Inspector?" Ames took a swallow of tea. "Whose?"

"Why, that gentleman who was with you yesterday afternoon, Miss Ames," Crippen replied, turning to Caroline. "Mr.—ah—Theophilus Clay. According to my men, you and him was at a—whatchamacallit."

"Séance," Caroline said. "A séance at Mrs. Sidgwick's. But, Inspector—"

"Right. Mrs. Evangeline Sidgwick. Lights went out, mumbo jumbo took place, and when the lights came back up, there he was. Dead."

MacKenzie wished he'd taken his oatmeal. He didn't particularly like it, but over the past several months he'd gotten used to it, and he felt now the need of a little sustenance for what was obviously going to be an unpleasant time with the inspector. He tensed as Crippen, who ordinarily refused to acknowledge his existence, turned to him.

"But not dead of natural causes," Crippen went on, his voice tinged with malice. "Not what someone there at the scene— someone who calls himself a doctor—said it was, heart attack or some such. No, indeed."

Caroline's hands had suddenly gone cold and trembly, and she refrained from lifting her cup lest she spill her tea.

"When my M.E. got onto it," Crippen said, "he found something very interesting. As is often the case."

"But—" Caroline began. In the face of Crippen's hostility, she wanted to spare Dr. MacKenzie further embarrassment. "Murder, Inspector? But how can that be? We were all there in the room with him—"

Crippen nodded. Carefully, precisely, he clasped his stubby hands and rested them on the snowy tablecloth.

"That's it in a nutshell, Miss Ames. How could it be? That gentleman, sitting there with all of you in that room, how could he have been murdered? In plain sight—"

"The room was dark," Caroline interjected.

"If Theophilus Clay was murdered, Inspector," Ames said, "may I ask what was the cause of death? Did someone stab him? As I understand it, there was no blood. Shoot him? No gun went off. How, then, did he die?"

Crippen narrowed his eyes. "Well, now, Mr. Ames, I don't mind telling you, it was a very clever trick. My M.E. is the best in the business—the only one in the business, pretty near, since most police departments don't have such a man; I understand that in Europe they're more numerous—but mine is the best, as I say, and even he was fooled at first."

With an elaborate gesture, Crippen unfolded his hands and pointed to his collar. MacKenzie noted with satisfaction that it was a cheap celluloid thing.

"Right here," Crippen said. "Hard pressure on the carotid artery. My man found severe bruises on the neck. It's an Oriental trick, I've seen it before. If you know how to do it, and if you're strong enough, you can kill a man in seconds. Quick and quiet, no need of a weapon."

There was a little silence as they absorbed it.

"But that means—" Caroline began.

"Yes," Crippen said. "It means—and I won't mince words, Miss Ames—it means that someone in that room got to him and did the deed. Did it quiet—so quiet that no one heard him—or her," he added. He had taken on a menacing air; MacKenzie was glad to see that she faced him bravely, not intimidated by his suddenly threatening attitude.

"Well, Inspector," she said, lifting her chin a little, "then I suppose you must begin your investigations."

"That's right, Miss. So I must."

"And you wish to know—?"

"Everything you can tell me."

She glanced at MacKenzie, who sat immobile. He wanted to warn her, but of what he wasn't sure.

"I can't tell you much, Inspector," she said, turning back to Crippen.

"Whatever it is, I need to hear it. You have known Mrs. Sidgwick how long?"

"I first met her yesterday afternoon."

"You never attended a—ah—séance with her before?"

"No."

"And when you went there yesterday afternoon, you met the others in attendance for the first time?"

"I went with Dr. MacKenzie, whom of course I know fairly well. I am acquainted with Mrs. Leicester—she is Mr. Clay's daughter. I know—knew—him also, although not well. The others—no."

Crippen flicked a glance at MacKenzie as if to say, I'll get to you in good time. "And you had the opportunity to speak to all of 'em before the—ah—proceedings began?"

"A little, yes."

"Anyone seem ill at ease? Upset?"

"No. One of the ladies—a Mrs. Ellis, I believe her name is; she is elderly, rather frail—seemed rather nervous. She was trying to contact her son, who was killed at Gettysburg."

"My men tell me you was all sitting around a table, holding hands."

"That's right."

"And whose hands were you holding?"

"On my right—Dr. MacKenzie." Again that hostile glance flicked at MacKenzie and coming back to her. "On my left—Mr. Clay."

"The deceased."

"Yes."

"You did not see or hear or—ah—feel anything unusual? Aside from—what is it she does, exactly? This—ah—medium?"

"She tries to contact those who have gone over to the majority, Inspector."

" 'To the majority.' Well, that's one way of putting it, I suppose. And did she succeed?"

"For some people there, yes."

"For you?"

"No."

"You were trying to—ah—contact who?"

It was obvious that Inspector Crippen had no more use for mediums and séances than Addington did.

"My mother."

"Did you do it?"

"No."

"And this business went on for how long?"

"I'm not sure. About an hour, I'd say."

"And at the end of it, you were holding Mr. Clay's hand—"

"As I had done throughout."

"As you had done throughout, yes. And you did not realize that he had—ah—expired until the lights came on?"

"No, I did not."

Suddenly, startling them, Crippen stood and walked around to Caroline. "I need to see your hands, Miss Ames."

She held them out. Although her heart had begun to pound painfully in her breast, her hands were steady.

Crippen took them in his own. Slowly, thoughtfully, he looked at them; turned them over; looked at them again.

"Hold mine," he said abruptly.

For a moment she did not know what he meant; then she did. His nails, chipped and dirty, needed tending to, and his fingers were stained with nicotine. Reluctantly, she grasped them.

He nodded as if he had settled something in his mind. Then he released her and took his seat once more.

"Well?" said Ames. He had been watching the proceedings with a skeptical eye, wondering exactly how necessary it was for Crippen to go through this little exercise, if the inspector was using it as an excuse to have some physical contact, however brief, with Caroline. Now Ames reached out himself and took one of her hands and looked at it. "I appreciate your dilemma, Inspector, but I have to tell you I think you must pursue your investigations elsewhere. My sister's hands are clever enough—she does beautiful needlework—but they hardly have the strength that would have been necessary to squeeze the life out of a man."

"I don't say I disagree with you, Mr. Ames, but you understand—I need to speak to everyone who was a witness."

"Including Dr. MacKenzie here," Ames replied.

Crippen flicked his glance to MacKenzie again and held it there. "Yes," he said. "Including him."

"Doctor," said Ames, "would you be so good as to display your hands to the inspector?"

MacKenzie, resting his elbows on the table, held up his hands. They were good hands, Caroline thought; broad and strong, capable-looking like the man himself. And clean—very clean. For an instant, she allowed herself to remember how one of them had gripped hers yesterday afternoon.

Crippen did not go to MacKenzie, but for a long moment he looked at his hands. Then, as if he were still unwilling to address the doctor directly, he said to Caroline, "He sat on your other side?"

"Yes."

"And he didn't get up—didn't move at all?"

"No."

Crippen nodded. "The way I see it, the person who killed Mr. Clay was the person sitting beside him. Otherwise, there would have been too much commotion, getting up and moving around the room. You didn't hear anything unusual?"

"I heard—I hardly know how to describe it. A kind of scratching noise."

"Scratching?" Crippen peered at her suspiciously. "How d'you mean?"

"I didn't know what it was, but then when the lights came up I saw that she—Mrs. Sidgwick—had been writing something."

"In the dark?"

"Yes. It is called automatic writing. It comes to her from the beyond. She doesn't need to see to do it."

Crippen made an exasperated sound, as if to show his contempt for Mrs. Sidgwick and all her kind, and returned to his interrogation. "So it was you on Mr. Clay's right side. And on his left—?"

"A Mr. Jones."

"First name?"

"I don't know."

"You know him at all? Ever met him before?"

"No."

"Description?"

"Well, I—" She cast a glance at MacKenzie, appealing to him for help. What had Mr. Jones looked like? She couldn't remember. "Nothing in particular, Inspector," she said slowly. "I mean, he was a perfectly ordinary-looking little man. Ordinary features, ordinary attire."

"Black hair? White? Spectacles? Come now, Miss Ames, you must remember something about the man."

"Really, I can't." Caroline realized that she was trembling. Her voice sounded faint, and she tried to strengthen it. It would not do to have Deputy Chief Inspector Elwood Crippen think she had something to hide. "He was—just a very ordinary-looking little man. Brown hair, I suppose—I really didn't notice. I hardly had a chance to look at him before the lights went out."

Crippen cast her a skeptical glance. "As I understand it, this Mrs. Sidgwick gets her—ah—clients through word of mouth. People recommend other people, and so forth."

"That's right."

"So someone must have recommended this fellow Jones."

"I assume so, yes."

Crippen grunted. "I'll get his address from the lady herself. See him before he does a midnight flit."

"So you may wrap up your case by noontime, Inspector." Ames spoke soberly enough, but Caroline and MacKenzie could see the gleam of humor that lurked in his dark eyes.

What does he find amusing in poor Mr. Clay's murder? thought Caroline. Or is it Crippen's predicament—having to deal with the likes of Mrs. Evangeline Sidgwick—that amuses him?

And MacKenzie thought: Do not antagonize this officious little man, Ames. If he fixes on your sister as a suspect, he can do her great harm.

"I may, yes," Crippen said in answer to Ames's remark. He turned back to Caroline. "You did not see anyone come into the room during the proceedings?"

"No."

"No crack of light at the door?"

"No."

"No phantoms lurking about? I've heard they do that, these—ah—mediums. Provide a little excitement for their sitters."

"No phantoms, Inspector. Nothing out of the ordinary. Well—the entire proceeding was out of the ordinary, I suppose. But aside from the contacts Mrs. Sidgwick made through Roland—no. Nothing."

Crippen pricked up his ears. "Roland? Who's that? I don't have him on my list."

With a great effort, Caroline stifled her laughter. It was nervous laughter, MacKenzie knew, but Crippen, thin-skinned as he was, would surely misinterpret it as mockery. "He is Mrs. Sidgwick's control. The one who allows her to speak to the departed."

Crippen stared at her, suddenly suspicious all over again. "But who is he?"

"I have no idea. I've never seen him."

"You mean, he came in after the room was darkened?"

"Yes. That is exactly what I mean."

Crippen had whipped out a small notebook and pencil. "Last name?"

"I don't know."

"Address?"

"None, I should imagine."

Glancing at MacKenzie, she saw him shake his head. She understood: This was a murder investigation, not some joke to be played on Elwood Crippen.

"I beg your pardon, Inspector. I should have been more explicit. Roland is the disembodied spirit who allows Mrs. Sidgwick to make contact with the departed souls who are being questioned by the people—like me—who attend her séances."

" 'Disembodied spirit'—you mean, he isn't real?"

"Oh, he seems to be real, all right. But he doesn't exist the way we do, in a physical body. He lives on another plane, and he speaks only through Mrs. Sidgwick when she goes into trance and summons him."

Crippen stared at her as if he doubted her veracity—or her sanity. Then, to Ames: "You don't know of any enemies Mr. Clay might have had?"

"No. None."

"Well liked, was he?"

"Since he was one of the most generous philanthropists in the city, I would say he was very well liked indeed."

"A rich man, he was."

"Extremely."

"A rich man's death is always interesting to his relations," Crippen commented sardonically.

"I suppose it is. Your point being, Inspector, who benefits from Clay's death?" Ames nodded at Caroline. "My sister might know, better than I do, about the family."

"Miss Ames?" Crippen peered at her.

"Family? Oh—he had just the one daughter, Inspector. April Leicester. She is married to David Leicester, and they have one child, I believe."

"Who else?" Crippen said.

"In his family? I don't know. His late wife's sister, a Mrs. Briggs, accompanied him and Mrs. Leicester yesterday afternoon. It seems to me, now that I think of it, that Mr. Clay had a brother, but I believe he died some years ago." She shook her head, forcing herself to smile at him. "That's really all I know, Inspector."

"No enemies that you know of?"

"He was such a very good man. How could he have had enemies?"

Crippen stared at her accusingly. "Well, Miss Ames, he had one enemy, didn't he? Someone wanted him out of the way, that's one thing we can be certain of."

Ames said, "Perhaps you should not only speak to this Jones, whoever he is, but also inquire of Mrs. Sidgwick if she had any acquaintance with Mr. Clay before yesterday afternoon."

"All in good time, Mr. Ames. All in good time." He shot a hostile look at MacKenzie. "Anything you can add?"

MacKenzie forced himself to stay civil. This odious little man had the power to cause a good deal of trouble for the Ameses, and for him as well. He didn't want to antagonize him any more than he had already, by the mere fact of his presence.

"No."

"You examined him. You didn't see anything suspicious?"

"I— No." MacKenzie longed to make a believable excuse for his mistaken opinion of the cause of Theophilus Clay's death, but he could think of none. He'd simply been wrong. Nothing could be done to rectify that now.

"All right. Notify me if you have anything to add. And now—" Again Crippen pushed back his chair and stood up. "I must speak to my office before I move on. If I could have the use of your telephone?"

Caroline averted her eyes. How embarrassing to have to admit to Elwood Crippen that they didn't have one.

Ames was not embarrassed at all. "We don't subscribe to the telephone, Inspector. Damned noisy nuisance, bell going off at all hours anytime someone chooses to disturb you. I refuse to have one in the house."

Crippen seemed sincerely surprised. "You do? And I thought—well, never mind, Mr. Ames. We all have our little eccentricities, don't we? Most people find a telephone a very handy thing to have, keeping up with the times and all. But I imagine you make do with Western Union when you want to get in touch with someone. Makes it hard for people who want to get in touch with you, but that's their lookout, isn't it?"

And with that parting shot, to Caroline's vast relief and Dr. MacKenzie's as well, the little police inspector took his leave.

CHAPTER
4

A SHORT WHILE LATER, ADDINGTON AMES CROSSED MT. Vernon Street and headed down Willow toward the Common, beyond which was Crabbe's, his athletic club.

It was a perfect spring day, a trifle chilly but the sun in the cloudless sky would soon warm things up. On Boston Common, the elm trees lining the walkways were in full leaf after a slow start during a rather dank April. Children too young to be in school ran ahead of their smartly attired nursemaids, some of whom pushed high-wheeled wicker perambulators with infants tucked up inside. Old men lingered at the benches, gossiping; women marched along with a determined air, holding their bonnets against the stiff breeze, headed, perhaps, for the shopping at Eben Jordan's department store.

Ames nodded to the many passersby he knew, touching the brim of his hat to the ladies. Another few weeks and it would be time to take out his straw boater. Perhaps this year he would buy a new one. He'd never had a new one, not since nearly twenty years ago, when he'd been at the College. Recently, however, what with Dr. MacKenzie's board money paid promptly every Monday, the Ameses' finances had improved considerably. He was grateful for that, more for Caroline's sake than for his own.

As he strode down the walkway, his thoughts veered to the far less pleasant topic of Elwood Crippen.

An unpleasant surprise to see Crippen this morning. He'd had dealings enough with the little police inspector over the winter, and his opinion of him hadn't improved.

The effrontery of the man to suspect Caroline of murder! Crippen had once wanted to court Caroline; was his visit to No. 16½ his way of pushing himself forward into her life?

An opening appeared in the traffic on Tremont Street. He took his opportunity and ducked in front of a pair of grays, his thoughts still with Crippen.

In January, Crippen had arrested, wrongly, an Irish boy, Garrett O'Reilly, suspected of killing some poor girls over in the South End. And before that, in November, in the business of the death of Colonel Mann, Crippen had decided—wrong again—that Serena Vincent was the person he sought.

Serena Vincent.

Ames had stopped in front of a small store that sold tobacco and newspapers and sundries. For a moment the clatter and clamor of the busy street scene vanished. In the store's front window was a display that had caught his eye. A photograph—many photographs and all the same, all of an exquisitely beautiful woman. She was wearing an elaborate gown and a handsome four-strand pearl choker. In the sepia-toned photograph the color of her hair did not show, but he saw it nevertheless: a dark, lustrous auburn. Her eyes were greenish, her mouth very red. The photographer had posed her facing half away, looking over her shoulder. Even so, he could see that she was tightly corseted in a low-cut dress that showed off far too much of her stunning figure. A provocative pose; she seemed to be saying, Shall we become better acquainted? Unfortunately, she seemed to be saying it to the entire world.

She was an actress at the Park Theater, very popular.

Serena Vincent.

Several people jostled him, but he did not move on. His mind was filled with the image of Mrs. Vincent: tall, statuesque, beautiful beyond men's dreams. He was with her once more. It was no longer a bright May morning but a dreary day in the January thaw, and he'd called on her at her elegant apartment hotel on Berkeley Street. She was telling him her secrets, and he—yes, he admitted it—was glad to receive them. Greedy, even. Despite the protests he'd uttered, he'd wanted, that rainy January afternoon, to listen to her speak for hours, enchanting him with her low, husky voice, her beautiful eyes. He'd felt as if he could listen to her forever.

It was not until he'd left her, gone out into the cold, that he'd come to his senses and reminded himself that Serena Vincent—Serena Sohier she'd been before her ill-fated marriage—was not the woman who had once moved in his own circle but someone very different who, cast out of Boston Society, had taken up a life on the stage.

A few days later, he'd gone to her again to give her bad news, and when she'd begun to weep, he had taken her into his arms. For just a moment she'd stayed there, allowing him to embrace her, and then she'd moved away. He would go to his grave remembering that sensation, he thought now as he stared at her photograph.

Beautiful woman, how are you? How do you do these days?

At that last meeting, she'd asked him to stay in touch. And so he'd called on her once or twice in the weeks afterward, but she'd never been at home—or not, at any rate, to him.

Had she, those times, been entertaining someone else—some other man? She had a number of men in her life, he knew; one of them had killed himself at least in part because she refused to go away with him.

Her theater—the Park—was a block away. For the past month, they'd been running a vaudeville revue imported from New York—a surprising comedown, he'd thought, for an outfit that prided itself on the high-toned comedies and dramas that were its usual offerings.

And what had their resident leading actress been doing all that time? Was she even still in the city? Or had she already left for her summer vacation, which she would undoubtedly spend in dubious company? Taking in the races and the casinos at Saratoga Springs, or venturing farther afield to Monte Carlo and Nice, yachting through the Mediterranean . . .

Suddenly he realized that he wanted to find out. Crabbe's could wait.

At the Park Theater, he saw that fresh posters had been put up. They announced a new comedy of manners, a limited run of four weeks. Starring, of course, Serena Vincent. Opening night, Saturday next. So she'd be in town for a while longer, at any rate.

She'd send him tickets for it if he asked her. Did he want to do that? Did he want to spend an evening in a box—her box, reserved for her friends—watching her as she displayed herself for all the world to see in some bewitching gown, her graceful form moving about the stage, perhaps being embraced by whatever actor she'd approved of to play opposite her, speaking in that voice that could reach the highest seats in the second balcony, but which could also—as he well remembered—speak low, speak intimately, speak of the secrets of her heart . . .

"Sorry, sir!"

Some clumsy fellow intent on his own business had nearly knocked him down.

He straightened his hat, gave himself a mental shake, and moved on. What he needed was an hour or two at Crabbe's—a good workout, fencing, boxing, followed by a hard massage and a cold shower.

What he didn't need was any further contact with Serena Vincent.

"ARE YOU SURE YOU FEEL WELL ENOUGH TO GO OUT?" said MacKenzie. He waited for her at the bottom of the stairs as she descended with her sewing basket.

"Of course." She stopped two steps from the bottom, enjoying the unusual sensation of being taller than he. He was not as tall as her brother, who was well over six feet, but he was tall enough—and stocky, as opposed to Addington's spare frame. She didn't mind. His stockiness, his broad, honest face adorned with a well-kept mustache, his kind gray eyes—all of him was exactly right.

She could hardly remember a time when she didn't know him. He'd come to them in September to recuperate after his knee had been shattered by a Sioux bullet on the western plains, where he'd served as an army surgeon. I need a place for just a few months, he'd said. But the few months had passed, his knee long healed, and still he stayed. She hardly had the courage to ask him if—when—he planned to move on. His board money was useful, of course, but it wasn't the money she thought of when she thought of him. It was his friendliness, his kindness, his dependability. So unlike Addington, who tended to be a trifle eccentric in his habits, spending long hours over in Cambridge consulting his former professors; or at Crabbe's, where he took some little pride, she knew, in his athletic prowess; or at one or another of his clubs; or at the Athenaeum, reading for long hours, lost in thought . . .

Not that she didn't appreciate Addington. But Dr. MacKenzie was different. More approachable, more companionable, less critical. He seemed to value her opinions in a way that Addington never did, and he seemed to take real pleasure in her company in a way that Addington often did not.

"Sewing Circle?" he asked, stepping aside for her.

"Yes. It is our last meeting of the year. We don't even try to get together in the summer, with everyone scattered, so we must finish all our projects."

Sewing Circle was a time-honored tradition; no one could remember when it had begun. Every woman in Boston Society, having made her debut, joined her debut year's circle to sew garments for the deserving poor. Caroline's circle sewed mostly for immigrant Italians and Irish in the North End, where the items produced—shirts, jackets, trousers, knitted caps and mittens and stockings—were distributed by the staff of the settlement house on North Bennett Street. Caroline and all her friends took Sewing Circle very seriously; one had to be at Death's door, or very nearly, to miss it.

The hall smelled of fresh furniture polish—Margaret had been hard at work since breakfast—and the residue of last night's hearth fire. It would be warmer today; Margaret could clean the grates and put up the tapestry fire screens for decoration until the fall.

"May I walk with you?" MacKenzie asked.

She laughed. "You may if you wish, Doctor. But I warn you—it is just across the square, at Emmie Lodge's house."

She saw disappointment cloud his face, quickly replaced by a smile in answer to her own. "Then I'll make the most of it, and take you around by the long way."

While Caroline fetched her bonnet and a light cashmere shawl from the hall tree, Dr. MacKenzie took his bowler, glad that he no longer needed his cane. It was by now a glorious day, sunshiny and bright, a chilly breeze coming up from the river but nothing like the raw, cold winds of April. As they set off, Caroline accepted MacKenzie's proffered arm, since the cobblestones were treacherous and the frost-heaved redbrick sidewalk hardly less so.

"I was wondering—" MacKenzie began after they had gone a little way.

"Yes? What were you wondering, Doctor?"

He cleared his throat. Even though he'd become accustomed, over the winter, to speaking easily to her, he still had moments when his words, so carefully formed beforehand in his mind, refused to come.

"The swan boats," he said.

"Yes?"

"They have started up, I believe."

"Yes, they have. Mr. Paget is always very prompt. He has them freshly painted and on the water by the first of May, every year."

The swan boats in the Public Garden lagoon were a Boston institution. There were six of them, each with a large white wooden swan at the front. Propelled by boys pedaling at the back, they made their stately way through the water, around the tiny islands and under the miniature suspension bridge. Ever since she'd first told him about them, MacKenzie had been longing to escort her there for a little excursion.

"I was wondering," he said, "if you would care to accompany me some afternoon this week, while we have fine weather?"

Although it might not be fine for long. Boston weather, as he knew by now, was notoriously unpredictable; today's sunshine could vanish in an instant, replaced by fog or rain or even, once, as she'd told him, by snow. In May. He had come to understand that Bostonians took a peculiar perverse pride in their weather; they boasted of its unreliability, and smiled as they told tales of climatic vagaries, each more unbelievable than the one before.

"Why, Doctor." She stopped and turned up her pretty face to smile at him. "What a delightful idea. Yes, indeed. Let us go on the swan boats—on Thursday, perhaps?"

She had a busy schedule, he knew: charity work, her Saturday Morning Reading Club, various committees at her church.

"Thursday?" he said. "Excellent. I look forward to it."

She was laughing again. "Do you wonder why I chose that day in particular?"

"Well, I—"

"It is my birthday."

Her birthday! And he never knew, never even thought to ask—

"When a lady reaches my advanced age, she shouldn't tell, should she? But I don't care about it. If Aunt Euphemia can tell people how old she is, surely I can, too."

Aunt Euphemia Ames, their late father's sister, was seventy-five if she was a day and the most fearsome old female MacKenzie had ever encountered.

"But surely your brother will have made some arrangement—a celebration, perhaps?"

"Addington? Celebrate my birthday? Hardly." She rolled her eyes. "He doesn't believe in celebrating such things. What would he do? Have a party? Never! Which is fine by me, I don't mind telling you. But, yes, Thursday is my birthday, Doctor, and we will celebrate it, as you say, with an excursion on the swan boats. It's been years since I've done that, and I look forward to it."

They were at Mrs. Lodge's. Since he could think of no excuse to keep her with him any longer, he lifted his hat and bade her farewell. He would go down to Charles Street and buy some tobacco. She'd given him permission to smoke his pipe when he'd first come, and very grateful he was to her for that, among so many other things.

She stood on the Lodges' front steps, watching him go; then, steeling herself, she turned and lifted the door knocker.

A circle of a dozen eager faces awaited her, voices rose in greeting, curious eyes raked her—in the friendliest possible way, of course.

After only a few moments, as she took out her sewing and began to work at it, she realized that the mysterious and vibrant network of communication that wove itself through her small, insular world had been in full force ever since last evening. Gossiping maids (Mrs. Sidgwick's had been hysterical, but she'd surely calmed down soon enough, eager to talk), tattling butlers, an observant mistress of the house wanting to know what was the matter. And even, now, the telephone, a useful instrument for spreading gossip despite the fact that one needed to shout into it, thus eliminating any chance to tell secrets.

So most of the women here—women Caroline had known all her life, women who were, for the most part, her friends—knew she'd attended a séance at Mrs. Sidgwick's yesterday afternoon. They knew that at that séance, Theophilus Clay had traveled over to the other side. Caroline took some small comfort in reminding herself that they probably did not know—not yet—that the police believed Mr. Clay's death was murder. She imagined the rumpus it would cause if she told them now. Perhaps she would.

"I saw a police wagon at your door this morning, Caroline," said Mrs. Lodge.

There was a sudden hush as every woman in the room leaned forward, sewing momentarily forgotten, to hear her reply.

"Oh?" she said. She was annoyed with herself because her voice sounded so faint.

"I suppose it is only to be expected that they would come calling under the circumstances," Mrs. Lodge added.

"What circumstances?" Ida Curtis asked eagerly. She was a

notoriously giddy and frivolous little woman; even now she could barely suppress a giggle.

"Why, that Theophilus Clay should die so suddenly," replied Mrs. Lodge. "And at a séance, too, which makes it even more strange."

"Dear Caroline," breathed Julia Norton, "do they think— but no, they couldn't possibly."

Caroline lifted her chin. Deliberately she met the eyes of each woman as she looked around the circle of eager faces. Poor things, they had so little excitement in their lives, she could understand why they were so avid to hear about Theophilus Clay. She would be avid herself in their shoes.

But what would you all say if you knew your suspicions are correct? she wondered. She picked up the shirt she had let fall to her lap and threaded her needle afresh. She was glad—very glad—that her hands were steady enough to do so.

"Who inherits?" asked Mrs. Curtis, giving voice to the next question uppermost in everyone's mind.

"Probably the daughter," said Mrs. Lodge.

"You're sure?"

"Fairly, yes."

Mrs. Curtis turned to Caroline. "And she was there with you?"

"Well, yes, she was, but—"

"His sister-in-law was there as well, wasn't she?" asked Amalia Crowninshield. They glanced at her, grateful to her for voicing the curiosity they all felt about this truly delicious little— well, it wasn't a scandal just yet, but it certainly had the makings of one. "Was she sitting next to him?"

"No." Now, Caroline thought, comes the test of your friend- ship. "She wasn't sitting next to him. I was."

There was a moment of shocked and horrified silence as they absorbed it. Then: "But that means—" someone said.

"Yes. That means I was sitting next to him when he died."

"Caroline!" shrieked Mrs. Curtis. "That means you were *holding his hand*! When he *died*! Were you? Tell me! Ooooh, I am going to faint! I *am*! I can feel it coming on!"

"Oh, hush up, Ida!" snapped Mrs. Lodge. As hostess for the day, she felt duty bound to rescue the morning from the brink of disaster. "If Caroline could bear to live through such an experience, you can bear to talk about it." She turned to Caroline. "And the police called on you because—"

They all realized they were far beyond the bounds of propriety now. It was bad enough that Caroline had attended the séance where Theophilus Clay had died. That she'd been visited by the police was shocking—and enthralling—beyond belief. None of them had ever had such a visit, and none of them wanted one.

But to hear about it—yes, that they could endure. More than endure. They longed for it, for every last delicious detail of it. Thrusting aside the reticence and good manners they'd learned from infancy, they fixed their eyes on Caroline and practically salivated to hear what she would say next.

"The police called on me this morning because—" Caroline began. She heard the warning voice of caution at the back of her mind, but she ignored it.

"Because of the unusual circumstances of Mr. Clay's death," she finished.

With a little surge of defiance she looked at the circle of astonished faces that surrounded her, their mouths fallen open, their sewing dropped into their laps.

"What do you mean, 'unusual,' Caroline?" breathed Mrs. Lodge.

"I mean—his death may not have been natural."

Silence in Mrs. Lodge's parlor. A dead silence, in fact.

Then: "Not natural?" squeaked Mrs. Curtis. "Not *natural?* But, Caroline, what do you mean?"

"What do you think she means?" snapped Mrs. Crowninshield. "She means—"

"Murder," said Caroline. She spoke calmly, deliberately; she even managed a small, tight smile as she saw that single word drop among them like a stone disturbing the smooth surface of a pond. She didn't want to frighten them, but she wanted them to understand, for once in their sheltered, restricted lives, the terror that lay just beyond the boundary of those lives. A terror that could strike anyone, anytime—even privileged women like themselves. It would be good for them to realize that, she thought; it would shake them out of their complacency.

Mrs. Curtis seemed to be fainting at last, but no one paid any attention to her as, dramatically, she fell back in her chair.

"Murder?" breathed Julia Norton. She and Caroline had been good friends since babyhood, but now Caroline thought she saw something in Mrs. Norton's eyes that was very far from friendship.

"Yes, Julia. You know what murder is. It is the most extreme violence from one person toward another."

"And the police called on you because—"

"Why do you think?" She was irritated with her friend— with all of them—now. "The police called on me this morning because I was holding Mr. Clay's hand when he died. And because his death may have been murder, I am a suspect in the case."

And now at last a great distance—a yawning chasm— seemed to have opened between herself and them. She could almost feel them withdrawing from her. It was as if she'd suddenly become someone alien, someone foreign, even more foreign than the aliens who flooded the city week after week and needed to be supplied with the charitable sewing she and her friends were doing that morning.

They feared her, she realized. Because she would taint them? Because she would infect them with the disease—scandal, notoriety—that now infected her?

A suspect in the case?

She stabbed her needle through the unfinished seam of the shirt she was making, folded the material, and thrust it into her basket.

"Thank you for a lovely morning, Emmie," she said to her hostess with no hint of sarcasm. Mrs. Lodge, in the face of this social disaster, looked ready to cry. "I'm afraid I will not be able to stay for luncheon today."

She stood up; drawing on her last reserve of strength, she nodded good-bye. "Good morning, ladies."

Mrs. Lodge did not urge her to remain. In another moment, Caroline found herself outside, squinting in the sunshine. She saw a man's figure just turning into the square from Mt. Vernon Street. To her enormous relief, it was Dr. MacKenzie.

CHAPTER
5

"I SAY, AMES!"

It was Harold Edgeware, calling to him as he entered the lobby of the St. Botolph Club on lower Newbury Street. He knew Edgeware slightly—an older man, a friend of his late father's—but had not seen him in weeks. Now Edgeware advanced, hand outstretched; he was smiling but his eyes held worry and fear.

"Could I have a word?" Edgeware asked.

"Of course." After his workout at Crabbe's, Ames was hungry, but he followed the older man into the members' room, empty now at lunchtime.

They stood by the front windows. Edgeware was a sharp-eyed, vigorous man who looked much younger than his years; his heavy Dundreary side-whiskers waggled a bit as he spoke in lowered tones despite the fact that he and Ames were alone.

"It's about this incident yesterday at Mrs. Sidgwick's," he began.

"You know the lady?" Ames was surprised. As far as he knew, Harold Edgeware was a rock-solid Bostonian, nothing flighty about him, a member of a prosperous family firm, the owner of a handsome house on Marlborough Street. He and all his relations were as securely ensconced in Boston's upper circles as were the Ameses themselves. Two sons and a daughter, Ames remembered, all married; Edgeware himself had been a widower for some time.

"Yes," Edgeware replied. "I know her—fairly well."

"And do you know that the police consider the—ah—incident to be a case of murder?"

"Yes. I know that also." Edgeware's face was grim.

"May I ask—"

"How I know her?" Edgeware shrugged. "I met her a few years ago. It was my daughter's doing. Come with me to a séance, she said. See if we can contact Susan. That was her sister, my older daughter. She died years ago. Pneumonia." His voice roughened, and he paused for a moment to clear his throat. "I told her I didn't have any truck with such nonsense, table-tilting and disembodied voices and such, but to please her—she's always missed Susan very much—I said I'd go."

Ames nodded. "My sister wanted to contact our late mother."

"And did she?"

"No."

"Ah. Well, we were luckier—if you want to call it luck. I don't mind telling you, Ames, you could have knocked me over with a feather when I heard that fellow Roland—"

"Mrs. Sidgwick's control."

"That's right. Scamp of a fellow, never know what he'll say next. But at any rate, there he was, coming through loud and clear, and answering my daughter's questions with the most amazing accuracy! I tell you, he knew things that no one but family could have known. Every time, he got it right!"

"And did your daughter take some comfort from the exchange?"

"Indeed she did. Much comfort. She was in tears at the end, but they were tears of joy. She'd made contact with her sister—or thought she had, at any rate. She'd learned that Susan was well and happy up there in the beyond, wherever it is, and she had the added comfort of knowing that when she herself passed over, they would be together for all time. Yes, it was a great solace to her."

Edgeware's eyes had moistened, and he dabbed at them with his white silk handkerchief.

"So you came away convinced of Mrs. Sidgwick's spiritualistic powers," Ames said.

"Yes, I did. I admit it. I went in a skeptic, I came out a believer. Mrs. Sidgwick herself—have you met her? No? She is a most admirable woman. Not what you might think at all. Modest, not forward in any way. At that time she lived over on Shawmut Avenue in very reduced circumstances—not that she'd ever had any money to begin with—and she solicited her clientele through advertisements in the newspapers. She put herself at some risk by doing that, of course. Put an advertisement in the public prints, and you never know who will turn up on your doorstep. But she had to do it; she had no other way to make her living."

"She charged a fee for her sittings?"

"Yes. A dollar a head. Think of it, Ames. A woman alone in the world, and with a child to support—yes, she has a child, a daughter. I am happy to say I have been able to help provide for her. She wants for nothing now: dancing lessons, pretty frocks, her own governess. She won't be able to have a coming-out, of course—or not here in Boston, at any rate—but I'll give her a year at a good finishing school, and see to it that she marries suitably."

Edgeware had taken on a faint flush, and Ames understood it was not an easy thing for him to speak so frankly.

"And the house on Lime Street?" he asked.

"That's my property. I've always rented it out, and it seemed the sensible thing to offer it to Mrs. Sidgwick."

"After you came to know her better," Ames said.

"After I—yes." Edgeware flushed more deeply. "It isn't what you think, Ames. I mean, she's a perfectly respectable woman. I suppose you think that what she does is no better than a cheap trick, but your sister feels differently, does she not?"

"She—was curious," Ames replied.

"That's right. Curious. Wanted to see if the thing worked. And there are a lot more like her. Look at that great pile of a building up the street—that took some doing, sure enough. Some serious interest there, wouldn't you say?"

He referred to the First Spiritual Temple of the Working Union of Progressive Spiritualists, a massive Richardsonian Romanesque building of rough stone that had gone up, eight years before, at the corner of Newbury and Exeter streets.

"Indeed," Ames replied. "I don't deny the interest, just the thing itself. But it is not my intention to argue with you. You wanted something of me?"

"Yes." Edgeware nodded emphatically. "I wanted you to—ah—pay a visit with me. To her—to Mrs. Sidgwick."

Ames's eyebrows rose. "Why?"

"To see if you can help her. This business of Clay's death yesterday afternoon during her séance—it will harm her."

"Because it was murder, or—"

Edgeware made an impatient gesture. "So say the police. Even if it had been a natural death, it would have been bad enough. But murder! Great heaven, man, think about it! It is difficult enough for her to keep up her reputation, what with all the charlatans about. Every traveling carnival has its resident medium—or crystal-gazer, more like it. Gypsies, palm readers, what have you. If people come to believe that when they attend her séances they will not only make contact with the other side but will actually go over to it themselves, and not of their own volition—why, no one will patronize her! She will be ruined! And that"—he leaned in, tapped Ames's shirt bosom with a bony finger—"would break her heart. In her own way, she's an artist, Ames. A real artist at what she does, and people know it. She's beginning to get a little reputation. Did you know that Professor James studies her?"

Ames was surprised. William James, one of the brightest stars in the Harvard firmament, a scholar whose wide-ranging brilliance touched on perhaps too many things, thus fragmenting and perhaps dimming it, was nevertheless not a man easily deceived. "No," he said. "I didn't know that."

"Oh, yes. He's had many sittings with her. Got up a committee of his people over there at the College to study her as well. They try to trick her, you see, catch her out in some kind of fraud. But they can't do it. No, sir. Never once. Ask him yourself. I don't think he's here today, but he comes often enough. He'll tell you. He's fascinated by her. Can't explain it—can't explain what she does or how she does it—but he believes it. She has powers, he says. What kind, he doesn't know, but that she has them—absolutely. That, he believes."

They heard a burst of laughter from the dining room: the members, seated around the large communal table, enjoying their noontime meal. What was it today? Ames wondered. Boiled cod? Overdone Yankee pot roast? One did not join the St. Botolph Club for the food.

"Mr. Edgeware, I think you should know that we had a visit

at home this morning from Deputy Chief Inspector Crippen. Do you know him?"

"Unfortunately, yes. He called on Mrs. Sidgwick as well."

"Were you there?"

"Yes." Edgeware's expression darkened. "It is beyond my comprehension why we allow these public servants to bully us like that. The man is a barbarian!"

"Barbarian or not, I will tell you that once he gets an idea into his head, it is very difficult to dislodge it. He came to question my sister as a suspect in Theophilus Clay's death. You know how it goes at a séance, a darkened room, people sitting around the table holding hands—and it was she who held Clay's hand."

"But your sister could not possibly—"

"Of course not. But from Crippen's point of view, until he has the matter cleared up, everyone is a suspect, including Caroline."

Edgeware chewed his lower lip. "Someone called Jones sat on Clay's other side."

"Right. No one seems to know who he is—or if he had any relationship with Mr. Clay."

"All the more reason, then, for your sister's sake, why you should take an interest—"

"So it seems."

"So you'll come with me to Mrs. Sidgwick's after lunch?"

"Is she able to receive visitors? From what Caroline told me, Clay's death, even when it seemed to be only of natural causes, was a great shock to her."

"It was, but she will be able to see you, at least."

Ames cocked his head. "Why me in particular?"

Edgeware flushed again. "I know you have had some dealings with the police. With Crippen, was it? Good. As I have explained to you, this is a delicate matter for Mrs. Sidgwick. And since you tell me your sister is involved, you might see your way clear to—ah—asking around a bit, finding out something that might be useful. I will tell you for a start, I have heard that Clay's son-in-law seems to be running through his wife's money at a good clip. So if one is looking for a motive—"

"Clay's son-in-law was not present at the séance," Ames replied. "So I hardly see how he could have done the deed."

"True enough, but still. It is a point to consider, don't you think? That the young man might be eager to inherit some part of Clay's fortune, or even for his wife to do so—as one must assume she will—instead of living off the old man's largesse, no matter how generous it might have been?"

Another burst of laughter came from the dining room.

"Shall we eat?" Ames said, not wishing to speculate further about Theophilus Clay's son-in-law. "And then—although I cannot imagine how I can help her—I will go with you to see Mrs. Sidgwick."

"I⊤ IS GOOD OF YOU TO CALL, MISS AMES," SAID PAULINA Briggs.

She was a woman of late middle age, once rather attractive, now faded, particularly in her severe, high-necked mourning. "May I offer you tea?" she added.

After Caroline's unnerving morning at Sewing Circle, she had been unable to eat lunch, nor did she want anything now.

"Thank you, no."

Mrs. Briggs's parlor was done up in the latest fashion: dark, leathery, patterned wallpaper; dark, carved walnut and ebony wood; a crimson velvet ottoman before the fire; fringes on all the draperies and much of the upholstery; knickknacks scattered on every available surface. Although the day was bright, the room was dim, the heavy draperies drawn, the gas turned low. A handsome mourning wreath adorned the front door of the house, and the maid, as was correct, had shown no touch of white on her attire. One wore mourning for six months for a brother-in-law; Mrs. Briggs would have to get through the summer, all the hot months, swathed head to toe in heavy black.

Mrs. Briggs sat stiffly on a brocade sofa, her hands folded on the black fabric of her skirts. Etiquette dictated that women in mourning wear no adornment save their wedding rings, if they had one, and a mourning brooch made of the deceased's hair. Apparently she didn't have that. How close had she been to Theophilus Clay? Caroline wondered. Her sister, who had been his wife, had been dead for some time; perhaps Mrs. Briggs had seldom seen Clay recently until she went with him and his daughter to Mrs. Sidgwick's séance yesterday afternoon.

Caroline cleared her throat. It was obvious from her hostess's attitude—somber but hardly distraught—that Mrs. Briggs had not yet heard Inspector Crippen's news.

"Mrs. Briggs, I am so sorry to trouble you after the shock you must have had yesterday, but—I came here to ask your help, and I apologize for intruding on your grief."

"Yes," Mrs. Briggs replied. "It was a shock, as you say. But at least he—we—had the solace of making contact with Fanny before he . . . went to join her."

"It must have been a great comfort to you."

"It was. You were trying yourself to contact your mother?"

"Yes. But as you know, I didn't."

Mrs. Briggs made a small moue of sympathy. "These things are not always predictable. Perhaps you will try again?"

"Yes, perhaps." Get on with it, Caroline thought. "Mrs. Briggs, I must tell you that something has happened. Have the police visited you today?"

"The police? No. Why do you ask?"

"Because this morning at breakfast, one of their inspectors came to see us. I am afraid he had very bad news."

Mrs. Briggs's eyes became wary; her mouth tightened. "What was it?"

"He told us—I am very sorry to have to be the one to tell you, but he said that your brother-in-law did not die a natural death."

Fool, she chastised herself. You should have brought *sal volatile* with you. You do not know this woman well, you do not know how she would receive your news.

"What do you mean, he did not die a natural death?" snapped Mrs. Briggs. "What are you talking about?"

"I mean—apparently someone killed him."

"Killed him?" Mrs. Briggs repeated as if Caroline had spoken in a foreign language she didn't understand.

"I'm afraid so," Caroline said gently. It didn't matter that she didn't know this woman well. She hated bringing bad news to anyone. "Can you—would you like me to ring for some water, or smelling salts?"

Mrs. Briggs ignored her. She sat immobile, letting Caroline's news sink in. "But that is not possible," she said after a moment. "We were all there in the room with him. How could—surely the police are mistaken."

"Inspector Crippen has complete faith in his medical examiner. He said no weapon was used. It was an Oriental trick, he said—pressure to an artery in the neck."

She heard her words drop into the silence of the room. The only other sound was the soft ticking of the little Gothic clock on the mantel, which somehow made the silence seem more oppressive. In all this spacious house, a house of mourning now, there was no evidence of the usual domestic routine, servants hurrying through the halls, the faint *chink* of china and glassware in the dining room as the butler laid the table for dinner, a child's voice, perhaps, calling to its nurse. Was there a Mr. Briggs? A maiden aunt? Grandchildren?

Mrs. Briggs had seemed to wilt momentarily, but she collected herself and said with some spirit, "That is unbelievable, Miss Ames. More, it is outrageous. It is a slander on Theo's good name."

Caroline understood: It was almost as much a disgrace to be the victim of a murder as to be the murderer oneself. Illogical, perhaps, but true.

"I shall consult my attorney," Mrs. Briggs went on. "It is unthinkable that poor dear Theo should be caught up in a scandal now, when he can no longer defend himself."

"Your attorney?" Caroline said. "I don't—"

"Yes! I shall sue! For slander! Theophilus hadn't an enemy in the world. Everybody liked him. He was the most generous philanthropist in the city. Perhaps when you came in you saw the condolence cards on the tray in the hall? Half a hundred, at least, and the day is not over. Theo was a perfectly wonderful man. Why should anyone want to kill him? It is ridiculous!"

"Well, yes, of course it is, but—"

"I am in your debt, Miss Ames, for warning me. Now, if the police come, I shall be prepared. They will see they cannot tarnish the good name of a man like Theophilus Clay."

Suddenly Mrs. Briggs's eyes softened, and a faint smile came to her lips. "He was always so very kind to dear Fanny," she said. "Well, now he is with her for eternity, and although I will miss him, I can take comfort from that, at least." She sniffled, searched for her handkerchief—black, of course—and blew her nose.

It was always difficult dealing with people newly bereaved. Caroline remembered the awkward speeches of some of her friends when her mother died. People sympathized with loss, but they didn't always know how to express their sympathy.

"Mrs. Briggs," she began hesitantly.

Her hostess looked up sharply. "Yes?"

"I wonder—I know how widely admired, and even loved, your brother-in-law was, but if we are to believe the police, we must face the fact that someone was his enemy."

"I have told you, Miss Ames—"

"Yes, you have. But—and I realize that I am treading on shaky ground here—but the fact remains that someone killed him. And since I myself am a suspect in the case, I feel that I must make some effort, at least, to discover—"

"Discover what? I have told you—and I repeat—there is nothing to discover. Theo hadn't an enemy in the world. Think of all the charities he funded, for a start—all his good works."

"Surely he made appropriate bequests to those charities in his will?"

His will. Caroline watched, fascinated, as a succession of emotions played across her hostess's face. Contempt, envy, anger . . .

I have touched on something, she thought, but what?

"Yes," said Mrs. Briggs after a moment, in a rather strangled voice. "I am sure he did."

"And aside from those bequests," Caroline went on, still feeling her way, "the family was to receive the rest?"

Mrs. Briggs's mouth twitched, her eyes grew cold, and her left forefinger began a little tattoo on her black bombazine lap. "To my niece, April," she said, biting off the words. "It all goes to her."

A fact of which you obviously disapprove, Caroline thought. "She was with us at the séance yesterday," she said.

"Yes. It was she who prevailed upon Theo to attend."

Caroline remembered the young woman: a pretty little thing, devastated by her father's death even when it had been thought to be of natural causes. What would she say now, when it was believed to be murder?

"She lives on Commonwealth Avenue?" she asked.

"In half a double house Theo built when she married, three years ago. He lived in the other half. He doted on her and didn't want to be separated from her."

"And her husband—"

"David Leicester." Mrs. Briggs's voice was as cold as her eyes.

"I can't place him," Caroline fibbed. "What—does he do?"

"Do? Why, he does nothing, Miss Ames. Except live on his wife's money, and spend it with a very free hand."

"I see." Caroline had a memory of a handsome young man, not very bright. His sister was in Europe with the Ameses' young cousin, Valentine Thorne.

"So the news that April is to inherit must be very welcome to him," Mrs. Briggs went on, "even if it will probably be in trust for her alone. I am sure Theo would have put it in her name, and thank goodness for the married women's property act. I shudder to think what would happen to that fine fat fortune if David Leicester were given access to it."

So here was a little family difficulty, Caroline thought. Some-one—Theophilus Clay's son-in-law, in fact—with a motive. But a motive for what? Greedy and free-spending he might be—the kind of young man for whom "spendthrift trusts" had been created by canny Boston fathers—but surely he was not a murderer.

And besides, he hadn't been there. The daughter had, but she'd been seated across the table, no chance to reach her father until the lights came up, and when she'd raced to his side, he was already dead.

"Have you seen your niece today?" Caroline asked.

Mrs. Briggs frowned as if the very mention of the young woman were distasteful. "No. We telephoned to David from Mrs. Sidgwick's yesterday, but he wasn't home. Not surprising. So I took her home in my carriage. I offered to stay with her, but she declined." She sniffed. "I sent a note around this morning—I am not on the telephone—but there was no reply."

Still, Caroline thought, you intend to help manage the funeral.

"I had thought to pay a visit to the family plot over at Mt. Auburn, perhaps tomorrow afternoon," Mrs. Briggs went on. "Fanny's grave is there, of course. I want to make sure it has been properly tended, so that when we go there with Theo's coffin, we will have no unpleasant surprises. Would you care to accompany me? It is a beautiful place, Mt. Auburn, at this time of year."

"Why, certainly, if you wish," Caroline replied. But what about the inquest? she thought. Will Crippen release the body for the funeral?

"The funeral arrangements will be difficult," Mrs. Briggs went on, "since we can expect an overflow crowd. I shall insist to April that the services be by invitation only. Will you come?"

"Why—yes, thank you." Funerals and weddings were always of interest; Caroline had been to many of both, and she never tired of them. Weddings were (almost) always happy occasions, and funerals, unless one were distraught with grief as she'd been at her mother's, were often a treasure trove of information for someone like herself, always interested in genealogy.

And besides, she'd wanted to get a look at David Leicester, and this would be a convenient way to do it.

Mrs. Briggs was eyeing Caroline with new interest. "This—what did you call it? Oriental trick? Do the police believe that someone—some Oriental, perhaps—came into the room, in the dark, to attack poor Theophilus? But you say that you yourself are a suspect, Miss Ames. How very distressing for you. Have the police questioned you?"

Caroline managed a small dismissive laugh. "Inspector Crip-

CYNTHIA PEALE

pen asked to look at my hands." She held them up now. "He said they didn't look strong enough to have applied such pressure. But he made it very clear that for the moment, at least, I am a suspect in the case."

"Stuff and nonsense," snorted Mrs. Briggs. "Why, you didn't even know Theophilus. Or not very well, at any rate. Why on earth should you want to kill him? But it does put you in a delicate position, doesn't it?"

"For the time being, yes. That is why I came to see you, Mrs. Briggs. To see if you could tell me if anyone might possibly have had a reason—"

"I don't blame you. If I were a suspect in a murder case— and who knows? Perhaps I will be. Perhaps everyone in that room will be—I would do likewise. You want to take care that your good name is not harmed, Miss Ames. As the Bible says, a woman's good name has a price above rubies. Once lost, never found again. But as for the question of your killing poor Theophilus—no, it is impossible. No one would have wanted to do that. He hadn't an enemy in the world. You can tell that to your police inspector, Miss Ames, with my compliments. Not one enemy did Theophilus Clay have, and everyone who knew him will tell you the same."

CHAPTER
6

LIME STREET, A NARROW WAY BETWEEN CHARLES STREET and the river, had once, like lower Chestnut Street, housed the stables for the families up on the hill. In recent years, many of those stables had been converted to dwellings or torn down altogether, replaced by flat-fronted, ill-matched houses, some of them quite large, squeezed directly onto the sidewalk.

The house where Mrs. Sidgwick lived was an oddly arranged place, no particular design to it, rooms sized and shaped any which way and with no apparent logic to their placement. She received her guests in a small parlor at the second-floor front; Ames assumed that the room where she held her séances was behind the closed door he'd glimpsed down the hall.

"How are you, Evangeline?" said Harold Edgeware. He went to her at once, clasped both her hands, and looked deep into her eyes. She did not rise, but she held his gaze, and Ames saw on her rather plain face a look of trust, of devotion even, that immediately gave him a glimpse into the nature of their relationship.

"I am well enough, thank you," she replied. She removed her hands from his and glanced inquiringly at Ames. When Edgeware introduced them, she shook Ames's hand firmly, with none of the usual shrinking feminine modesty.

"Mr. Ames," she said. It was obvious she was puzzled at his visit, and yet, he thought, she trusts her protector's judgment. If Harold Edgeware thought it wise for her to receive him, she would comply.

The men seated themselves and Ames looked around. He wondered if Edgeware had furnished the place, or if that task had been left to her. The room was done up in Oriental style, wicker and bamboo, lacquered wood, painted screens and potted palms. Despite the warmth of the afternoon, a fire burned in the grate, and the windows, which might have let in a breeze from the river, were closed. Ames felt his high collar uncomfortably tight around his neck, and he was perspiring under his wool sack suit.

"Now, my dear," Edgeware began. "I have asked Mr. Ames to come here today because of all this trouble."

Mrs. Sidgwick nodded. She was a small woman, with brown hair whose color looked not quite natural, and pale eyes whose color Ames could not quite discern. Blue, green, gray—they seemed to change with the light as she turned her head. She wore a dress of brown silk, lace trim at the high collar, ruching across the bodice, and a handsome jewel at her throat. Had Edgeware supplied that brooch? Ames wondered—and the dress as well?

Although she had nothing pretty about her, she had a certain tranquillity—a strong confidence in herself, a sense of being comfortable in her own skin, that made her seem attractive even though she was not. As plain as she was, he realized, she was an intriguing woman. No wonder Edgeware was taken with her.

As he obviously was. He sat beside her and held her hand, as if he thought she needed reassurance. But she was quite calm, not the fluttery, fainting female one might have expected after such an appalling occurrence.

"I met your sister yesterday, Mr. Ames," she was saying. "But I never learned whether I was able to be of help to her."

"You don't know?"

She shook her head. "No. I never know what I—what comes through, or what happens in the room. I am in trance, you see. I know only what people tell me afterward."

"So you were not aware of—ah—anything untoward? Any unusual movement, or a sound, perhaps?"

"No."

"And the police have told you about the medical examiner's findings?"

"Yes."

"My sister has been informed that she is a suspect in the case."

"As I suppose we all are," Mrs. Sidgwick replied with what Ames thought was remarkable calm. She might have been speaking of the weather. What would it take to disconcert her?

"The next time," Edgeware said with some heat, "I will insist that Frank Shattuck be here. You should not be interrogated without counsel."

Mrs. Sidgwick frowned. "Such a *fussy* little man, that inspector was. So self-important."

"Fussy and self-important he may be," Ames replied, "but once he gets an idea into his head, it is well-high impossible to get it out again. What did you say to him?"

"Why, just what I would say to you—or anyone." She gazed at him with perfect composure. "I don't remember anything. I never do when I am in trance. I know that Roland comes—"

"Your 'control,' as you call him," Ames interjected.

"Yes. My control. I know—because my querants tell me—

that he appears. Not in the flesh, of course, but his spirit. He takes questions through me, and through me he gives what answers he can. Nothing is guaranteed, of course. Sometimes no message comes."

"Why is that, do you suppose?" Ames asked.

"I have no idea. I do not claim to understand the process, Mr. Ames. I am merely its instrument."

"Have you always been, even as a child? Or did this—ah—ability come to you after you were grown?"

He couldn't be sure, but he thought he saw her tense slightly. Good, he thought, so she is not so tranquil, after all. It did not seem right that a woman in her position would be so calm, so seemingly unperturbed by the fact that a visitor to her house had been murdered. Surely any normal woman would be more upset? But Mrs. Sidgwick did not claim to be normal, he reminded himself; on the contrary, she claimed to be anything but.

"When I was a child," she replied, "I fell from a wagon. I suffered a blow to my head. I was unconscious for some days. When I came to, I was—different from what I had been before."

"Different? How?"

She made a movement of her narrow shoulders, as if she were impatient with his questions. "I discovered that I could go easily into trance. And when I was in trance, I was able to make contact with those who had gone before."

"But about this business yesterday," Edgeware put in impatiently. "I asked Mr. Ames to see you, Evangeline, because he has some experience with—some connection to—the authorities, and yet he is free to act independently. It seems to me that this matter must be settled quickly, or your reputation will be irreparably harmed."

He was interrupted by a soft knock. At Mrs. Sidgwick's bidding, the door opened to reveal a female child and her attendant.

"I beg your pardon, Ma'am," said the attendant, a pleasant-looking young woman in a plain dark dress. "We thought to say hello to Mr. Edgeware. I didn't realize—" She cast an apprehensive glance at Ames, as if she were afraid the police had returned.

"It's all right, Miss Kent," said Mrs. Sidgwick. "You may come in. Hello, dearest."

This to the child, who was not, Ames realized as she stepped cautiously into the room, a child at all but a girl of about fifteen or so—he couldn't tell for sure. Small and slight, with a shy, almost fearful air to her, she was a pretty little thing with large blue eyes and brown hair a shade lighter than her mother's. She wore a dress of blue silk, rather fussily trimmed with satin bows and lace, that seemed too fancy for everyday.

She advanced to stand before Edgeware (as if it was her habit to do that, Ames noted) and rapidly bent her knees in a charming little half curtsy.

"Now, then, Louisa, how are you today?" Edgeware asked, smiling at her as he patted her cheek.

"Very well, sir." Her voice was like herself, shy and hesitant. Was it the mother's almost preternatural self-confidence, Ames wondered, that had made the daughter so unsure of herself? He remembered his sister at that age: confident and merry and bright, chin up, ready to meet the world and all it had to offer, good or bad.

"This is Mr. Addington Ames," Edgeware said.

The girl glanced at Ames and murmured a greeting.

"Now, Miss," Edgeware went on. "Have you mastered that sonata I brought you last week?"

"Yes, sir."

"Good. I will come later to hear you play it for me."

At this, an expression very nearly like terror flitted across the girl's face, but she quickly recovered and said faintly, "Yes, sir."

"We are going for our walk," Miss Kent said to Mrs. Sidgwick. "So perhaps, if we are not back in time—?"

"Yes, yes. Tomorrow will do as well," Edgeware replied heartily. His gaze lingered fondly on the child. "And the new dress is ready, eh?"

"Yes, sir," Miss Kent replied.

"Excellent. Well, I will want to see that, also. Off you go now, catch the day at its best."

And with a final pat to the girl's pale cheek, he smiled at her in an encouraging way, as if he understood her shyness, her fears. She kissed her mother; then, with her attendant shepherding her, she went out.

Edgeware cleared his throat. "Fetching little thing," he said to Ames. He looked vaguely embarrassed, as if his concern for the girl was not quite proper.

Mrs. Sidgwick stood and went to the window. Was she trying to catch a glimpse of her daughter as she left the house? Ames wondered. To make sure that the girl—or her governess—had not been making an excuse to leave this room but really had gone out?

"Now," said Edgeware. "Where were we? Ah. Yes. I was saying, Evangeline, that Mr. Ames has very kindly agreed to see you, and perhaps—yes, Ames?—to look into the business—"

"Look into it?" said Mrs. Sidgwick. She came back to them, but she did not sit. "I don't understand. What can Mr. Ames do that the police cannot?"

"I don't know. But he has managed to be of some assistance to them in the past, and since this is a particularly delicate matter—confound it, Evangeline, do you want your reputation ruined?"

"My reputation." She seemed to think about it. "No. Of course I do not. I must say, the police were rather intimidating. They seemed to think that I was responsible—"

"Well, there you are," Edgeware said as if that settled the matter. "You can't live with such a cloud over you. Sooner or later they will find out who killed Clay. And of course it won't be you, my dear, nor your sister either, Ames. But by that time, the damage will have been done. No one will want to come here. And you've worked so hard to establish yourself—"

He turned to Ames. "You understand, there are many fraudulent mediums. People—men and women both—who seek to prey on the bereaved, to trade on people's longing to speak to their loved ones who have passed on."

Ames nodded. "Yes."

"And so when someone comes along who is genuine, like Mrs. Sidgwick here, it is very important—for the cause, you understand—that she not be disgraced."

"The cause," Ames repeated. "You mean, the cause of spiritualism?"

"Yes. That is exactly what I mean. It is difficult enough to separate the wheat from the chaff. We don't need scandals like this as well."

"Apparently Mr. Ames does not share your concern," Mrs. Sidgwick said. She gazed at Ames with that same tranquil, self-assured look. "Do you, Mr. Ames?"

"Well, I—"

"Excuse me," she said, turning toward the door. "I have something I think you ought to see."

After she left the room, Edgeware said, "You see she is perfectly genuine, Ames. I know you don't share your sister's belief, but—"

"Hope," Ames interjected. "I would call it hope rather than belief."

"As you wish. The point is, and I am asking you as a friend of your late father's, I would like you to look into this affair. I cannot believe that Clay's death was not natural. The police have been known to make mistakes before, as I do not have to tell you."

"Inspector Crippen has every faith in his medical man."

"But your own sister is under suspicion, is she not? I would think, for that reason if for no other—"

He broke off as Mrs. Sidgwick returned. She carried several sheets of paper, which she gave to Edgeware.

"I thought perhaps Mr. Ames might want to look at this," she said. "What with all the confusion yesterday, I neglected to tell Miss Ames about it. I would have notified you myself, Mr. Ames, had you not come here today."

Edgeware scanned the sheets. "I did not know you had received this," he said. "I can't make—but, yes. Look here, Ames."

He handed them to Ames. They were several pages of indecipherable scrawls, here and there a legible word: "fate," "death," "love."

"What is it?" Ames asked.

"Automatic writing," Edgeware said. "She always keeps a pencil and paper to hand when she is in trance. Sometimes messages come to her, not through her control, but in some other way. She writes them down."

Ames glanced at Mrs. Sidgwick. As before, she was not at all embarrassed, as he would have been, to have such an outrageous claim made for her.

"You mean, you hear voices that others with you do not hear?" he asked her. "You—ah—take dictation, so to speak?"

"Yes," she said. He thought he saw a faint gleam of sympathy in her eyes.

"And you don't know what it is that you write?"

"No. No more than I know what Roland says."

"Does it ever make sense—this 'automatic writing'?"

"Sometimes. Sometimes not."

He started to hand the sheets back to Edgeware. "I don't think—" he began.

"Look, man," Edgeware interrupted. "You haven't seen what is there at the end."

Ames looked. He saw the pages of meaningless, indecipherable scribbles—and, at the last, two words. He could not repress the shiver that traveled up his spine as he read them, and yet, by themselves, they had little meaning.

"You see?" said Edgeware.

"Yes," Ames replied. "I see."

Little meaning, but still they were oddly, unnervingly, sinister.

The words were "Ames next."

CHAPTER
7

THE SUN WAS JUST SETTING WHEN AMES BOARDED THE NEW electric cars that would take him across the river to Cambridge—the "electrics," as they were known. As he lowered himself onto one of the slatted wooden seats, he gazed out across the shining surface of the water reflecting the sunset, lavender and silver and rose. Looking over his shoulder, he could see the golden dome of the State House, the highest point on the landscape, glittering in the last of the light. He could remember when they'd gilded it, in seventy-four. Too extravagant, some of his father's friends had complained, but it had been right to do it. Even a city as straitlaced as Boston, not wishing to seem too showy, needed a little show once in a while.

He settled himself for the journey. He'd used this new conveyance often enough, but he was still not accustomed to it. He kept looking for the horses at the front, and when he didn't see them, he felt a little stab of concern.

We are hurrying too fast toward the end of the century, he

thought, everything speeding up. There was even a movement afoot in the city to build an underground railroad like the one in London: iron rails tunneled through the earth, subterranean railway carriages traveling at some incredible speed, unimpeded by the traffic that clogged the city's streets, carrying people ever faster to where they wanted to go.

He sighed. Perhaps, hating change as he did, he was traveling too rapidly himself, straight into middle age. He was thirty-nine—forty, come September. It was some kind of milestone, he supposed. He didn't like to think about it.

As they came into the twilit streets of Cambridge, the river behind them, he thought about what he would say when he arrived at his destination. He'd not asked for an appointment, so perhaps he'd not have the chance to say anything at all. William James was a busy man, much in demand; Ames didn't even know if he'd be at home.

But if he was—what to say? To ask? Harold Edgeware had said Professor James had taken an interest in Mrs. Sidgwick. Perhaps that wasn't entirely true, or perhaps the interest had faded. Perhaps she had disappointed him in some way, as she had disappointed Caroline yesterday afternoon.

Caroline. If she hadn't insisted on attending that séance, none of this would have touched them. Clay would still be dead, yes, but it would be no affair of theirs. Now she was mixed up in a murder investigation—was a suspect in it.

How Crippen must enjoy this, Ames thought with some bitterness. Did he know that his desire to court Caroline made her frantic with disgust? If he did, at the very least he could make her life unpleasant for the duration of this inquiry. And—Ames wouldn't put it past him—all the more so as a kind of revenge for knowing that Caroline would not welcome his paying suit to her.

She'd gone to see Clay's sister-in-law, she'd told him at dinner. He wasn't sure he approved of her doing that, but since she'd already gone and done it, he wouldn't chastise her. She was upset enough as it was; he didn't need to add to her distress.

He'd promised their parents he would always look after her. But it wasn't always easy, looking after Caroline. She had an unfortunate streak of independence that in some other woman, a woman not so charming, would have been called Amazonian—unwomanly. He often had the sense that Caroline, left to her own devices, would have been an Amazon herself—striding about uncorseted in ankle-short skirts, demanding the vote. But her demeanor was usually so sweet, so docile, he was taken off guard when every now and then she opposed his dictates. Or, worse, as she had done yesterday afternoon, when she deviously evaded them.

They were passing through Central Square: a busy place, stores on every side, the lights just coming on now in the dusk. People clambered on, people clambered off. The bell clanged, warning the horses—and their drivers—who had not yet learned to avoid this new conveyance. Would there come a day when horses were no longer seen on the city's streets? Ames couldn't imagine a world without the pervasive odor of horse dung.

He alighted just short of Harvard Square and, threading his way through the crowds of students along the sidewalks, made his way to James's house on Irving Street. Here it was quiet, with large, gracious dwellings set well back, streetlamps shining through the new-leafed trees that lined the way. He could see families gathered in the lighted parlors; children's voices carried out on the mild night air, and now and then he heard a snatch of song, a few notes from a piano.

Family life. He'd never felt the need for a family of his own. His life was eccentric, perhaps—he was an autodidact, a solitary—but it suited him. And he didn't particularly like children.

He strode rapidly up James's front walk, crossed the veranda, and rang the bell. A boy answered, and when Ames asked to see the professor, he said, "Come in, sir."

William James should not make himself so accessible to every casual caller, Ames thought even as he stepped across the threshold. He'd never been here—his acquaintance with the professor was confined for the most part to their mutual membership in the St. Botolph Club—and as he looked around him, he realized that this was exactly the kind of place he would have imagined James lived in: a spacious, fireplaced front hall, clutter lying about, books spilling off the wide settle by the hearth, a tennis racket atop a carved chest of drawers, a woman's shawl draped over the newel post. From somewhere above he heard children's laughter, and then the thump of small feet, running.

He'd given his card to the boy—one of James's brood, obviously—and now here was the professor himself, emerging from the back hall, hand outstretched, a smile of greeting to welcome his caller.

"Mr. Ames! What a pleasant surprise."

"I hope I am not disturbing you, sir."

"Not at all, not at all! We've just finished dinner. Can I offer you coffee? Or something stronger, perhaps?"

William James was a slight, nervous man of some fifty years with a high, domed forehead and a neat, graying beard. His clear blue eyes were the brightest Ames had ever seen, and his mind— the mind behind those eyes—was by far the most brilliant he'd ever encountered. With the publication two years before of his monumental work on psychology, James had acquired a reputation that went far beyond the confines of Harvard Yard, and yet here he was, a paterfamilias in the midst of this domestic scene, shoving aside with his foot a stray roller skate, reaching down to deter the family dog from slobbering over Ames's pant leg.

"No, thank you," Ames replied. "I merely wanted a word. If this is not a convenient moment, I can see you at the club—"

"No, no! I was prepared to spend the evening reading something of my brother's that I haven't had the chance to look at—*The Princess Casamassima*, have you seen it? I realize that Henry has a great talent, but I sometimes think it is a talent I am destined never to appreciate. Come along, come along—"

As he spoke, he led the way back along the hall to his study. This was a large room that seemed small because of all that was in it: glass-fronted shelves crammed with books and journals and stacks of manuscript; more books and journals on tabletops and on the surface of the vast partners' desk; upholstered chairs before the tiled fireplace; a fainting couch by the window; a standing globe; a glass display case filled with—Ames saw as he stepped close to look—the preserved corpses of several tiny monkeys, stuffed birds, a human skull, a tray of dead insects each neatly pinned and labeled, a scattering of rocks, several fossils, a bird's nest with three speckled eggs . . .

"Smoke?" said James, offering a box of what looked like excellent Havanas. "I smoke here, not anywhere else in the house. Wife objects to it. No? Don't mind if I do?"

They settled themselves by the empty hearth, and James clipped the end of his cigar, lit it, and drew heavily. "Now," he said. "What is it? Another serial killer?"

Ames had consulted him, in the winter, in the matter of a series of murders in the South End, which a hysterical public had attributed to the infamous Jack the Ripper.

"Hardly that." Ames put his hat on a side table and looked away from James's kindly but very keen gaze. What he was about to say made him feel faintly ridiculous. "Professor, I have been told by Mr. Harold Edgeware that you have an interest in spiritualism, and that you have in fact some acquaintance with Mrs. Evangeline Sidgwick, who calls herself a medium."

"That is correct." James nodded slightly, his head wreathed in smoke.

"And so—I hardly know how to ask you this, but I wondered if you could tell me anything about her."

"May I ask why?"

"You haven't seen the late papers?"

"No."

"Yesterday afternoon, my sister attended a séance with Mrs. Sidgwick at which a man was murdered. As outrageous as it may seem, she—my sister—is now a suspect in the case."

"Is she? Yes, I would say that is outrageous indeed. A most delightful lady. Please remember me to her. But about this séance—you were not there, I take it?"

"No."

"You are not a believer in the *Geisterwelt*—the spirit world." It was not a question.

"No."

"And yet Professor Harbinger tells me you are an enthusiastic amateur of Greek and Egyptian history."

"That is so."

"Then I do not have to tell you that both those civilizations had an active belief in the afterlife. You were to have been a member of Harbinger's expedition to the Valley of the Kings this past winter?"

"I was, yes."

"A pity he had to cancel. Ah, well, a broken leg is nothing to sneeze at. Too bad he couldn't have broken it over there. Then at least you'd have been on the site, no need to leave."

This rather cold-blooded comment did not disturb Ames, who knew all about academic ruthlessness.

"But about this woman, Professor—"

"Mrs. Sidgwick, yes." James took a puff or two and then removed his cigar from his mouth and stared at it as if doing so helped him to think. "I met her seven years ago—seven years, almost exactly. My wife had gone to her with my mother-in-law; they were trying to contact my wife's late father."

"And did they succeed?"

"Yes. Or so they believed. When they came home, they couldn't wait to tell me about it, could not say enough in praise of Mrs. Sidgwick. They planned to visit her again, and nothing would do but that I must accompany them. I was reluctant to do so. Not so much because I feared harm to my reputation—my reputation, such as it is, can take care of itself. For me it was simply a matter of time. There are never enough hours in the day for me to accomplish what I must, and to take an entire evening, travel across the river, sit with this woman who, I was sure, was almost certainly a fraud—no, I did not want to do it."

"But you did."

A faint breeze stirred the sheer white curtains at the window; from the garden, Ames caught the scent of lilac, almost strong enough to overpower the professor's cigar.

"Yes. I did. My wife is such a very good woman, I find it difficult to deny her occasional requests. So I went. I met Mrs. Sidgwick, and very carefully I observed her as she went into trance."

"The room was dark?"

"Not completely. A faint light came from a candle on a sideboard. She went into trance quite easily—I have often hypnotized people; I can tell the difference between a real and a fake trance—and then it began. Questions put to her, and her answers. Or, rather, the answers given to her by her control."

"Roland."

"Roland, yes."

"Did you question her?"

"I did. I asked her very particular questions that needed very particular answers."

"And?"

"And I received those answers with every question I put. I will not deny it: I was astonished."

James leaned toward the hearth to knock off the thick ash at the tip of his cigar. He peered at his visitor intently for a moment; then he sat back once more and said, "I do not blame you for being skeptical, Ames. Skepticism is the basis of all science, all knowledge. But I tell you, I put questions to that woman to which she could not possibly have known the answers. And, more, she volunteered information that she—out of trance, I mean—could not possibly have known."

"For instance?" Ames asked.

"For instance: On the very first night the three of us went to Mrs. Sidgwick—my wife, my mother-in-law, and myself—her control warned us that a close relative—in New York, mind you—would soon die. When we returned home, a telegram awaited us, informing us that my wife's aunt in New York had passed on. We hadn't even known she was ill—she hadn't been, in fact, so no one could have been warned that she might die."

"Yes, but—" Ames frowned. It seemed a fragile foundation upon which to build an entire edifice of belief.

"But it may have been a lucky guess. Is that what you're thinking? I agree with you. So I went back again. That time I took not my wife and her mother, who are believers, after all, and hardly objective about the matter, but a colleague of mine from the medical school. He is a well-known man of science, and a devout atheist with no belief in anything but what he can see and touch. Certainly he does not believe that we survive death, that we live for eternity in some kind of afterlife. He put a series of questions to Roland that Roland—or Mrs. Sidgwick, either—could never in a thousand years have known the answers to. Questions about his childhood—and remember, Mrs. Sidgwick had no idea that I would bring anyone with me, let alone who it might be."

"And was this man convinced?"

James smiled. "Let us say that if he was not convinced, he was at least a little shaken in his disbelief."

"And you?"

"Oh, I have an open mind always. It is the only way to proceed. If a thing seems to be, and proves to be, then it probably is. But I was not done with Mrs. Sidgwick—not yet. Since then I have visited her at least two dozen times. And I have written her up for the Society for Psychical Research in England as well as for our own branch over here."

"So you do believe in her," Ames said.

"As much as my scientific training allows me to, yes."

"Can you explain it—what it is that she does?"

"No."

"But you believe it."

"I do." James leaned forward, a fervent teacher with a captive pupil. "You see, my friend, we are fortunate to live in a great age of invention and discovery. The telephone, the typewriting machine, Edison's electric light, the camera, the bicycle—have you tried a bicycle? Amazingly difficult to keep one's balance—all kinds of things are being discovered or invented, or are about to be. Right up to the end of the century and beyond. The end of the century, Ames! Think of it! And one of those discoveries may be—I say 'may'—that we survive Death."

It was full dark outside now. In the cluttered room overflowing with the myriad interests of this brilliant man—this genius, even—the lamplight pooled down on his forehead and made a little halo of his hair as his last words echoed in the silence.

After a moment he went on. "I see your doubt, Ames, and I cannot say I blame you. It is a startling thing to say, is it not, that we survive Death, that Death is not the end. But what if Death were merely a passage to another life—a passing over to the majority, if you will? That view of Death has been a belief of mankind since the first primitive man, in the Neander Valley in Germany, buried his dead with grave goods to see them on their way through the next world.

"Every civilization we have known since then has believed in life after death—the survival of the human soul: the Greeks telling us of Odysseus and how Circe taught him to contact the dead Tiresias, sheep's blood and all. The Egyptians with their *Book of the Dead*—a complete instruction manual on how to live in the afterlife. The poet Dante, guiding us through purgatory and beyond. Jesus Christ Himself telling us that 'In my Father's house are many mansions'—how do you interpret that? Not to mention the very basic Christian belief in life after death—it is the very foundation of the religion, and one it shares with many others. I could go on, but you take my point."

Ames sat silent. He reminded himself that he was in the presence of a world-famous scholar—a man widely respected, even revered, for his knowledge, his brilliance. And yet . . .

"The Fox sisters," he said.

He referred to a pair of notorious table-rappers who had come to prominence some years before, subsequently disgraced as frauds.

James waved his hand dismissively. "The Fox sisters were a couple of charlatans, I grant you. But don't condemn it all because of them. Think of people like Andrew Jackson Davis. Like David Dunglas Home, over in England. I could name half a dozen more—well-known mediums, all of them, and amazingly impressive in their *Wissenschaft vom Übersinnlichen*, their knowledge of the supernatural, the world that lies beyond what our senses can tell us."

"But—" Ames shook his head. He felt battered by the professor's enthusiasm, but he was not persuaded by it.

"Think of this," James went on. "Think of a vast cosmic

reservoir of human thought. That is what remains when we die—the product of our minds. And some of us—some of us still alive here on this plane—have the light. Do you know that expression? It means some of us can tap into those thoughts, some of us can communicate with those spirits that were once flesh and blood like ourselves. People like Davis, and Home, and Mrs. Sidgwick. I know it's hard to believe. At first I had some trouble believing it myself. There are plenty of frauds out there, no question. People who look to pick up easy money, preying on the susceptibilities of loved ones left here behind. Oh, yes. I've seen those, too. *But Mrs. Sidgwick is not one of them.* Even if there were no other medium in the world who had her powers, she alone proves that such powers exist. I put it this way: If you seek to prove that not all crows are black, you need only one white crow. And Mrs. Sidgwick is my white crow."

From somewhere in the house, Ames heard a woman's voice calling, and a child's high, fluting tones in reply. A carriage rumbled by in the street. A clock chimed the hour: nine. He realized that he was trembling, and his throat was dry, so that for a moment he could not speak.

"Sorry," James said then. He threw the stub of his cigar into the hearth, stood up and flexed his shoulders, and nervously began to walk around the room. As he went, he stopped to examine a book, a sheet of manuscript, a curious carved object made of stone. "I've given you too much," he added. "I admit that sometimes I get carried away."

"No. It's just that—"

"You are, by temperament, not a believer."

"That's right."

"Not in anything?"

"Not in anything—beyond myself, and what I can see, and touch, and hear. What I can—find believable."

"You should have stayed on at the College after you received your bachelor's degree," James said. "You should have taken advanced work, gone on the faculty—"

"No." Ames shook his head, thinking of it: a lifetime of confronting callow, impudent, overprivileged youths who didn't want to learn, mountains of blue books to grade, faculty teas. "Not for me, I'm afraid."

"There are many advantages to such a life."

"I'm sure there are. But as Socrates said, 'Know thyself.' "

James chuckled. "Quite. Came to a bad end, though, old Socrates."

"I don't know. Hemlock has its virtues."

James paused in his perambulations and peered into the middle distance. "When I go . . ." he said softly, "I mean to try to come back." He smiled as he met Ames's astonished eyes. "I've told my wife to attend a séance, to try to contact me. It will be quite a feat, don't you think? Assuming that I—or my disembodied mind—realize what is happening. Write it up, I've told her. Send off a paper to the SPR—the one over in London if our own group won't have it." He chuckled. "I hope you don't think I'm mad."

"No. Not at all."

"Well, you may think it. I have to tell you that I care not. I am privileged, here, to follow my curiosity where it leads me. Harvard is a nurturing place, and she nurtures even wayward children like me. And as you have seen tonight, perhaps my curiosity leads me to chase after phantoms—will-o'-the-wisps, things that can never be proved to the satisfaction of some of my more hardheaded brethren at the medical school. But I tell you again, my friend, we are in an age of discovery. There is a man in Vienna—Freud is his name, Sigmund Freud; he was a student of Charcot's, in Paris—who is doing some fascinating work.

Exploring his patients' hidden memories, exploring the darkest recesses of the human mind, and what will he discover, eh? Think of it!"

But Ames couldn't think of it—couldn't begin to imagine it. The darkest recesses of the human mind undoubtedly contained nothing but a lot of garbage that should never see the light of day.

He stood up. Suddenly he felt trapped—confined in the cluttered room, listening to William James's outlandish speculations. He'd been wrong to come here, and now he wanted to get away as quickly as possible.

James understood. "Wait," he said. "You came to me tonight for help, and I haven't helped you at all, have I?"

"Well, I—"

"Let me arrange a séance with Mrs. Sidgwick. You say Miss Ames is somehow caught up in the investigation? Then she must be in some distress. By all means, we must do what we can to assist her."

Ames realized he hadn't mentioned the medium's automatic writing, and he did so now. The professor's eyes brightened even more, if that were possible.

"Automatic writing! Very good—yes, sometimes we get interesting messages that way, and from the living as well as the dead. 'Ames next'—but that could mean your sister, could it not, as well as yourself?"

Ames's heart skipped a beat as he realized the truth of it. Caro in danger—and he hadn't given it a thought.

"That hadn't occurred to you?" James said. "But after all, she was there and you were not. So quite possibly— Yes. We must have a séance with Mrs. Sidgwick as soon as possible. I will telephone her tonight. Do you subscribe to the telephone? No? Then I'll be in touch with you by Western Union."

CHAPTER
8

DEPUTY CHIEF INSPECTOR ELWOOD CRIPPEN TAPPED HIS forehead with a nicotine-stained finger and peered at Ames with angry red-rimmed eyes.

"She says she can't remember," he grumbled. "She's a woman with so-called extraordinary mental powers, and she tells us she can't remember who recommended this Jones person to her."

"Perhaps she is telling the truth," Ames replied. He and MacKenzie sat perched uncomfortably on straight-backed wooden chairs before the little inspector's overladen desk. It was the following morning. They had come to pay a courtesy call on Crippen and had found him rather cranky. He is well out of his depth in this case, MacKenzie thought with some satisfaction.

"The truth, Mr. Ames?" Thoroughly exasperated, Crippen blew out his breath. "From a person like that? A woman who is no better than a carnival shill?"

"She takes no money, Inspector."

Crippen threw him a scornful look. "Not in so many dollars

and cents, perhaps, but she makes a living somehow, don't she? Somebody set her up in that house and pays the bills, don't he?"

"His name is Harold Edgeware. I believe you met him yesterday morning when you interviewed her."

"Aha." Crippen seized a pencil and scribbled a note. "I thank you for that. He passed himself off as her 'friend.' Now you tell me he has an irregular relationship with her. So what else about him is irregular, hah?"

"As far as I know, he is a law-abiding man."

Crippen grunted. "All the same. He may have had some connection with the deceased, some business deal gone bad."

But if Harold Edgeware had had some grudge against Theophilus Clay, Ames thought, he would hardly have chosen a séance at Mrs. Sidgwick's to do away with the man.

"You have spoken to everyone who was there, Inspector?"

"Almost. The daughter was hysterical, couldn't tell us anything. Son-in-law not at the séance, nothing to say about it. Sister of his late wife, nothing there either. Daughter claims she doesn't know if she inherits. Sister-in-law says she does. Sister-in-law gets nothing. No family trouble."

"And the others?"

"Well, there was Miss Ames, of course." A sly grin slid across Crippen's ugly face. MacKenzie gritted his teeth and looked away.

"But we can dismiss her, surely," Ames said easily.

"For the moment, Mr. Ames, we can't dismiss anybody. But I grant you, she's not at the top of my list. As for the rest of 'em— woman who wanted to contact her brother. Woman who wanted to contact her son killed at Gettysburg. And"—he darted a hostile glance at MacKenzie—"this man here."

"Who, unlike my sister, wasn't sitting next to Clay."

MacKenzie hated even to speak to this odious little man, but now his natural instincts of self-preservation surfaced. "I'd never met Mr. Clay before, Inspector, and I had no reason to—"

Crippen waved his hand dismissively. "Right. So unless we can find someone who slipped into the room, did the deed, and slipped out again without being noticed—which I doubt we can—it comes down to this man Jones. Who no one seems to know, and who seems to have disappeared."

"You had his address from Mrs. Sidgwick?" Ames asked.

"Bowdoin Street. I've put a man on the place, but Jones—if that's his name—hasn't been in or out. And if you ask me, that makes him smell to high heaven."

"The fact that he seems to have disappeared?"

"And the fact that although this Mrs. Sidgwick denies knowing him, she may be—shall we say—not coming clean."

"You mean, she somehow conspired with Jones to kill Mr. Clay? But why would she do that? As far as we can tell, she didn't know Clay either."

Crippen contemplated him, tapping the pencil against his desktop. "So she says, Mr. Ames. So she says. But she may not be what she seems. You ever been to one of her—ah—little gatherings?"

"Never."

"You believe in it?"

"In spiritualism? No."

"But your sister, now. She's a believer."

"She—I'm not sure."

"Went there, didn't she? Tried to contact your late mother?"

"That's right."

"But she didn't succeed."

"No, she didn't."

"Well, there you are, then." Crippen leaned back in his chair, nodding as if he had scored a telling point. "Stuff and nonsense, all this talking to the dead."

"I should tell you, Inspector, that some rather prominent people—including, I believe, Queen Victoria herself—take spiritualism quite seriously."

"Oh? The Queen, eh? Well, good luck to her is all I can say. Dotty old thing. Ought to have stepped down years ago, if you ask me."

"And on this side of the water, one of the most prominent men over at the College also takes spiritualism—or Mrs. Sidgwick's version of it, at any rate—very seriously indeed."

"Oh? And who might that be?"

"Professor William James."

Crippen sniffed. "Don't know him."

"He is a world-famous scholar, Inspector. A brilliant man."

"Even the smartest ones can be a bit off balance, if you ask me."

"True. But if you were to meet Professor James, I daresay you'd find him as sane as any of us. And—perhaps I should not tell you this, but I will—he is going to arrange for Mrs. Sidgwick to hold a séance to see if it can be learned—from the late Mr. Clay—who killed him."

Crippen stared, openmouthed. Then he began to laugh. "From the late Mr. Clay? That's rich. What's he going to do? Tell her who did it, and you expect me to believe it?"

Ames shrugged. "Believe it or not, as you please. I will be in attendance, and if we learn anything of interest, I promise you I will make a full report."

Crippen was still laughing. "You do that, Mr. Ames. You come right down here to City Hall and tell me everything. Testimony from a dead man! I'd like to see the judge who allows that kind of evidence into his courtroom!"

"It is good of you to see me, Miss Ames. I hope I'm not interrupting—"

"No, not at all," Caroline replied.

Miss Jennie Price was small and dark, and some years older

than Caroline. They had never met before Monday's séance at Mrs. Sidgwick's. All the same, because of that shared experience, Caroline felt as if she and Miss Price were good friends.

She'd asked Margaret to bring tea, which now appeared. Then, when they were alone again, she said, "Have you been visited by the police?"

Miss Price nodded vigorously. "That's why I wanted to speak to you, Miss Ames. It was dreadful, the way they carried on! As if they thought *I* had killed poor Mr. Clay! *Oh!*" She shuddered at the memory, whether of the police interrogation or the macabre ending to Monday's séance, it was impossible to tell.

Caroline handed her her tea. "You were sitting between Mrs. Sidgwick and the man who called himself Mr. Jones."

"Yes."

Caroline forced a laugh she did not feel. "I can imagine that your interrogation was unpleasant enough, Miss Price, but I will tell you frankly, I doubt they accused you of the crime the way they did me."

Miss Price stared, her teacup halfway to her lips. "They accused you—but that is absurd!"

"I agree with you. But there it is. I was unlucky enough to be sitting next to Mr. Clay, and Inspector Crippen—"

"A fat little man who smokes a cigar?" Miss Price interrupted. "Hateful creature!"

"That's him, yes. He asked to look at my hands, to see if they might be strong enough to have exerted the fatal pressure to Mr. Clay's neck."

Miss Price sipped, set her cup onto its saucer, and leaned forward, causing her corset to audibly creak. "So it really was murder, then?" she said in a whisper, as if she feared being overheard. "I couldn't believe it, Miss Ames. Murder!"

"I'm afraid so."

"But *why*? It doesn't make any sense!"

"Murder doesn't, often enough."

Miss Price frowned. "I think the police are mistaken. I think they are making a mountain out of a molehill. Mr. Clay suffered an attack—apoplexy, heart, who knows what—and died, and that is all there is to it. To say that he was murdered when none of us heard a thing, no cry, no shot, nothing—"

"According to the police," Caroline said, "only the two people sitting next to Mr. Clay would have had the opportunity to—to do what was done to him. Since I did not do it, Inspector Crippen thinks that Mr. Jones is his man."

"And that is why they questioned me so closely?" Miss Price asked.

"I suppose so, since you were sitting next to him. Did you—did he do anything unusual that you remember?"

"No, not that I recalled when I was speaking to the police. At the séance, I was so caught up in the proceedings—my dear brother, and I was able to speak to him at last. How I have missed him all these years!" Miss Price sniffled and paused to drink the rest of her tea.

Then she went on. "But when I stopped to think about it later—after the police left, I mean—I remembered that at one point Mr. Jones let go of my hand. I suppose I didn't notice it at the time. And it must have been then that he—*if* he—"

She covered her mouth with her hand as if she would keep back her next words.

"It must have been then that he stood up and attacked poor Mr. Clay," Caroline finished for her.

Her words lingered in the air, alarmingly out of place, she thought, in this bright, familiar room illuminated by the morning sun. But out of place or not, she needed to proceed; Miss Price might know something important, even something she didn't realize she knew.

"Did you speak to Mr. Jones at all before the séance began?" she asked.

"No. Not a word. He didn't even speak to me when we took our places. I was pleased to sit next to Mrs. Sidgwick, of course, but I would have been just as happy not to hold his hand." She shuddered. "It was so clammy, and he didn't have a good, firm grip. I was worried the whole time that he would break the connection because he wasn't holding my hand tightly enough, and yet I could hardly squeeze his, could I? He might have gotten the wrong impression of me," she added primly.

"Try to think, Miss Price," Caroline urged her. "Did he say or do anything at all that might help us?"

Miss Price shook her head. "No. But what does he have to say himself? Surely the police have questioned him, too?"

"I don't know. I suppose they must have. Inspector Crippen, when he came here to question me, didn't know about him— didn't know who was sitting on Mr. Clay's other side."

"And you told him?"

"What little I could, yes."

"Oh!" Miss Price exclaimed. "I just remembered something!"

"What?"

"About Mr. Jones!"

"Yes?"

Miss Price shot Caroline a triumphant look. "He left early! Don't you remember? He wasn't there when the police came!"

Caroline blinked. No, she hadn't remembered that. And you should have, she chided herself. That is an important detail. More than a detail. Not that it helps us much. But she would tell Addington, of course, and perhaps he would be able to make something of it.

"Are you sure?" she said.

"Yes, I am, because Mrs. Ellis—she was the elderly lady—said it was too bad there was only one gentleman to help lift Mr. Clay onto the settee."

"Dr. MacKenzie." But he hadn't done that in the end; Clay was too heavy for him to lift by himself, and so he'd lowered him onto the carpet.

Caroline rehearsed the scene in her mind: Clay's hysterical daughter, Mrs. Ellis frightened half to death, the medium still partly in trance and not entirely aware of what was happening, the maid shrieking in the hall . . .

And where had Mr. Jones been? She'd seen him muttering to himself in a corner, she remembered that clearly enough, but then, when the police came—

Miss Price was right. He hadn't been there. He'd vanished, gone as mysteriously as he had come.

Who was he? And where was he now?

CHAPTER
9

IN THE HUSHED AND SHADOWED CONFINES OF THE SOMER-
set Club, a few doors down from the State House, Addington
Ames was not so frequent a visitor as he was to the rather livelier
St. Botolph, over on Newbury Street. All the same, he came here
often enough to know nearly everyone and for nearly everyone
to know him.

Accordingly, as he entered the Somerset that afternoon, just
as the luncheon crowd was emptying out from the dining room,
he knew whom he was looking for, and in a moment he had
found him: Endicott Minot, not only a fellow Somerset member
but also a classmate from the College.

"Ames. How are you?" Minot said, not sounding terribly interested. However, since Ames's sister's name had been in the
newspapers—again—he cast a somewhat more inquisitive eye
over Ames than he would have ordinarily, and nodded when
Ames asked him if he had a moment.

"What is it?" Minot asked. "My cousin Leicester?"

Score one for you, Ames thought, for saving me the trouble of explaining what I want. "Yes."

"He doesn't get a penny. The old man didn't like him. Old Clay couldn't deny his daughter when she wanted to marry him, but he didn't trust him, either."

"Why not?"

Minot shrugged. "Far be it from me to tell tales out of school, but—well, you didn't know old Clay, did you?"

"I knew of him. I suppose everyone did. But I didn't know him personally more than to say hello to, no."

Minot smiled sourly. "A most generous man. Oh, yes, quite the philanthropist. As he could well afford to be. But—I tell you this privately, of course, and I know you can keep the confidence because my pater knew yours. The finest kind of gentleman of the old school, was your father. Your sister is involved in this affair, is she not? Too bad."

Ames agreed that it was. But about the late Clay?

"Well," Minot went on, "it is just that while he may have been a paragon of generosity as far as philanthropy was concerned, I think he was rather more tightfisted when it came to his family. His daughter, of course, had her private way into his heart—she never would have been allowed to marry my cousin otherwise—but from what I heard, he kept his wife, and his late brother, who was not the success that he was, and there was an aged aunt, I believe, totally dependent on him—all those folks, I heard, were kept on a rather short leash."

Ames nodded. When a man had such a lot of people needing money from him, he thought, he had better keep them on a short leash or he would be beggared in no time.

"Do you think your cousin would speak to me?" he asked. "Under the circumstances," he added.

"Oh, I imagine he would," Minot replied. "I don't think

the—ah—circumstances are bothering him at all. I mean, he doesn't seem to be terribly cut up about old Clay's death, but then again, why should he be, considering that his wife is about to become one of the richest women in Boston?"

"Is he here?"

"Yes. Have you met him? Yes? Well, go ahead and speak to him, then. Don't say I told you to, we don't get on."

David Leicester was a long-limbed young man, very fair, with blue eyes slightly too close together and a slightly dissolute look to him. He glanced up from his newspaper as Ames approached him in the members' room. This was a spacious chamber overlooking Boston Common, sparsely populated now in the early afternoon.

"Hello, there," Leicester said, offering a lazy, languid smile and a rather limp hand. Shaking that hand was like taking hold of a dead fish, Ames thought; in his opinion, a weak handshake was an even greater indication of a man's bad character than his physiognomy.

" 'Afternoon," he said, settling himself in a leather chair opposite. "Please accept my condolences on your father-in-law's death."

"Thank you. How is your sister?" Leicester replied.

"Caroline? Oh, she's all right. But as you obviously know, this is a rather more serious case than it seemed at first."

"Rather," Leicester drawled. "Or so the police told us." He was wearing appropriate mourning, black neckcloth and a black band around the left arm of his dark gray coat, but somehow he didn't seem to be in mourning. Rather, he seemed like a man who harbored a delicious secret.

And what might that be? Ames wondered. That he had just come into a large sum of money? Caroline had reported what Mrs. Briggs had said, and what Minot had just confirmed: that

Clay's money had gone to the daughter. Perhaps, after all, that wasn't so; or perhaps Leicester thought he would benefit from it all the same. Which, undoubtedly, he would.

"I told the old man," Leicester went on, "I said, don't get mixed up in that mumbo jumbo of table-turning and spirit-rapping and all that nonsense. But April—my wife—insisted that he go with her, and so he went." He lifted one well-tailored shoulder in a dismissive shrug. "And now look. The old boy's dead, and not only dead but murdered, and we are all"—he rattled the newspaper—"in the public prints."

"How is Mrs. Leicester taking it?" Ames asked.

"Oh, she'll be all right," Leicester said airily. "Once she realizes how much money she's going to come into, she won't give him another thought."

Ames remembered that this man's sister had been traveling with his cousin Valentine in Europe for the past several months. He hoped the sister was made of sterner—and better—stuff.

"The police tell me they are looking for a man who calls himself Jones," he said.

Leicester lifted his pale brows. "An obvious false name, wouldn't you say? Jones? It doesn't say anything about such a man in the *Herald*."

"Yes, well, I don't imagine the police give out all the information they have," Ames said dryly.

"You are privy to confidential information from them?"

"Some, yes."

"I just remembered. Your cousin sits on the Board of Commissioners, doesn't he?"

"Yes. But he has nothing to do with—"

Leicester snapped his fingers. "Now I understand! Your sister was not only in the room, she was sitting next to the old man. And the police think she was somehow involved?"

Ordinarily, Ames gave not one thought to people's opinions—of him, or of his sister, either. Now, however, despite himself, he looked around to see if they were being overheard. They weren't.

"I would remind you that you soil a lady's good name with such talk," he said, leaning in toward Leicester. "But, yes, it has been mentioned—and dismissed. Inspector Crippen concluded that even though she sat next to Mr. Clay, her hands were not strong enough to have done the deed. Quite aside from the obvious fact that she didn't do it. So he is looking for this Jones, who sat next to your father-in-law on his other side."

Caroline had told him that Miss Price had reminded her that Jones had left before the police arrived. All the more reason to make him the chief suspect in the case, it seemed.

But the question remained: why? Why would he have wanted to kill Theophilus Clay, who had been one of the best-loved, most-admired men in Boston?

Could this extraordinarily unimpressive young man conversing with him now know the answer to that?

Leicester frowned and pulled out his pocket watch to ostentatiously check the time, even though a tall clock stood plainly visible in one corner.

"You must excuse me, Mr. Ames. I have a rather pressing engagement, and I must be on my way."

He made as if to rise but sank back again into his chair as Ames put out a restraining hand.

"One moment more, if you please. My sister describes this man who calls himself Jones as being small, inoffensive-looking, nondescript-looking, in fact. He may have been someone your late father-in-law knew. Can you remember ever seeing such a person?"

Leicester shook his head impatiently. "Such a person? Hard

to remember such a person as you describe him, Mr. Ames. 'Nondescript?' But the world is filled with men who are nondescript. How can one be expected to remember them?"

"You must have known some of Mr. Clay's acquaintances," Ames persisted. "Might you not have seen such a man? Even someone who might have approached him in a public place—in a restaurant, say?"

"My father-in-law did not approve of restaurants. He thought it was a waste of money to pay double or triple for food that one could eat so much more cheaply at home. It was all I could do, a year or so ago, to persuade him to accompany me to Locke-Ober's one evening, and even then he consented to go only because they do not admit women. He did not approve of women dining in public, either, with or without men," he added with a sarcastic half-smile.

"But all the same," Ames said. He knew he was being too pushy; at any moment, this young man would cut him off, and rightly so, for theoretically, at least, David Leicester was in mourning, and if one spoke to him at all, it should be only to offer one's condolences.

Leicester stood up. "Please remember me to your sister," he said. "My own sister is with your cousin Valentine in the South of France, is she not?"

"That's right," Ames replied, rising also.

"We are in mourning for the next year," Leicester said, not troubling to conceal his unhappiness at that fact. "But after that—perhaps we will see each other socially. My wife is very fond of entertaining."

Ames watched Leicester thoughtfully as he walked away. A strangely disappointing young man, he thought. The kind of weak and shiftless young man who looks to find an heiress and, having found her, marries her.

Odd that a shrewd businessman like Theophilus Clay—and

for all his philanthropy, he'd been known as a shrewd, hard man when it came to the business of business—should have failed to discern what kind of man it was whom his beloved daughter wanted to marry.

But then, often enough, the human heart had a wayward streak, as he of all people should know well enough by now. Caroline's misadventure, for one thing, years ago with that feckless fellow who had done a midnight flit, never to be seen again.

And his own wayward thoughts of Serena Vincent, for another?

Nonsense. He was far too set in his ways to allow himself to become involved with Serena Vincent or any other woman. Yes, she was often in his thoughts. Yes, she was beautiful—beyond beautiful. That was not a word that could begin to describe her.

He stared out the window at Boston Common, a symphony of gold and green. But what he saw, in a half-dream, lulled by the warm afternoon, the peace and quiet of the members' room, was a tall, statuesque woman with auburn hair and wide greenish eyes. She was smiling at him.

Stop it.

He shook himself awake.

Had David Leicester had a part in Theophilus Clay's death? And if he had, what had he done, and how?

Had he hired the elusive Jones to kill Clay?

A dangerous business to hire someone to do such a deed. If you hired a man for that, he could turn on you—blackmail you, thus forcing you to do away with him as well, involving you in yet another murder.

A certain amount of sturdy backbone would be required to undertake such an enterprise.

Was David Leicester the kind of man who had such a backbone?

Ames didn't think so.

On the contrary, David Leicester had struck him as the kind of man who might well wish his wealthy father-in-law dead, but who lacked the necessary intestinal fortitude to make that wish come true.

CAREFULLY, CAROLINE EASED ASIDE AN OVERGROWN strand of ivy to read the inscription on the gravestone. It was a family name she knew, but she hadn't known this particular member of it. It was a lovely stone, she thought as she moved on, its white marble only just beginning to weather.

Mrs. Briggs, intent on her errand, had gone on before, but Dr. MacKenzie was waiting. Caroline felt the satisfying crunch of gravel beneath her high-button shoes as she hurried toward him.

It was a glorious day, and Mt. Auburn Cemetery was at its best. On every side, flowering trees and shrubs were at the height of their bloom, purple and pale lavender and white lilacs perfuming the air with their sweet scent, a pink dogwood just ahead covered with blossoms. Scarlet tulips and rosy azaleas lined the paths, and against the bright blue sky the wine-colored leaves of a young Japanese maple fluttered in the breeze.

Caroline loved Mt. Auburn, loved the thought that when her time came, she would lie here for eternity next to her parents in the Ames family plot. She knew it really didn't matter where she lay after she died, but she was glad it would be here.

"I must take you to see the War Memorial," she said as she came up to MacKenzie. "It is my very favorite thing—the Sphinx, just up there, by the chapel."

He'd never seen a cemetery like this. The ones he'd visited in the Midwest had been plain affairs, not much ornament to the plots, every now and then a modest monument atop the grave of some prominent man. But Mt. Auburn was different—almost like a museum, he thought, with all this statuary. Winged angels, cherubs, miniature Greek temples, Gothic arches—and all this lush botanical display, bursting now at the peak of its springtime bloom.

They trudged up to the Sphinx, which had the body of a lion—enormous paws, he noted—and a stern, female face. Caroline closed her eyes for a moment, and MacKenzie, seeing her lips move, realized she was saying a prayer. For the war dead, he assumed; the Civil War, thirty years ago, had claimed many hundreds of thousands of men's lives. He wondered if the Ameses had lost a family member.

"And now," she said, "we can visit Mama."

She led the way along one of the curving paths to a tall granite obelisk. "Ames" was engraved on it in large letters, and in smaller letters, Christian names and dates beneath. She bowed her head while he lingered respectfully behind.

Dear Mama. I so wanted to speak to you. Did you know that? Did you hear me?

For a moment the spring blooms all around her blurred as tears came to her eyes. Her mother was gone, and her father, as well. They would never come back, probably not even through Mrs. Sidgwick's control.

As they moved on, she saw Mrs. Briggs ahead, walking purposefully down a path.

"I don't know exactly where the Clays are buried," Caroline said, "so let's not lose her."

As, he realized, it would be easy to do in this place: curving paths, hills and valleys, extravagant statuary, acres of shrubbery and vegetation to conceal a person. As a rule he didn't like cemeteries; they depressed him. He'd never been in one this large, either, which made it more depressing than ever. And if one were inclined to believe in spiritualism (which he was not), here was an entire community of spirits to commune with—if they could be summoned.

Rounding a bend, they saw Mrs. Briggs in the distance, making her steady way. Closer, standing before a fenced-off family plot, was a youngish woman gazing at the flat marble tombstones within. She looked up as she heard their footsteps and smiled as she recognized Caroline.

"Miss Ames."

"Miss Hereward!" Caroline responded with genuine pleasure. "I haven't seen you in an age. How are you? This is my friend, Dr. John MacKenzie."

They shook hands. Caroline glanced at the gravestones but made no comment. Then Miss Hereward said, "My fiancé. Do you remember?"

"I—oh, dear. Yes. I do."

She hadn't remembered quickly enough, however, and she was ashamed of herself for that. Poor Miss Hereward—and that awful case that had involved Addington, and dear Papa . . .

Sudden tears came as she recalled the events that had led—she was sure of it—to her father's death, ten years before, and she turned away for a moment to collect herself.

Miss Hereward watched her, sympathy shadowing her face. Once, MacKenzie thought, this woman might have been pretty. Now, well past her first youth, she looked—what? Haunted, he thought. Her fiancé lives for her yet, in some way, so that she cannot get on with her life.

"How is your brother, Miss Ames?"

Caroline had blinked her tears away, and now she faced Miss Hereward once more. "He is very well, thank you."

"I have never forgotten what he did. I will always be in his debt."

"Yes, well, he did only what had to be done."

Caroline turned to MacKenzie to explain. "There was a case, ten—no, eleven years ago now—in which a man organized a stock swindle. I can't tell you the details. I didn't fully understand them then, and I certainly can't remember them now. But at any rate, it turned out that Papa—who was the most honest, the most honorable man in the world—had been taken in, and had lost a great deal of his clients' money as well as his own. Some of them sued him. And then the confidence man who had organized the swindle was tried for fraud. Addington looked into the matter, and he testified against him."

"Chester Snell." Miss Hereward looked as though she'd bitten into a particularly sour lemon. "It was Jonathan"—her voice broke as she turned toward the tombstone she'd been contemplating—"who first identified him."

MacKenzie looked at the inscription. "Jonathan Dwight. 1847–1881."

"Yes. That's right," Caroline said. "And Mr. Dwight passed away—"

"Under mysterious circumstances," Miss Hereward said flatly. She threw a defiant look at MacKenzie, as if she feared he would dispute what she said next. "Jonathan named Chester Snell as the man responsible for swindling Mr. Ames—and many others—and the very next day he died beneath the wheels of a speeding carriage. Since he was not inebriated—Jonathan was not a drinker—I have never believed it was an accident."

"So tragic," murmured Caroline. "Dear Miss Hereward—"

"The police investigated?" MacKenzie asked. He was uncomfortable in the face of the woman's obvious pain, and he wished the day had not been spoiled by this encounter.

Miss Hereward allowed herself a bitter smile. "Oh, yes. They investigated. They found nothing, of course. Snell was a clever man. Clever enough to kill poor Jonathan and get away with it—but not clever enough to outwit your brother, Miss Ames. It was his testimony that sent Snell to the penitentiary. It is fortunate that he is incarcerated, or he might try to harm your brother, too. I hope he rots there," she added savagely.

To this, neither Caroline nor Dr. MacKenzie could think of a reply, and so after an awkward moment followed by a promise from Miss Hereward to call soon at Louisburg Square for tea, they moved on. When they'd gone a little distance, MacKenzie turned to look back at the solitary figure standing before the Dwight family plot. The sight of her there, grieving not only for her fiancé but surely for herself, as well—no husband, no children—stirred his feelings more than he would have thought possible.

"You heard Miss Hereward say it could never be proved that Mr. Dwight was killed by that awful man, Snell," Caroline said as they walked on. She was looking down, studying the tips of her shoes as they peeped beneath her skirts: right, left, right, left. "It is the same for me—I could not prove that dear Papa died as a result of that terrible case, but I know Addington always believed it. He—Papa, I mean—was never himself afterward. He had been badly humiliated. Imagine it—to have been sued by his clients! He went into a decline, as if his faith in himself—his faith in his own judgment—had been so badly shattered that he could never believe in himself again."

"Everyone makes mistakes—" MacKenzie began.

"Of course. But not when you have been paid all your life, as Papa was, to make prudent decisions for your clients. And then to be deceived yourself, in your old age, by a slick confidence man with a stock swindle— No. It was very hard on him. All during Snell's trial, I could see him visibly withering as he stood before the world, exposed as a dupe, a foolish man who had succumbed to Chester Snell's lies. I really do believe it was the public shaming that killed him. Can such a thing be, do you think?"

He had no idea. His medical expertise was army surgery: a gangrenous leg, a bullet in the arm, an emergency appendectomy. The idea of the mind's ability to bring about a man's physical demise—as if one could will one's own death—was beyond him.

After climbing a little slope, they found Mrs. Briggs at the Clay family plot, at the grave of her late sister. It was a good-sized space, with neatly trimmed grass and an urn of fresh flowers.

"Theo provided for the flowers in perpetuity," she said now as they came up. "And I shall do the same for him if April does not. Such a dear man," she added. "I shall miss him." For a moment her face crumpled in grief.

"Mrs. Briggs," breathed Caroline, "if there is anything we can do—"

"You have come here with me today, Miss Ames, and that was kindness enough." Mrs. Briggs gazed over the landscape: a white wilderness of statuary.

A veritable city, MacKenzie thought. A city of the dead. But were the dead truly dead? Or did they exist in some unknown dimension, able to make contact with the living, but only through a few gifted ones like Evangeline Sidgwick?

Despite the warmth of the sun, he shivered. Let them lie in their eternal sleep, he thought. He wanted no communication with the dead; communication with the living was difficult enough.

CHAPTER
1 0

WITH A LOUD *CHINK*, AUNT EUPHEMIA AMES SET HER
teacup onto its saucer and pursed her withered lips, preparatory
to making—Caroline just knew it—some important, and probably unwelcome, announcement.

Aunt Euphemia was a tiny, wrinkled creature, well into her
seventies but defiantly healthy, determinedly active, who considered Boston Society—her Boston, the city of her ancestors—to
be her own special province. Long ago she had been one of the
fiercest, one of the most dedicated of the abolitionists, running
escaped slaves to Canada, flouting authority, breaking the law
with impunity. Now, in her old age, she was grimly law-abiding,
aghast at what she considered the breakdown of morality in the
city's youth. She dressed always in black (for the Union dead),
she was invited to all the best social occasions (although she did
not always attend), and she never hesitated to say exactly what
she thought.

What she thought this afternoon was that Caroline should

not have wasted the day by traipsing about over at Mt. Auburn Cemetery.

"We will all go there soon enough," she said sternly, fixing Caroline in her dark, intense gaze that was so like Addington's. "Why do you need to rush it?"

"It was a beautiful day, Aunt, and it is such a beautiful place, after all." A weak reply, Caroline chided herself, but no reply was ever strong enough to fend off Aunt Euphemia.

On the other hand, she did not want to admit that she had gone to Mt. Auburn at the behest of Mrs. Briggs, whose brother-in-law had been, apparently, murdered on Monday afternoon at a séance that Caroline had attended. Aunt Euphemia did not approve of séances, and she most certainly did not approve of murder. Fortunately, she subscribed only to the *Boston Evening Transcript*, which did not publish sensational news, even news as sensational as the murder of Theophilus Clay at a séance in one of the best neighborhoods in the city.

"Nonsense. Go to the Public Garden if it is such a fine day," Euphemia replied. She shot a glance at Dr. MacKenzie, who sat cradling his teacup, hoping not to be noticed. He was not a timid man, but Euphemia Ames was a terror such as he had never met; having met her, over the winter, his only aim now was to avoid her.

"I plan to," Caroline replied, glancing at Dr. MacKenzie also. He winked at her and she stifled a giggle. Yes, she would go to the Public Garden tomorrow—with him—and ride on the swan boats, but Aunt Euphemia did not need to know that.

"But that is not what I wanted to say to you, Caroline," Euphemia said. "What I wanted to say to you is that Valentine is coming home next week."

"She is? I didn't know that!" Euphemia's ward, who was her orphaned niece and Caroline's young cousin, had spent the winter in Rome and spring on the Côte d'Azur, recovering from a broken engagement. She was not a reliable correspondent; Caroline hadn't had a letter from her in over a month.

"Yes. On the *Olympia*. Due in a week from today if they keep to their schedule. And I am planning a party for her."

"You are?" This surprised Caroline even more; Euphemia hadn't entertained for years.

"Yes. I thought she should be properly reintroduced. After—what happened."

Caroline understood. Val's broken engagement had been a minor scandal, but hardly the scandal it might have been had the full facts of the case come out. Fortunately, Euphemia had never learned the whole story.

"That's very good of you, Aunt," she said.

Euphemia snorted. "She made some kind of misstep—oh, yes, don't think I don't have my suspicions. Not that I would expect you to tell me about it. You covered up for her, didn't you? No,"—she held up one wrinkled claw in protest; MacKenzie noted her large emerald ring, loose on her shrunken finger—"don't tell me now. You know my heart is not as strong as it should be."

Caroline knew nothing of the kind, and in any case she didn't believe it.

"But how delightful, Aunt, that you are going to entertain. Val will be thrilled. And if I can help you at all—"

Euphemia nodded. "I expect you can. I'll let you know."

"You have everyone's name," Caroline said. She meant the name of everyone in Val's set, all of whom were connected by arcane intertwinings of marriage going back two hundred years and more.

Caroline had attempted, once or twice, to explain to MacKenzie the interconnections of Boston families. She'd drawn vast family trees, each with its lush sproutings of branches and twigs and little trailing vines, but he'd been confused at her talk of second or third cousins once removed marrying back into a family that once, two centuries before, had all lived under one roof. Cabots and Lodges and Lowells, Saltonstalls and Ameses and Lawrences and Peabodys—no, it was all too much for him. He'd come away thinking that Boston Brahmin blood must be running thin; they'd need to start marrying out fairly soon, or they would all wind up as idiots over at the McLean Asylum.

"Yes," Euphemia replied. "You'll probably want a new dress," she added. She squinted a little as she studied Caroline's costume. It was a perfectly respectable spring walking dress of pale gray serge that Caroline hadn't worn for two years because last year she'd been in mourning for her mother. Today, when she'd put it on, she'd been dismayed to find that it was a trifle tight. More than a trifle. Well, when she went to Mrs. O'Donovan to order a new dress, she'd ask her to let this one out. And all her others, she thought. She longed to be slender like Val, but she knew she never would be.

"Yes, Aunt. I'll go to see Mrs. O'Donovan as soon as I can."

"I cannot understand why you have an Irishwoman for your seamstress." Although Euphemia had been devoted to the effort to free the slaves, she'd never taken an interest in other oppressed classes.

"Because she is clever and quick, and she has a tremendous sense of style," Caroline replied. And, she thought but did not say, because she never overcharges the way some more fashionable dressmakers do.

"Hmmph," Euphemia said, but then she moved on to more important matters. "Now, Caroline, I will want to let you know at once when Val arrives. I cannot believe that you still have not taken a subscription to the telephone."

Oh, dear. As Euphemia spoke, Caroline heard Addington coming in. The last thing she wanted was yet another argument about whether they should have a telephone. Euphemia, who had had one since the winter, was thrilled with it; she'd urged all her friends to subscribe, as well, so she could call them. As old-fashioned as Euphemia was about many things, she was apparently determined to keep up with the latest inventions. Caroline had even heard her say that she hoped, soon, to have electric lights in her house—the first resident of Chestnut Street to have them.

"Don't you want one?" Euphemia was saying now, just as Addington pushed open the pocket doors and came in.

"Hello, Aunt," he said, smiling at her. He was very fond of her—fonder, Caroline admitted guiltily, than she herself was. "Don't we want one what?" He crossed to place a swift kiss on Euphemia's withered cheek.

"A telephone!" Euphemia exclaimed. "We are on the brink of a new century, and we must keep up! I cannot believe that a man of your intelligence wants to be left behind. Everyone is getting a telephone—even Hattie Ordway, who is as deaf as a post and cannot possibly hear what anyone says to her in person, never mind through a machine."

Ames accepted his tea from Caroline and stood at his usual place by the hearth.

"Don't you mind the interruption, Aunt?" he replied, still smiling at her. "Bells ringing at all hours—"

"Pshaw," she retorted, waving her claw again. "At my age, I like to know that people still want to talk to me. That they remember I am still alive, for goodness' sake! I tell you, Nephew, just as I told Professor Bell himself the last time he was in Boston, 'That is a most wonderful invention,' I said. 'Nothing ever like it before!' He didn't mean to invent it, of course. It was an accident—he was trying to think of some device to help deaf people." Swiftly she turned on Caroline. "You'd like one, wouldn't you? With all your committee work? Surely you would find it helpful."

"Yes, Aunt, but perhaps—"

"Very well, then," Euphemia said, nodding emphatically so that the black feathers on her black bonnet fluttered a little. "I will order one for you. I will speak to Mr. Goodrich himself. He is the manager of the Boston office," she added. "I will tell him to install it at once. He won't do it personally, of course, but he'll send someone immediately. With luck, you should be connected by the end of the day tomorrow."

Caroline did not dare glance at her brother. Would he think she had put Aunt Euphemia up to this? And how was Euphemia on such good terms with the telephone company's manager? Possibly, Caroline thought, because she made frequent complaints about the service. Euphemia never dealt with underlings.

Euphemia was standing, preparing to take her leave. "You'll see," she pronounced. "You'll like it. You won't be able to imagine how you ever lived without it. Call me immediately, as soon as you are connected!"

And with that, declining Ames's offer to escort her the short distance to Chestnut Street, she took her leave. When he came back from seeing her out, Caroline said at once, "Addington, I hope you don't think that I—"

"No, Caro. You can be devious enough when you like, but no, I do not think that you asked Euphemia to insist that we subscribe to the telephone." To her relief, he laughed. "I can hold my own against you, but against Euphemia—never!"

"So you don't mind?" she breathed.

"I do mind. But Euphemia is right, after all. We must keep up with the times, must we not?"

"Yes, Addington. We must." She watched as he—as thin as a whippet—selected a plate of pastries from the tea tray and settled himself in his chair. "Did you have an interesting afternoon at the Athenaeum?" she asked him.

"Interesting enough. I was reading up on Professor James's

hobby horse. There is a surprising amount of literature on the subject, some of it written by him."

"You mean spiritualism?"

He'd told her something of his interview with William James, who had confessed to her several months before that he was a devotee of her own favorite novelist, Diana Strangeways. He preferred her sensation novels to the weightier efforts of his brother, Henry, he'd said. Caroline had been delighted to learn that now she had something else in common with that world-renowned scholar: a belief—or at the very least, an interest—in spiritualism.

"Yes. A great many people take it very seriously, and they have written it up at some length. What about you? How was Mt. Auburn?"

"It was glorious—of course. And we met—"

He quirked an eyebrow. "Yes?"

Too late, she reminded herself that he would not want to hear about Miss Hereward and her late fiancé.

"It was Miss Hereward, Addington. Do you remember her? She was visiting the grave of Jonathan Dwight, who was—"

"Yes. I remember who he was." His face had darkened, and Caroline berated herself for having upset him.

"And?" he asked. "What did Miss Hereward have to say?"

"Well, nothing much. I mean, she—"

"What, Caro? I can see from your expression that it was not just the usual chatter."

"No," she replied softly. She looked down at her hands, which were clenched tightly in her lap. "It was not that."

"Well?"

She met his eyes. "She said—oh, Addington, she is so very unhappy. She has never recovered from losing Mr. Dwight. She believes very strongly that that terrible man who was sent to prison—"

"Chester Snell."

"Chester Snell, yes. She believes it was he who pushed Mr. Dwight under the carriage. Do you think that could be? I know the man was a swindler, but surely he was not a murderer, as well?"

Ames frowned. "Chester Snell was—is—a complete black-guard," he said. "And since it was Dwight who first identified him, he may well have decided to get his revenge while he could."

"So you agree with Miss Hereward?"

"Let us say—I do not disagree."

"But, Addington, if it was Mr. Dwight who first identified Chester Snell, it was *you* who—I mean, it was your testimony at his trial—your testimony about Papa's affairs—"

"Yes," Ames said curtly, ending the exchange.

Ames next, he thought.

He shook his head to rid himself of the image of his father on his deathbed, weeping, confessing his gullibility. Suddenly over-come by the memory of the old man's torment, he moved to the window. Through the lavender-glass panes he saw the shadowed oval with its oddly purplish springtime bloom. Twilight was coming on, and then the night. Soon the lamps would glow around the square as darkness settled over the hill. Stars would come out. And somewhere—beyond the stars?—did his father's soul live on, unquiet, longing to see his death avenged?

Ames next.

Should he tell Caroline about that?

He turned back to the room. Margaret was just coming in to turn up the gas, and in the sudden illumination, Caroline's face—her familiar, beloved face—was strikingly vivid.

Of course he must tell her. Even if those two words meant nothing, he must not take the chance, however slight, that they might mean danger. For her? How could he know?

She was staring at him. "What is it, Addington?"

"Probably nothing of consequence."

The "probably" alerted her even more than his expression.

"What?" she asked more urgently.

He left the window and came back to her.

"In fact," he said, looking down at her, "I am almost sure it is nothing. But Professor James said—"

"Addington!" Trained up all her life to defer to him—to all men—she ignored that training now. Her pretty face was pale with concern, and her soft brown eyes held a hint of their aunt Euphemia's iron will. MacKenzie, looking on and loath to intrude, silently cheered her on. She would never be an Amazon—thank heaven—but she had her share of gumption, and he was happy to see it.

"Tell me," she demanded.

Ames took a deep breath. "When I visited Mrs. Sidgwick yesterday afternoon, she showed me a sample of what she called automatic writing. Apparently, it came to her during her trance on Monday afternoon, when you were there. In the confusion, she neglected to examine it at the time."

"Yes. I remember. It was just before— What did it say, Addington? Oh, I wish I'd seen it!"

"It was mostly indecipherable scrawls. There were only a few legible words, and only two that need concern us."

"And what were they?"

"Ames next."

She stared at him. "Ames next? But—"

"I know, Caro. Not very helpful. Obviously it is some kind of threat."

"Or a warning," she said thoughtfully. "It could be a warning, Addington."

"Threat or warning, it means nothing. I refuse to believe that a message of any kind can be transmitted in that way. The very idea is ridiculous."

"But even if—for the sake of argument—you were to believe it," MacKenzie put in, "you don't know who sent it."

"No," Ames agreed, "I don't."

"What did Professor James say?" Caroline asked.

"He said . . . that although I assumed it was a message for me, it might not have been. It might have been meant for you."

CHAPTER
1 1

WINCING AT THE SLIGHT TWINGE IN HIS KNEE, MACKENZIE knelt and ran his fingers over the floorboards of Evangeline Sidgwick's séance room. It was a solid rock-maple floor, no loose boards, no gaps through which a confederate might project his voice, pretending to be the medium's control.

"Nothing," he said to Ames as he moved on his hands and knees to the carpet under the round séance table. Foolish, he thought, to crawl about like this; if he wasn't careful, he'd be back on Dr. Warren's operating table. He lifted an edge of the carpet and felt along the floorboards underneath it. "If she does use an assistant, he doesn't work from below."

Ames nodded and turned back to the wainscoting. He pressed each panel, searching for the hidden mechanism that would allow it to open. An assistant could crouch in a secret cubbyhole behind, could crack open the panel and project his voice.

MacKenzie, stifling a groan as he stood up, contemplated

the tall cabinet to the left of the door. It was more than eight feet high, and about four feet wide and two feet deep. Made of some dark wood, walnut perhaps, it was flat-fronted with double doors secured by ornamental brass hardware. "How about this?" he said, nodding at it.

"By all means," Ames replied, still working his way along the wainscoting.

He'd been surprised when Mrs. Sidgwick had given him and MacKenzie permission to search the room before that night's séance. He'd expected her to refuse him, but with Harold Edgeware at her side, she'd received him cordially, taken no offense, and told him to search all he liked.

Edgeware had been the offended one. He'd assumed an injured air, as if he thought Ames's request was an insult to Mrs. Sidgwick's honor.

As it was, Ames supposed. On the other hand, the woman must know that people were skeptical about the powers she claimed. And she must know, further, that to have refused would cast suspicion on her—more than rested on her already.

So either she had nothing to hide, or she thought herself sufficiently clever to outwit him.

"Find anything?" he asked MacKenzie.

The doctor was half in the cabinet, feeling along the back, where the wood was joined. "No," he said after a moment. "It seems quite solid."

Ames came to inspect as MacKenzie retreated from the cabinet's interior. "Such a large piece of furniture, with nothing inside," he murmured. "Not even shelving. Now, why do you suppose she has such a thing—and has it here—with no apparent use for it?"

"It would easily hold a man—or even two," MacKenzie offered, flexing his bad knee.

"Yes." Ames reached in, felt the wide, smooth panels. "But

unless he had some secret means to enter it—a means that we cannot find—he would either need to be here before the proceedings began, or he would need to come in after the lights went out, open the cabinet door, and step inside." He shot a glance at the doctor. "You heard nothing like that on Monday afternoon?"

MacKenzie shook his head. "Before her control spoke, it was absolute silence. I'm sure I would have heard—or seen—someone coming in."

Ames grunted. "Yes, I'm sure you would. And in any case—"

A tap at the door, and Edgeware appeared. "Miss Ames and Miss Hereward have come," he said.

Caroline had wanted to invite the young woman she'd encountered at Mt. Auburn. You never knew whose spirit might appear, she'd said, and if Miss Hereward attended, perhaps her presence could bring the spirit of Jonathan Dwight. And perhaps he could tell us more about—how he died.

"Good," Ames replied easily. He took out his gold pocket watch—his father's watch—and flipped open the lid. It was ten minutes till nine. "As soon as Professor James arrives, we can begin."

"You found nothing?" Edgeware asked in a rather belligerent tone.

"Nothing."

"I knew you wouldn't. Great heaven, man, how many times do I have to tell you, Mrs. Sidgwick is no fraud!"

"I understand, sir." Ames felt a brief spasm of pity for Edgeware, who was so obviously enamored of Evangeline Sidgwick. A dubious business all around, he thought; no wonder he is so protective of her. "But you understand that my sister has been implicated in a murder investigation, and in all fairness to her—"

"Yes, yes," Edgeware replied testily. "But surely no one in

his right mind would believe that Miss Ames had anything to do with—ah—what happened on Monday afternoon."

"Surely not," Ames agreed. "But all the same—"

The maid looked in. "Professor James is here, sir," she said to Edgeware, "and the mistress said to tell you she's ready to begin."

A SHORT TIME LATER, THE SIX QUERANTS SAT IN THE DARK-ened room, waiting for Roland.

Dr. MacKenzie, as before, sat on Caroline's right, having maneuvered himself there, eager to have the chance to hold her hand again; Professor James was on her left. On his left was Mrs. Sidgwick, now in trance. Beyond her was Harold Edgeware; then Miss Hereward; then Ames, completing the circle, sitting beside MacKenzie.

Caroline heard a chair creak as someone shifted position. She heard the medium's breath come heavy and harsh as she descended deeper into trance. She felt—was glad to feel—Dr. MacKenzie's large, strong hand gripping hers. As long as he and Addington were there with her, she would fear nothing—not even the voice of the late Jonathan Dwight, gone these past ten years; not even the voice of the late Theophilus Clay, gone for only forty-eight hours.

Was it really only two days ago that she had sat here, trying to contact her mother? No seeking you tonight, Mama, she thought, and perhaps not ever again. Rest easy, wherever you are.

She started as she heard a loud moan. It seemed to come from Mrs. Sidgwick, although in the darkness she could not be sure. But it meant something, she knew; perhaps the control, the temperamental Roland, was coming in. Professor James's grip tightened. He must have heard it, too. They had agreed that it would be the professor who would put the questions, at least in the beginning; if he made contact with Jonathan Dwight, he said, he'd defer to Miss Hereward.

"Ames next" might refer to herself, Addington had said. She hadn't been frightened by that warning—not really—but she'd certainly given it more credence than Addington had.

"Ames next"—but who, in the spirit world, would want to harm her? Or even to warn her—of what? Of whom?

Another moan, louder this time. Then, startling Caroline so that she jumped, three loud raps. That hadn't happened before. What did it mean?

"Are you there, Roland?" said Professor James.

"Yes."

"We seek the spirit of Theophilus Clay."

"TheophilusClayClayClay."

Caroline couldn't be sure, but she thought she detected a hint of laughter in Roland's rather petulant voice.

"Yes, Roland. We seek the spirit of Theophilus Clay. Is he with you?"

No reply.

"Roland? Are you there?"

No reply. The other day, Roland had been rather coy, not to say irritating, in his responses. Caroline wondered why Mrs. Sidgwick couldn't find a control who was more accommodating—or, at least, more polite.

And perhaps, after all, they should have invited Mrs. Briggs and Mr. Clay's daughter to attend. Surely, if Mr. Clay's spirit were to appear, it would be in answer to people who had been close to him in life?

But Addington had said no. If in the highly unlikely event that either of them had in fact murdered Mr. Clay, he might not wish to appear to them. Not that Addington believed that Mr. Clay's spirit would come at all. It had been enough that he had agreed to attend the séance, had agreed that Miss Hereward could come. She hadn't dared to push her luck by arguing with him about who else should attend.

"Roland. Please answer me." Caroline thought she heard a note of irritation in Professor James's voice.

Rap-rap-rap!

What was that supposed to mean? she wondered. How should they—how could they—interpret it?

Mrs. Sidgwick moaned again and then uttered a loud, unintelligible cry. Reflexively, James's hand squeezed Caroline's hard, and he shouted, "Roland! Are you there?"

Silence. Oh, why couldn't the blasted control behave properly? Was he playing games with them? Was Mrs. Sidgwick? Did Roland exist at all, or—

"Dead."

"Yes, Roland. Theophilus Clay is dead. We are trying to contact him."

"Deaddeaddead."

Caroline could sense movement beyond James, where Mrs. Sidgwick sat. She seemed to be swaying back and forth as if she were in pain, although in the darkness it was hard to tell.

"Murdered!"

The word hung in the air, seeming to echo through Caroline's mind. Murdered! So Mr. Clay's spirit knew, after all—

"That's right, Roland. Mr. Clay was murdered. Does he have any idea who—"

"Hurt."

They waited in silence for what seemed, to Caroline, a long time. James's hand was trembling a little in hers.

"Roland? Are you there?"

"So long ago . . ."

This was faint, as if it came from a greater distance than before.

They waited.

"Clara." Loud again.

Caroline froze. "Clara" was Miss Hereward. So it was not Mr. Clay whose spirit spoke, but—could it be—Jonathan Dwight?

"Yes, Roland? There is a Clara here."

"Tell her . . . tell her . . ."

After an excruciating moment, they heard a noise like a grunt, as if someone were struggling. Then came the sound of a woman's soft sobs. Miss Hereward, thought Caroline.

She felt her heart pounding heavily, painfully, in her bosom. She longed to take a deep breath, but because of her corset, she could not.

"Tell her what, Roland?"

A long pause. Then: *"Dark. Dark. Didn't see."*

"Didn't see what?"

"Oh, please!" The strangled cry came from Miss Hereward. "Is that you, Jonathan? Are you there?"

A long pause. Then: *"Yes, Clara. I am here."*

"Oh, my God." Miss Hereward again, but her voice was stronger now. Please don't faint, thought Caroline; it would undoubtedly break the connection. "Jonathan—Jonathan, can you hear me? I must know—please tell me—was it an accident?"

"No."

"Then how—?"

"Pushed."

"Who, Jonathan? Who pushed you? Oh, dear heaven, I knew it! I knew it! I have known it for ten years, and now— Who was it?"

Silence.

"Jonathan, for God's sake, tell me! Who was it who pushed you in front of the carriage? Who killed you?"

Silence again, and then, when the answer came, it was as if it came from far away, as if the voice—the spirit—were retreating back into that ether where it dwelled. *"Snell."*

There was a small commotion across the table. Caroline could not see, but from the sound of it, she thought Miss Hereward must have fainted at last. Someone—Addington?—was moving, trying to help her.

"Roland!" shouted Professor James. "Are you there?"

No answer.

"Turn up the gas!" Ames barked. "She's fainted. Doctor, can you help?"

MacKenzie let go of Caroline's hand and pushed back his chair; she heard him moving in the darkness, trying not to stumble.

"Damn," muttered James. He, too, removed his hand from Caroline's, stood up, and stepped away from the table. A moment later he had turned up the gas in the twin globes beside the mantel.

Caroline blinked and looked around. Miss Hereward was lolling back in her chair, her face deathly pale, her breath coming in gasps. Addington hovered over her while Dr. MacKenzie had loosened her collar and was muttering at her, chafing her hands, gently patting her cheeks.

Mrs. Sidgwick sat immobile, her eyes closed. Was she still in trance? And was it dangerous, Caroline wondered, to jolt her so quickly back to them, back to this room when she had been—where? Caroline couldn't imagine. Now Edgeware was speaking to her, gently trying to awaken her, and, yes, her eyelids were fluttering, she was coming to.

"All right, my dear?" he said softly.

"Yes. What—what happened?"

"Roland spoke."

The medium turned to Professor James, who had come to sit by her once more. "Did you learn anything helpful?" she asked.

"About Mr. Clay—no." He glanced across the table at Miss Hereward, who was now sitting up, weeping inconsolably. "But I believe the young lady had some information."

"Ah." Mrs. Sidgwick was still not quite fully returned to them, Caroline thought. Returned to the living? Was that the right way to put it? The medium seemed oddly subdued, her eyes vacant, and she looked exhausted—completely worn out.

"Well, my friends," said Professor James, "we have done all we can for now. I thank you, Mrs. Sidgwick, for so kindly helping us."

LATER, LYING SLEEPLESS IN HER BED AND LISTENING TO the bell in the Church of the Advent tolling the small hours, Caroline's thoughts drifted. Poor Miss Hereward. She'd been distraught; Addington had seen her home in a herdic-phaeton. Caroline and Dr. MacKenzie had waited up for him, but when he came in he'd obviously not wanted to talk. So they had soon retired, leaving him alone, brooding, sunk into his chair. He was much given to brooding—or thinking, as she preferred to call it.

Ames next. Was Addington in danger? Was she? From whom? From Chester Snell, who may have pushed Jonathan Dwight to his death? Snell was safely in prison—for how long, she didn't know. But if he were to be released—

She started up, and after a moment she swung her legs over the side of the bed, her heart hammering, her thoughts racing. A convict released. She'd read something like that—where?

Diana Strangeways, of course: England's premier lady novelist, whose sensation novels appeared from across the sea every October with the fall of the leaves, when the dark came early and the lamplight in the parlor—or here in her bedroom—beckoned with the promise of delicious hours lost in the wilderness of Miss Strangeways' outrageous plots. Caroline allowed herself few secret pleasures, but Diana Strangeways was one of them. Every autumn, having saved up her pin money, she bought that lady's new novel, and every autumn she succumbed all over again to the magic of Miss Strangeways' rather overwrought prose, her tales of love and (often) forbidden passion, her breathtaking chapter endings that drew one helplessly on so that one read (rather sinfully) late into the night, never mind that one had Sewing Circle in the morning, or some church committee . . .

Silvery moonlight lay in a broad swath across the flowered carpet, so she did not need to turn up the gas. The bookshelf by her fireplace still held many of dear Mama's favorites, this having been her mother's room, but with a generous selection, now, of the productions of Miss Strangeways.

Where? In which one? She scanned the spines of the well-worn volumes (for she was never content to read a Diana Strangeways only once; she read them over and over). The titles were easily legible, their gilt letters winking at her invitingly— *The Ashton Affair, The Hellfire Club, The Sun Is My Undoing* . . . Yes. Here it was: *The Dark Prince.*

She sank onto the rose velvet slipper chair before her empty fireplace and began to leaf through the volume, but the moonlight, as bright as it was, wasn't quite bright enough to read by.

She stood, turned up the gas, returned to the book. Quickly she flipped through the ragged pages. She'd cut them carelessly, so eager she'd been to get on with the truly enthralling story, love and death, honor and betrayal, jealousy and thwarted passion and deeply, deeply satisfying revenge . . .

Here it was. She read the passage once, and then again to make sure. Yes, it was as she'd remembered.

She'd tell Addington in the morning. He might scoff at her, but it was worth a try.

CHAPTER
12

"ESCAPED?" SAID AMES. HE SAT AT HIS PLACE AT THE
breakfast table, sipping the last of his tea. The morning *Globe* lay
beside his place. He'd been annoyed to find that for the third day
in a row, it displayed a prominent headline about Theophilus
Clay's murder.

It was the very stuff of sensation, of course: one of the
wealthiest, most respected men in the city, murdered at a
séance—and not some hole-in-the-wall séance, either, some
dingy room over in the South End, but a séance at the elegant
home of Mrs. Evangeline Sidgwick, who ministered exclusively
to Boston's upper crust. It was a case made for the city's journal-
istic scribblers; even the stuffy *Transcript*, so "proper" that it carried obituaries only once a week, on Saturdays, might run a few
lines about it before it was done.

"Yes, Addington," Caroline replied. He was being deliberately obtuse, she knew, because he did not approve of Diana
Strangeways. "Escaped. It turns out in the end, of course, that

he was never guilty at all, and so that makes it different from Chester Snell's case. But the point is, he escaped from prison and Lady Ghislaine and her father didn't know it! Don't you see?"

He shook his head and shot a glance at Dr. MacKenzie, who was concentrating on his oatmeal. Had the two of them been by themselves, they could have enjoyed a laugh at Caroline's insistence on the relevance of Miss Strangeways' outrageous plots to their own lives, but as it was, MacKenzie kept his eyes on his porridge and didn't venture any comment.

"Frankly, Caro, I don't. You are trying to say—"

"I *am* saying, Addington! You told me yourself that Mrs. Sidgwick showed you her automatic writing that said 'Ames next.' Don't you think you at least ought to pay a visit to Inspector Crippen—"

"Again?"

"Yes, again! And again after that, if necessary!"

Uncomfortable under her assault, Ames shifted in his chair. He held her gaze, however, as he replied, "If I understand Mrs. Sidgwick's—ah—methodology correctly, Caro, she receives messages from the dead."

"From those who live, but on a different plane," she corrected him.

"As you wish. The point is . . ."

He remembered what Professor James had said: Sometimes automatic writing came from the living. Should he tell her that?

Definitely not.

"The point is, Caroline, if Chester Snell is dead, he cannot possibly harm us. And if he lives, he lives in Charlestown Prison. Either way, he may send us all the messages he cares to, automatic writing or not, and still he is powerless against us."

Undaunted by his logic, she persisted. She'd felt a terrible sense of urgency last night when she'd found the relevant passage, and nothing her brother said this morning could make it go away. "Addington, I know you don't believe in Mrs. Sidgwick's powers, but—"

"No," he said flatly. "I do not."

"Not even after last night?"

"Not even after last night. What did last night tell us, after all? Nothing. If we are to believe Crippen's medical man, which I suppose we must, someone killed Theophilus Clay at Mrs. Sidgwick's séance on Monday afternoon. We went there last night to try to learn who that someone might be, and we failed. I never believed that we would succeed, and I never would have gone to it if Professor James hadn't organized it."

"But we heard Miss Hereward's questions answered—"

"Yes. But the information was useless as far as I can see. If we are to believe what happened last night, the spirit of Jonathan Dwight spoke to her and told her that it was Chester Snell who pushed him under a carriage. Given what we know about Snell, that news is hardly surprising. But it doesn't help us in Mr. Clay's case, and it doesn't help us in the death of Jonathan Dwight, either, since I know of no judge or jury in the land who would credit such evidence."

"But, Addington—"

He gave her a look, and she understood it. He was saying to her, Go carefully, dear sister, for my patience is wearing thin.

"What is it, Caro?" As his dark, brilliant eyes raked her, his long, lean face settled into lines of disapproval.

She felt a wave of defeat wash over her. All her life she had tried to live up to his strict standards. Four years older, he had always been her dear brother, protecting her (as he ought), guiding her, judging her . . . Sometimes it was exhausting, trying to measure up. She'd known before she began that he would pooh-pooh her mention of Diana Strangeways. "I'm sorry, Addington. I just thought—it might be useful."

"I know what you thought, my dear. But we must—"

A soft knock at the dining room door, and Margaret came in bearing the early mail on a silver tray. Caroline sifted through it. There were bills—of course—and a few invitations, an announcement of a showing of new paintings at the Vose Gallery. Nothing from Val. But here was something odd—a letter from the Park Theater addressed to Ames, and in a woman's handwriting.

The Park Theater. Where Serena Vincent was the resident star. Cautiously, Caroline separated the envelope from the others and handed it to her brother, watching closely for his reaction.

At first he stared at the envelope without obvious recognition, as if he did not know what the Park Theater was. Then he slid his thumb beneath the flap, extracted a folded sheet of paper, and scanned it.

For a moment too long, Caroline thought.

Then, to her intense disappointment, he tucked it back into its envelope, tucked the envelope into the inside breast pocket of his jacket, and held out his cup for more tea.

He is not going to tell us what it is, she thought. But she very much wanted to know, and so, feeling very daring, she said, "What is that from the theater, Addington?"

"A note from Mrs. Vincent. She invites us to the opening night of her new play."

Oh, dear. Over the winter, Caroline had worried that her brother had become attracted to Mrs. Vincent, but recently—as far as she knew—he hadn't seen her, and Caroline hoped he'd forgotten about her.

But obviously Mrs. Vincent had not forgotten him. Was she going to pursue him? Decent women did not do that, or at least not so blatantly, but Mrs. Vincent, as everyone knew, was not a decent woman. She'd been caught out in adultery, divorced by her husband, and banished from proper Boston Society. The fact that she had gone on the stage and made a great success of it made her no less persona non grata to the small circle of upper-crust Bostonians that was Caroline's world.

"Her new play? What is it?"

"I saw the hoardings downtown. A comedy, I believe. A limited run before the summer closing."

"I really don't think we can go, do you?"

Was she imagining it, or did she see a faint gleam of wicked mirth in his dark eyes? "Why not? It is on Saturday evening. We have no other engagements, do we?"

"Well, no, but—"

"Good. That's settled, then." Ames pushed back his chair and stood up. Suddenly he was restless. He wanted to get out of this room, out of this house, and stretch his legs as he so often did, walking the streets of the city. Usually he made these excursions at night, but now, in the bright May morning, he could not bear to be confined a moment more in this quiet domestic setting.

"I am going to Crippen," he said abruptly.

"You are?" This was a surprise. "And you will tell him—?"

"I have nothing to tell him, but I will try to get him to tell me something that may be useful."

Usually, on such visits, he asked MacKenzie to accompany him. The fact that he did not do so now was evidence enough, Caroline thought, that he was somewhat unsettled. By that invitation from Serena Vincent? She hoped not. Mrs. Vincent was nothing but trouble. Somehow she must make Addington understand that.

As Ames left No. 16½, he heard the sound of distant but fast-approaching music. Circus music, in fact: the thump of a bass drum, the oompah of tubas, and a calliope's cheerful whistle. When he reached Mt. Vernon Street and looked down the hill to Charles Street he saw the crowd awaiting the parade—the annual publicity extravaganza of the newly arrived Barnum & Bailey Circus.

Amused, he strolled down the hill. When he was a boy, he'd always loved to see the elephants. They were awesome, mysterious creatures, and no matter how undignified the stunts they were compelled to perform, they always, somehow, retained their majesty.

A shout went up, and here it came—an advance guard of gaily dressed clowns running and jumping, followed by the ringmaster in top hat and tails, acrobats riding their prancing horses, the uniformed musical contingent blaring and pounding away, several barred, red-and-gold wagons carrying lions and tigers that roared now and then to delight the onlookers, and then, finally, the elephants, linked trunk to tail as they lurched along, each with its rider high above the crowd.

For a moment Ames had a brief pang of nostalgia for the heady days when, having saved up his allowance, he was permitted to go to the circus with his chums. So little, then, it took to make him happy.

And now? What did it take now?

He turned away toward Beacon Street and the Common.

Now, he thought, it took the solving of a murder, and even then, his happiness was not assured.

CRIPPEN WAS IN. HIS UGLY LITTLE FACE WAS CREASED IN smiles, and his stubby fingers beat a happy tattoo on his overladen desk as he listened to his caller. "You don't say, Mr. Ames," he said.

"I do say, Inspector. And a most interesting evening it was. Speaking of which, have you found the missing man from Monday's séance?"

"The one who called himself Jones?" Crippen's face soured. "I've got corroboration from the rest of 'em that he was there, next to Clay, but nobody knows who he is."

"Description—anything more helpful than what my sister was able to give you?"

"Not much. Ordinary-looking, like she said. No distinguishing features."

"She has remembered something about him that she asked me to tell you, by the way. She thought it might be important."

Crippen brightened. "Oh? And what might that be?"

"She said that in the commotion after Mr. Clay was found—ah—indisposed, this man Jones, whoever he is, left before the police came. Rather suspicious, wouldn't you say, Inspector? So when you find him, you will undoubtedly have found your murderer. You can telephone me to give me the news, by the way."

"Needle in a haystack," Crippen grumbled, gloomy again. He shot a wary glance at his visitor. "You're finally subscribing? About time. But tell me about this thing last evening, Mr. Ames. Enjoy yourself, did you? Mumbo jumbo, voices from the beyond? Don't tell me you believe in all that. I've always thought of you as a very intelligent man. Hardheaded, not easily fooled. And now you're telling me some carnival fortune-teller has hornswoggled you?"

"No, Inspector, I am not telling you that. What I will tell you, however, is that Miss Clara Hereward made contact with her late fiancé, dead these ten years—"

Crippen interrupted with a loud guffaw. " 'Made contact'? Did you look in the cabinet, where the voice was coming from?"

"It did not come from the cabinet."

"But there was a cabinet in the room? And some ghostly figure came out of it, pretending to be the dead man?"

"No. Nothing like that, Inspector. I examined the room—and the cabinet—beforehand."

"Then where did the voice come from, eh? Tell me that."

"I have no idea. It may have been a fraud, or it may not. All I am saying is that everyone in the room heard it. It purported to be the voice of the spirit of Jonathan Dwight, and it claimed that Chester Snell—you remember him, surely?—pushed Dwight in front of a carriage ten years ago. Which makes Dwight's death not an accident, as was claimed at the time, but murder."

Crippen picked up a half-smoked cigar from the battered metal ashtray on his desk and without relighting it, clenched it between his teeth. "Hard to prove at this point, I'd say. Particularly on that kind of—ah—testimony. I told you, Mr. Ames, there isn't a judge and jury in the state—in the country—that would convict a man on evidence like that. Chester Snell is locked up over in Charlestown on another charge. We have to leave it at that."

"A charge of fraud," Ames said grimly. His father's agonized face rose in his mind's eye. I've been swindled, his father had said. And by that miscreant Snell.

"Inspector . . ." He'd been gritting his teeth so hard that his jaw ached. "When is Chester Snell due to be released?"

Crippen's eyes narrowed. "Why d'you ask?"

"I'd just like to know. Can you find out?"

Crippen kept still, his eyes fixed on Ames. He seemed to be thinking. "It wouldn't do for you to take the law into your own hands, Mr. Ames. You aren't planning anything like that, are you?"

"Not at all, Inspector. And in any case, I would imagine that even a character as brazen as Chester Snell would hardly choose to set up shop in Boston again. He will undoubtedly move on to greener pastures."

"Hmmm. You're probably right about that. And you want to know when he's due out? I'll ask my sergeant."

While Crippen was gone, Ames stood and paced the cluttered little lair. Files were stacked high on the desk and bulging from half-open filing cases that lined the walls, and on top of an overcrowded bookshelf Ames saw a wooden box camera and a stack of glass negatives gathering dust. Cartons were piled in a corner, a pair of India-rubber overshoes perched atop them. A waterproof was draped over a chair, an umbrella leaning against it.

It was difficult to believe that anyone managed to operate in such chaos, and yet, often enough, Crippen got results. Ames had to believe that the Boston police were sufficiently well run that they would not retain, never mind promote up through the ranks, someone like Crippen if he were completely incompetent. Ames's distant cousin, Standish Wainwright, sat on the Board of Commissioners, and Wainwright was a solid man, an intelligent man. He wouldn't allow someone like Crippen to remain on the force if—

Crippen was back.

"What is it, Inspector?"

The little policeman's former bravado had vanished. Before he answered, he lighted what remained of his cigar.

"Gone," he said, exhaling a stream of foul-smelling smoke.

"What do you mean, gone?"

"Chester Snell. My sergeant has the lists. Snell was released on good behavior two months ago."

Released. Ames felt the shock of it rocket through him. Shock—and a sudden hot, flaming anger. Why hadn't he been told? But his anger was quickly replaced by a vision of two legible words in a maze of scribbled incoherence: *Ames next.*

But which Ames? Himself—or Caroline?

And now, for the first time, he felt a shadow of fear. Had that message come from a soul that had passed on? Or had it come from someone still alive? Snell, perhaps?

"And no word of where he might have gone?" he managed to ask.

"No." Crippen shrugged as if the matter were of no importance to him. "He served his time, got his going-away outfit—we give 'em decent clothes so they can find work, not that most of 'em want to—and he's off our books."

CHAPTER
1 3

OFF THEIR BOOKS. HARDLY A HELPFUL PIECE OF INFORMA-
tion, Ames thought as he made his way down the broad granite
steps outside. School Street was busy, the Parker House across
the way thronged with guests going in, coming out. A bright,
busy morning, reassuringly normal.

Behind him lay King's Chapel Burying Ground, a small oasis
of tranquillity that was the resting place of one of his ancestors,
one Jepthiah Ames, a stouthearted Puritan who had come over
on the *Arbella* with John Winthrop. What would old Jepthiah
have done, confronted with spirit-voices that warned him of
some impending disaster? The Puritans, clever, educated men
that they were, had nevertheless believed in witchcraft, so perhaps they would have believed in Mrs. Sidgwick's powers, as well.

Or perhaps they would have hung her for a witch.

Ames next . . .

He turned down School Street toward Newspaper Row on
Washington Street. Soon he came to a doorway cluttered with

small signs, one of which announced the BOSTON LITERARY JOURNAL. In a moment more he had bounded up the tall, narrow stairway and entered the office of his good friend, Desmond Delahanty, the *Journal*'s proprietor.

"Ames!"

Delahanty was a slightly built, red-haired Irishman with sparkling blue eyes and extravagant mustaches that nearly reached his jawline. Somehow—Ames never knew how—he eked out a living by publishing his periodical, his days and nights consumed by reading manuscripts submitted by hopeful scribblers. But for all his unrepentant Irishness, he had made himself welcome (thanks in part to Ames's sponsorship) at many wealthy homes in the city, and was ushered into many Brahmin drawing rooms that Ames, a Brahmin himself, refused to patronize. Delahanty claimed to enjoy the hours he spent with the city's ruling class, if only as an ambassador of his own.

"How are you today, Desmond? Any geniuses turn up?"

Delahanty had been reading a manuscript written in a tiny, indecipherable scrawl; now he threw it down and rose to shake his friend's hand. "No," he laughed. "Not this week. But what brings you downtown? On your way to Crabbe's?"

"Not today, unfortunately. I have a rather more pressing matter to attend to."

In a few moments, Ames had told his friend of the events at Mrs. Sidgwick's séances. He'd expected Delahanty—a man with even fewer illusions about the world than he had himself—to scoff, but to his surprise, he did not. The Irishman nodded gravely, looked around for his keys, and said, "Let's take lunch at the Oyster House. It's quieter there than at Durgin-Park, and the bartender owes me a drink."

The Union Oyster House, in the Haymarket, was a dark, ancient, low-ceilinged place, filled now with the early lunchtime crowd but, as Delahanty promised, with a less frenetic atmosphere than the bustling Durgin-Park Market Dining Rooms. They sat at the semicircular oak bar at the front, with a view to the street. Having collected his drink from the barkeep, and ordered one for Ames and littlenecks for both of them, Delahanty focused his attention on his friend and said, "Now. Tell me the real story."

The real story. What was that? Ames wondered. That he had begun to believe in Mrs. Sidgwick's powers? That he feared—for Caroline, if not for himself—the specter of an ex-convict on the prowl to do them harm?

Or was the real story that he wanted, at last, to avenge his father's death?

"The dead man—" he began.

"Yes—Theophilus Clay. I read about him. And your sister was there?"

"Crippen came to the house to interrogate her," Ames said, hearing the outrage in his voice. "Can you believe it? My sister, a suspect in the case?"

Delahanty smiled sympathetically. "It would have to be a copper even more thickheaded than our Crippen to believe that Miss Ames would kill a man she hardly knew. Or any man, for that matter. And how would she have done it, after all? With her bare hands?"

Ames swallowed one of the briny, icy delicacies before him. He'd often come here with his father, years ago. In season, they'd ordered oysters, which the elder Ames had preferred to littlenecks, but his father had never told him about oysters' supposed aphrodisiacal powers. Being here now brought the old man back to him more forcefully than ever. That scoundrel Snell had killed him as good as if he'd taken a knife to him.

"No," he said in answer to Delahanty's question. "She couldn't have done that. Even Crippen agreed she couldn't—after pestering her for half an hour with his questions. Damn the man!"

Delahanty sipped his Guinness stout and eyed Ames with concern. When he'd first come to Boston, Addington Ames, unlike so many Boston Brahmins, had been quick to befriend him—a penniless Irishman come from the old country, like so many others, to seek his fortune. Well, his fortune had eluded him, what with the perilous state of his little publication, but the friendship had been strong and true. Ames had sponsored Delahanty for membership in one of the Brahmin clubs, the St. Botolph, whose members fancied themselves to be artistic and intellectual and who were, therefore, willing to allow a literary man like Delahanty to join despite the fact that he was Irish. Delahanty often had the notion, at the St. Botolph, that he was watching a tribe of eccentrics called Anglo-Saxons disport themselves, all unaware that an alien Celt like himself was paying close attention. Most of those men he didn't care about, but Ames—yes, Ames was a good friend. He would always do what he could to help him.

"It seems to me that you have two separate problems here," he said. "One, a man was killed at Mrs. Sidgwick's séance, where your sister—and Dr. MacKenzie, too?—was a querant. At that same séance, Mrs. Sidgwick received a message through automatic writing that said, 'Ames next.' "

Spoken in the familiar surroundings of the Union Oyster House, Delahanty's words sounded as if they came from another world. As, presumably, they did.

He went on. "Now, what did that message mean? Automatic writing sometimes comes from the living, so did it mean that the man who killed Theophilus Clay intended also to kill you? Wait—before you speak, Ames, let me work it out. Now we come to the second problem, the séance of last evening, in which—what is her name? Miss Hereward?—received a message from her late fiancé, dead these past ten years, naming Chester Snell as his killer. This morning you learn from Crippen that Snell was released from prison two months ago. Now, consider. Do those facts fit together?"

Ames swallowed his last littleneck and took a sip of beer. "It depends, I suppose, on whether you put any faith in Mrs. Sidgwick."

"Oh, but I do," Delahanty exclaimed.

"What! Have you met her?"

"No, but I've heard of her. There is a woman in South Boston—an Irishwoman," he added with a wry grin, "whose powers may equal hers."

Ames stared at him. "You really believe in all that nonsense?"

"Nonsense?" Delahanty frowned. "I wouldn't call it that. We are possessed of the second sight, you know—we Irish, I mean. Oh, yes. My mother has it. She always knows when something is to happen—something bad, I mean. Good things haven't happened to her very often, and when they do, she doesn't seem to know about them beforehand. She heard the banshee's wail when my da was about to die." He shuddered and looked away.

"But about this woman in South Boston," Ames said. "You have attended séances with her?"

"I have. My da, God rest his soul, has spoken to me through her control more than once. Don't look at me like that, Ames. There are people who have this ability, call it what you will, to go beyond the physical world, to make contact with those who have gone before—"

"William James is a believer," Ames interrupted.

"Well, then. There you are. A world-famous scholar, the leading authority on matters of the mind—and he believes? What more do you need? Does he know Mrs. Sidgwick?"

"Yes. He says he has sat with her many times, and she always transmits information she could not possibly have known out of trance. He can't explain it, but he believes it, and will continue to do so, he says, until he sees proof that Mrs. Sidgwick is a fraud. He calls her his 'white crow'—on the theory that if you seek to prove that not all crows are black, you need only one white one."

Delahanty, satisfied, sat back. "I don't need William James to back me up," he said, "but I am happy to know that such a brilliant man keeps his brilliant mind open to . . . the possibility."

"What possibility?" asked Ames, irritated. He felt as if he walked on thin ice that at any moment would give way, plunging him into a swamp of superstitious nonsense.

"That 'there are more things in heaven and earth, Horatio, than are dreamt of in your philosophy,' " Delahanty quoted.

Ames gave him a look. "My philosophy be damned," he said. "I want to find Chester Snell."

"Why? Do you think he killed Theophilus Clay—made himself invisible and managed it without being seen by anyone in the room?"

But Ames was not thinking of Theophilus Clay. He was thinking of "Ames next"—and the man who, two months before, had been released from Charlestown prison.

"No," he said. "I do not think that. I have no idea who killed Theophilus Clay, but I have unfinished business with Chester Snell, and if he is still in Boston, I mean to attend to it."

Delahanty pushed back his empty plate, swallowed the last of his stout, and said, "Come on, then. Let's pay a visit to Martin Sweeney. He may be of more help, at the moment, than all the mediums in Christendom."

MARTIN SWEENEY'S PLACE, THE GREEN HARP SALOON, was on Atlantic Avenue, hard by the docks. At this mid-afternoon hour, it was half empty, Sweeney himself deep in conversation with a man at one end of the bar. When he saw Delahanty and Ames, he came to greet them.

"Desmond. Mr. Ames." Sweeney was a tall, solid man in an immaculate white shirt, sleeves anchored by sleeve garters, and an equally pristine white apron over his trousers. Ames had met him, had been helped by him over the winter in the matter of the deaths at Bertram's Bower. A lad named Garrett O'Reilly, now one of Sweeney's employees, had been wrongly arrested in the crimes. Ames saw him now across the room, sweeping up.

"Martin, my friend. How are you keeping?" Delahanty settled himself at the bar and accepted the glass of stout the barkeep put before him; Ames declined.

"Not so bad." Sweeney rested his hamlike fists on the polished mahogany surface and flicked a glance toward Garrett. "The lad's doing well, too."

"You have him here full-time now?"

"I do. His ma thinks it's a step up from the Bower."

Garrett had been a boy-of-all-work at Bertram's Bower until the place closed under a cloud of scandal. "Now, what brings you today, Desmond?" he added. Unlike many Irish, Sweeney always got directly to the point.

Delahanty deferred to Ames, who told Sweeney in a few words what he wanted: a way to learn the whereabouts of one Chester Snell, late of Charlestown prison.

Sweeney, impassive as always, thought about it. "An ex-con, is he? I see all kinds in here. I could ask some one of 'em. I suppose you don't want it known you're lookin' for him?"

"Hardly."

Sweeney thought about it some more. "I'm in your debt, Mr. Ames, for what you did for Garrett. They'd have hanged him by now if you hadn't had a hand in the matter." His eyes shifted to a place behind Ames, and Ames turned to see Garrett watching them. He'd have a word with the boy, he thought, before he left.

Sweeney was speaking again. "I know a man with Barnum's circus," he said. "He keeps up his contacts. He might know something."

"Excellent," Delahanty said. "And you'll let us know when he shows up?"

"I will. He always stops by to see me." Sweeney's impassive face softened slightly in what might have been a smile. "He did me a service some years ago, and he's never forgotten it."

Sweeney's attention was diverted then by the arrival of a supplier, and Ames and Delahanty moved over to Garrett, who had finished his sweeping, and seemed to be waiting for them. He was as tall as Ames, even more thin, a strikingly handsome youth with black hair, blue eyes, and fine, sharp features. Because he'd had infantile paralysis, he walked with a limp.

"Mr. Ames. Mr. Delahanty." As they shook hands, Ames noted a new confidence in him. This was not the terrified, distraught lad who had been arrested by Crippen and charged with murder.

"How are you, Garrett?" he said. He glanced around. "Is Sweeney keeping you busy?"

"Busy enough," Garrett replied easily. "He wants me to take classes at the settlement house. Learn to read and all."

"Good idea," Delahanty said. "If you want to get ahead in the world, reading's a start."

"It is. My ma thinks so, too."

"Someday you could have a place of your own," Delahanty added.

Garrett shrugged. "I might. If I could get the capital to start. Or—"

"What?" Delahanty asked, his eyes alight with interest. "You have something else in mind?"

"I was thinking of talking to Johnny Fitzgerald. He might have something for me."

Ames repressed a grimace. Garrett lived in the North End, where John Fitzgerald, popularly known as Honey Fitz for his propensity to sing while he campaigned, always in a mellow, honeyed tenor voice, was one of the new breed of Irish politicos who were building strength in the wards, undoubtedly preparing to take over the city government. Boston had already had an Irish mayor—a time of mourning for the Yankees—but he'd been voted out in the last election, and in any case the Common Council had kept him in check. But there would come a time, Ames knew, when the Irish would control the council as well, and then an Irish mayor could run the city as he saw fit, and the Yankees be damned.

Still, he liked this lad and knew that Caroline did also. "Keep well, Garrett," he said. "And if I can ever be of help to you, come and see me."

"You've already been a help to me, Mr. Ames. But—yes—I will if need be."

Or would it be the other way around? Ames thought as he and Delahanty left the saloon. Would the day come when his own class, outnumbered, outvoted, needed to go to John Fitzgerald—or to Garrett O'Reilly, for that matter—to ask for help in a time when the Yankees no longer controlled this small, bustling city clinging to the edge of the vast continent, the United States port nearest to Ireland and therefore the place that had grudgingly received so many of her children?

The sun was low in the west when they came out onto Atlantic Avenue. Here at the water's edge, bowsprits extended over the sidewalk above their heads, and the smell of fish and tar and salt water permeated the air, overlaying the city's usual odor of gas and horse dung.

Ames looked about. This was not his usual stomping ground, but he felt comfortable here, as he did in all districts of the city. It was at India Wharf, just down the street, that his grandfather, who had built the family's house in Louisburg Square, had had his warehouse, built by an Ames at the end of the last century, shortly after the Revolution. From here, the Ameses' ships had set sail to the Orient; here they had returned with their cargoes of tea and silk and porcelain, some few pieces of which last reposed now at No. 16½. An adventurous life, Ames thought; he could still remember his grandfather and his tales of the mysterious East, where pigtailed, silk-clad Chinamen bargained with the Americans in their hongs. Family fortunes made in the China trade were Boston's most prestigious, even if, like the Ameses', they had dwindled over the years as the trade fell off.

"What are you thinking about, Addington?" Delahanty asked.

"Tea and silk and porcelain." He smiled. "A different era, that was. The great days."

Delahanty sniffed. He knew a little history, Ireland's as well as Boston's. "Not so great in Ireland," he said dismissively. "But listen. I've had a card to an early reception this evening at the Stoddards'. Will you come?"

The Stoddards, Ames remembered, lived around the corner from the Berkeley Arms, Serena Vincent's apartment hotel. She was probably not at home; her new play was to open in two days, and she was undoubtedly at the Park Theater, rehearsing. Still, there was always the chance that he might have a glimpse of her; just to be in her neighborhood would give him pleasure.

"Would that be Snookie Stoddard?" he asked. "He was in the class ahead of me at the College."

Delahanty laughed. "Snookie? Is that what you called him? Not these days, I'll warrant. Or not to his face, at any rate."

"No," said Ames dryly. "Not to his face these days. And yes, Desmond, I will come with you."

CHAPTER
14

CAROLINE TUCKED ONE KID-GLOVED HAND INTO THE CROOK
of Dr. MacKenzie's arm and lifted her skirts a bit to keep them
clean as she and the doctor crossed Arlington Street and entered
the Public Garden. At the corner, the hurdy-gurdy man was
grinding out a lilting tune, and she hummed along, causing
MacKenzie to smile at her. He was pleased to see her so happy,
her cares, for the moment, forgotten.

It was nearly twilight. Around the lagoon, and along the
winding paths, shadows were gathering beneath the trees, and
on the streets around the garden the lights were just coming on.
Above the brownstone spire of the Arlington Street Church, a
silver-gilt moon shone in a sunset sky stained pale pink and
peach; a narrow red cloud hovered over the rooftops along the
Commonwealth Avenue mall. The French called this hour, the
hour between daylight and dark, *"l'heure bleu."* It was, every day
no matter what the season, her favorite time.

She sighed with delight. It had been really a very uneventful afternoon. She'd visited her dressmaker and, as Aunt Euphemia had instructed, had ordered a new gown. It promised to be quite the loveliest gown she'd had since her debut, and Mrs. O'Donovan, reliable as always, had promised to have it ready by Saturday. As much as Caroline didn't want to go to the theater on Saturday evening, as much as she didn't want to lay eyes on Serena Vincent ever again, at least having a beautiful new dress would make the occasion a little less unpleasant.

Later, she'd come out with Dr. MacKenzie, and what they'd done hadn't been, she admitted, all that exciting: a ride on the swan boats followed by an ice cream tea at Bailey's. So why should she feel so happy, so utterly content? She couldn't imagine a place she'd rather be on this, her birthday, or any other day: not being presented at Court to Queen Victoria, not basking in the South of France with Val, not even voyaging up the Nile to see the splendors of Egypt.

"Shall we take the last excursion of the day?" MacKenzie asked. The swan boats were still gliding around the silvery-dark waters of the lagoon, around the miniature islands and under the miniature suspension bridge.

"Oh, yes. Let's." She couldn't remember when she'd been so happy—not since she was a girl, a giddy girl who had lost her heart to a faithless young man who had gone away and never come back. Although she'd vowed never to do that again, Dr. MacKenzie's solid, comforting presence in the household over the winter had made her think she might do so, after all.

Did she want that? She lectured herself as they approached the boat dock: You are thirty-six years old today, Caroline Ames. You are an old maid, a spinster with no fortune. Remember that, and behave accordingly.

Old Mr. Paget, the proprietor of the swan boats, nodded a greeting to them. "Last call, Miss Ames," he said. She'd known

Mr. Paget since he'd started up. Often, when Val was younger, she'd brought her here for rides.

They boarded. There was only one other party, a trio of young women who sat at the back, just in front of the boy on his high seat. He started to pedal and they were off. Caroline and MacKenzie were at the front, and as the little craft with its white wooden swan began to make its stately way through the water, she felt the familiar twinge of excitement she'd always felt riding on the swan boats. As they headed toward the southern side of the lagoon and rounded the little island there, she was aware that her hand, which had been resting properly in her lap, had somehow found its way into Dr. MacKenzie's. I shouldn't allow this, she thought; it is not proper.

But even with her glove, and his, between them, it felt good. Secure, and somehow just right. As it had felt at the séances at Mrs. Sidgwick's.

"If we were in Venice, the boy would be singing," MacKenzie said. She caught the smile in his voice, and she laughed.

"But I'd rather be here, wouldn't you?" she replied. Venice! What did Venice have to offer that Boston did not, aside from a lot of antiquities that she didn't care about? Boston was good enough for her, always had been. Particularly with Dr. John MacKenzie in it.

Willow trees in their first yellow-green bloom were spaced out around the edge of the lagoon, their branches trailing in the water, swaying in the soft evening breeze. As the darkness came on, here and there she could see people walking along the paths, and once, startling her, a live swan flapped its great white wings as it lifted itself from the water to cross the lagoon to reach its mate. Two pairs of swans lived here in the warm months; she had no idea where they went in the winter. She'd heard that swans mated for life, and that their beauty belied a nasty, hostile nature. When creatures mated for life, she thought, they should try to refrain from nastiness—even if they were only swans.

They'd passed under the bridge, and now they were rounding the other islet, the one nearer Beacon Street. The girls in the back were chattering and laughing, but they were doing it quietly, not disturbing the lovely tranquillity of the moment. Impulsively Caroline turned to MacKenzie. "This is the nicest birthday I've had in years," she said. "Thank you, Doctor."

"My pleasure," he replied. "And—what is it they say? Many happy returns." He'd wanted to give her a present as well as this little excursion, but he hadn't wanted to be too forward.

She laughed. "I thought, last year, that I wouldn't count my birthdays anymore. You've made me go back on my word."

"Am I forgiven?"

"Of course. My conscience doesn't bother me a bit."

That was something, MacKenzie knew. Like her brother's, hers was a New England conscience—a Puritan conscience, in fact—and, as he'd learned, a stern guardian of her behavior. She was too hard on herself, he thought, always doing for other people, never doing enough—or much at all—for herself.

He glanced at her profile. He thought she was the loveliest woman he'd ever seen. Why had she never married? What was wrong with the bachelors of Boston that none of them had ever claimed her?

And—he cautioned himself—why, now, well settled in her comfortable life, would she have any interest at all in a man like him: pensioned off from the army on a small allowance, no visible prospects to offer her?

The excursion was over. The swan boat drifted up to the dock, bumping gently against the wooden pilings. MacKenzie handed Caroline out. It was nearly dark now, the globe lamps on the bridge and along the pathways flaring into yellow-white light. As they started along the path toward the corner of Charles and Beacon streets, he said, "I hope your conscience will allow you to take this excursion again before your next birthday? Sometime in the summer, perhaps?"

"Oh—yes, of course it will. But we are to go to Nahant, you understand—we always do. Will you come?"

He hadn't thought about that, although it had been mentioned once or twice: the family's summer home, on the ocean north of Boston.

"I don't—" he began.

"Oh, do, please, Doctor," she said, and then she warned herself, Do not be too eager, or he will think you forward. "I mean," she added hastily, "if it would suit your plans."

His plans. He had no plans. Some months ago he had been invalided out of the army; now he had the rest of his life to live on his own, with his meager army pension to support him. He could try to set up practice in Boston, he supposed, if he could get his Massachusetts medical license. And there was that female physician, a friend of Miss Ames's, over in the South End. Much as he disapproved of lady doctors, he could work with her, perhaps, if he couldn't build up a practice on his own.

"Well," he began, "I might be able to—"

"Oh, *look*!" She'd darted away from him, across the grass to where the water lapped at the granite coping. There, beneath a clump of shrubbery and a thick cluster of trailing willow branches, was a covey of tiny ducklings, quacking loudly as their mother paddled quickly toward them from the islet. "Aren't they adorable? See how fluffy their feathers are, and their little bills, opening so wide. Why, they must be hungry for their supper!"

When Val had been a child, they brought stale bread to feed to the ducks. She wished she had some now. She edged closer. They were enchanting, those tiny balls of fuzzy, fluffy down, all crowding noisily around their mother, insistent—

Something caught her gaze, but in the dusky light it did not immediately register.

Something . . . that did not, as the ducklings did, belong here.

She froze.

Something.

A hand. It lay half-hidden beneath the shrubbery, and what with that, and the trailing branches of the willow, this particular place was dense with growth, a good blind for the ducklings, a good cover for anything else.

A *hand*.

She put her own hand to her mouth to stifle her scream. Her knees went weak, and she would have fallen if MacKenzie, hearing some small sound she must have made, had not swiftly come to her side and gripped her elbow to support her.

"What is it?" he asked. But then, following her horrified gaze, he looked for himself, and saw it: a hand emerging from the water. It was attached to an arm, which was covered by the sleeve of a man's suit.

Dear God.

"Come away at once, Miss Ames," he said more harshly than he had intended. "At once, do you hear me?"

But if she heard, she did not obey him. She stood frozen in place, staring down at the hideous thing at her feet. It would begin to move, she thought; it would reach out for her and seize her by the ankle—

"Miss Ames," MacKenzie said. He was pulling her away, forcibly moving her toward a nearby bench. When she reached it, her knees finally did give way and she sat down, quite hard, on the wooden slats.

MacKenzie hesitated. Should he take her home and summon the police? Or should he try to pull the body—surely there was a body attached to that arm—out of the water? The man could not possibly be alive. He glanced at the hand. It glimmered whitely in the shadows, and he had the sudden, awful fear that it would beckon to him.

"Stay here," he told Caroline. He stepped to the edge of the lagoon. He stood for a moment, deciding what to do, and then, gingerly, as if he approached a snapping turtle or some poisonous snake, he reached down and seized the hand and pulled.

Something moved under the surface of the water.

He pulled again, and this time—ah, God, how hideous it was!—a head emerged, and shoulders.

There was just enough light remaining to see the face. It was a face MacKenzie knew, because he'd seen it just three days before, at Mrs. Sidgwick's séance in Lime Street.

"It's him," said a voice at his side—Caroline's voice, oddly strangled. "It is Mr. Jones—the man Inspector Crippen has been looking for."

"And now," MacKenzie replied, "we know why he couldn't find him."

CHAPTER
1 5

"KILLED THE SAME WAY," CRIPPEN SAID. "PRESSURE TO THE carotid artery." He gestured to a livid bruise on the corpse's neck. "Well, I was looking for him, and here he is. You say you can positively identify him, Doctor?"

"Yes. He is the man I met at Mrs. Sidgwick's séance who called himself Mr. Jones," MacKenzie replied.

It was later that evening. The three of them, Ames, MacKenzie, and Crippen, were at the city morgue. Caroline, somewhat recovered from her shock, was resting at home, since they had agreed that her presence here was not needed.

"Called himself that," Crippen grunted. "Not likely it was the name he was born with."

Jones was a small man, his naked body lying on the slab before them very white in the glare of the gaslights in the white-tiled room. His chest and arms and legs were nearly hairless, and his left forearm was crooked, as if it had been broken and improperly set. His hands, gnarled and worn, looked to be extraordinarily powerful.

Powerful enough to have caused the deadly pressure on Theophilus Clay's neck? Ames wondered. Probably.

"So now you have your murderer, Inspector," he said, turning away from the revolting sight. The air in the room was heavy with chemical stench, and although he'd had no dinner, his stomach felt queasy.

"I imagine I do," Crippen said, frowning. "But now I've got a new one to look out for, don't I? And he has a little imagination, wouldn't you say? Dumping this fellow in the Public Garden lagoon—that's a new one! Almost as if he wanted us to find him. Nasty shock for your sister, though, Mr. Ames. How is she?"

"Fairly well, under the circumstances."

She'd been calm—too calm, he'd thought. MacKenzie had told him how she'd stood at the edge of the lagoon, staring down at that face swimming up at them, and she hadn't fainted, hadn't even turned to him for support. But at last she'd allowed him to walk her away, and she hadn't objected when he'd insisted on flagging down a herdic-phaeton, even though they were so close to home. Then he'd summoned a passing patrolman to deal with their discovery while he'd accompanied Caroline to No. 16½.

Ames glanced at the doctor now. A good man, an honest, solid, thoroughly decent man. And so very concerned about Caroline. The two of them hadn't told him beforehand what they were up to that afternoon, and he'd been mildly surprised when he'd learned of it. He himself never celebrated her birthday because he thought she didn't like to be reminded of her age. Some women her age were grandmothers, while she—

"One more thing, Mr. Ames, before you go," Crippen was saying. He beckoned them back to the corpse, and as easily as if he were upending a stone, he seized one shoulder and half lifted, half turned the body. "See this?" He pointed to the skin covering the right shoulder blade.

Ames, trying not to gag, looked. "It is some kind of tattoo," he said. It was a simple design in dark blue ink, a Greek cross of equidistant arms enclosed by a circle.

"Right," Crippen replied, letting the body ease flat once more. "It's the only identification—if you can call it that—that he had on him. And I don't see how it helps us connect him to Theophilus Clay."

"If someone hired this fellow to kill Clay, and then killed him to silence him," Ames said, "this man will have had no connection to Clay other than being chosen to kill him."

"I wonder what he was paid," Crippen said. "Amazing, what people will do for practically no money."

"It would be important," Ames went on, "to discover—as you have doubtless tried to do, Inspector—whether Theophilus Clay had any enemies. His reputation was that of a widely respected and even loved man, but you may have learned differently."

Crippen motioned to the attendant to cover the body and turned to lead the way out. "Well now, Mr. Ames, as a matter of fact, I have not. Learned different, I mean. From what my men can discover, Mr. Theophilus Clay was a man of impeccable reputation, no enemies, many friends, no reason on earth for anyone to want to kill him."

They were standing in the corridor, where the air was only slightly less nauseating than in the dead-room itself. Ames's thoughts moved on. In his mind's eye, he saw the scribbled sheet of automatic writing that Mrs. Sidgwick had—she claimed—received while she was in trance, during the same séance at which Theophilus Clay had been killed.

Ames next.

But neither he nor Caroline had been next, had they? It was

that poor fellow lying on a slab in that stinking morgue who had been "next."

THAT NIGHT AMES DREAMED THAT A WHITE-FACED CORPSE was pulling him into the waters of the Public Garden lagoon. As he struggled to free himself, he shouted for help but no sound came from his lips. The water was deep—fathoms deep, far deeper than the lagoon really was. He could feel it closing over his head, could feel his hand in that death-grip from which he could not free himself, and then, just when he could hold his breath no longer, he awakened, shaking, sweating, his bed-clothes tumbled—had he cried out?

He sat up, his heart pounding, listening for sounds of Caroline coming to see to him. Dear Caroline. He sometimes thought he had perhaps not been the brother to her he should have been. He'd never taken employment, so that their purse, before the advent of Dr. MacKenzie, had grown perilously thin. Nor had he found a husband for her after the departure of that one young man with whom, so long ago, she'd fallen in love. She'd never fallen in love again. Once burned, twice shy, he supposed. Still, it was too bad she'd resigned herself to spinsterhood.

His heart slowed. The night breeze stirred the filmy white curtains at his windows, and shadows of the trees in the square moved on the wall. He heard the screech of a wandering tom-cat—an eerie sound, but familiar, too, reminding him that he was awake and safe in his own home, his own bed. He'd had a bad dream; now he was rid of it.

But when he lay down again to try to sleep, the memory of the dream came to him again, more intense, more terrifying than before, himself dragged down to the bottom of that deep lagoon by a white-faced corpse, his lungs near to bursting, his panic as he realized he was about to die.

At last he gave up trying to sleep. He sat at his window, the breeze cooling his face while he watched the eastern sky pale toward dawn. William James knew about dreams. He'd ask him, next time he saw him, how to keep from having this one.

A<small>T BREAKFAST THE NEXT MORNING</small>, C<small>AROLINE NOTED</small> her brother's drawn face, the shadows under his deep-set dark eyes, and she regretted all over again having gone to Mrs. Sidgwick's séance against his wishes. If I had obeyed him, she thought, none of this would have happened.

His mood was not improved, she knew, by the fact that once again her name was in the newspaper, as she saw when, silently, and with a warning glance, he handed the morning *Globe* to her.

Most people in their circle scorned the *Globe* as too plebeian and subscribed instead to the reliably Republican *Herald*. But Addington preferred the *Globe*, she wasn't sure why, and so it and the stodgy *Evening Transcript* were their daily source of news.

She scanned the story—she could hardly bear to read it carefully—and then she gave MacKenzie his coffee while she cast about for some reassuring thing to say to her brother. She'd promised Mrs. Briggs she'd go to Theophilus Clay's funeral that morning, but somehow she didn't think that would reassure Addington at all. He sat silent in his accustomed place at the head of the table, not eating, not drinking the tea she'd put before him.

"Addington," she began tentatively, "I've been thinking about that message Mrs. Sidgwick received—the automatic writing."

He glanced up at her, but he did not reply.

"And it occurred to me that if Mrs. Sidgwick receives messages from—from people who have passed over, then that message, too, must be from someone who is no longer alive. So even if Chester Snell was released from prison, if that message came from him, doesn't it mean he is dead?"

"Professor James told me that automatic writing can come from the living as well as the dead, Caro."

"He did?" she replied faintly.

"Yes. It is a kind of thought transference, I suppose."

He cringed inwardly as he heard himself speak. Was he beginning to believe in all that nonsense?

Caroline refrained from answering as Margaret came in with the morning mail, which she presented to Ames. There was nothing of interest, only a bill or two, but now he suddenly perked up and withdrew a folded slip of paper from his pocket.

"Margaret, will you take this to the Western Union office for me?" he said.

And when she had left the room: "I want to ask Mrs. Sidgwick about that tattoo—and I want Harold Edgeware present when I do so. That woman knows more than she has told us so far."

He broke off as they heard the front door knocker. Margaret came back to announce that it was the man from the telephone company.

"Oh, dear! I forgot all about that!" Caroline exclaimed. "We must have it done. Euphemia will be very upset if we don't, since she went to the trouble of ordering it put in so quickly. He was to have been here yesterday. I said I'd call her at once, and she will wonder why I didn't. Where do you think it should go, Addington?"

"Nowhere, if I had my way," he replied shortly. "But you are right, Caro. Euphemia would be mortally offended if we refuse it. Where to put it? In the front hall, I suppose. Blasted thing," he added, picturing the months and years ahead when they would be jolted out of their tranquillity by the jangling of the bell. He knew a fellow at the St. Botolph Club who, after six months of subscribing to the telephone at his wife's insistence, had suffered a nervous breakdown.

Caroline went into the hall to deal with the man, who looked at her with marked respect; he'd never been instructed to fill an order for service so quick, he said. And, yes, right here on the wall at the foot of the stairs was where most folks wanted it, a central place, the bell would easily be heard all through the house. She'd get used to it soon enough, he told her with a reassuring smile; after a week, what with all her friends ringing her up, she wouldn't know how she'd lived without it.

Caroline felt as if she stood at the edge of a precipice and was about to jump off into the void. She wasn't sure how, but she knew this modest little wooden box with its dangling cord attached to the little thingamajig that you put to your ear—this little contraption would somehow change their lives. It was a perfectly marvelous instrument, she knew, an example of the exciting new age of invention in which they lived—the typewriting machine, the bicycle, the camera, the electric cars to Cambridge, and, soon, houses lit by Edison electric lights instead of gas. People could hardly adjust themselves to one new thing before the next new thing arrived. Now, standing in her front hall, she had a sense of breathlessness, of some little panic, even, the way she'd felt, once, when she'd been a passenger in a runaway carriage. She hadn't been able to control the horses, just as she couldn't control the swift pace of change all around her; she could only hold on for dear life and hope she survived.

"Do you recognize this?" Ames asked.

Evangeline Sidgwick looked at his sketch of the cross-in-a-circle tattoo, but she did not take it from him to examine it closely.

Harold Edgeware, however, did. As he studied it, he frowned a bit. "Odd," he said after a moment. He glanced up at Ames, and then at MacKenzie. "What do you make of it, either of you?"

MacKenzie shrugged and shook his head. "I have no idea," he said. "Some secret sign?"

"It is a Greek cross," Ames said, "and the circle is an ancient sign. The sun, the moon, the wheel of time—"

"Some esoteric religion, perhaps?" Edgeware asked. He turned to Mrs. Sidgwick. "You don't know what it is, do you, Evangeline?"

"No." Mrs. Sidgwick looked more than usually pale. "I have never— No. I have no idea what it is—what it might mean." She cast an imploring glance at Edgeware, as if she were begging him for help.

Perhaps she is worried that her trade will fall off, what with this crime—a double crime now—connected to her, MacKenzie thought. She seemed calm enough, and yet he saw something in her eyes, some shadow of fear, of dread, that belied her composure.

"And you are sure you never met this man before, this so-called Jones?" Ames persisted.

"I have told you, Mr. Ames—"

Edgeware silenced her with a hand on her arm. "Let me speak for you," he said softly. And, turning to Ames: "She has told you, she never met the man before Monday afternoon," he said. "The appearance of this—insignia—whatever it is, will not change her mind."

Or her story, Ames thought. All women were a mystery to him, but this woman, with her pale, unreadable face, her soft, uninflected voice, her air of being, somehow, as otherworldly as the spirits she claimed to summon up—this woman was a mystery twice over.

"How did he come to you?" he said.

She held his gaze, but her bloodless lips trembled slightly. "I don't remember."

Crippen had been angry with her for that.

"From what I understand, you receive only those people who are recommended to you. Is that so?"

"Yes."

"So this man Jones could not simply have walked in off the street, announcing that he wanted to participate in one of your—ah—sittings?"

"No. He could not."

"But you say you cannot remember who sent him to you—who vouched for him?"

She seemed to think about it. As she gazed into the middle distance, her mouth worked almost as if she were trying not to cry. At last she turned to him and said very softly, "No."

And now at last Edgeware seemed to lose all patience. "Really, Ames," he exclaimed, "she has told you what she can, which I acknowledge is not much, but can't you see she is severely troubled by all this? If you are going to persist in questioning her—"

"At your request, sir," Ames reminded him.

"I realize that. And I am grateful to you for what you have done. But now that Theophilus Clay's killer has been apprehended—"

"As far as we know," Ames interrupted. "Hard to prove a dead man's guilt, wouldn't you say?"

Edgeware stared at him. Obviously, he regretted this interview, regretted their presence here. He wants us gone, MacKenzie thought. Why, when at first he was so eager to ask Ames's help?

"I imagine it is, yes," Edgeware replied. "But as you see,

Mrs. Sidgwick knows nothing about this—this whatever it is. Tattoo, d'you call it?"

From beyond the closed parlor door, they heard a jangling bell—a telephone bell, Ames thought. He sighed to himself. Soon enough, such a noise would intrude on his own home. He wished he had been more firm with Euphemia, had had the strength of character to refuse her insistence that they have a telephone of their own.

A maid appeared. "It is Mrs. Hall, Ma'am," she said. "I told her you were engaged, but she says she must speak to you."

Mrs. Sidgwick, far from being annoyed at this interruption, seemed to welcome it. "If you will excuse me," she said to Ames and MacKenzie.

Edgeware took his opportunity. "You will be going, Ames?" he said, rising as if to see them out.

Ames gave him a look. "Certainly," he replied. "I am sorry to have intruded on you—on both of you."

Outside on Lime Street, the flat-fronted houses basked in the warm spring sunshine. An S. S. Pierce delivery wagon pulled up. A nursemaid followed a toddler in walking strings along the uneven brick sidewalk. From an open window, they could hear someone practicing scales on a piano.

Nothing here out of the ordinary, thought Ames, and yet he felt oddly ill at ease.

What did Mrs. Sidgwick know that she had not told?

Did Edgeware know it, too?

"What did you make of that, Doctor?" he said.

"I thought it rather odd," MacKenzie replied. "She claims not to know what the tattoo signifies, and yet she seemed discomposed. Hard to say exactly, but—"

"I had the same impression. Blast the woman! If she knows something, why won't she reveal it?"

"Because she is somehow connected to Clay's death?" MacKenzie wondered. "But if that is so, surely Edgeware, as her protector, would not have wanted to involve you in the first place."

"Unless he didn't know of that connection. Which puts him in an awkward position, wouldn't you say?"

Ames gave himself a little mental shake. Why, now, should either of the Ameses care—about Mrs. Sidgwick or the unknown Jones, either? Crippen was satisfied he'd found Clay's murderer, so whatever threat of arrest and prosecution Caroline had faced no longer existed.

Why, then, strolling along this familiar street, did he feel that some menace still awaited him—or her?

They paused at Charles Street, waiting to cross. The sun was hot. Soon it would be summer. He would row and sail on the Charles, and at the end of June the household would decamp to Nahant to escape the city's summertime heat. There had been a cholera scare last summer; conditions in the poor quarters of the city were worsening every year. There had been talk of setting up a special hospital for slum children. They should do that, he thought, and the sooner the better. Epidemics knew no bounds; everyone was vulnerable.

Why had Mrs. Sidgwick not told him what she knew?

They crossed. At Bright's Apothecary, at the corner of Mt. Vernon Street, a man who had been standing outside backed into the store. Ames had had no more than a glimpse of him, but even that brief sighting had triggered a response.

He knew that face.

It was a face he hadn't seen in years, and yet he would recognize it anywhere, anytime.

With a muttered oath, he darted inside. The man had vanished. No, sir, the startled clerk said, no one here but us.

Ames sprang to the other door, looked up and down Charles Street.

Nothing.

But he'd seen the man—and recognized him.

He was perspiring, and not just from the heat. He removed his hat and wiped his brow.

The last time he'd seen that man, he'd been in court and the fellow had been in the dock, about to be sent away to Charlestown prison.

But recently, Crippen had said, he'd been released.

Ames next.

CHAPTER
16

TRINITY CHURCH IN COPLEY SQUARE WAS FILLED TO CA-
pacity, a fitting tribute to the memory of Theophilus Clay. The
organist played softly as people in the tightly packed pews
waited for the service to begin. Muffled sounds of weeping could
be heard throughout the church, and every now and then a man
coughed, as if to conceal a sob.

Caroline had a seat on the aisle, about halfway down. She
knew many of the people here, of course—Choates, Paines, Lymans, Cabots—because although she had not known Clay well,
he had moved in the outer fringes of her own circle.

She saw several men who were obviously not gentlemen
standing at the rear and sides of the church. Although they were
not in uniform, she thought they must be policemen. Looking
for—what? Or whom? Crippen had found Clay's murderer
(thanks to herself); did he believe that the person who had killed
Mr. Jones would turn up at Theophilus Clay's funeral?

Hardly, she thought. If that person has any sense, he'll have left the city.

She nodded circumspectly to ladies left and right, while turning every minute or so to catch a glimpse of who was coming in. She wanted to acknowledge Mrs. Briggs; more, she wanted to see Clay's son-in-law, who was now, even at one remove, about to become a wealthy man.

"Hello, Caroline," said a woman standing in the aisle next to her. It was Caroline's good friend, Julia Norton. "Can you move in a little?" she added, glancing around. "There isn't a seat anywhere."

Caroline did so, as much as she could and to the annoyance of the gentleman sitting next to her.

"Why are you here, Caroline?" Mrs. Norton whispered behind her kid-gloved hand. "Don't you think you'll draw attention to yourself?"

Caroline remembered the awkward, painful interval she'd spent at Sewing Circle on Tuesday morning. Her friends—including Julia—had been horrified once they'd learned she was tainted by scandal.

"I don't care," she whispered back. Not true, but almost. "I told Mrs. Briggs I'd come. She's his late wife's sister, and I gather she doesn't altogether approve of— Oh! There they are."

Coming down the aisle was a woman draped in heavy mourning, a young man at her side. Caroline recognized him as David Leicester, Clay's son-in-law, so presumably the woman was Clay's daughter. She was unrecognizable behind her heavy black veil, so Caroline turned her attention to the young man. People said he was a high liver. He looked it: sunken eyes, his face a little too fleshy (from drink? or merely from literally too rich a diet?) and rather weak-looking, a loose-lipped mouth. And undeniably, she thought, he looked angry. As they passed, she heard him mutter to his wife, "For heaven's sake, don't start blubbering. I'm sick of hearing it."

In a moment they were past and moving toward the empty right front pew. But before she took her seat, Clay's daughter sank to her knees at her father's coffin, which rested on a bier before the altar under a large spray of white lilies. Her sobs could be heard throughout the church. After a moment or two, she stood up and moved slowly, shakily, to her place in the pew.

The service began. A hymn; a prayer; a homily. The minister spoke at some length of how generous Clay had been to the less fortunate population of the city, looking pointedly at Clay's daughter and son-in-law.

Good luck in that quarter, Caroline thought. Although she knew she shouldn't judge people she didn't know, she'd heard enough about those two to guess they wouldn't match Clay's generosity or even come close.

Several people took turns at the pulpit to declaim upon Theophilus Clay's goodness. These encomiums lasted for the better part of an hour, and Caroline began to fret that she would miss her appointment with her dressmaker. She looked around. People were weeping silently or sobbing out loud, nodding in agreement with all the wonderful things that were being said about the late—unfortunately late—Theophilus Clay.

But then at last the minister said a final prayer, the choir sang another hymn, and the ceremony was over.

Outside, there was a great crush of people. Carriages lined Clarendon Street and Boylston Street in every direction; at the church door stood the funeral cortege, a line of closed black carriages drawn by black horses, each with its black rosette and cockade.

Caroline lingered with Mrs. Norton, who was speculating about Clay's fortune. "I heard it was tied up tightly in a trust for the daughter, so he can't get his hands on it."

But Caroline didn't answer, for here came the man in question with the Clay family contingent. David Leicester's face was like a thundercloud, and his voice carried clearly as he spoke angrily to his wife.

"Don't give me that excuse," he said. "I've waited long enough, and now I have a right to expect something for myself."

From behind her heavy veil, April Leicester murmured something unintelligible, but if it was intended to shush him, it failed.

"I don't give a damn about that!" he snapped. They were abreast of Caroline and Mrs. Norton now, heading for the lead carriage, which would take them to Mt. Auburn and the family plot that Mrs. Briggs had inspected on Wednesday. "If your father had had any decency, he would have provided for me, as well! I was given to understand that he would do so!"

Just then, his angry eyes met Caroline's over the top of his wife's black bonnet. It was a glance that lasted for only a second or two, and yet Caroline had the distinct impression that he was the most unpleasant young man she'd ever encountered.

The moment passed; he helped his wife into the carriage and they were gone.

"Well!" breathed Mrs. Norton as the crowd began to disperse. "Have you ever? What a very rude young man! One wonders why he was allowed to marry into the family in the first place."

"There is no accounting for love, Julia," Caroline replied. Thinking of love made her think of Dr. MacKenzie. Should she tell Julia about her adventure with him in the Public Garden yesterday? No. Definitely not. It was too unbelievable. She could hardly, now, less than twenty-four hours later, believe it herself. And besides, she'd carried enough scandal with her at Sewing Circle; she didn't need to add more.

They parted, and Caroline turned down Boylston Street. If

Addington had his way, they were going to have to go to that play tomorrow night, so Mrs. O'Donovan would have to be quick as well as clever.

AN HOUR LATER, THE DRESSMAKER WAS SMILING AT HER approvingly. "I'd say that's about right, wouldn't you, Miss Ames?"

Caroline looked at herself in the pier glass. She seemed a different person. Her new gown, a truly handsome creation of fawn-colored silk trimmed with black velvet ribbons down the bodice and ecru lace at the neck and sleeves, was as beautiful as one of her young cousin Val's costumes. Val always dressed in the height of fashion; but then, she had a slender figure that showed off clothing far better than Caroline's.

The truth of it was, she was too plump. Since women's clothing had many yards of fabric, tucked and ruffled and layered, if a woman wanted to look graceful, she had to begin with a slender form, and Caroline hadn't been slender since her debut.

Nevertheless, this dress flattered her—how clever Mrs. O'Donovan was!—and she knew it. She turned a little and looked at herself over her shoulder. Yes, the lines of the skirt made her waist look smaller—thank heaven bustles were going out—and the slightly puffed sleeves set off her bosom nicely.

Her bosom. Surely it showed too much?

Mrs. O'Donovan, who had much experience with hesitant customers, spoke up. "Now, you don't want to go altering that neckline, Miss Ames. You have lovely skin, really you do, and you want to show it off. I know you were in mourning all last year, but now you're out, you need to catch up with the new styles. This is a much more flattering shape for you than those big bustles—and more comfortable, too."

"Except for the waist," Caroline said. Her corset was laced

tighter than ever; she didn't see how she'd be able to eat a bite at Val's party, wearing this dress.

But it *was* lovely, she couldn't deny it. She turned again, staring at herself. People had often told her, when she was young, how pretty she was. Well, she might not be so pretty anymore, but she'd do. She liked herself in this dress; it made her feel young, and slightly giddy, the way she'd often felt years ago, getting ready for party. And now she was getting ready for a party again, wasn't she? How delightful, how very clever of Euphemia to propose it. There would be music and laughter, and the conviviality she'd missed since her mother died . . .

"Very good, Mrs. O'Donovan," she said, still gazing at herself. "You can have it delivered—tomorrow?"

"For sure, Miss Ames." The dressmaker stood up and brushed stray threads from her dark skirt. "And you'll get compliments on it, see if you don't."

Caroline could not repress a smile at her reflection before she turned away. "And I'll pass them right along to you, Mrs. O'Donovan, since it is your creation that will inspire them."

Fifteen minutes later, she made her way down the crowded sidewalk along Washington Street, past Eben Jordan's department store and up to the Common. She'd walk across to Charles Street, she thought, and stop at S. S. Pierce for a pound of tea.

The sun was warm, much warmer than it had been an hour ago, a typical Boston spring day, when you never knew from one minute to the next how to dress. Surreptitiously, she opened the top button of her jacket; she longed to take off her gloves, but that would have been too great a breach of etiquette. She nodded to the many people whom she knew, and now and then she stopped to talk, so her progress was slower than it might have been.

But it was pleasant to know everyone; she always had. From the time she'd been very young, her mother had taken her on calls, had introduced her, so that even though she had only one brother, she'd always felt that she had quite a large extended family. The intertwined Boston genealogies of Cabots and Lymans, of Carys and Howes, Codmans and Perkinses and Parkers—and Ameses—had given her a vast pantheon of folks who were, if not actually blood relations, then relations in spirit, linked to her by a common heritage and way of life.

Dear Mama. Caroline stopped near the Frog Pond to adjust her bonnet, which had blown slightly askew in the breeze. How difficult it had been those last years of her mother's illness, and how she missed her mother now.

Was it the wind that made her eyes water, or sudden tears? She blinked them away and walked on, her mother's beloved image filling her thoughts. I'm sorry I couldn't contact you at Mrs. Sidgwick's séance, Mama. Do you know that I tried? I'm not sure I will try another time, but that doesn't mean I'm not thinking of you. I hope you know that. But the séance turned out to be so disastrous—if Dr. MacKenzie hadn't been there . . .

She saw the doctor in her mind's eye. As she walked on, she imagined his reaction when he saw her in her new dress. He would smile at her, perhaps—that shy, warm smile she had come to treasure. And she would see he thought she was attractive—more than that.

Did she want him to think that?

Or perhaps he won't have any reaction, she told herself sternly. Men didn't, often enough. Addington probably wouldn't, beyond the enigmatic arching of an eyebrow. Not that Addington would begrudge her the money she was spending with Mrs. O'Donovan. He wasn't fussy about money; she admitted to herself that they might have been better off these past few years if he were. He'd always left the juggling of the household accounts to her, and she never liked to plague him about their finances because she always had the sense that he was thinking about other, more important things, although how anything could be more important than the question of how they were to live, month after month, on their increasingly strained budget, she didn't know.

Someone was calling her name. She looked around.

"A moment of your time, Miss Ames!" He was a tall, slovenly looking man wearing a battered bowler tilted back on his greasy hair and a shapeless jacket bulging at the pockets with scraps of paper.

"Babcock of the *Globe*," he said, coming up to her. "Just give me one statement and I won't ask for more. You were at the séance where Mr. Clay was killed?"

Caroline froze. She'd watched Addington deal with pushy journalists, but she'd never had to do so herself. Suddenly she felt helpless—as vulnerable as if he'd approached her with a weapon.

She glanced around. All across the Common, people hurried along intent on their own business. Of course, just at the moment she needed a friend, she saw no one who might stop to help her rid herself of this pest. All right, she'd deal with him on her own.

She reminded herself that she was Caroline Winslow Ames of Louisburg Square, Beacon Hill. She reminded herself that no decent female wished to have her name in the public prints save at her birth, her marriage (should that happy event occur), and her death. To have one's name appear in the newspapers in any other connection, let alone in connection with a murder, was embarrassing in the extreme. The fact that this unfortunate thing had happened to her more than once was all the more reason to prevent it from happening again.

She straightened her already ramrod-straight shoulders, lifted her chin, and said coldly, "I do not know you, sir."

At once she turned away and began to walk again, very fast.

But of course he was not so easily discouraged. He loped alongside her and said, "Just a word—it is Miss Ames, isn't it? I had you pointed out to me by one of your neighbors up there on the hill."

Caroline gritted her teeth. Surely he lied? Would a fellow resident of Louisburg Square betray her like that?

She walked faster, trying to ignore the pain in her side from her tight lacing. For a little way he kept up with her, but then, seeing his quest was hopeless, he gave up and stopped. "Don't talk to the *Post*," he called after her. "They won't even spell your name right!"

Dear heaven, what an unnerving encounter! By the time she reached the corner of Beacon and Charles, she was panting and feeling rather faint. She glanced around to make sure the journalist wasn't following her.

Coming toward her were several people, men and women both, but Babcock wasn't among them. Good. She met a man's eyes—a different man—and then turned and moved forward into the little crowd waiting to cross. This was a notoriously busy—and dangerous—corner, because the vehicles coming down Beacon Street from the top of the hill always picked up speed, and they raced across Charles Street, where traffic came fast in both directions without stopping. Almost every day there was a more or less disastrous collision here.

She never felt the jolt to her shoulder as someone pushed her. Later, she remembered only that she was hurtling off the curbstone, falling under a pair of bays tearing around the corner of the Common. The last thing she saw was their hooves about to come down on her.

Then the world went dark.

CHAPTER
17

IN LOUISBURG SQUARE, THE NIGHT WIND RUSTLED SOFTLY through the trees in the oval as Ames and his companion strolled slowly along toward Mt. Vernon Street. They had been silent since leaving No. 16½ and Caroline's rather tentative hospitality. She'd recovered from her fright—from her near death, Ames had judged, although he'd kept that opinion to himself—and was resting now, as she had done all afternoon, in the parlor with Dr. MacKenzie at her side.

What exactly had happened to her?

She hadn't known—couldn't say.

"All I remember, Addington, is that I glanced around to make sure that dreadful man from the *Globe* wasn't following me, and I saw a man—a different man, I mean—who seemed to be watching me."

At that, Ames had berated himself. He should not have told her about "Ames next." He'd thought to warn her, but he'd succeeded only in frightening her.

Unless—

The face he'd glimpsed that morning at Bright's Apothecary, a face he'd last seen in a crowded courtroom, rose up in his mind.

Jonathan Dwight had died under the wheels of a carriage.

Chester Snell had recently been released from prison.

And this afternoon, at the heavily traveled intersection of Charles and Beacon streets, Caroline had nearly died as Jonathan Dwight had died—run down in traffic.

And if Evangeline Sidgwick's spirit-voices—her "control," rather—were to be believed, Jonathan Dwight, like Caroline, had been pushed. Murdered.

When Harold Edgeware had called a short while ago, at an unexpectedly late hour, Ames had seen at once that he'd wanted to speak to him privately. Since Caroline was in any event in no condition to receive callers, now here they were, perambulating the square.

Edgeware, so obviously eager to speak, had nevertheless been silent since they left the house. Now Ames turned to him and said, "What is it, sir? I assume you did not visit me tonight to inquire after my health."

In the darkness, which the few streetlamps did little to dispel, Ames could not see his companion's face clearly, and in any case it was partly hidden by the brim of his hat. But he heard Edgeware sigh deeply, and then: "No, I did not."

"Something troubles you—about Mrs. Sidgwick?" He put it as a question, even though he knew the answer.

"About Mrs. Sidgwick—yes. It is that tattoo you showed us this morning."

"I thought it might be," Ames replied evenly.

Edgeware made a strangled sound, as if the words were caught in his throat and he lacked the strength to force them out. "It is very difficult for me to say this, you understand."

"I do, yes."

"But aside from being rude to you this morning, Ames, I also told you an untruth. And so did Mrs.—Evangeline." Ames heard in the older man's voice the agony this confession—for surely it was that—caused him.

"I guessed as much."

"You did? How did you—but no, I suppose it is all very obvious, isn't it?"

"Obvious?"

"I mean, my relationship with her. I can't—I don't apologize for it. She has brought me much happiness. She is—as you have seen for yourself—a most extraordinary woman."

"Yes, she is."

"But it is not because of her powers—her spiritualistic powers—that I have become—ah—close to her. Quite aside from what she may be able to achieve in the realm of—I know you are not a believer, Ames, but I am not speaking of belief here. I am speaking of—"

He cleared his throat, as if he had suddenly choked up. "I am speaking of my affections for her."

"I see."

"I wonder if you do. You never married, never had the solace of a wife and children—not that I criticize you for that, I understand that not every man is fortunate enough to find his life's mate—but for someone like me, having had that, and then having lost it—"

They had come to Mt. Vernon Street, and now they turned back along the eastern side of the square, opposite the Ameses'. "I missed it," Edgeware said simply. "The comfort of a female companion, someone to care for, someone to care for me, someone who treasures my protection, my affection for her—"

"You needn't explain," Ames said. "I understand." Edgeware's was a sentiment, he knew, that most men held. He himself did not. The pleasures of a family, the dependence upon him of some good woman, the knowledge that he was the center of her world—his sister had given him those things at one remove, as it were. He'd never wanted a closer relationship with any woman.

The image of Serena Vincent rose up in his mind, and for a moment—a delicious, weak moment—he savored it. Then he put it aside.

"Well, then," Edgeware said. "You will understand, too, when I tell you that I have seen that tattoo you showed us this morning."

"Where?"

"Oh her. On her back, to tell you the truth."

Ames felt a small frisson of revulsion pass through him, but immediately he chastised himself. Many men had irregular relationships, and it was not as if Edgeware were committing adultery, after all. His wife was dead; for all practical purposes he was a free man. The question of why, feeling so strongly toward Mrs. Sidgwick, he had not married her, was one best left unexplored.

"Obviously neither she nor I could have told you that this morning," Edgeware added.

"Of course not." Why not? Ames thought. To preserve the all-important appearance of propriety? For whose sake? Did Mrs. Sidgwick have such an unsullied reputation that Harold Edgeware needed to keep it pure?

"It would have been too embarrassing for her, you understand," Edgeware went on. "She is not someone who is accepted socially, but still, she is a very good and decent woman who does not deserve to be disgraced."

But she will be disgraced in the end, Ames thought, if this affair is not brought to a speedy conclusion.

"Has she told you what it signifies?" he asked.

"No."

"Or where she came by it? It is not a usual thing, after all, for a lady—of whatever station—to carry such a brand. It is a permanent mark, something she can never erase."

"I asked her about it, of course," Edgeware said.

"And what did she tell you?"

"Nothing. She would not say what it was, or where she'd gotten it. Her past—" He paused, cleared his throat, and went on. "Her past is largely unknown to me. She came from somewhere in the Midwest—you can tell that by her accent—and arrived in Boston some years ago. She spoke vaguely of earning a living as a seamstress before she came here, and I believe at one point, in Indianapolis, she ran a small grocery store. She had the child, of course, to provide for—never an easy thing for a woman alone."

"And her husband?"

"She—I don't know anything about a husband. She never mentioned one, and I did not feel it was my place to inquire. People have their secrets, you understand, and it is not always wise to try to pry them out."

"Nevertheless," Ames said, "we must assume—obviously— that she knows where and when she acquired that tattoo, and, more, that she knows what it means."

"Yes."

"And now, since the man called Jones, whose body my sister and Dr. MacKenzie discovered in the Public Garden lagoon, has been seen to have that same tattoo—"

"Yes! Yes! Do you think I do not realize the implications of what you say? I have spent the entire afternoon struggling with it—whether to implore her to tell me what she knows, or whether to go to the police, or to do what I have finally done, and come to you—do you not think I have not wrestled with it? I don't know what to do, Ames! I care for the woman—yes, I admit it to you! I care for her deeply! And to subject her to all the indignities—all the horrors of a murder investigation, more horrors even than she has had to endure so far—it is a difficult thing." ·

"You believe she is somehow connected to this man Jones," Ames said flatly.

"I don't know! Perhaps she is, perhaps not! The fact that he appeared at her sitting on Monday afternoon and was found dead three days later, added to the fact that they both bear this— this mark, this brand, call it what you will—what am I to make of it?"

"Very little, I think, until she is willing to reveal to you exactly what it is—what it signifies, where she acquired it, and whether it somehow connects her to Jones and thus to Theophilus Clay's murder. It hardly seems a coincidence that a man bearing an identical mark would turn up at one of her séances."

"No, I don't think it was a coincidence." Edgeware's voice, anguished, trailed off.

They stopped at the Pinckney Street end of the square under a lamppost, and suddenly Edgeware put out his hand and leaned against it, as if he were about to collapse.

"Here—are you all right?" Ames moved to support him, but the older man shook his head and motioned him away.

"A momentary weakness. This affair has been a strain, I don't mind telling you."

"Of course it has. Come back with me now, and I'll give you a drink of brandy."

Which prospect seemed to appeal to Edgeware, and in a moment more they were approaching the little flight of granite steps at No. 16½. Lights still shone through the shutters, but Ames hoped that Caroline had retired; Edgeware was in no condition to make polite conversation just now, even as she was not.

But when they entered, and Ames pushed apart the pocket doors to the parlor, he saw that Caroline and MacKenzie both were still there, and that MacKenzie must have said something amusing, because she was laughing as if she'd never had, earlier in the day, the fright of her life.

Her face sobered as she saw the two men. "Hello, Addington. Mr. Edgeware. We were just—"

Rrrring-rrring! Rrrring-rrring!

Caroline started badly, and even Ames jumped a little.

Rrrring-rrring! Rrrring-rrring!

It was a dreadful sound—harsh and unsettling, terrifying, even. What on earth—?

"The telephone!" Caroline exclaimed. "Oh, Addington! What a noise! I had no idea!"

Ames had remained standing in the doorway, and now he was aware of a commotion at the rear of the hall. It was Margaret, thudding up the back stairs. "Mr. Ames! What's that noise? Is it that?" She pointed to the little wooden box on the wall. The ringing continued—a sound that could wake the dead, Ames thought. And was he to live with it now, for the rest of his days, liable to be disturbed at any moment by this insistent, jangling, maddening noise?

"Someone had best answer it," MacKenzie said with his usual good sense. But already Ames had seized the receiver, lifted it gingerly to his ear—yes, that was the way—and spoken to the box. To the box!

"Yes?" He was aware that Margaret stood as if transfixed, watching him with wide eyes. For some reason, she irritated him, and he made a little motion with his hand to tell her to go back downstairs. She didn't seem to notice.

A voice was coming into his ear from the receiver. It had a high, singing sound, and he could imagine it whisking along the wires through the dark. It faded in and out—like Roland's voice, he thought, it had an eerie sound, a faraway sound as if it traveled from some great distance, as if it were a spirit-voice coming to him from some other world.

"I can't understand you!" he shouted. He'd been told that it was not necessary to shout on the telephone, but he couldn't imagine how anyone—where? where was that person who was trying to speak to him?—could hear him if he didn't. "Speak slower, please!"

And again that eerie voice came at him, singing along the wires. It seemed to be a woman's voice, and she sounded frightened; perhaps she felt no more comfortable than he did, using this strange new contraption.

He put his hand against the wall to steady himself and concentrated on trying to make out what was being said to him. And now at last the voice came clearly, and he realized who it was on the other end of the line, and what she was telling him.

"All right," he shouted into the box. "Mr. Edgeware is with me. We'll be there at once! Five minutes!"

He replaced the receiver. What a very odd experience—like talking to someone from the beyond. And how very appropriate it was, he thought, that his first conversation on his very own telephone was with a woman who made it her business to communicate with that beyond.

He turned to Edgeware. "That was Mrs. Sidgwick," he said. "She was looking for you. I wonder why she thought to contact me? At any rate—"

"She's had bad news, I'll wager," Edgeware muttered. His eyes were filled with alarm, and a nervous little tic worked at the corner of his mouth.

"Yes. Very bad. Her daughter has been kidnapped."

THE SOUND OF WEEPING GREETED THEM AS THEY ENTERED the house on Lime Street, but it came from one of the maids, not from Evangeline Sidgwick. She was quite calm, paler even than the last time Ames had seen her, but otherwise almost unnaturally in control.

"Evangeline, my dear," Edgeware said with heartfelt emotion as he crossed the room to greet her. She had risen as they entered, and now she stood still, allowing him to hold her hands and then, as if Ames were not there, allowing him to embrace her for a long, silent moment.

Then she stepped back and acknowledged Ames. "Thank heaven you are on the telephone," she said. "I had no idea where to turn."

"Yes, well, we have just—"

"How did it happen?" Edgeware interrupted. "Was she here in the house? Someone broke in?"

"No. Miss Kent took her to the Friday evening dancing class at Papanti's."

Papanti's classes, Ames knew, were closed affairs, open only to the children of the city's best families. How had Evangeline Sidgwick's daughter been admitted? Obviously, Edgeware had pulled a string or two.

"Yes?" Edgeware said. "And so they went—?"

"Yes. They took the carriage, as they always do. Miss Kent told me—but you should hear it from her."

Mrs. Sidgwick went to the bellpull by the fireplace and pulled it twice, hard.

"She is in a condition to speak to us?" Ames asked.

"She will speak to you no matter what her condition," Mrs. Sidgwick said with startling ferocity, and suddenly her calm expression changed to one of fury. "The stupid chit, to allow such a thing—"

"Have you sent for the police?" Ames asked.

"Not yet. I wanted to speak to Mr. Edgeware first. The police—" She turned to Edgeware. "I suppose they will have to become involved?"

"I don't see how we can avoid it, my dear. But I can't understand how such a thing could have happened."

"Louisa and Miss Kent were the last out when the evening

was over. And they—but here she is—" The door opened and the frightened-looking governess came in. She did not meet her mistress's eyes, keeping her own downcast, her hands folded over her skirts. Her mouth was trembling, Ames saw, as if she only just managed to hold back her sobs.

"Well?" snapped Mrs. Sidgwick. This was a new woman, Ames thought—a lioness fighting for her cub. "You had better tell everything to these gentlemen. Stupid girl!" she added viciously. "I do *not* understand how you could have been so careless—"

"Oh, please," the governess cried. She raised her clasped hands to a point under her chin, as if she were praying to her employer. "It wasn't my fault—honestly it wasn't! I told you—"

"Why don't you start from the beginning," Ames said firmly. "And perhaps we should sit—and perhaps we could have some tea, or"—this to the frightened governess—"would you prefer a glass of warm milk?"

She threw him a grateful glance as she sank onto a straight-backed chair. She declined any refreshment, however, and after a moment she began to tell them, as coherently as she could, what had happened.

"We were at the end of the class," she said, "and Mr. Donati—he is the assistant—wanted to show Louisa just one last little improvement in her waltz step. You know, she is so very light and quick on her feet, she cuts a beautiful figure on the floor and Mr. Donati always pays special attention to her, I suppose because he feels she is worth it. Some of those girls are so clumsy, they stumble over their own feet—"

"Yes, yes," Mrs. Sidgwick interrupted. "Never mind about the other girls. Just tell us what happened."

The governess swallowed hard and took a deep breath. "Well, by the time Mr. Donati finished with what he wanted to show her—a neat little turn, and she did it perfectly—all the others had gone. So we were alone when we went out on the street."

"Where was the carriage?" Edgeware asked.

"Oh, it was there, waiting. But it was a little way down, and so by the time Peter had seen us and had ordered the horses to walk on, to come to us—"

She broke off. Her face crumpled, and she began to sob. Mrs. Sidgwick watched her impassively for a moment, and then, with startling suddenness and savagery, she leaned in and slapped her face hard.

"*Oh!*" cried Miss Kent.

"You stupid bitch," snarled the medium. She was no longer the calm, ladylike seeress who presented her tranquil face to the world, nor even an angry lioness defending her cub, but an infuriated virago striking out at the culprit she knew to be responsible for her daughter's injury—and her own.

"Easy, my dear," Edgeware cautioned, obviously alarmed at this display. He put a warning hand on her arm, and a glance passed between them.

At once, Mrs. Sidgwick quieted. She sank back onto her chair while the hapless governess sobbed uncontrollably. Ames, unsettled, got up and began to pace the room. It was too warm; he wanted to part the heavy draperies and open the window, but he didn't quite dare.

"All right, Miss Kent," Edgeware said. "You were standing on the sidewalk, waiting for the carriage to pull up—"

"Yes." The governess's sobs lessened; she removed a handkerchief from her cuff and blew her nose, and then, with a frightened glance at Mrs. Sidgwick, she continued. "And it all happened so quick, I didn't realize—two men jumped out from—I don't know where. They must have been waiting for us.

CYNTHIA PEALE

They grabbed Louisa and threw a shawl over her head and hustled her away, around the corner. Before I could collect my wits—"

"Your wits," snapped Mrs. Sidgwick. "You have no wits, you stupid slut! Why did you not cry out, call for help?"

"Oh, but I did!" the governess exclaimed. "I screamed something awful. And right away, people came—Peter jumped down from his seat, and the doorman at Papanti's ran out, and two or three gentlemen stopped. But it was too late." Her voice quavered and broke. "She was gone."

"In a carriage?" Ames asked.

"I don't know, sir. I didn't see a carriage, but they might have had one around the corner."

"If they did, they did not drive past you, but in the other direction," Ames said, thinking about it. "Is that correct? You did not see them—or any suspicious vehicle—drive by immediately afterward?"

"No."

Papanti's studio was on Tremont Street, not far from Crabbe's. A small carriage—a hack cab, a stolen herdic—could have waited on a side street, headed away from Tremont, and could have made its escape down toward the waterfront—and a fast ship. Or toward the South Cove, that notorious den of iniquity, a haven for all kinds of nefarious goings-on, including, no doubt, white slavery. Or—to anywhere.

He turned to the medium. "Mrs. Sidgwick, you must notify the police, and the sooner the better. The trail, as faint as it is, will only grow increasingly cold as time passes. If even one other witness could be found, it might make all the difference."

"Between what and what, Mr. Ames?" Evangeline Sidgwick asked. Her voice was hard, not the voice of a lady. But then, he'd never believed her to be that; he was sure her origins, whatever they were, were not the kind that produced ladies.

"Between success and failure," he replied.

She gave him a long, searching look. "Do you have faith in them—in the police?"

Now, why did she ask that? Did she somehow know his own opinion of the police? "Yes," he said at last. "I do."

Still, she hesitated, until his irritation with her burst from him and he cried, "For God's sake, woman! Your child's life might be forfeit!"

Her eyes seemed to darken as she met his gaze. "Do you think I don't know that, Mr. Ames?"

"Then why will you not do the most obvious, the most necessary thing, and notify the authorities that she has been taken?"

Mrs. Sidgwick had been sitting as all women did, her back straight, her shoulders squared; their corsets did not allow them to slump. But now she did slump a little, her entire posture seeming to signal defeat.

"He is right, my dear," Edgeware put in. He took her hand. "As difficult, as painful as it might be, we must send for the police."

"Twice in one week?" she replied bitterly. "Whatever will they think of me?" She thought for a moment, seeming to withdraw into herself, as if she communed with some inner voice. Then: "All right." She turned to Edgeware. "Will you telephone them, Harold?"

"Of course." At once he was on his feet and heading for the door. Ames followed him. As they went out, they heard Mrs. Sidgwick say to the governess in a hateful tone, "Get out of my sight."

In the next moment, that unhappy young woman brushed past them in the hall and fled up the stairs.

Edgeware looked after her. "I don't suppose—surely she could not have been a party to some plot to take the child?"

"Anything is possible," Ames replied. Particularly anything

connected to this irregular household, he thought. "But on the face of it, I doubt it. She seems genuinely distraught."

"Yes." Dispatched to telephone the police, still Edgeware hesitated. "I don't suppose you need to stay, Ames—to talk to the police, I mean. But may I see you tomorrow?"

"Of course." They had started downstairs to the front hall, where the telephone was, Edgeware in the lead. "But if I might make a suggestion?" Ames added.

"Yes?"

"The matter we were discussing earlier."

They had reached the front hall. Edgeware looked around as if he suspected that one of the servants might overhear them, but the hall was empty.

"The tattoo?" he asked.

"Yes. You must discover from her what it is, what it signifies, where she acquired it. It might be the key—to this, and to Theophilus Clay's death, as well."

Edgeware's face fell as he nodded agreement. "I understand," he said. "And I do not necessarily disagree with you. But at such a moment, when she is so distressed—it is a delicate matter."

"How delicate can it be?" Ames replied. "What secret—I assume there is one—could Mrs. Sidgwick have that is so terrible she fears to reveal it, not even to hasten her child's safe return?"

Edgeware hesitated. You fear it also, Ames thought. Whatever it is, you fear that its revelation will destroy your bond with her.

"Of course you are right," Edgeware said at last. "I will ask her about it. Perhaps she will tell me before the police come, and perhaps it will be nothing they need to know."

"Perhaps," Ames said, retrieving his hat and taking his leave. But not likely, he thought as he stepped out into the breezy

May night. He'd spend an hour with his telescope, he decided. Stargazing always soothed him, helped him to put the problems of this world into perspective against the immensity of the universe.

But long after he'd climbed onto the roof and taken out the telescope, long after he'd put his eye to the lens and scanned the heavens, the thought nagged at him: What was that odd, enigmatic cross-within-a-circle he'd seen on the man called Jones—and that Harold Edgeware had seen, as well, on an intimate part of Evangeline Sidgwick's person?

What did it mean?

Mrs. Sidgwick knew. Of course she knew—she wore it, didn't she? So why would she not tell them?

CHAPTER
18

"HE SAYS HE'S BEEN SENT TO YOU, SIR." AS MARGARET looked into the dining room, they saw that her face was suffused with outrage.

"Well, then, Margaret, you may show him in," Ames replied from his place at the breakfast table.

"Oh, but—" The maid turned to Caroline. "He's a tramp, Miss. He looks like—I don't know what. I don't like to let him in the house."

"Then perhaps you should go and talk to him at the door, Addington," Caroline said, trying to stifle her curiosity. "Since Margaret feels he is not a proper sort of person to invite inside," she added. You had to be alert to the delicate sensibilities of servants, she knew, or else they up and left, complaining that you did not have strict enough standards and therefore that working in your household sullied their own reputations.

As soon as Ames left the room, Caroline followed. It was *not* fair that Addington—and, often, Dr. MacKenzie, as well—had all the interesting encounters. This man might not be fit to have in the house, but all the same, he might have some crucial information. She wanted to hear it, too. As she tiptoed along the hall to the front door, she was aware that MacKenzie was behind her, and she threw him a conspiratorial smile over her shoulder.

As Margaret had reported, the caller was disreputable-looking in the extreme. Of medium height and powerfully built, he wore a tattered jacket and a shapeless cap. As Caroline stopped at the vestibule door, she heard him say, ". . . sent by Martin Sweeney."

"That's right," Ames replied. "And you may know of a certain felon, recently released?"

"No, sir, I don't know nothin' about that. I put up the tent, y'see, an' then I help with th'elephants. They're stubborn beasts, they are, need a firm hand."

"But you may know of someone who could help me?"

"Well, now." The man shifted his weight while he chewed meditatively on a length of straw. For a moment his eyes traveled beyond Ames to where Caroline and MacKenzie stood; then, as if he were considering his options, he looked back to Ames.

"Perhaps I do, at that," he said. "Might it be worth somethin' to you?"

Ames was aware of the onlookers to his rear. Had he been alone with this man, he would have cut him off at once, but with Caroline and the doctor looking on, he was reluctant to seem too quick to dismiss someone who might, after all, be of help. He reached into a trouser pocket, withdrew his leather change purse, and took out a dollar coin. Before he handed it over, he said, "You can give me a name?"

The stranger eyed the coin. "All right," he said. "It's Jocko Frary."

"And he is—?"

"Ringmaster. He's down at the fields." This meant, Ames knew, the playing fields on Huntington Avenue, where Barnum's circus annually set up.

When the caller had gone, and they had finished their breakfast, Ames and MacKenzie set off to find the ringmaster. As Caroline finished her second cup of coffee, she heard the rumble and thump of the dumbwaiter in the back passage. It was time to be about her business; Margaret would want to start clearing away. She thought of the day ahead—and the night. They were to attend the opening of Mrs. Vincent's new play that evening, much as Caroline wished they were not. She hoped her new dress would arrive promptly, as Mrs. O'Donovan had promised. Addington had said there was to be a party afterward, and Mrs. Vincent would surely be resplendent in some fabulous creation. Caroline wanted to look her best, even though her best might never rival that beautiful creature's.

Yes, Serena Vincent was beautiful. She couldn't deny it. Beautiful—and disreputable, a woman of dubious moral character who lived a fast life in what, in Diana Strangeways' novels, was called the demimonde.

Was Addington attracted to Mrs. Vincent? She'd asked that question of Dr. MacKenzie last fall, when it seemed he might be. MacKenzie had reassured her. Ames was a steady man, he'd said, far too sensible to succumb to an actress, even an actress who, once, had moved in their own small, chilly social circle.

She went to the window, which looked onto the tiny, brick-walled back garden. It was a bright, warm morning, the kind of day that beckoned. With a twinge of guilty relief, she was glad that her Saturday Morning Reading Club had disbanded until the fall; the last assignment had been Edward Bellamy's *Looking Backward*, a utopian fantasy about life in a socialist America—

in Boston, in fact—in the year 2000. She'd found it alternately tedious and frightening, and, compared to Diana Strangeways, hardly worth looking at. If Bellamy was right about what the year 2000 would be like, she was glad she wouldn't have to live in it.

In the kitchen, Cook was chopping vegetables for the noontime soup. With a word to her, Caroline went through the back pantry to the garden door. On this miniature patch of earth surrounded by high brick walls, she felt as if she were in a secret place, a hidden, private place, never mind that any neighbor, looking out, could see her. The houses on West Cedar Street that backed onto their own gardens were somewhat lower down the hill than the houses on Louisburg Square, and so a fair amount of light, and even occasional afternoon sun, was let into the Ameses' garden. Caroline grew violets here, and begonias and bleeding hearts and lilies of the valley; a small boxwood hedge lined the miniature stepping-stone walk, and the corners were filled with ferns and ivy. At the far end was a small arbor with a stone bench, a birdbath, and a trellised rose that somehow, despite the paucity of sun, managed every June to put forth glorious scarlet blooms. She went to it now, clippers in hand, to trim away the deadwood she hadn't pruned in the fall.

As she reached for a stem over her head, she felt a twinge in her right shoulder and, without making the cut, lowered her arm. For the moment she'd forgotten yesterday's narrow escape, but now it came back to her. She had a large dark bruise on that shoulder, and although Dr. MacKenzie had looked at it (very professionally, no embarrassment for either of them) and had assured her she'd suffered no broken bones, he'd warned her that she would doubtless continue to have some pain for another week at least.

Suddenly feeling weak, she sank onto the bench. Even through her several layers of petticoats and skirt, she could feel the coldness of the stone. She didn't care that it was cold. She needed to sit just then, as memories of her misadventure came flooding back.

She'd been standing at the corner of Charles and Beacon streets, waiting to cross. A carriage had sped around the corner, heading up Beacon to the top of the hill. Someone had pushed her in front of it. She could feel it now—that hard, savage thump against her back, propelling her into the roadway, helpless to re-gain her balance. If someone else had not seized her and pulled her back, she would have fallen under the horses' hooves, would have been badly injured at least, and quite possibly killed.

She glanced around at the high redbrick rear walls of the houses, each with its many windows. The windows were blind—empty; she couldn't see anyone looking down at her. Still, she felt as though someone did; all of a sudden now, despite the fact that she knew everyone in each of those houses, she felt terribly exposed to the eyes of a hundred unfriendly strangers, and she shivered hard enough to hurt her shoulder again.

Who had wanted to injure her—even kill her?

Why?

She remembered Mrs. Sidgwick's automatic writing: *Ames next.*

Was that a threat to be taken seriously, after all?

Suddenly she didn't want to be in the garden any longer. She wanted to be inside, where she felt safe. She could not possibly be in any danger here in the garden, but still, she felt uneasy—vulnerable. She rose and stepped quickly to the back door, to the familiar back pantry and kitchen, with Cook working at the scrubbed deal table and Margaret folding linens in the drying-room.

As she went up the back stairs to the front hall, she heard the door knocker, and a moment later Margaret ran up past her to answer. It was the delivery of a large parcel: her new dress.

She'd go up to her room now and try it on, she thought. It was the loveliest dress she'd had since her debut. Wearing it, she was sure she could face even Serena Vincent with confidence.

Barnum's circus, at this mid-morning hour, was a maelstrom of activity. The huge tent having been raised with the help of the elephants, now laborers hauled the wooden grand-stand seats into place. Clowns and acrobats practiced their rou-tines in the big center ring, while rough-looking men in bowlers and loud vests and shirtsleeves hurried back and forth shouting orders.

In one corner, a dozen or so musicians were running through some rousing marches. High overhead, the famous Flying Fisch-binders were anchoring their high wires; MacKenzie, glancing up, was forced to look away because the thought of rope-dancers performing on those slender, nearly invisible wires made him feel dizzy and sick. The place smelled of animals and sawdust and sweat, and the air was filled with the cries of the performers, the shouted commands of the workmen, and, from somewhere in the distance, the roar of wild beasts. MacKenzie had never seen a circus, but he knew they had tigers and lions jumping through fiery hoops, and elephants that walked around the ring, trunk to tail, carrying costumed performers.

After several inquiries, Ames and MacKenzie found the man recommended to them: the ringmaster, now divested of his top hat and tails, in shirtsleeves like everyone else. He was MacKen-zie's height but thinner, with shifty dark eyes and a grim, tight mouth that in MacKenzie's opinion betrayed a bad character.

"Yah?" he said when Ames addressed him. "I'm Frary. Who wants to know?"

Ames introduced himself and MacKenzie, and told Frary what he wanted: someone who while he was in prison might have known a convict named Chester Snell.

Frary's glance traveled over them and then away, up to the high reaches overhead, where one of the rope-dancers, a girl in pink tights, had seated herself on a trapeze and was beginning to swing back and forth on it.

"Wait," Frary said, still watching the high-wire artist. She was swinging higher and higher, making huge arcs in the air; then she stood up, balancing her feet just so on the slender bar of her trapeze.

Then—and Ames felt his heart lurch in his chest as he watched her—she leapt off, made a double somersault, and flew through the air to grasp—just—the hands of her catcher, swinging toward her. With amazing strength and agility, she pulled herself up to sit triumphantly beside him, and the two of them made a graceful bow to the empty grandstands.

Frary turned to his visitors. "One of these days, she won't make it," he said somberly.

"It seems a hazardous business," Ames agreed. "But about this man—"

"What was he in for?" Frary asked.

"Fraud."

"Money fraud?"

"That's right."

Frary looked him up and down. "I don't want no trouble," he said.

"No trouble will come to you. I am simply trying to trace this man."

"You the police?"

"No."

"He owe you money?"

"No. But I may owe him something." I do, he thought. I do owe him something. A great deal, in fact.

"A slick kind of fella? Talk you right around yourself if you don't watch out?"

"So you did know him."

Frary looked him up and down again. "Maybe. If he's the same. I been out now three years, I don't want to go back in."

"Of course not."

"The fella I knew had a tattoo."

The high-wire artist was now standing alone on the trapeze, swinging back and forth in ever-widening arcs. Both Ames and the ringmaster were watching her, but MacKenzie couldn't. If she falls, he thought, I may have to tend to her. Hitting the hard-packed earth from that height, her bones would be jelly. He turned away, not even wanting to watch Ames watching her.

"A tattoo," Ames repeated, and MacKenzie wondered at his sangfroid.

"That's right," Frary said. "That mean anything to you?"

"It might. Can you describe it?"

"Sure. It was a cross inside a circle."

Now the high-wire artist seemed to be preparing to leap off her trapeze once again into the arms of a different catcher swinging toward her. They needed to time their joining exactly to the split second, or one of them—the girl—would plummet to her death. Right in front of us, MacKenzie thought, watching her again in spite of his queasy stomach, drawn by a kind of horrid fascination that was, he understood, a great part of the rope-dancers' appeal.

Ames went on, cool as ever. "And have you any idea what that meant—the cross in a circle?"

Frary shrugged. Then he waited a moment, until the rope-dancer had made her leap and was safe in her partner's grasp. Then he said, "He told me it means you're a carny."

"A carny?"

"A carnival fella. That's your life—you travel with 'em, work with 'em. Why d'you want to know?"

"I can't say. It is—a personal matter. You have been in town—how long?"

"Since yesterday."

"Have you seen him?"

"Snell? No. Didn't know he was out."

"He is," Ames replied tersely. Without offering his hand to the ringmaster, he added, "You have been helpful, and I thank you."

Would this man, too, ask for money? MacKenzie wondered. But he didn't. Seeing that they had no more questions for him, he nodded once and returned his attention to the high-wire artist.

Ames was furious as they made their way out, narrowly avoiding a trio of elephants just going in. Furious with himself for never having discovered that Chester Snell had been a carnival traveler—no wonder the man had been such an accomplished trickster!—and, more, furious with Evangeline Sidgwick. Damned prevaricating woman! She wore the tattoo, so surely she'd been a "carny" herself. Probably she knew Chester Snell—undoubtedly she did, and possibly Jones as well.

Jones: Whom Caroline had discovered in the Public Garden lagoon, who had undoubtedly murdered Theophilus Clay— why? *why?*—and who was linked to both Snell and Mrs. Sidgwick by that same cross-in-a-circle tattoo.

"Come on, Doctor," he said. "We are going to pay a visit to Mrs. Sidgwick, and this time she will tell us the truth."

CHAPTER
19

AT THE HOUSE ON LIME STREET, AMES PEREMPTORILY brought down the door knocker. He had been preoccupied with his anger with Mrs. Sidgwick, but now, focusing, he noticed a gash in the wood at shoulder level. He was sure it had not been there before.

The frightened-looking maid who answered told him her mistress was not at home. But before she could shut the door, a man's voice came from within the house, asking who the caller was.

In a moment more, Harold Edgeware appeared. He looked the worse for wear, his hair mussed as if he'd been clawing at it, his cravat loosened, his face unshaven.

"It's all right, Betty," he told the maid. And to Ames and MacKenzie: "Come in, come in. I thought of sending for you, but now you are here, after all."

He ushered them upstairs to the medium's sitting room. As she rose to greet them, they saw that her face was streaked with tears, her eyes red-rimmed. Despite the warmth of the room, she wore a paisley shawl pulled tight over her shoulders and up to her throat.

"My dear, you must tell Mr. Ames what you have told me," Edgeware said. "I do not want to press you, but—"

She silenced him with a look, nodded to MacKenzie, and took Ames's hand. As she held it, she stared up at him as if she were assessing his character, his trustworthiness.

He stared back. Mendacious woman, he thought, not caring if his disgust with her showed plainly on his face. Somehow you are connected to Chester Snell, and now at last you will acknowledge it.

She did not speak, and neither did he. She released his hand and motioned the men to sit while she stood before them. It is as if she is preparing to testify, MacKenzie thought—and, indeed, that proved to be the case. Turning to Edgeware, she held out her hand. "May I have it, Harold?"

He hesitated. "You are sure?"

"Yes."

With some reluctance, and yet with a palpable air of relief, he opened the drawer of a small table by his chair, took out a ragged-edged sheet of heavy paper, and handed it to Ames.

With a shock, Ames saw that it was a crude drawing—in bloodred ink—of the cross-in-a-circle tattoo.

"Where did this come from?" he asked Edgeware.

"One of the maids found it this morning. It had been impaled by a knife onto the front door."

"Ah." Ames looked up at Mrs. Sidgwick, who had remained standing motionless before them. "Will you tell us, now, what this is?" he asked her. "You recognize it, do you not?"

"More than you know, Mr. Ames."

"Dr. MacKenzie and I have just had an encounter with a man who was released from Charlestown prison three years ago.

While he was there, he knew a man who called himself Chester Snell—and who wore that same tattoo. Snell was sent up for fraud—on the strength of my testimony, among others. Ten years ago, he may have killed Miss Hereward's fiancé, Jonathan Dwight, whose spirit—supposedly—spoke to her here through what you call your control." And he killed my father, as well, he thought—an unprovable crime, but a crime all the same.

"Yes." The medium's voice was calm—eerily so, MacKenzie thought.

"You remember that?" Ames asked sharply.

"I remember Miss Hereward. I don't remember whom she spoke to while I was in trance."

How easily she referred to her strange powers, MacKenzie thought. He eyed her warily. A perfectly normal woman to look at, and yet, what depths of unholy communion did she have with the spirits of the dead?

"What did the police tell you last night?" Ames asked, fixing her in his dark, intent gaze.

"About Louisa? Nothing. They took our statements and left."

"And you have not heard from them today?"

"No."

"Nor have you contacted them to tell them about this—ah—message on your front door?"

"No."

All right, he thought. Let us get on with it. And then he thought, *Ames next*, and in his mind's eye he saw Caroline, nearly trampled to death under the hooves of a speeding pair, and he gritted his teeth to keep from lashing out at this woman before him, who held—he was sure of it—the key to the meaning of that threat.

Mrs. Sidgwick had been standing very still, both hands clutching her shawl to her throat. Now, suddenly, she threw her arms wide, and her shawl slipped to the floor. She whirled around, presenting her back to them. Above her corset, which reached to just below her shoulder blades, she was naked.

The tattoo leapt out at them, dark blue against her pale skin: a cross-within-a-circle on her right shoulder.

MacKenzie heard Edgeware's sharp intake of breath. "My dear—" he began.

She ignored him. Retrieving her shawl and draping it around her once more, she turned to face them. "The cross-within-a-circle is an insignia of the carnival," she said.

"We know that," Ames put in, startling her.

"You do? How?"

"It doesn't matter. Go on, please."

Momentarily distracted, she began again. "It signifies a wheel—because carnival people are always on the move. It brands people, marking them forever as belonging to that world, which is different from any other. Its people are clannish, secretive—and yet, wearing that brand, one can go anywhere and be assured of a welcome from his or her own kind.

"I was born into that world," she went on, gazing steadily at each one of the three men in turn, as if she defied them—dared them to think the less of her for that admission. "When I was still a girl, a new man joined our little troop. He was very skillful at games of chance, and at working a crowd, enticing people to play. They always lost, of course. And he was skillful, too, at . . . other things, as well."

MacKenzie was uncomfortable at this recitation, and, more, at what he feared would come; he wished he didn't have to hear it.

"At length," the medium went on, "he and I . . . became close. Became lovers, in fact, although our union, such as it was, was never sanctified by the formality of a marriage ceremony." She lifted her chin a little, still defiant. "I bore him a child—a

daughter. You have met her, Mr. Ames, and you, Harold, have—
I think—grown fond of her."

"Yes, my dear," Edgeware murmured. "You know I have."

"One time, he—the man I knew as Thomas Dowd—fell into
an argument with a man who had just joined us. They fought—
physically, I mean. I saw it happen. It was night. There had been
a heavy rain. The light from the wagon lanterns glistened on the
puddles of water, and it threw their shadows so they looked like
giants. They struggled for what seemed like a long time, but
I suppose it was no more than a few minutes. And then . . .
Thomas pulled a knife, and he . . . stabbed the man."

"Killed him?" Ames asked.

"Yes."

"He was never arrested for the crime?"

"No. He dragged him away. He never told me where, but I
believe he left the body in a lake nearby. We moved on the next
day. Thomas had become violent with me before that, and now I
was afraid that he would somehow harm me—or our daughter.
More, I feared that somehow I would be implicated in his crime,
perhaps arrested as an accessory. He threatened me with that,
warned me never to tell anyone about it. I didn't, but I grew
more and more afraid of him. So one day, when he had been
drinking heavily and had fallen asleep, I stole his money—I
knew where he kept it hidden—and I took the child and ran
away. The money didn't last long, of course, but after that I managed to support us. I changed our names, and we moved from
town to town. I did what I had to do—worked as a seamstress,
had charge of a little grocery store. I even learned Pitman short-
hand so I could take a position in an office. We kept moving east.
I was always afraid he would catch up with us. At last we came
to Boston. When I saw that the Spiritualists had put up a grand
new church here, I knew I could make a living as a medium."

Edgeware turned to Ames. "We must assume that the

insignia found on the door this morning is some kind of message—a warning—"

"Of course it is that!" Mrs. Sidgwick exclaimed. "It is exactly that. It is from *him*. Don't you see? He has caught up with us at last, and it is he who has taken our—*my*—child!"

She began to cry. At once, Edgeware sprang up; putting his arm around her quaking shoulders, he guided her to a chair and eased her into it. "I will ring for tea," he said, "or would you prefer coffee, or something stronger?"

"Brandy," she said, and at once Edgeware fetched it from the sideboard. Ames waited until she had taken a few restorative sips. Then: "Mrs. Sidgwick, why would this man—Thomas Dowd—kidnap your daughter?" He had an answer for that, but he wanted to hear hers.

She looked at him, and he thought he saw in her eyes something like contempt. Because compared to her, he'd led a sheltered life? Because she thought he knew nothing of the harsher ways of the world—lessons she'd had to learn at her mother's knee?

"Revenge," she said simply. "I took his child—our child—I took his money, never mind that it was my money, too, and I left him to face a possible murder charge alone. Why would he not want to take his revenge on me? Even though I was right to do what I did," she added. "He was not—a good man. I was right to leave him, and to take the child, as well."

"Yes," Ames replied softly. "I would agree with you. But now we must consider something else—not only the fact that the man found in the lagoon" (a similar method of disposing of a body, he thought) "bore the same tattoo, but also the fact that a man who calls himself Chester Snell has recently been released from prison. But even that is not the most important thing."

She waited, frozen, as if she dreaded what he would say next.

"The most important thing," he said, speaking slowly, as if

he feared she would not understand him, "is that this man—the ex-convict—also bears the cross-within-a-circle tattoo."

She stifled the cry that sprang to her lips, staring at him as if he had pronounced a death sentence on her.

"Well?" he said at last, growing uncomfortable under her scrutiny. "Do you agree—that we are dealing with the man you knew as Thomas Dowd? He came to Boston before you did, about eleven years ago. But let us make sure we are talking about the same person. What did he look like?"

She blinked, as if she were returning to them from some far place. "What did he—" She closed her eyes, as if to call him up in her mind. "About five foot ten," she said slowly. "Light hair, so blond as to be nearly white. Hard blue eyes. A narrow face, small nose. A scar across his right eyebrow." She made a strangled sound that might have been a laugh. "He was thought to be good-looking. Or at least I thought so, when I—when we first met."

Ames nodded. "Yes. That is the man I knew as Chester Snell." He looked around their little circle. He felt as though he had been in this small, airless room for hours instead of only a brief while. All the outside world, the bright spring day, the busy city, might not have existed. Then, from the street, he heard the muffled sound of horses' hooves clop-clopping along the cobblestones, and he reminded himself that this woman had given him a message, and the message was *Ames next*.

Now he knew who had sent it—not a spirit from the beyond, but someone alive and dangerously well, right here on earth. How had the message gotten through to Mrs. Sidgwick? Telepathy? Or was she somehow in league with Snell? But for what purpose?

He dismissed the thought. She seemed genuinely distraught, as well she might be, over the abduction of her daughter.

By Chester Snell, whom she'd known as Thomas Dowd?

They were one and the same, he'd stake his life on it. Snell had taken this woman's child—and his—and would undoubtedly do more damage until he was stopped. And he had almost certainly killed the man known as Jones, who had almost certainly killed Theophilus Clay at Mrs. Sidgwick's séance on Monday afternoon.

At Snell's direction?

Why Theophilus Clay?

"You are sure you didn't know Jones?" he asked Mrs. Sidgwick now.

"No, I didn't. But—" She broke off, trying to puzzle it out.

Ames leaned forward, his elbows on his knees, and as if by the force of his will, held her gaze. "I am going to put a hypothesis to you," he said. "What if Chester Snell, who was released from prison two months ago, discovered that during his time behind bars, a certain woman—a woman with whom he had once had a close connection—had come to Boston and set herself up as a medium? For we may assume he did not forget the supposed wrongs he believed you did to him.

"More, when he came out of prison, he may well have believed he had a score to settle with me, also, since it was primarily by my testimony that he was sent up. He may have been planning to take his revenge against me when he learned you were in the city, and he may have decided to act against you first. So he found his mark—Jones—and put him up to his mischief. It is my belief that Jones was sent to you to make trouble for you—to ruin your reputation. I don't think he knew Theophilus Clay. In fact, I believe Clay's killing was a random act. Anyone at that séance might have been Jones's victim."

He caught MacKenzie's eye and broke off, instantly reading his friend's thoughts: It might have been MacKenzie who was killed . . . or Caroline. Suddenly, he choked up, and before he could continue, he needed to clear his throat. But then Edgeware interrupted.

"You mean, Ames, if I understand you correctly, that the man whom Mrs. Sidgwick knew as Thomas Dowd came to Boston all those years ago. He got himself into trouble, for which, thanks to your testimony, he was imprisoned, and now has come out of prison and discovered that the woman he knew years before in the carnival had also settled here."

"Yes. And that bizarre—that cold-blooded—killing here on Monday was his warning shot across her bow, so to speak. He wants to make trouble for you, Mrs. Sidgwick—and he is succeeding. Do you think he might harm your girl? Or does he simply want to take her away from you, possibly to initiate her into the carnival life?"

"I don't know," the medium whispered. "If that man is the man I knew as Thomas Dowd, he wants to torture me—and he is doing so! Oh, my poor child! To be in his power!"

"There, there, my dear," Edgeware said soothingly. "You must not upset yourself. We must stay calm, so that we may deal with this—this miscreant." He shot an inquiring glance at Ames. "I would not be surprised if he demands a ransom, wouldn't you agree?"

"He might." Ames thought about it, thought about the vengeful man who had kidnapped his own child.

What would such a man do to avenge himself on the man who sent him to prison for ten years? He had killed once, twice—many times, perhaps—so what would stop him from killing again?

"Snell will have gone to ground," Ames said, "if he is still in the city at all. A search must begin at once. At least now we know whom we are looking for. Will you telephone the police?" he added to Edgeware.

"Of course." Edgeware drew himself up, prepared to duel with the entire world, if necessary, to help the woman he loved. "And I am going to offer a reward for Louisa's return. What do you think of that?"

"I think— Yes. Why not? Someone may know something, may be willing to offer it to us. How much?"

"I don't know. Five hundred?"

Hard to put a value on a human life, Ames thought. Five hundred would do as well as anything.

"All right. And I will speak to Crippen, urge him to put out posters with the reward noted on them."

He would describe Chester Snell to the police artist, he thought. No need to trouble Mrs. Sidgwick about it.

He approached her to take his leave. She seemed stunned, slumped in her chair, hardly acknowledging his presence.

"Take heart," he said softly to her as if they were alone. "Your daughter will be found, Mrs. Sidgwick. You must believe that."

She met his eyes. "Thank you," she whispered. "I am so grateful for your help. I know you do not . . . believe . . . in my work."

This startled him. Had he shown his agnosticism so plainly?

"What I believe is that we will find your daughter," he said. "And you must believe it, as well."

Outside, he walked with MacKenzie for a time without speaking. His thoughts were not of Evangeline Sidgwick, but of the man with whom, with such unhappy results, her life had been entangled.

Would Snell kill his own daughter?

More, having exacted his revenge on Mrs. Sidgwick, would he decide to come after Addington Ames, who had sent him to prison for ten precious years of his life?

He looked around. The blind, closed fronts of the houses

baked in the sun. Here on Lime Street, away from the bustle of Charles Street, it was quiet. Almost too quiet, he thought. A sinister kind of quiet, in which he felt suddenly watched—threatened—from all sides. Despite the heat of the day, he shivered.

MacKenzie noticed. "All right?" he said quietly.

"I felt a sudden chill. It's gone now."

But it wasn't gone, he thought. It would not be gone until Chester Snell—carnival charlatan, swindler, kidnapper, killer—was safely behind bars once more.

Until then . . . does he search for me even as I search for him, Ames wondered.

Yes. He knew it—could sense it, as if he were an animal being stalked. The hunter had become the hunted, and which of them would find the other?

He felt suddenly energized. Very well, he thought. Let us get on with it.

"Come on, Doctor," he said, turning at Charles Street toward the Common. "I am sure Inspector Crippen will be happy to learn that Harold Edgeware has offered a reward for the Sidgwick girl."

Afterward, he would go to Crabbe's to work off some of his nervous energy.

The theater tonight. He'd see Serena Vincent again. At the thought of that delight, he was aware of a sharp, delicious frisson of desire. He could hardly wait.

CHAPTER
20

CAROLINE RAISED HER CHAMPAGNE FLUTE AND TOOK AN experimental sip of the pale gold, fizzy liquid. She'd tasted champagne only a few times, most notably at her coming-out party years ago, and as she tasted it again now, she remembered that she didn't really like it. You were supposed to like it, she knew, because it symbolized all that was gaiety and luxury in life. Since her own life had seldom been either gay or luxurious, she'd never acquired a taste for it.

Dr. MacKenzie, sitting beside her at one of the small tables circling the room, nodded at her and lifted his own glass. The laughter and chatter rising around them made conversation difficult, and in any case he wasn't good at small talk. If he said anything to her now, it should be something meaningful, something to reassure her, to erase the telltale vertical line that had marred her smooth brow ever since they'd come in half an hour before. Obviously she wasn't enjoying herself. He wondered how long they needed to stay before he could suggest they leave.

He glanced toward the door, where several people, already seemingly inebriated and talking and laughing very loud, were coming in. This was a celebratory gathering after the opening night of Serena Vincent's new play which, at her invitation, the Ameses and MacKenzie had watched from her private box. MacKenzie had enjoyed it—a light comedy that showed off to perfection Mrs. Vincent's glamorous persona—but now he was tired. He wanted to go home, and he knew Caroline did also.

He followed her gaze to a place across the room where Ames, handsome and debonair in his evening clothes, was deep in conversation with the star of the evening, Serena Vincent. When she'd made her entrance at the party some few minutes ago, he had gone to her at once and had been, as it were, kept at her side by her gravitational pull ever since. Several other men were jockeying for position, but he hadn't given way.

MacKenzie tried to think of something to say that would lessen Caroline's concern, but he couldn't. He was acutely aware that he himself was losing his head—over her—and so despite his desire to comfort her, he could not repress a small twinge of sympathy for his friend across the room who was, to all appearances, in a similar state over Mrs. Vincent.

There was a burst of laughter louder than the rest from the table where the theater manager was holding court as he waited for the early editions of the newspapers that would carry the critics' reviews. It had been a successful evening, the audience wildly applauding at the end, many curtain calls for the cast, but as MacKenzie knew, the reviews were important, too, and waiting for them was a nerve-racking business for the people concerned.

The leading man, an actor imported from New York, seemed to be drunk. Now he lurched to his feet and unsteadily made his way across the floor to where the musicians were setting up.

"A waltz!" he cried. He clutched the arm of the conductor to keep from collapsing. "We must dance until our destiny is proclaimed!"

MacKenzie leaned in to Caroline. "When the dancing starts," he said, "we can make our exit if you like."

She tore her eyes from her brother. He was going to make a perfect fool of himself tonight, she thought, and I can do nothing to stop him.

"Do you think we should?" she replied. "I don't know that Addington will want to leave so soon."

"No, he won't," MacKenzie admitted. "But that doesn't mean we have to stay here and suffer while he—ah—amuses himself. He seems rather preoccupied at the moment."

Caroline bit her lip. She was only too well aware that Addington was preoccupied. That was the problem. Oh, that terrible woman! Beautiful and deadly—Caroline was sure she was deadly; she would ensnare Addington—had already done so—and lead him to utter ruin.

She took another sip of champagne. It was giving her a headache. Or perhaps the headache came from the noise, or, more likely, the sight of her brother—her dignified, reserved, levelheaded brother—acting like a callow, smitten youth caught in the clutches of Serena Vincent.

She wished they hadn't come. She wished she were at home in her own parlor, a Diana Strangeways novel in her lap, her petit point handy. Dr. MacKenzie would be sitting across from her, lighting his pipe, Addington just coming in from an hour in his study with some interesting thing to tell them, the three of them cozy and comfortable, no constraint, no dark secrets.

Mrs. Vincent was going to be Addington's dark secret, she just knew it.

She glanced down. She'd spilled champagne on the skirt of her beautiful new dress. Just as Mrs. O'Donovan had promised, she'd been quite happy with it. She'd seen Dr. MacKenzie's eyes light up when she came downstairs earlier that evening, and even Addington, who normally paid no attention to what she wore, had murmured an approving word.

But now she didn't care about her dress, or even that she'd stained it. Probably, after tonight, she would never want to wear it again. She'd wear her old gray silk to Valentine's party and put this one away in the guest-room closet, just as she would try to put away her memories of this unhappy night.

She looked back to Mrs. Vincent, who was speaking to Addington. He was bending down to her; even from a distance, Caroline had the sense that the two of them felt they were alone. Oh, why were men such fools? Mrs. Vincent would be nothing but trouble for Addington—for any man caught by her allure. Hadn't that poor Richard Longworth committed suicide over her last fall? And in the winter, during the dreadful time when Agatha Montgomery's girls were being killed, Serena Vincent had made some sort of confession to Addington—just what, he'd never said—about Agatha's brother. The Reverend Montgomery hadn't killed himself, of course, but he'd come to a bad end all the same. Caroline could not help but feel, even though she knew it was unfair, that Serena Vincent had somehow been responsible.

The music began: a waltz, as requested. But no one moved, and Caroline realized they were waiting for Mrs. Vincent to go first. The leading man made his tipsy way to her, and Caroline could see he was asking her to dance, but she shook her head. Then, almost as if *she* were the one doing the asking, as if *she* were the one in pursuit, she turned to Ames, extended her hand to him, and the two of them stepped out onto the floor.

Caroline really didn't think she could bear to watch them. But of course she did watch; the scene had the horrid fascination of a bad dream. She couldn't have looked away even if she'd wanted to.

Addington was a beautiful dancer. If only he were dancing now with their young cousin Valentine, whom he had escorted to the cotillion last November. That was before he'd become acquainted with Mrs. Vincent, and Caroline had thrilled to watch him then, tall and slim, graceful as only a well-conditioned athlete could be, darkly handsome in his evening clothes, whirling Val around the floor . . .

This was a very different scene. Mrs. Vincent, stunning in her claret-colored gown that showed far too much of her bosom, was allowing herself to be held much too close to Addington, for one thing. Around and around they whirled, one-two-three, one-two-three, in perfect time to the music, the center of attention, as they must have realized, but they didn't acknowledge it. They seemed aware only of each other, gazing into each other's eyes, making some wordless communication that only they could know . . .

Abruptly, Caroline turned to MacKenzie. "Yes, Doctor," she said. "Let us go home."

I T WAS LATE—HOW LATE, AMES DIDN'T KNOW. THEY HAD left the party, had been dancing in this small, out-of-the-way café—how long? He didn't know that, either. He knew only that she was in his arms, and to have her there was a kind of ecstasy he'd never known and could not bear, now, to end.

The lone violinist sawed away at his fiddle. He knew every waltz ever written, it seemed, and now, having run through his repertoire once, he was beginning all over again. They were the only customers left. They had come in over an hour before, had taken a table, and ordered wine, since the café did not offer champagne and then had risen and stepped to the tiny dance floor, there not to dance, not to whirl around the room, but simply to stand, barely moving, in each other's arms.

The violinist eyed them wearily: lovers with no place to make love. He had seen many such in his long career. He always felt sorry for them, and always he played on and on, past closing time, to give them a few more moments of aching bliss.

Ames pressed his face against her glorious hair. She smelled of violets, and something deeper, more sensuous. It was her own scent, he thought, not something artificial.

He'd thought, briefly, of asking to take her home. But her watchful duenna of a maid would be waiting up for her, would listen, perhaps, to what passed between them. No. They were better off here.

The music stopped. They stood still. She cast her eyes down, but he could see her bosom heaving from the force of her emotion that was, perhaps, too strong to reveal in her glance.

"It is time to go, I think," he managed to get out. He was aware of the violinist watching them. No more music tonight, his silent figure seemed to be saying.

Very well. Ames dropped his arm from her back, let go her hand. With a small, intimate nod, she cast him a melting glance and turned away to retrieve her velvet evening cloak from where it lay across a chair.

Ames left a dollar on the table and they went out. The streets were deserted, the night air cold. They were far from the Back Bay, where she lived. He looked up and down, searching for a cab. Behind them, the lights in the café suddenly went dark.

"We are stranded," she murmured beside him. She didn't seem upset; he heard a hint of laughter in her voice, and he felt her hand in the crook of his arm, the pressure of her body as she pressed close to him. He was seized with the sudden, desperate need to embrace her, and he was reaching for her when they heard the sound of a carriage coming toward them.

A vacant cab. A miracle. Ames stepped out from the curb, raised his arm, and the cab pulled up—not a herdic-phaeton, but a closed four-wheeler. A miracle twice over. The driver touched the brim of his bowler and muttered a greeting, and Ames gave his hand to Serena to help her in.

"Where to, sir?" the cabbie said as Ames climbed in beside her.

Before he could answer, she put a warning hand on his arm. "Tell him just to drive for a while," she said softly. "I don't want to go home—not yet."

Ames's head was whirling as they started off. Inside this small, closed, private space, they might have been alone in the world. She sat close beside him, her face turned up to his. He couldn't see her clearly, but he didn't need to. He caught her scent again, and he felt her tormenting presence, the press of her bosom against his arm.

I will drown in you, beautiful woman. It was his last coherent thought before he embraced her. Her mouth was lush and soft, and he was aware that even as she returned his kiss, she was murmuring something that he could not quite catch.

Her skin was warm and silky-smooth. He touched it, stroked her with a mounting sense of wonder that he was there, that she was in his arms, yielding to him, but more than that. She was as ravenous as he. No coy withholding, no modest, ladylike pretensions, her hunger matched his own. He saw her face in the dim glow of the streetlamps as they passed, light, dark, light, dark . . .

She smiled at him—a slow, sensuous smile. "We have the night," she murmured, and her voice was low and throbbing as she reached up and drew his head down to hers once more and took his mouth to her own. Drew him down into the dark, into the darkness of his desire for her, desire that nearly maddened him, threatened to overwhelm him. His need for her was agonizing, unendurable, and now, tonight, it must be satisfied.

The cab drove on through the silent, sleeping city.

CHAPTER
2 1

"MORE TEA, DOCTOR?"

At the breakfast table, Caroline set her face into a determined smile. As was her custom on Sundays, she'd dressed for church upon rising instead of bothering to change after breakfast. She was wearing an old brown dress that had been her Sunday-best before she'd gone into mourning for her mother. It was too tight, its bustle too large. It was also too warm, but she hadn't had her summer things made ready yet, and in any case . . .

She realized MacKenzie was still holding out his cup and she hadn't poured. He was looking at her with a curious mixture of sympathy and concern, as if he knew exactly what was on her mind and couldn't think of anything to say to reassure her.

She poured a cup for him and another for herself. But her hand was unsteady, and as she slopped a bit into her saucer, she uttered an exclamation of annoyance.

Addington hadn't come down yet, which was not surprising

considering he hadn't come home until four in the morning. She knew, because she'd lain awake with her headache, listening to the bell in the Church of the Advent toll the hours. At last, just when she thought she could bear the suspense no longer, she'd heard him come in and climb the stairs and walk past her closed bedroom door. She'd wanted to go to him then, demand to know where he'd been, demand to know what he'd been doing. But she knew where he'd been; that was the terrible truth of it. She knew, or she could almost—almost—imagine what he'd been doing, and with whom, and that was a more terrible truth.

He'd been with *her*—Serena Vincent. Caroline imagined they hadn't stayed long at the party after she and Dr. MacKenzie left. Not when she'd seen them dancing like that, so close, so oblivious of everyone else.

Oh, how she hated to think of it! Her own sane, steady brother, who had been the guardian of her life, the firm monitor of her own sometimes wavering inclinations. He had always been there to guide her, to protect her—and now what? Now he himself was in need of guidance, in need of protection, and she had no idea how to tell him so.

That woman was trying to ensnare him. If Caroline knew nothing else in the world, she knew that one thing. Serena Vincent had set her cap for him, would try to use him as her means to gain reentry into the world of her birth.

And who better for that purpose than Addington Ames? The sanest, steadiest, most proper Bostonian of all, the scion of a proud Brahmin family, and never mind that their money had run low; their bloodline was as fine as any and better than most. Serena Vincent, with her wiles, with her cunning, was going to force her way back into the small, chilly circle that had cast her out, and she was going to try to use Addington to do it.

So Caroline's thoughts had run, all the night, and it was only with the greatest self-control that she had refrained from accost-

ing her brother in the darkened hallway to demand an accounting from him of his whereabouts.

But of course it would have been pointless to have done
that—pointless, and tactically very unwise. Within limits, he had
always been indulgent with her, and she knew it. He had indulged her when she'd demanded that he help Val in that awful
mess with the late and unlamented Colonel Mann; had indulged
her again when she'd demanded that he look into those dreadful
murders at Bertram's Bower; had even (and she'd been espe-
cially grateful to him for that) not been too critical of her only
this past week when she'd gone against his wishes and attended
a séance at Mrs. Sidgwick's, thereby landing herself in a most
alarming predicament that had resulted in Deputy Chief Inspector Elwood Crippen's practically accusing her of murder.

And now, when Addington himself seemed in danger of acting unwisely, even recklessly, should she—could she—indulge
him? Or should she try to reason with him, make him see that his
behavior was most unwise, that it could only lead to disappointment, disillusion—even disgrace?

Now, at breakfast with Dr. MacKenzie, uncomfortably
aware of her brother's empty place at the head of the table, she
sighed and pushed back her chair as she heard the thump and
rumble of the dumbwaiter in the back passage. Margaret would
want to be clearing away. She'd tell her to leave Addington's
place so that when he came down—*if* he came down—he
wouldn't take its absence as some kind of reproof.

"Will you come to church, Doctor?" she asked.

He'd often accompanied her, although she could tell that he
had no more use for organized religion than Addington had.
Addington, having been brought up with her in their parents'
Unitarianism, had long since given up going to church, and had
raised a skeptical eyebrow when she'd announced, some years
ago, that she had decided to forgo Unitarianism's cheerful toler-

ance and adopt the much more stringent doctrines of the High Episcopal Church of the Advent down on Brimmer Street on the flat of the hill. He had murmured something about the denizens of Mount Olympus, and the gods of the Egyptians, and had let it go at that. She'd not understood what he'd meant, but she'd been glad that at least he hadn't raised any objection. Her mother had been somewhat more apprehensive, but in her kind and loving way hadn't raised any objection either.

A short while later Caroline walked determinedly along the square to Mt. Vernon Street (Dr. MacKenzie, for once, having declined her invitation), racking her brain about how to speak to Addington about Mrs. Vincent. She'd try to put it out of her mind during the service, she thought; the Reverend Nightingale, always so eloquent in the pulpit, would surely have a sermon for her to meditate on today, and she had no doubt the mental exercise would do her good.

Two hours later, trudging back up the hill, perspiring a bit in the warmth of the sun, she felt no better. The sermon had been unwontedly dull, the hymns somehow lacking their usual appeal. She'd had a thought while the reverend was speaking, that perhaps she should go to him with her troubles, explain her fears about Addington.

But no. The Reverend Nightingale was a small, intense man who seldom acknowledged weaknesses of the flesh. He would not understand her concerns even if she managed to find the words to tell him. Better that she wrestle with this problem by herself, or perhaps—yes, why not?—with Dr. MacKenzie's help.

She arrived back at Louisburg Square out of breath and with her mind firmly set on confronting her wayward brother. It was her duty to do so, she told herself, just as it was his duty to confront her when he thought she'd done something wrong, or even slightly foolhardy.

The sight of the trees and shrubbery inside the little oval in their springtime foliage was a sight she was usually overjoyed to see: the end of the long New England winter, the start of the warm months that led to the glories of the fall. But not today. Today she had more important matters to attend to, and so she strode briskly toward No. 16½, screwing up her courage to confront her brother.

The house was quiet. Standing in the front hall, divesting herself of her hat and gloves and cape, she caught the odor of roasting lamb from the basement kitchen. Good. They would have a fortifying Sunday dinner, and then she would find—or make—the opportunity to have a word with Addington.

Cautiously sliding apart the pocket doors to the parlor, she peered in.

Addington and Dr. MacKenzie were sitting in quiet companionship, the air pungent with the odor of the doctor's pipe.

"Addington," she breathed. "I am so glad to see you."

He looked up at her. His face was drawn with fatigue, as if he hadn't slept, and his eyes held—what? Something. Some new thing that she hadn't seen there before—a kind of defeat, she thought, as if his evening with Mrs. Vincent hadn't gone well.

Her heart lifted at that happy thought. Perhaps Mrs. Vincent wasn't setting her cap for him, after all; perhaps she'd let him know she wasn't interested in him.

He didn't reply to her greeting but merely nodded and turned back to the Sunday newspaper he'd been reading. Dr. MacKenzie rose as she came in, and smiled at her in what she thought was a reassuring way.

She perched on a small brocade settee and stared at her brother. She'd meant to wait until after dinner, but now, confronted with his maddeningly opaque presence, she realized that she couldn't wait, after all. Even with Dr. MacKenzie there, even though Addington might not be in the best of moods (as he obviously wasn't), she couldn't refrain, right this minute, from saying to him what she knew she shouldn't have as soon as the words were out of her mouth.

"You came in very late, Addington."

He continued to hold the newspaper high, hiding his face.

"Addington? I was very worried about you."

The newspaper came down. She flinched a little at the sight of his dark, brilliant eyes (but they were not so brilliant just then) meeting hers again. "No need to worry, Caro."

"I think there was. I had no idea what you were doing out so late."

His mouth settled into a severe line, as if he were gritting his teeth. Well, she'd begun; she might as well finish.

"I mean, it was four o'clock when you came in, and I—"

"I wonder," Dr. MacKenzie put in gently, "if dinner might not be ready?"

She threw him a distracted glance and turned back to her brother. Dinner was not ready. If it were, Margaret would have come in to announce it.

"I appreciate your concern, Caro," Ames said flatly, "but I assure you, it is not necessary."

"Not necessary! When you were—"

"When I was what?"

"With that woman." She lifted her chin. I am saying these things for your own good, dear brother, she thought, just as you, so often in the past, have done the same for me.

MacKenzie tried again. "I really don't think—"

Ames silenced him with a look. "Never mind, Doctor," he said. "My sister obviously has something on her mind, so let her continue. What woman, Caroline?"

"Mrs. Vincent." She hated even to say the name.

"My acquaintance with Mrs. Vincent is hardly your affair."

"Oh, but I think it is. When she is so obviously trying to use you—"

Ames threw down his newspaper. Use him! Hardly! If anything, it had been the other way around. He flushed slightly now, remembering the enchanted hour he'd spent with her in that cab, driving through the dark, deserted city. Not that she'd objected to his behavior—far from it.

"I think you have seriously misinterpreted matters," he replied. "And if you were wise—"

"Misinterpreted!" She felt her temper rising to a dangerous pitch, and she clenched her hands, digging her nails into her palms to try to quell it. "Don't tell me you were out by yourself until four in the morning! You were with her, and I have to tell you honestly, Addington, I think it is most unwise of you to associate with her! What will people say? You know what she is, you know she has been disgraced! No one will receive her, no one will even speak to her!"

"Then I would say that is their loss," he retorted. "She is a most interesting woman."

"Interesting! Is that what you call it? She will try to insinuate herself back into Society by using you, and not only will she fail, she will ruin your reputation, as well!"

He did not reply. He looked down, he looked away, and she could tell that his thoughts had suddenly veered away from the topic at hand.

He was remembering Mrs. Vincent's parting words to him, and thinking that no, she was not trying to use him for any purpose other than—what had it been last night? An hour of passion, as much for her delight as for his, an hour of dalliance and nothing more?

The tense silence in the room was broken by the sound of a jangling bell, very loud. Caroline started, not knowing what it was, but then she remembered: the telephone. How inconvenient.

Ames sprang up at once and hurried to answer, not troubling to close the pocket doors behind him.

"Yes?" he shouted. "Oh, Crippen! Yes! Yes!"

During this one-sided exchange, Caroline sat frozen, not looking at MacKenzie. She'd been wrong to light into Addington the way she had, and not only did she know it, she knew the doctor knew it also.

"No, I don't think so," Addington said loudly.

Caroline felt the beginnings of shame creep over her.

"Good! Well, Inspector, do what you can."

Over the winter, she thought, MacKenzie had become a good friend—possibly the best friend Addington had ever had, and herself, as well—but even so, he was not family.

"I'll see you tomorrow, then!"

And even family should not know the shame of Addington's possible infatuation with that woman. Even family should not know—

Addington had not returned. Apparently he was trying to place a call. She heard him cranking the handle, and then his angry tone as he struggled with the operator.

"Yes!" he shouted. "Sidgwick! Lime Street! Hello? Hello?"

Silence.

"The wonders of modern technology," MacKenzie murmured in a vain attempt to lighten her mood.

"Hello? Mrs. Sidgwick? Did Professor James contact you? He did? It is arranged? Good. In one hour? I will see you then."

Ames came back into the room looking somewhat less desolate. His eyes sparkled with a hint of their usual lively interest, and Caroline thought she saw a faint grim smile on his lips. Good, she thought. Anything was better than the bleak, devastated look he had had earlier.

"Crippen has had no word on our friend Snell," he said, "but at least he has done as much as he could. Railroad stations being watched, police in all the northeastern cities alerted, a description of Snell and the girl telegraphed everywhere. He has even promised that the WANTED posters announcing Edgeware's reward will be out today, but I doubt the police artist will make a decent likeness."

"You spoke to Mrs. Sidgwick just now," MacKenzie said. "You are going to her?"

"For another séance, yes. It was Professor James's idea. If nothing else, she may receive some telepathic message from her daughter as to her whereabouts."

"Or such a message might mean the daughter is dead," MacKenzie replied. "Could Mrs. Sidgwick stand to hear that?"

"Since she has agreed to do the séance, we must assume that she could," Ames replied. "She must know that the possibility exists. Doctor, will you come? Or—no, perhaps you had better not," he amended, seeing Caroline's expression. Let MacKenzie stay here, he thought, and try to cajole her into a happier frame of mind.

"But—don't you want dinner, Addington?" Caroline asked as Margaret appeared.

"What? Dinner? No. I'll take something later."

And with that, he vanished. They heard his boots clatter on the tiled floor of the vestibule, and then the front door slammed.

Ah, well, Caroline thought as she and MacKenzie made their way back along the hall to the dining room. At the very least, her involving Addington in Mrs. Sidgwick's affairs had the virtue of distracting him—as she hoped it would—from the dangerous charms of Serena Vincent.

But as she and MacKenzie began to spoon up their soup, she caught his glance and gave him a rueful smile.

"I didn't do very well, did I, Doctor?"

No use pretending he didn't know what she meant. "Well, it is a delicate thing, after all, to throw a man's indiscretions up to him."

"So you agree with me that he was indiscreet?"

He shrugged. "I imagine so. They call your sex the weaker one, Miss Ames, but I have my doubts about that. Many men confronted by a woman's wiles are very weak indeed."

She was amazed that he would make such an admission. Is he giving me some kind of message? she thought. Does he think that I, too, have wiles? Does he want to avoid them?

And then she thought: Don't be silly, Caroline Ames. You are a spinster of advancing years, and you have about as many wiles as Margaret. Which is to say, none.

"Well, then, Doctor," she said (and he was delighted to see a smile lighten up her pretty, worried face), "we will just have to strengthen him, won't we?"

CHAPTER
22

As Ames made his way down the steep slope of Mt. Vernon Street to the flat of the hill to Mrs. Sidgwick's house on Lime Street, he had almost—almost—forgotten his encounter with Serena Vincent. His memory of it was still with him, but as only a faint shadow, a painted theatrical flat as it were, in front of which, now, was occurring the immediate business of a séance with Evangeline Sidgwick.

Concentrate on that, he thought. Do not think about last night, do not remember it: the way she felt in your arms, the way she responded to your kiss, her ardor, her total absence of any modesty . . .

He had stopped at Charles Street, waiting to cross, when he heard someone shouting his name.

"Halloo, Ames!" He turned to see Desmond Delahanty loping along from the Common. The Irishman was hatless as usual, his fiery red hair rumpled in the breeze.

"How are you, Desmond?"

"Coming to see you, as a matter of fact. How goes the search? Did Martin's man catch up with you?"

"He did." Briefly, as they crossed and walked along the flat of Mt. Vernon Street, Ames told his friend about the circus ringmaster.

"I saw the news about the daughter's being kidnapped," Delahanty said.

"Yes."

"Any word for a ransom?"

"No. But a reward has been posted, and we've a good idea of who took her." He explained about Mrs. Sidgwick's previous life in the carnival.

Delahanty emitted a low whistle. "She's got herself caught up in a nice mess, for sure," he said. "And even with all her mental talents, she can't help?"

"I don't know. I'm on my way to her now." A thought struck him. "Would you come, Desmond? Professor James has asked her to hold a séance in the hope that she can learn something about the girl. Since you are a believer, your presence there might—ah—help her along."

Delahanty peered at him. "You mean it, Ames? I would surely love to see the famous Mrs. Sidgwick in action. You don't think she'd mind if I sat in?"

"I don't see why she would. Particularly if you might be helpful—merely by believing in her powers, if nothing else."

They turned a corner and came into Lime Street, still and empty in the sun. Delahanty stopped. "You think the girl might be dead?" he asked.

"She might be, yes. Even though the man who took her is her father."

Delahanty emitted a low whistle. "Would her own father harm her?"

"Given what he is, it is possible. Crippen has cast his net, but

I doubt he will catch anything. Either the man left town imme- diately upon taking the girl, or he has gone to ground here in the city. He might be anywhere," he added gloomily.

"Yes, I see. Well, then," Delahanty said with some enthusi- asm, "it is all the more important for Mrs. Sidgwick to exercise her fabled talents. And, yes, Ames, I will come along, thank you very much. I won't stay if she objects, of course," he added.

But she hardly seemed to notice that Ames had brought an extra man. She sat in her upstairs room, Harold Edgeware at her side, Professor James perched on a spindly carved chair oppo- site. He was leaning forward, looking intently into her eyes; he didn't move, nor did she, when Ames and Delahanty were shown in.

Edgeware approached them. "He's trying to hypnotize her," he said softly, "but it doesn't seem to be working."

"Ah." Ames nodded. Hypnotism, like spiritualism, was a foreign notion to him. Give someone else power over your thoughts? Answer questions that, awake, you could not—or would not? Never.

The room, as before, was too warm, the draperies drawn against the light. He and Delahanty edged in, standing along the wall, not wanting to interrupt James's concentration.

". . . asleep," he was saying. "You want to sleep, you are go- ing to sleep . . ."

Mrs. Sidgwick's frail form suddenly shuddered violently. Her eyes were wide, her face contorted in—what? Agony, Ames thought. She is in mental agony—not surprisingly—and she ei- ther cannot or will not surrender, even to the great Professor William James.

"It is no use," she said. She stood up, and James did also. "I am sorry, Professor. I know you have hypnotized me before, but today—I cannot do it."

"Gentlemen." James came to greet them—he knew Delahanty from the St. Botolph Club—and after shaking hands, took out his handkerchief to mop his high, broad brow. "May Mr. Delahanty attend?" he said in answer to Ames's question. "I don't see why not. Mrs. Sidgwick?"

She stared at Delahanty for a moment. He stared back. "Of course," she said. "If you approve, Professor."

"Oh, absolutely," he replied, smiling at Delahanty. "I would imagine a good Irishman knows all about séances and second sight, isn't that so?"

"Perhaps not all, but something, yes," Delahanty replied.

At Edgeware's word, they moved down the hall to the room where Mrs. Sidgwick held her séances. The men arranged themselves around the table with the medium at her accustomed place near the tall cabinet. The maid, obviously well trained, stepped in to turn down the gas, and then they sat in darkness.

Ames heard a sound that might have been the rustle of Mrs. Sidgwick's skirts, and heavy breathing that he thought came from Edgeware. He was sitting between Delahanty and Edgeware; Delahanty's hand in his was slim and cool and firm, while Edgeware's was heavy and damp.

Mrs. Sidgwick moaned, a sound that made Edgeware flinch and, for a second, tighten his grip. Ames strained to hear, listening hard for the sound—the very eerie sound—of the temperamental Roland's voice.

But nothing came. After that one low moan from Mrs. Sidgwick, and a stifled cough from Delahanty, the room was completely silent. Dead silent, one might say, Ames thought with grim humor. So silent that when, at last, Professor James spoke, it startled them all.

"Roland?" said James very low. "Are you there?"

Nothing.

He tried again. "We are waiting for you, Roland."

Still nothing. Roland, it seemed, was otherwise engaged.

"Come on, come on," Edgeware muttered impatiently under his breath. He was sweating more now, so that Ames felt the sticky wetness cover his own hand, and only just managed to keep from letting go.

Mrs. Sidgwick moaned again, and Ames could feel—or thought he could feel—the sudden rise of tension in the room. Everyone here except himself devoutly believed this woman could, and would, produce messages from the beyond, or at the very least, in automatic writing from someone else's thoughts. They waited with nearly palpable longing for her to do so now. He could feel it, could feel their yearning to make that connection. Even Delahanty, who had no personal stake in the business, was nevertheless a believer, was nevertheless aware of Evangeline Sidgwick's reputation and wanted, today, to see her live up to it.

But nothing came. No eerie greeting from Roland, no messages from that vast population—"the majority"—that had passed on, no hurried scribbling in the dark. A minute crawled by; two. Ames's thoughts began to drift. All unbidden, Serena Vincent's voice—low, throaty, infinitely seductive—came to him, and he was aware that his heart, which until then had been perfectly quiet, had begun to beat hard.

Stop it, he thought. Concentrate on the business at hand. With difficulty, he forced himself back to the darkened room, the little circle of querants intent on this urgent exercise. Would the girl speak to her mother? And if she did, what would that mean? That she was dead?

But nothing—no one—came through. Roland had abandoned them. The girl was nowhere to be found—or not in the spirit world, at any rate.

Which could only be good news, Ames thought. He shifted in his chair and wondered what harm it would do to remove his hand from Edgeware's. He started to do so but stopped when Edgeware spat out at him: "Don't!"

So he didn't. But we had better get on with it, he thought. With every passing hour, the girl was more endangered, her captor more likely to escape.

Suddenly there was a flurry of movement from where the medium sat in trance, a chair pushed hurriedly back, someone murmuring to her—Professor James, apparently.

"Can someone turn up the gas?" James said sharply.

Edgeware, extricating his sweaty palm from Ames's, did so. They blinked in the harsh glare of the light.

Mrs. Sidgwick sat fallen back in her chair, her head lolling, her eyelids fluttering. James hovered over her, patting her hands, her pale cheeks. "All right now, you are here with us, it is all right," he was saying.

She didn't seem to hear him at first, but then after a moment she opened her eyes, staring up at him and clutching his hands. Then slowly she sat upright, gazing around the room as if she did not know where she was, or with whom.

"My dear," Edgeware exclaimed at her side. "Are you all right?"

She ignored him, turning instead to James. "Did I—did Roland come?" she asked.

"No."

At that, she seemed to crumple, and with an exclamation of concern—or perhaps annoyance at James's blunt reply—Edgeware seized her by the shoulders. "Evangeline! Listen to me! You mustn't despair! It means nothing—nothing at all!"

At last she looked at him. "What are you talking about, Harold? Of course it means something! It always means something."

"What? The fact that Roland didn't come through? But there could be a dozen reasons why he didn't. Perhaps he couldn't hear you, perhaps the connection was broken—anything! Oh, please, my dear, you mustn't cry. Here—" He fumbled about his person, producing a large white cotton handkerchief with which he began to dab ineffectually at her face until she snatched it away from him and, quite forcefully, blew her nose.

"I think," said James slowly, "that Mr. Edgeware might be correct." He looked around at them as if they were students in one of his classes and then at the medium. "If you did not make contact, might it not be because there was no one to make contact with?"

There was a little silence as they thought about it. "You mean—" Delahanty began.

"Exactly," James said. "I mean that if the girl were dead, she might well be trying to get through to her mother. And since she did not do that, should we not assume it was because she has not yet passed over?"

Delahanty glanced at Ames, and Ames saw his own thought reflected in his friend's eyes: Or it might mean that the medium's powers had been weakened by her worry over her missing child, and therefore she had been unable to summon her control as she normally did.

But we should not voice that notion, Ames thought. At this point, the woman is fragile enough; she does not need any such negative opinions to weaken her further.

"Perhaps tomorrow," Edgeware murmured.

She nodded, but without conviction. "Yes. I must try again. Even though—" She broke off, her tears choking her.

William James said, "I suggest that we take this result today—or lack of result, more precisely—to mean that your daughter is alive and well. But if you feel strong enough, then yes, of course you should try again. Telephone me tomorrow to let me know how you do."

AMES TOOK HIS SUNDAY MEAL WITH DELAHANTY AT THE Parker House, and then he walked home alone. It was late afternoon. The city was quiet, only a few vehicles rattling by, a pleasant respite from the usual workaday traffic and noise.

As he walked along Tremont Street, past the Old Granary Burying Ground behind its high iron fence, he paused for a moment, thinking to go in. Like King's, a block down at King's Chapel, it was a small, tranquil oasis in the midst of the bustling city. He liked it there: the ancient table-tombs, the slate headstones carved with winged angels or death-heads slanting among the grass, the tall elms arching over them, pigeons fluttering high among the branches. When he'd been a small boy, his mother had occasionally taken him there to gaze upon the tombstones, some of which marked the graves of their ancestors—Bowdoin, Hull, Hancock, Sewall. They would visit, too, the grave of Mrs. Elizabeth Vergoose, the fabled "Mother Goose," whose tales, brightly illustrated, had been part of his and Caroline's childhood.

But that was a long time ago, he thought. The elms had seemed taller then, the table-tombs much larger. And where was she—his mother? Her grave was in the family plot over at Mt. Auburn, but where was *she*? In some place where she could be spoken to, even as Caroline had tried to do? He didn't think so—couldn't believe it to be so.

He walked on. Thinking of Caroline had removed all his momentary desire to visit the Old Granary. If Caroline had not gone against his wishes—his dictates—she would not have been present at that séance on Monday afternoon last. And he would not have become privy to the fact—the unnerving, disconcerting fact—that one of the men he most admired, one of the men he most trusted to look upon the world in a sane and rational manner, Professor William James, was a devotee of spiritualism.

Yes. That was what stuck in his craw: the fact that William James was a believer. A brilliant man of science, dabbling in claptrap like spiritualism. If William James could believe in such rot, what hope was there for ordinary mortals to rid themselves of ancient superstition? The world was on the brink of a new century—a new age of scientific discovery and wondrous invention. Spiritualism had no place in it.

At Brimstone Corner he turned up Park Street. The day had been warm, but now a welcome cooling evening breeze blew up from the Common. He would stop at the Somerset, he thought. He wanted to think—had to if he ever hoped to extricate himself and Caroline from this morass of séances and mediums and voices from the beyond.

Because somewhere there, in that treacherous quicksand, lay the menacing figure of the man he'd known as Chester Snell.

If Caroline had not gone to that séance, he would never have learned that Snell was once again at large, that he was perhaps intending to take some revenge on Ames, whose testimony had sent him to prison.

If Mrs. Sidgwick's "automatic writing" were to be believed . . .

But how could it be? How could he, Addington Ames, a rational, intelligent man, a product of the height of civilization, Boston in the late nineteenth century, a man who had lived all his life disdaining other men's ignorance—how could he put any credence in such a thing as automatic writing?

Still. Snell was at large, and that was a fact he needed to remember. Because sooner or later—preferably sooner—he was going to have to deal with it.

He crossed Beacon Street, passed the State House with its golden dome gleaming in the westering sun, and walked down the hill. The gray granite neoclassical front of the Somerset Club loomed before him. He bounded up the steps and went in.

CHAPTER
23

"YOU ARE NOT FORGETTING ABOUT THIS EVENING, ADDING-ton?" Caroline said at breakfast the next morning.

He lowered the newspaper. He had had a bad night—again—and he didn't want to talk to anyone, not even to her.

"What about this evening?" he replied.

"The musicale at Mrs. Gardner's. Surely you remember? It will be that new Hungarian pianist, Lazlo something-or-other. He is supposed to be as fine as Lizst."

Ames closed his eyes. "Yes," he said. "I had forgotten."

"Oh, Addington! When she's invited us at last! I've wanted to see her house for years!"

She turned to MacKenzie to explain. "Isabella Stewart Gardner is our—well, I hardly know what to call her. She isn't a Bostonian—her father was the New York department store magnate Alexander T. Stewart—but she married John Lowell Gardner thirty years ago and has lived here ever since. She's never really been one of us, however. She's a little—well—strong-minded. Some people might even call her eccentric. She travels a lot, buys tons of objets d'art, and where she puts them all I have no idea. Her house on Beacon Street is supposed to be a fabulous place, chockablock with all the things she's collected on her journeys. They say it's almost like a museum, but I wouldn't know because I've never been invited. Mr. Delahanty told me, Addington, that she regularly invites you to her big 'crushes' but you never go. I cannot imagine why. You might meet some interesting people there. Mrs. Gardner is quite the patroness of artistic young men, Doctor. She displays their paintings and sculptures, gives them a place to perform at her salons, like the one tonight. Oh, please say you'll come, Addington! I can hardly go without you, and I so want to see her house!"

Ames flicked a dark glance at MacKenzie, who had seemed less than enthralled at Caroline's description of the eccentric Mrs. Gardner. "Doctor, will you accompany us?" he said. "If I can be assured of another male in our party—"

MacKenzie sighed to himself. Several times, over the winter, he'd accompanied Caroline to Friday-afternoon Symphony, and aside from the delight of her company, he hadn't particularly enjoyed it. Classical music was lugubrious stuff; he preferred a rousing Sousa march or a lilting tune from the Waltz King, Johann Strauss. "Yes," he said, smiling at Caroline. "I would be happy to."

"Good," she breathed, returning his smile. "You see, Addington, you will have male company. And I'm sure there will be a lot of men there in any case, since Mrs. Gardner is notorious for inviting gentlemen alone, without their wives."

Ames grunted. An evening perched on an uncomfortable chair in a crowded room, listening to the efforts of some young sprout polishing his technique at the expense of Isabella Stewart Gardner's guests, was not his idea of an evening well spent. Better to be alone in his study, thinking, or reading some scholarly treatise borrowed from his academic friends over at the College. Better even to spend his time at Crabbe's, or at the Somerset, as he had done last evening.

And Monday, he recalled, was Serena Vincent's night off. Would he hear from her today? Did he dare go to see her on his own, without an invitation? Considering what had happened between them on Saturday night, he could probably do so without seeming too presumptuous, but as much as he wanted to see her again, he didn't want to go to her until she let him know that his visit would not be unwelcome.

So he needed to get through the day, to see if she might contact him, ask him to call. She'd done that before, but only because she'd wanted his help in the matter of Agatha Montgomery's girls at Bertram's Bower. Would she summon him for a more personal reason, merely because she wanted to see him?

"In any case, whether I go or not, Dr. MacKenzie can escort you," he said to Caroline. "And you can tell me all about it afterward," he added.

She bit her lip. It was almost, he thought, as if she knew he was thinking about Serena Vincent. Had she somehow—from Mrs. Sidgwick?—picked up the ability to read his mind?

He devoutly hoped not.

DEPUTY CHIEF INSPECTOR ELWOOD CRIPPEN STOOD behind his overladen desk, a smoldering foul-smelling cigar clenched between his teeth, and peered up at Ames with a patronizing gaze.

"It's like this, Mr. Ames," he said. "I've done all I can, and now we must wait for him to show himself."

"He's killed at least one man and kidnapped a young girl, and you say we must wait, Inspector?"

But I will not wait, he thought. I cannot. I have a score to settle with Chester Snell beyond anything the law may bring to bear on him.

"Where did he live before?" he asked.

"Before he got sent up, you mean?" Crippen frowned. "It's in his file. Just let me see—" He shuffled through the tall stack of papers on his desk, not seeming to care that a few of them slipped to the floor. "Ah. Yes. Here it is." He extricated a file, opened it, and leafed through the several sheets of paper. "Last known address—Seaver Street. But you can't expect to find him there. Why would he—and we have to give him credit for some little bit of brainpower, don't we?—why would he go back to a place where he was known?"

Seaver Street was in Roxbury, a pleasant middle-class neighborhood. Since Snell probably hadn't bought property, he must have lived at a boardinghouse. Or perhaps he'd had an apartment, where some other tenant might have known him and might have seen him since his release. A slim chance, but one that offered, if nothing else, an opportunity to be doing something—anything—to get through the day. Ames had promised himself when he'd left home that morning that he wouldn't go back until late afternoon, by which time he might have had some message from Mrs. Vincent. He'd give her all day, and perhaps, if he waited long enough, if he didn't rush back now at midday, he would be rewarded with some word from her.

Crippen was speaking again, and he was missing it.

". . . exactly what you have in mind, Mr. Ames?"

"I don't know. It simply seems to me that we must do something—anything. A young girl's life is in danger!"

And my sister's, he thought grimly. Should he tell Crippen about Caroline's narrow escape? Would that impel the little police inspector to take more urgent action?

Crippen eyed him suspiciously. "I am perfectly well aware of the seriousness of the matter, Mr. Ames. But I have told you, I don't see what more we can do at the moment. We have our Wanted posters everywhere, we have men at the railroad stations and the docks, we have alerted the police all up and down the eastern seaboard and well into the Midwest. The man won't be able to show his face."

"Which is something he must know," Ames interjected.

"I assume so, yes. So what would he do? If he wants to spirit the girl out of the city, he must hire a private conveyance, and if he has decided to stay here, he has gone to ground. In either case, he has her on his hands, and he must keep her quiet and hidden. Not an easy task, but not impossible."

All too possible, Ames thought, particularly for a man who once traveled with a carnival, a man who knew many tricks and would not scruple to use them.

But they must do something to find him—anything. Crippen had other demands on his time, true, but he, Addington Ames, did not.

"Do you have Jones's things?" he asked.

Crippen frowned. "You mean, what we found on him? A soaking mess, that was. But, yes, we do."

"Any helpful information in the mess?"

"No identification. Pawn ticket for a pair of cuff links."

"Could I see what you have?"

"Why?"

"I'm not sure. I just want to have a look."

Crippen shrugged. "If you please. My sergeant will get them for you, just tell him I said so."

The sergeant was none too happy to be sent on an errand to the storage rooms, but he returned bearing a cardboard box labeled "Jones" and handed it to Ames without comment.

Ames sat in the outer office and opened it. Aside from the clothing, none of which had identifying labels, there was nothing much: a dirty, sodden handkerchief; a few coins; a penknife. Assuming that Jones's corpse was intended as a warning, Snell would have counted on the other attendees of the séance—like Caroline—to identify the body when it was found in the lagoon.

But how could Snell have known who would find the dead man? Anyone could have found him; it was only coincidence that Caroline and MacKenzie did, and immediately recognized him.

So perhaps Snell hadn't cared if Jones was identified. Perhaps, having bribed him to murder someone—anyone—at the séance, he'd wanted only to dispose of him. He must have met Jones in the Garden and killed him there, and used the lagoon as a handy place to dump the body.

There was something else in the box: a pawn ticket, still damp. Had anyone followed up on that? He rose, intending to ask Crippen about it, but just then the little inspector hurried out of his office, obviously bent on a suddenly important errand, and vanished down the corridor.

Ames handed the box back to the sergeant. "I'm taking this for an hour or two," he said, holding up the ticket. "I'll return it by the end of the day. Yes, I'll sign for it."

Out on School Street once more, he paused to savor the sour salt smell carried on the chilly breeze. The day had been bright at the start, but now the sky had clouded over and he knew there would be rain before nightfall.

He set off. The pawn ticket was from a shop in Scollay Square. This well-known red-light district, near Faneuil Hall and the Haymarket, was a place frequented by the riffraff of the city, by sailors on shore leave, by every kind of dubious character who wanted an hour in a burlesque palace, or who sought to purchase literature or photographs not seen in more respectable districts. Ames never went there now, but he'd sometimes visited when he was at the College. Harvard boys considered it part of their education to frequent Scollay Square; he'd gone along not because he'd enjoyed it, but because he'd wanted to look out for some of his more reckless friends. On the whole, he'd found the area dreary and uninteresting, repellent to his austere nature. The streetwalkers who had offered themselves to the eager college boys had been unattractive at best and diseased at worst, and the burlesque extravaganza at the Old Howard, the few times he'd seen it, had been embarrassingly bad and not in the least arousing.

Along the way he passed the secondhand bookstores in Cornhill, where he sometimes went in search of an obscure volume, but he was not interested in book browsing today. In no more than ten minutes he was at his destination, a shop marked by its traditional three balls. The small, barred display window had an array of jewelry and watches and silver flatware: the detritus of people's lives, sad evidence that they had fallen on hard times.

The interior was dark, and at first he thought no one was in attendance. Then a voice spoke to him.

"Yes, sir?"

It was the pawnbroker, who had appeared behind a counter protected by a heavy grille.

Ames held out the ticket, but the pawnbroker, seeing what it was, did not move to take it.

"You people have already been about these," he said warily. "I can't be responsible—"

"I am not the police. I just want a quick look at them."

"And who might you be?"

Ames handed over his card. The pawnbroker studied it for a moment as he seemed to be waging some silent argument with himself, and then tucked it into his trouser pocket. He turned away to rummage along a shelf and came back holding a pair of mother-of-pearl cuff links.

Ames took them, examined them. Nothing: no initials, nothing to tell him anything about their owner. If in fact Jones had been their rightful owner; probably he hadn't. He handed them back.

"Murdered, was he?" The pawnbroker's face was in shadow. His voice sounded—not uninterested, but hardly surprised. Ames wondered how often the man had been visited by the police, telling him that one of his customers had been done away with.

"Yes," Ames replied shortly.

The pawnbroker sniffed. "If these links aren't claimed, I can sell them."

Ames wanted to leave this depressing place, but before he did: "Can you tell me when he brought them in?"

Despite the dim lighting, he could see the suspicion on the pawnbroker's face. "You're not the police, you say?"

"No."

"Who are you, then? Why d'you want to know about this fellow?"

"I have an interest in the case. Can you check your records?"

The pawnbroker hesitated.

"I could see to it," Ames added, "that you are given a good report. The police likely wouldn't—ah—bother you for a while if I told them you'd been of some help."

There was no reason for the pawnbroker to believe this, he knew, but it was worth a try.

The pawnbroker hesitated a moment more, and then he reached under the counter to pull out a ledger. After a moment he looked up and said, "Two weeks ago today."

"Did he have anything else to pawn?"

"No, just these."

"Do you remember anything about him?"

The pawnbroker shrugged. "No."

"What name did he use?"

"John Jones."

"Address?"

"One twelve Bowdoin Street."

Nothing helpful there. It was barely noon; he had hours before he wanted to return home. Well, then, he thought, Seaver Street it is. He'd take the pawn ticket back to Crippen's sergeant and catch the omnibus to Roxbury.

And tonight, if Serena Vincent hadn't summoned him by then, he would go to Mrs. Gardner's after all. He liked to indulge his sister when he could; he'd do that for her, go to sit for a couple of hours in that rich woman's mansion on Beacon Street, and with any luck he'd manage to get through the evening.

The city bustled around him as he walked back up Tremont Street toward City Hall. People everywhere, all manner of conveyances—carriages and omnibuses and delivery wagons—the sidewalks thronged with pedestrians. No one paid any attention to him, and yet . . .

He paused in front of King's Chapel Burying Ground and, feeling slightly foolish, looked back the way he'd come. He'd thought that someone was following him. He saw a man who met his eye and quickly turned away, plunging into the traffic, dodging the horses' hooves.

Now, why had the fellow done that?

Ames had always felt perfectly at home in Boston; it was his city, his and his ancestors'. No one had the right to make him feel uncomfortable in it.

But now he did. It seemed menacing to him now because it hid a man who menaced him. He could feel it, could feel the threat that Chester Snell posed, not only to Evangeline Sidgwick and her daughter, but to Caroline and himself, as well.

A dangerous man.

Ames next.

I will find you, Snell, he thought as he moved on, turning the corner at School Street. We have business between us to settle yet, and until it is finished, I will hunt you even as you hunt me.

CHAPTER
2 4

WITH A FEROCIOUS TOSS OF HIS IMPRESSIVE MANE, THE young man seated at the piano lifted his hands, fingers dangling theatrically, and brought them down on the keys with a loud, discordant crash.

Ames winced. He had been sitting on this spindly gilt chair for the better part of an hour, and his body ached with the need to stand up and move about. He glanced around. Caroline sat on his left, and beyond her, Dr. MacKenzie. Their faces were composed, dutifully attentive. All around him were the other members of the audience gathered in Mrs. Gardner's music room, perhaps fifty men and a few women, all of them looking equally appreciative of the young man's efforts. The previous performer had been another young man, a tenor who had sung mournful German lieder. Ames's German was passable, but even if he'd wanted to follow the lyrics, he'd not have been able to do so because the young man had an irritating way of swallowing his consonants and extending his umlauts.

The pianist thundered away. It was announced in the printed program that he was performing his own compositions. In Ames's opinion, the fellow was tone-deaf; there wasn't a harmonious chord in the lot. This wasn't music, he thought, it was simply noise. And unpleasant noise at that. What was the fellow thinking of to impose such twaddle on an audience? What, for that matter, was Mrs. Gardner thinking of to invite people to hear it?

He saw her now, sitting at the far end of the front row, nodding approvingly, smiling as if the young man were her own son and she a doting mother, blind—and deaf—to his many faults. She was hardly a handsome woman, but her money and her strength of will made her lack of looks unimportant. Faded reddish hair, blue eyes—and a good figure that even now, when she was well past her youth, never failed to impress. John Singer Sargent had painted a notorious portrait of her a while back, posing her in a low-cut black gown with her famous pearls draped around her tiny waist. Her husband, a starchy fellow, had been outraged and had demanded that the portrait be removed from the annual art exhibition at the St. Botolph Club.

Mrs. Gardner had found a moment, earlier, to take Ames aside to ask him—surprisingly—about Mrs. Sidgwick. Was she genuinely psychic, Mrs. Gardner wanted to know. Did she produce results?

Ames remembered that she'd had a child, a little boy who had died.

She would have done better to speak to Caroline, he'd thought, but Mrs. Gardner preferred to speak to men. He hadn't been able to tell her much when she asked him if she should attend a séance herself.

"I don't know, Mrs. Gardner. Perhaps, if you are curious about it, you should."

She'd gazed at him with her wide blue eyes, smiling a little, and he'd felt, faintly, the force of her imperious personality. Was that the secret of her attractiveness? She wasn't attractive to him, of course, but he could see how other men might find her so. He wondered that Gardner didn't curb her. Rumors about her eccentric behavior often penetrated even the male bastions of the Somerset and the St. Botolph, and all the other men's clubs of the city as well: She'd paraded down Tremont Street with two lions (or panthers, or leopards) on a leash; in typically ostentatious fashion she'd gone on her knees to scrub the steps of her church during Lent. Perhaps, since they'd lost their child, her husband felt sorry for her, wanted only to let her do as she pleased.

The piano-playing continued, but slightly less loud. The pianist was hovering over the keyboard like a lover caressing his beloved. Ames shifted his weight, tried and failed to cross his legs. There was no more than six inches between his knees and the chair in front of him; he felt cramped and confined, like a captive animal in a too-small cage.

Serena Vincent had not contacted him. He'd returned home at four o'clock, after a fruitless expedition into Roxbury, to learn that he'd had no telegram, no hand-delivered note. Nor had she telephoned. He didn't even know if she had a telephone, and in any case, even if she did, he felt very strongly that she would not use it to summon him. It was not a discreet thing, a telephone; everyone could hear what you said, and if you weren't there to receive the call, someone else would know your business anyway.

The thought occurred to him that perhaps she had telephoned, after all, and Caroline had "forgotten" to give him the message. But then he chided himself. Caroline was nothing if not honest and forthright; he did her a disservice to think she would stoop to conceal a message for him, even a message from Serena Vincent, whom she so heartily disliked and disapproved of.

Serena Vincent. He forced himself to block out the noise of

the piano while he summoned her into his mind. Where was she tonight? At home? Was she alone? Or did she have some man to keep her company? Or was she not at home, but with some man nevertheless, dining in some expensive restaurant?

He gritted his teeth. He couldn't bear to think of her with another man. Her beautiful eyes gazing into some other man's eyes, her beautiful mouth speaking enchantment to some other man's ready ear . . .

He winced at a particularly loud chord. He couldn't bear this noise, either. Not for one moment more could he sit quietly there, part of the captive audience summoned by the imperious Mrs. Gardner to hear her latest, newest genius. She had an inexhaustible supply of young geniuses, it seemed, and she never tired of imposing them upon people.

With a muttered word to Caroline, he stood up and managed to squeeze his way along the row to the side aisle. In a moment more he was in the foyer, with its cararra marble floor and giant antique bronze chandelier, its walls nearly covered by paintings acquired by Mrs. Gardner on her travels. Huge potted palms towered in the corners, and a liveried footman (liveried!) sprang to attention and hurried to open the door for him to the vestibule. No need to fetch his hat; as if by some presentiment, he'd kept it with him.

At last he was safe on the street. He stood for a moment taking deep breaths of the damp night air. As he'd known it would, it had rained earlier, but now the clouds were broken, racing white across the dark sky, and he knew it would be fine tomorrow.

He cocked an ear. Almost, he could still hear the dissonant sounds from within. He had a moment's thought for poor MacKenzie, trapped there with Caroline. She had gotten her wish at last, had seen the interior of Mrs. Gardner's famous house on the water side of Beacon Street. From the looks of the place, Gardner was going to have to buy—or build—a larger house, and soon, to make room for his wife's relentless acquisition of the art treasures of Europe. Her taste ran far beyond paintings: statues, tapestries, porcelains, display cases of illuminated manuscripts. He had even seen, in one corner, a tiny seventeenth-century sedan chair (had people really been so small back then?). He had a vision of Mrs. Gardner roaring through Europe, buying this, buying that, taking whatever she fancied at the moment. She should find someone to advise her, he thought, lest she spend herself into penury and have nothing but a hodge-podge to show for it.

And then he thought: Here was a woman with every luxury that money could buy, and still she was unhappy enough, probably over the loss of her son, that she seemed prepared to seek solace from a medium.

He began to walk. His footsteps sounded loud in the quiet night, and, he realized after a moment, they seemed to echo.

Or—

He stopped, and the echo stopped also.

Was he being followed?

He looked behind, down the long, dark stretch of Beacon Street broken at intervals by the light of the streetlamps. He saw no one. The shadowed street was silent, empty.

He started to walk again, and this time he heard no echo.

It was nothing, he told himself. His nerves were stretched tight, his imagination running wild. No one was there, no one followed him.

He came to the corner of Berkeley Street. If he went two blocks over, across Marlborough, across Commonwealth, he would come to the Berkeley Arms.

Where Serena Vincent lived.

He remembered the warmth of her body in his arms, and the

soft, maddening sound of her breath in his ear. Her lips, her scent, the touch of her fingers . . .

A herdic-phaeton approached, slowing as the driver saw him. He shook his head; the driver clucked to his horse and went on.

Two blocks over. And why not, he thought. He didn't intend to see her, to speak to her. He would simply stand across the street and look up at her windows. No harm in that. And now, having had the thought, he suddenly wished to do it—had to do it, knew he could not go home to Louisburg Square unless he did do it.

Rapidly his long legs ate up the distance. Ahead, at the corner of Commonwealth, a carriage had stopped. A man in a top hat alighted, turned, and handed down a woman. Ames could see the faint sparkle of gems at her ears and throat. The sound of their laughter reached him, and he felt a sudden pang of—what? Loneliness? Desolation? He'd been solitary all his life, but never lonely. Solitary was his nature. Even with all the dozens—hundreds—of friends and relations and acquaintances that a man like himself was heir to here in this small, close-knit, clannish city, he was known as someone who kept to himself. People didn't mind. For the most part, they understood. Every New England family had its eccentrics, many of them far more odd than Addington Ames. Who was, in fact, not odd at all, but merely solitary.

The couple had entered one of the imposing houses that lined the avenue. The carriage moved away. Ames walked on. Just ahead was the Berkeley Arms, an elegant new apartment hotel with its "French flats," its haughty concierge, its wealthy clientele. How did Serena Vincent, even given that she must make a fine high salary at the Park Theater, afford such a place? He hated to think she was accepting some rich man's largesse.

He came to it. He crossed the street and turned to stare up

at her windows. They were her parlor windows, he knew, and they were brightly lighted. She was in, then. His heart gave a sudden wrench. Should he call on her?

Why not? He was hardly a casual acquaintance, after all—not after what had happened between them. Surely she would not be averse to giving him a few moments of her time, even at this hour. He heard the bell in the Church of the Covenant tower, over on Newbury Street: ten o'clock. Not so very late. He could simply say he was in the neighborhood, had thought of her.

A woman's shadow passed the curtains. Hers. All right, he thought. Go across, walk into the lobby, give your name to the concierge.

He saw another shadow: a man's. Then hers came back, and the two shadows melted into one.

Damnation!

He stood as if rooted to the spot. He was aware of nothing but that lighted window, the shadows behind it. Now they parted; hers disappeared. The man's remained, but only for a moment, and then it, too, vanished.

She *was* seeing someone else. But she'd hardly been seeing him; she'd spent only a little time with him, with no promise ever to see him again. Their moments together, so burned into his brain, his heart and soul, had probably meant nothing to her. She probably spent such moments with many men, many different men, and thought nothing of it. Of them. Of him.

He realized he was trembling, and not from the chill night air.

The front doors of the Berkeley Arms were opening. A tall, heavyset man was coming out. Ames couldn't see his face clearly, but he was certain he was the man whose shadow he'd seen in Serena Vincent's window.

Suddenly Ames was seized with the impulse to follow him.

Who was he? Had he ever met him? Seen him at one of his clubs, perhaps, or working out down at Crabbe's? Or was he a stranger to the city—a New Yorker, perhaps? She was fond of New Yorkers, he knew—the fast crowd, with many men who would gladly accept the favors of the beautiful, the notorious Serena Vincent.

The man had walked quickly along Berkeley Street toward Boylston. Was he staying at the Hotel Brunswick, perhaps, a fashionable hostelry favored by many wealthy out-of-towners? No matter. He was gone—but Ames was still there. He looked up once more to her windows. They were still alight. Was she sitting before her fire, perhaps, thinking of what had just passed between her visitor and herself?

She wasn't thinking of him, Addington Ames, that was almost certain. She probably hadn't given him a thought since they'd parted early Sunday morning. He remembered how her scent had clung to his shirt, so that he hadn't put it into the laundry but had folded it and secreted it at the back of his bottom bureau drawer. Her scent. Her warmth. Her seductive, throaty voice whispering to him . . .

Suddenly, without looking out for the traffic, he plunged across the street and, before he lost his nerve, strode into the Berkeley Arms lobby.

It was deserted save for the concierge. He looked Ames up and down in his haughty way and said, "Yes, Monsieur?"

"Mrs. Vincent in?" Ames asked, presenting his card.

"Mrs. Vincent? It is not possible, Monsieur. She has requested that no one be announced for the rest of the evening."

"Just give my name, please." Ames heard his voice in his ears; it sounded rather more desperate than it should. Let these foreign fellows see you at a disadvantage, he thought, and they'd play it for all it was worth.

With a sniff, the concierge turned to his house telephone and rang a number. She wouldn't answer herself, Ames thought.

The maid would do that—a dour, middle-aged duenna who seemed to take unusual liberties in ordering her mistress about. He heard the concierge speak his name, pause, speak it again, pause again for what seemed a very long time. The maid was checking with her mistress, no doubt.

But at last, with an air of supercilious hauteur rather than defeat, the concierge told him he might go up.

In the elevator, he realized he was perspiring. Gingerly he mopped his face with his handkerchief. He shouldn't have come. She would think him a fool—no better than a callow youth, besotted with her. Many men were besotted with her, he knew. She was used to it—bored by it, undoubtedly. He should play a cooler game with her if he wanted to attract her. Did he want to do that? He had no idea. He knew only that he must see her—now—and that he would have been devastated if she had refused him.

The elevator doors clanged open. Down the thickly carpeted hall, her door was closed. He pressed the bell. Don't let the maid answer, he thought. He was not a man easily intimidated, but just now he felt rather fragile, reluctant to confront the maid's accusing gaze. How many of Serena Vincent's admirers had she gazed upon? he wondered, and immediately put the thought out of his mind.

The door remained closed. Why were they taking so long to answer? Was she going to refuse to see him, after all?

He had just lifted his hand to knock, when the shining wooden panel swung open. Serena Vincent stood before him.

For an instant—no more—he wanted to babble some foolishness about how grateful he was to her for admitting him. But he merely said, "Hello."

CHAPTER
2 5

"HELLO," SHE REPLIED SOFTLY, STEPPING BACK TO ALLOW him to enter.

She was wearing a gown of some soft, silky, dark green stuff, and a striking emerald necklace that fell into the cleft of her bosom. Her hand went to the necklace now, as if she were suddenly conscious of it.

She hesitated, then turned and went into her parlor. He followed. Her Yorkie, dozing on its silken pillow, lifted its head and growled softly at him, but at a word from her it quieted and went back to sleep. He wondered if the dog had growled at the man who had been here not half an hour before.

Mrs. Vincent waved him to a seat and sat opposite him on a pale green brocade settee fringed in darker green. From a silver box on the table next to her she took a thin brown cigarette and waited for him to light it for her. Did she remember that he'd done so before? Was it something she wanted only him to do, or would she have allowed any man to do it? The latter, he was sure.

He reached for the matches, took one and struck it, held it out. He was glad he wasn't trembling. She cupped her hand over his as she inhaled; then she let him go and he dropped the match into the china ashtray. It held several half-smoked cigarettes, only one of which matched the one she was smoking now.

"It is good of you to see me," he began.

She inhaled deeply and blew out a thin stream of smoke. "I am happy to see you," she said softly. She smiled at him. "Again," she added.

He felt himself flush. "Yes, well, I was passing, and I thought—"

"That you would look up to my windows to see if I was in."

She was different tonight, he thought. The passionate woman in the carriage had vanished, replaced by a cool, almost mocking, almost arrogant female who lacked any proper sense of womanly deference. But then, she'd never had that; it was her arrogance that had enabled her to survive.

"Yes," he said, realizing how inadequate it sounded.

"I had a previous caller tonight," she said. "Would you have come up if you'd known he was here?"

"I did know he was here."

"Ah. You saw him at the window."

"His shadow, yes."

"His shadow." That seemed to amuse her. "Yes, he is a rather shadowy character," she said, still smiling.

"You mean—"

She waved the hand that held her cigarette. "I mean, I don't know where he gets his money." She inhaled deeply again.

"Does it matter?"

"Not particularly. It is just that I don't want to become involved with—shall we say—some affair that might turn out to be messy."

Messy! Yes, she'd had at least two messy affairs that he knew of, one of which had resulted in her divorce, the other in the suicide of a man driven nearly out of his mind by his infatuation with her. Not to mention her entanglement in New York three or four years ago.

"You could simply tell him to go away—and stay away," he replied.

"Ah, but would he obey me? Men get so very involved in their attractions—and so possessive."

He pictured the man he'd seen, pictured him possessing her, and for a moment he could not speak. Then: "Who is he?"

"Just—a man."

"His name?"

"His name doesn't matter."

But it might, he thought. If he could find out who the fellow was, go to speak to him, tell him—what? That Mrs. Vincent found his attentions unwelcome? But perhaps, despite her protestations, she didn't.

"Is he a Boston man?" he asked.

"New York."

Of course.

"You have many—ah—acquaintances in New York," he said.

"Yes, I do. I like New Yorkers. They aren't as stuffy as Bostonians."

"May I take that personally?"

She laughed. "You are not stuffy, Mr. Ames. If you were, I would not take the pleasure I do in your—may I call it friendship?"

He could think of other names for it, but he relaxed a bit so that when she offered him a drink and told him to help himself—none for her, thank you—he was able to do so with some small sense of being at ease with her.

But her next words alarmed him all over again. "I will handle him, Mr. Ames. You needn't worry about me."

Oh, but I do, he thought as he sipped his brandy, and she read his thought in his eyes. "I am an independent woman, you know," she went on, smiling at him meaningfully. "And I can manage my life on my own."

An independent woman. What was that? Such a being had no place in his notion of the way of the world. Women were not supposed to be independent—were not, in the natural order of things, meant to be.

"A woman alone in the world," he began, "particularly a woman who is—ah—so exceptionally beautiful, as you are—"

Acknowledging his compliment, she inclined her head, crowned by its thick, glossy coil of auburn hair. The motion led his eye to her necklace.

Again as if she read his thoughts, she touched the stones as she had done before. "I suppose I shall have to return his gift," she said lightly. "I don't really like it in any case. Too showy, don't you think?"

He felt his stomach turn over. "He gave that to you?"

"Yes. This very evening."

And what did you do to earn it? he thought, but he could never have put the question into words.

"Does that bother you, Mr. Ames? That one of my—ah—admirers should give me such a token of his esteem?"

Now she was mocking him again. "It is hardly my business—" he began stiffly.

"No. It hardly is." She stubbed out her cigarette and leaned forward so that he had a startling glimpse of her décolletage. "My life is my own, Mr. Ames, no matter how close our friendship. I have not forgotten what passed between us on Saturday night, and I will not, not for a long time, if ever."

He felt himself beginning to blush. Most women—most ladies—having experienced such an interlude, would have refrained from mentioning it.

"But no matter what passes between us," she went on, "my life, such as it is, is my own. Please remember that."

She was warning him. Of what? Heartbreak? Abandonment?

"I do remember it," he said after a moment when the sudden tightening of his throat had eased a bit and he was able to speak in what he hoped was a normal voice. "But I would ask you to remember that you are vulnerable to all kinds of men who do not have your best interests at heart."

"As you do?" she replied softly. Her lips were parted a bit, and in her eyes he read what he thought was an invitation. He reached out, took her hand. The touch of her skin sent a shock clear through him. She allowed him to keep her hand for a moment, but then she took it back and sat up straight. Unselfconsciously, with that same hand, as if some sense of his touch remained on her, she caressed herself, running her hand over the thin fabric of the gown that covered her bosom.

He looked away. If she was trying to arouse him, she was succeeding. He needed to stand up, to try to calm his rebellious flesh; as he did so, he was aware that she watched him, smiling a little.

"How is your sister, Mr. Ames?"

He'd walked to the window. Was some other poor devil standing out there, looking up, yearning to see her?

"As well as you might expect," he said, his back still turned to her.

"I saw her name in the newspapers. So tiresome to be held up to public view like that."

Again she was mocking him. She herself was held up to public view all the time, and he thought she reveled in it.

He came back, sat across from her once more. "Caroline was briefly a suspect in Theophilus Clay's murder," he said.

"Suspected by Crippen?"

"Yes."

She made a moue of distaste. It had been Crippen who had arrested her last fall in the death of Colonel Mann. "I cannot imagine why they keep him on the force," she said. "He is a disgrace."

"He does his job as well as he can. Every now and then, unfortunately, he gets it wrong."

But Crippen had vanished from her thoughts. "Your sister believes in—Mrs. Sidgwick?" she asked, and he saw that it was more than a casual question.

"I'm not sure."

"She was successful at the séance? She contacted the person she wished to?"

"Her—our—mother. No, she didn't."

"Ah. And now there is some other difficulty. Mrs. Sidgwick's daughter kidnapped, a search for the man?"

"Yes."

"And you are involved?"

He didn't want to tell her why. "Somewhat."

She hesitated, as if she were considering whether to reveal some secret. Then: "I have been to Mrs. Sidgwick's," she said.

This surprised him. "You have? To—ah—contact someone in particular?"

"Someone in particular, yes."

Not Richard Longworth, he hoped, that miserable man who had killed himself at least in part because Serena Vincent broke off their affair.

"It was my father," she said. "When I suffered my disgrace when my husband divorced me, my father took it very hard. He felt that I had stained our family's honor, and he refused to allow me to return home. And then, not long after I joined the company at the Park Theater, he died. So we never had the chance to make it up. I always thought that if I could have spoken to him, if I could have explained why I did what I did, he would have understood, would have forgiven me. But I never had that opportunity. So . . . I thought I would try to contact him through Mrs. Sidgwick."

"And did you?"

"No." She saw his reaction and hastened to add, "But that doesn't mean that I don't believe in her powers. I do—very much. You don't, I suppose."

"No."

"But I know people—more than one—who have had much success with her. Only the other week, someone told me—"

Suddenly, startling them both, a bell rang somewhere in the apartment. A telephone bell, he realized.

After a moment, through the closed parlor door, they heard someone answer. Her watchful maid, undoubtedly. They stayed silent as they heard her say sharply, "No! She is not in!" followed by a little crash as she slammed down the earpiece.

Mrs. Vincent met his eyes as she smiled a wry little smile. "Hilda is very good at protecting me."

"Yes, she is."

"Sometimes she protects me more than I would like. But not just now. Just now she did what I would have wanted her to."

Ames cleared his throat. He wanted to ask her if she knew who had called (the man he'd seen earlier?), but he didn't quite dare. "I am surprised that you subscribe to the telephone."

She arched an eyebrow. "You do not?"

"We didn't until last week. I have an elderly aunt who, subscribing herself and enjoying it immensely, insisted that we do likewise. She likes to keep up with all the latest inventions."

"Then no doubt she will soon have you pedaling a bicycle."

They laughed together as they pictured it. Then, sobering, she said, "If you are now on the telephone, I should warn you that it is not a completely private method of communication."

"You mean, people nearby can hear what you say?"

"Well, yes, that, of course. But also, the operators listen in. You can hear them breathing, once you know what to listen for. And one time, if you can imagine it, I even heard the other telephone bells ringing in the office as the woman eavesdropped on my conversation. I never say anything of real interest on the telephone. Despite the fact that I display myself on the stage for all the world to see, I try to protect my privacy. Can you understand that?"

"Of course."

She looked, for a moment, quite forbidding. Her face was cold, her eyes hard. "People think that because I make an offering of myself onstage, I am to be allowed no shred of my own soul to keep for myself. Mind you, I am not complaining. Given my disgrace, my lot in life could have been far worse."

She stood up and held out her hand to him—a gesture of dismissal, he understood. But as he rose also, he saw some change in her expression, some softening, some small hint of a desire that matched his own. He ignored her hand and moved to embrace her, and she did not protest. For one long, exquisitely painful moment, she allowed him to hold her. She seemed suddenly fragile; he wanted to crush her to him, but he didn't quite dare. It was enough that she was in his arms, that she lifted her face to his and allowed him to softly, gently, press his lips to hers.

Then, surprising him, she lifted her hands and in an almost maternal gesture cradled his face between them, drawing back to stare deeply into his eyes. Briefly, he thought himself to be in bliss, but then she said very softly, "I shall be going away when the play closes in June," and his bliss vanished. Her wide, beautiful eyes searched his, as if she sought his reaction to her news.

"You—where?" Amazing, how those few words desolated him.

"On Commodore Vandergrift's yacht. We are to cruise the Mediterranean. The Riviera—Nice, Monte Carlo. And perhaps around Italy and up to Venice."

She released him and stepped away. "So we may not meet again before I go," she said.

For a moment he could not speak, so great was his sense of loss. And yet, as she had said, she was an independent woman; he had no claim on her.

"I see," he managed to reply at last.

"But in the fall—" she began.

He shook his head once, sharply. The fall! The fall was months away—an age, an eon. And to think of her all summer, on that luxurious floating palace, mingling with her rich friends, people who inhabited the demimonde, a world that was not his and never would be—no, he couldn't bear to think of it. Or of her, in such surroundings.

"Good-bye, then," he said. Suddenly he was angry with himself, and wanting to be away from her. Fool that he was to think that he meant anything to her, to this enchantress with her New York associations, her emeralds, her legions—he was sure they were legions—of dubious admirers.

"Not good-bye, surely, Mr. Ames?" she replied.

But already he was walking away from her into the little foyer, collecting his hat, pausing to try to think of one last thing to say to her. Something casual, he hoped, something impersonal to disguise his feelings.

She followed him. "I would rather say au revoir."

"Good night, then." He was glad his voice was cool—cold,

even—and glad, too, that he was able to meet her eyes steadily. Automatically he started to offer her his hand, but then, realizing how inadequate—how ridiculous—a gesture that was, he withdrew it.

"Good night, Mr. Ames."

As he met her eyes, he thought he saw there, as he had seen before, the devastating look that was not friendship, and certainly it was not anything more than friendship.

Pity, he thought. She feels sorry for me. He took it as a warning.

Outside, it was colder now, with a stiff wind that belonged more to March than May. He walked rapidly toward Boylston Street and turned there, hardly knowing where he went, wanting only to stride through the nighttime city, to stretch his legs, to inhale the cold, salty, gas-tinged air and try to banish from his thoughts the vision of Serena Vincent holding court on Vandergrift's yacht.

But by the time he reached the Common, he knew where he wanted to go, after all: to Crabbe's, that haven of male camaraderie where he and his companions worked off their animal energies. The place closed at ten, but like all permanent members he had a key, and he often went there late.

The Common was dark, and not safe. He knew he should go the long way around instead of cutting across, but he was in a hurry now, and he didn't want to take the extra few minutes. He plunged in. On this chilly night, not many people were about—only a shadowy form here and there, a few people sleeping on the grass. The police did their best, but the city's poor population, which mostly meant its immigrant population, grew apace, far beyond the powers of the police to control it. Any citizen walking across the Common at night ran the risk of being accosted by a footpad, robbed if he was lucky, assaulted if he was not, and like as not the words muttered at him would be in a foreign tongue—or, at the very least, English that was heavily accented.

Still. The Common seemed safe enough this night, no one about. Sometimes tramps slept among the graves in the little cemetery at the corner of Boylston Street, rising in the dark like so many ghouls to prey on the living, but Ames saw no such predatory shadows now, and in any case, in his present state of mind, he would have given any man who accosted him a good thrashing.

Automatically, as he passed the Parkman Bandstand, he looked behind him. Something—some shadow darker than the rest—moved, and then stopped. He peered into the gloom and waited for a moment, watching, listening. He heard the sounds of the nighttime city, nothing more: a lone cabbie going along Tremont Street, a distant train chuff-chuffing in to the Providence Station behind the Hotel Brunswick, the warning bell of an omnibus. He walked on.

At Crabbe's, he fished out his key and unlocked the door. The place was empty, echoing, the squash courts and massage room dark and deserted. No matter. Tonight of all nights, he didn't want company. He would go to the fencing court, he thought, and practice his lunge on the padded dummy.

Members coming in after hours were supposed to check in with the nightwatch, old Gibbons, and Ames did so now, descending to the murky region below stairs. A line of light showed beneath the watchman's door, but when Ames knocked, and even when he called the man's name, there was no answer.

He cracked open the door. The room reeked of liquor; Gibbons lay unconscious on his narrow cot, breathing stertorously. Ames pulled the door shut. He would speak to the management, he thought. No sense in paying the man if this was his way of performing his duties.

Upstairs in the fencing court, he inhaled the familiar smell of stale sweat as he turned up the gas and shed his clothing down to his shirt and longjohns. He took his face guard and walked along to the rack of swords. His was one of the best, a twenty-first-birthday gift from his father, who had never fenced in his life but had been proud of his son's athletic abilities: boxing, squash, crewing on the Charles, and this most exotic skill, dueling.

As he swiftly withdrew the weapon, he heard the satisfying scrape of the metal, and he felt a rush of energy course through him as he whipped the blade through the air, reacquainting himself with its heft. Yes, he thought, this is what he needed, a good workout. Some violent, demanding physical activity to engage his mind, to eradicate the image of Serena Vincent on Vandergrift's yacht, in another man's arms.

He was still struggling to erase that image when, the next moment, a voice came at him from out of the dark.

"Good evening, Mr. Ames. D'you fancy a duel?"

CHAPTER
26

AMES FROZE.

From the far side of the court, a man's figure emerged from the shadows.

The intruder was slightly built, and he moved with the ease and grace of a well-conditioned athlete. He wore a coat and trousers; he had dark hair and, Ames saw now as he approached, a neatly trimmed dark mustache. He carried a sword.

"Don't recognize me, do you?" he said, planting himself before Ames and smiling in a nasty way.

But now at last, with a sickening drop of his stomach, Ames did recognize him, dyed hair and all, and he felt his heart hammer at his ribs as he choked down his sudden anger. For a moment he stood frozen in place, staring at this man—this apparition, as he seemed to be.

"Remember?" said the man, grinning at him. "We have some unfinished business, you and me. What d'you say we tend to it now?" He had removed his coat as he spoke, and now he swirled his blade through the air before he pointed its tip at Ames's heart.

Ames's mouth was dry, his mind reeling with red fury. He heard a roaring in his ears, and from somewhere far away, a voice. This man's voice, in fact, but not from far away. From right there before him—the man he had seen in his mind's eye a thousand times, the man he had last seen in the flesh standing in the dock to receive his sentence.

Ten years for fraud. But really, it should have been the hangman's noose for murder twice over.

"I'll refresh your memory, Mr. Ames," the intruder said, the tip of his sword not an inch from Ames's chest. "You knew me as Chester Snell. I guess that name'll do as good as any, for now. D'you remember me yet?"

Do not give him the satisfaction of a reply, Ames thought. But as he made as if to step sideways, Snell was quicker than he, and now the sword's point was at his throat.

"Not so quick, Mr. Ames. I think I fancy a match with you. What d'you say? Just between the two of us?" Snell's voice was heavy with menace, but still he smiled.

The metal touched Ames's neck, its sharp point pressing against his flesh. Suddenly, he stepped back, whipping his own blade up to strike.

"Ah!" Snell leapt back and fell into the classic sideways stance, knees bent, one foot pointed forward, the other at a right angle, left arm curved and raised behind him for balance, hand dangling free to show he carried no other, hidden weapon.

They began. Before Ames had fully realized what had happened, Snell was on the attack with a fierce *balestra*—a quick jump forward in two or three steps that forced Ames to parry before he was quite ready. Then came a hard *coule,* the blades sliding along each other with a harsh scraping sound.

They broke, returned to lunge and parry, Ames's riposte, Snell's counterriposte.

Then: en garde and reprise, and they began again. Their blades clashed, scraped, came apart, and then Snell, very agile, swiftly lunged and struck again. Just in time, Ames parried, avoiding the lethal thrust, and made his riposte.

"Surprised I can handle a sword, Mr. Ames?" Snell growled. "I'm a carny—did you know that? Sure you did. Carnies have many skills."

A lunge, a parry, the scrape of metal on metal as Ames deflected the attack. Snell was good, Ames realized—quick on his feet and with a strong arm and a deadly accurate thrust.

"Oh, yes, Mr. High-and-Mighty Ames. I haven't forgotten you, not in all the years I sat in that stinking cell. I had plenty of time to think while I was there. And what I thought about—a lot—was you."

Lunge and parry again. *Beat beat beat* went the blades as they pounded and clanged against each other. Ames heard his heart as well, pounding in his ears, echoing the beat of the blades, the patter and thud of their feet on the wooden floor.

Ah! A close call, but he'd moved in time.

"You were right when you said I swindled your old man," Snell said.

Amazing, Ames thought, how Snell could speak and duel simultaneously. He moved with the grace of an acrobat, and he didn't seem winded at all—not yet.

"Sure I swindled him," Snell added. "Why shouldn't I? He was a prize mark. I took him as easy as you please, and he never knew what hit him. He died not long after I went up, I heard." Snell's teeth glistened beneath his mustache. "Poor old sod. My deepest sympathies to you—and your sister."

Lunge and parry, riposte and counterriposte. For a moment

their blades locked, and then with a harsh grating sound slid apart once more.

"They let me out six months early for good conduct, can you believe it?" Snell snarled with a grimace that might have been a laugh. "Very kind of 'em, wasn't it?"

They were circling now, each alert for the chance to strike.

"And I had a piece of good luck, too. I found that bitch who crossed me. Right here in Boston, she was. So I sent for old Jonesey, and I told him, go to one of her little gatherings and kill someone. Anyone. Didn't matter who. Could have been your sister. Ever think about that? Could've been her, easy. An' I showed him how to do it, press on the neck, press hard, it's all over in a minute. Why? Because she left me, took our girl, took all my money—oh, yes, I had a bit of business with her. An' I knew if word got out that the famous medium Evangeline Sidgwick—now, there's a fancy made-up name for you, isn't it?—had people turning up dead after her séances, she would see her business drop off sharp, for sure. People wouldn't go to her if they were afraid they'd die, now, would they? So I paid poor old Jones, taught him how to do it, and it worked. Of course, then I had to get rid of him, too, didn't I? Couldn't have him telling the police what he knew. And he would've. No more backbone than a worm, old Jones."

Lunge and parry— Ah! A near miss. Ames dashed away the sweat that dripped into his eyes and whipped his weapon around just in time to fend off the killing blade aimed at his heart.

"Jonathan Dwight," he panted.

"Him? Oh, yes. I took care of him, too." Snell was sweating now, too, and his eyes blazed with a fierce light.

Why is he confessing? Ames thought. Because he believes he will kill me?

"And I almost got your sister, Mr. Ames. If someone hadn't helped her out of the way, I would've."

"Where is the girl?" Ames said. He was breathing hard—too hard—but Snell didn't seem winded at all.

"The girl? You mean, my daughter? *My daughter*, Mr. Ames. That bitch whelped her, but she's mine. Yes, I have her. She's a weak little thing, but I'll train her up. She'll be a good carny when I've done with her."

"You can't get away—"

"Oh, yes, I can. I have her safe—from you, and from her mother. I could kill her, too—that jumped-up slut. She's so respectable now, isn't she? But it's worse for her if I keep the girl, and let the mother stew. Much worse, don't you think?"

"Where is she?"

But before Snell could speak again, Ames felt the hard impact of the blade, the sharp pain on his upper arm, the sudden burning as his sweat trickled into the cut. He shook his head hard and focused again. It was only a small flesh wound; it didn't count. This was a fight to the death, and they both knew it.

Snell repositioned himself, en garde. Lunge and parry. Lunge and parry. Step back, reposition, jump forward, thrust hard—*hard*— There!

Ames felt the reverberation of the blow all the way up his arm as his blade penetrated Snell's middle. A good three or four inches, it must have gone in. For a moment the two men stood frozen in place, their eyes locked. Then Ames pulled hard and saw the blood dripping from his sword's tip.

Snell seemed surprised. He staggered a bit and put his hand to his abdomen; when he took it away to look at it, Ames saw that it, too, was covered in blood. And blood was dripping onto the floor, slippery and gleaming in the gaslight. He could smell it, sharp and metallic.

With a sudden clatter, Snell threw down his sword and darted to the door. At once Ames was after him, but his foot hit blood and he slipped—fell—tried to right himself and slipped again—

Snell was gone. When Ames reached the hall, he felt the cold night air blowing in from the open front door.

The street was dark, deserted. Which way? He listened. Nothing. No dark trail of blood, no sound of a man's feet pounding on the sidewalk, no rat-tat-tat of a policeman's clacker sounding the alarm. Like the trickster he was, Snell had performed a vanishing act right there in the midst of the city.

But unless he died of his wound, he would surface again. And if he dies, Ames thought grimly as he went back inside, I will be charged with his murder. Either way, I am not shut of him yet.

Ames next.

He realized it was only luck, and not his own fair skill with the blade, that had resulted in Snell's being seriously wounded and not himself. He rolled up his slashed shirtsleeve and inspected the cut on his arm. It was about two inches long, not deep but still bleeding. MacKenzie could tend to it, and meanwhile, clumsily with one hand, he'd tie his handkerchief around it. Not surprisingly, he felt sick. He pulled on his trousers, retrieved his coat and hat.

Ames next.

The night air revived him. He walked quickly to Tremont Street to find a herdic. No need to fear that Snell stalked him now; the man had appeared, intent on mischief—or worse—and now he would undoubtedly go to ground once more and stay there until he healed. Or died.

And meanwhile, what about the girl?

CHAPTER
27

"YOU MAY HAVE A SCAR, BUT IT WON'T BE MUCH," SAID MacKenzie. He moistened a clean cloth with iodine and deftly swabbed the cut on Ames's arm. Then he began to bandage the wound.

Caroline winced, even though Ames did not. Iodine burned horribly, she knew.

It was past midnight. She and MacKenzie had returned an hour or so earlier from Mrs. Gardner's musicale, but she had not wanted to retire until she knew Addington was safely home. She'd been horrified when he appeared, disheveled and bloody—and profoundly upset, even though he'd refused at first to tell them what had happened. At last he'd relayed his misadventure with Chester Snell.

"But, Addington—for him to appear like that, in that deserted building, and to challenge you when you were all alone— you might have been killed!"

She fully realized that fact only after she'd spoken, and for a moment she felt quite faint.

"I might have been, yes," he replied. "But as you see, I was not."

"He was skilled with the blade?" MacKenzie asked.

"Yes, surprisingly so."

"But, Addington—" Caroline struggled with it. "He will come after you again! You will never be safe until he is behind bars—for good."

"No, I won't." Nor will you, dear sister, he thought but did not say. She was upset enough; he didn't need to add to her distress.

"The police?" MacKenzie ventured to ask.

"In the morning. Crippen is likely not there at this hour, and I didn't want to try to summon a patrolman. The swine had vanished in any case," he added bitterly. He remembered the eerie feeling he'd had, staring up and down the deserted street in front of Crabbe's. Not a sound, not a single footfall had he heard. If it hadn't been for the wound on his arm, he'd have thought he hallucinated the entire episode.

Yes, he'd see Crippen in the morning, and Mrs. Sidgwick, as well. Best to alert Edgeware to be there, he thought; he had no idea how the medium would receive his news, and she'd do better if her protector was with her.

Should he go to Edgeware now? Rouse him out of bed (if indeed he was in his own bed, and not in Mrs. Sidgwick's), call a conference in the middle of the night? He remembered that he'd recently acquired a telephone, but it seemed rude beyond belief to try to place a call to someone at this hour. And besides, it was difficult enough, during the day, to try to speak to someone you couldn't see; to try to do so after midnight (were there operators on duty after midnight?) seemed even more improbable.

Wincing a bit, he stood up. "Thank you, Doctor," he said, nodding at his friend.

MacKenzie's broad, honest face relaxed into a smile as he rose also. "A good night's sleep should see you in fine health in the morning," he said. "I wouldn't move that arm more than necessary. And if you should need me in the night, I can be with you at once."

"Addington . . ." breathed Caroline. She seized his hand and pressed it to her cheek. This surprised him; they were not, ordinarily, openly affectionate with each other. "Promise me that you will keep Dr. MacKenzie with you from now on. I mean, until they find this man—"

"At least now we know he remained in the city," Ames replied. "Badly wounded as he is, I doubt he will try to leave."

"Badly wounded—might he seek treatment?" MacKenzie wondered.

"He might, yes." Ames met MacKenzie's eyes and saw his own thought reflected there. "So we should contact the police, after all. They should inquire at the hospitals—now, tonight."

"I will try to reach them," MacKenzie said. But when he'd cranked up the telephone and waited for an operator to come on, he waited in vain. The telephone operators, it seemed, had gone off duty.

So he fetched his hat from the hall tree, bade good night to the Ameses, and set off to deliver his message to the police in person.

THE NEXT MORNING, MACKENZIE WAS AT POLICE HEAD-quarters again, this time with Ames for a meeting with Crippen. After Ames described to the inspector his encounter with Chester Snell, Crippen peered at him suspiciously. "You mean to tell me, Mr. Ames, that this fellow just happened to be there?

Came out of nowhere, and you never heard him? How'd he get in?"

"I imagine he's been a cracksman off and on."

"Hmmpf." Crippen stared at Ames with narrowed eyes. "Cut you, did he?"

"A bit, yes."

"And you say you cut him worse?"

"Yes. He was bleeding badly when he ran out."

"But you didn't see which way he went?"

"No. But at least we know he is still in the city."

"We know he was in the city last night," Crippen corrected him. "But by now—particularly since he's shown himself—he may have decided it's time to move on."

"He may have, yes. But with a bad wound? He may wait to make his escape until he recovers, at least somewhat. Your men had no luck at the hospitals?"

There were two, Boston City and Massachusetts General, and a number of private clinics.

"No." Crippen shuffled through the papers on his desk, found one, pulled it out. "Inquiries made—ah—two A.M., three A.M., following information provided by—ah—" He threw a venomous glance at MacKenzie, then struck a match to his half-dead cigar. "You're going to see the girl's mother?" he asked Ames, blowing a cloud of foul-smelling smoke.

"Mrs. Sidgwick? Yes."

Crippen squinted at him. "Perhaps she'll have another one of them séance things, eh? See if she can—ah—contact the girl? Be helpful if she could."

"If she contacts the girl, it probably means the girl is dead. Don't tell me you have become a believer."

"Not likely." Crippen grimaced. "But at this point—"

"I understand. And if she has any success at all, you will be the first to know of it. Good day to you, Inspector."

A SHORT TIME LATER, AMES SAW THAT MRS. SIDGWICK was in no condition to hold a séance. She sat near the window in her upstairs sitting room, fanning herself now and then with a handsome ivory fan. The day was unseasonably warm, no cooling breeze coming off the river, and so except for those moments when she felt strong enough to wield the fan, she looked as if she might faint from the heat. She wore a loose pale-gray tea gown, and her face very nearly matched it.

Ames was telling her about his encounter with Chester Snell. "I assure you, he spoke of your daughter as if she was alive. I think you need have no fear on that point."

"But nothing as to her whereabouts, eh?" Edgeware put in.

"No," Ames conceded, "nothing about that."

"The police—" the medium began, but then her voice broke and she began to sob.

"The police have been fully informed," Ames said as reassuringly as he could. He never knew whether Mrs. Sidgwick annoyed him or aroused his pity.

"They'd better get a move on," Edgeware put in. "It's an absolute disgrace, the girl gone for four days—no, five—and they haven't found her. I have doubled the reward. Perhaps simple human greed will bring results, if nothing else does."

"I think we would be well advised—" Ames began, but he broke off at the sound of a bell, very loud.

"*Oh!*" cried Mrs. Sidgwick. "Harold! The telephone! You don't suppose—"

At once Edgeware was out the door and running down the stairs to the front hall. He answered on the fourth ring. They could hear him shouting.

"Yes? Yes, it is I! Louisa? Is that you? Where are you, child? Tell me where you are! We will come for you at once, but we cannot— Louisa! Louisa, can you hear me? What? What? No— don't say that! Don't! Where are you? *Damn!*"

During this exchange, the three others had hurried out to the upper hall. Mrs. Sidgwick leaned against the railing as she stared down at Edgeware; her face had gone from pale gray to deathly white, and MacKenzie, fearing she might collapse, put out a hand to catch her if she did.

As Edgeware cursed at the telephone and slammed the receiver back onto its cradle, Ames called down: "That was the girl?"

Edgeware's grim, set face peered up at them. "Yes."

The medium uttered a low moan, and again MacKenzie moved to support her. But she moved away from him and started down the stairs. "Where was she?"

"She didn't say. Or couldn't," Edgeware replied.

"What did she say?" Mrs. Sidgwick demanded. Ames was interested to see that far from fainting, she seemed suddenly quite strong.

As she reached the bottom of the stairs, Edgeware stepped to her and took her hands in his own. "She said she called to say good-bye."

Stronger and stronger, Ames thought as Mrs. Sidgwick straightened her shoulders and lifted her chin.

"That brute," she said; and her voice, too, was suddenly steely and forceful. "He wants to see me suffer. That is his only purpose in allowing her—or forcing her—to communicate with me. So now we know he is still alive," she added bitterly. "If he were not, she would have come home at once."

Ames wondered if that was so. Did Snell, along with his other talents, have some power of mind control, so that he could somehow have turned the girl against her mother? So that even if he died she would refuse to return?

But no. That was too cruel a thought. Edgeware was right: That call from heaven knew where had been made by the girl under duress, and so they must believe that Snell lived on.

"I wonder—" he began, thinking out loud.

"What, Ames?" Edgeware demanded. "I confess, I am at a loss to know what to do. What's your notion?"

"My notion is that perhaps—perhaps—it might be possible to learn where the call came from," Ames said slowly, still thinking it over. "The telephone company has a central office, where the calls come in and are sent out again. And perhaps they could tell us whose telephone was used to make that call, and where it is."

Was that possible? Even as he voiced the thought, he doubted it. Finding the origin of a telephone call seemed as chancy as making contact with a spirit during a séance. Still, it seemed the only course of action.

"Good man!" Edgeware exclaimed. He let go of the medium's hands and turned her toward the stairs. "Put on your street clothes, my dear. And we will go to—ah—where, Ames? The telephone office?"

"Yes. Down in Court Street. And meanwhile, I will place a call here myself."

While he waited for this transaction to occur, he closed his eyes and leaned against the foyer wall. His arm hurt a bit, not much; with his free hand he reached for his handkerchief to mop his damp brow. Why was he here instead of resting in the cool, shaded back garden at Louisburg Square?

The vicious, grinning face of the man who called himself Chester Snell floated up into his mind's eye.

That face was why he was here. That face, which now would haunt him until he found it again.

Stay alive, Snell, he thought. As he listened to the clicks and whines coming along the wires into his ear, he gritted his teeth and whispered a curse—and a promise.

Stay alive, so that at last I may avenge my father's death.

THE MANAGER OF THE BOSTON OFFICE OF THE BELL Telephone Company was a small, balding man with a nervous tic, brought on, no doubt, by the heavy responsibilities of overseeing the workings of this fantastic innovation that was transforming people's lives. When Ames introduced himself, his eyes narrowed and he twitched more noticeably.

"Ames? You are—ah—connected to Miss Euphemia Ames?"

"Yes."

Goodrich swallowed hard. "A most—ah—charming lady."

Ames repressed a smile. "Yes, she is charming, isn't she? And she has assured me, Mr. Goodrich, that the telephone company provides excellent service. I have taken the liberty of asking the police to be present as well, so that— Ah."

The door opened and Elwood Crippen came in.

"The police!" Goodrich exclaimed. "But what—"

Crippen nodded to the men and stared openly at Mrs. Sidgwick, not troubling to hide his curiosity.

"Now, then, Mr. Ames," he said with the slightly irritated air of a man who has been called away from more important business. "You said you had a message from the girl?"

"Yes. A telephone call, in fact. And we have come to see whether Mr.—ah—Goodrich's operators can help us discover where that call came from. I mean, what number. Is that possible?" he added to the manager.

"Well, I—yes. Yes, it is."

"Good. Then if you would be so kind as to inquire which of

them might have taken that call this morning? They keep some kind of record?"

"Yes, they keep very accurate records. It is all in their books."

"And, if possible, we want to know the name of the subscriber."

"I would need to know the number called."

Ames turned to Mrs. Sidgwick. "Your telephone number?"

"Six seven four."

Goodrich gave a last alarmed glance around at them. "Six seven four," he repeated in a low voice, as if to himself. "All right—yes—if you would come with me."

The telephone company's operators worked in a large, high-ceilinged room brightly illuminated with electric lights. Perhaps twenty women wearing heavy metal contraptions on their heads (like monstrous earmuffs, MacKenzie thought) sat at individual stations unlike anything he had ever seen: tall boards with many wires plugged into them. Every few seconds, a bell sounded and one of the women seized a wire, unplugged it, replugged it into a new place, and then spoke into a mouthpiece attached to her headgear. The ringing bells and the constant low hum of female voices produced a noise that was profoundly annoying.

"Now," Goodrich muttered, surveying his employees. "Which one? Ah." He approached a young woman who sat halfway down the aisle, and they followed.

"Miss Robertson! I need you to tell me—no, just let me see your book, if you please."

The operator, startled, handed over a ledger filled with numbers. A bell was ringing on her call board, and she glanced at it apprehensively. Apparently, Ames thought, she could not deal with it—could not receive the request from someone to be connected to someone else—unless she could make a notation in her ledger.

Serena Vincent had told him she suspected that some of the operators listened in to calls. Would this young woman be willing to admit to that? He didn't think so.

"Now," Goodrich was saying as he ran his finger down the columns of numbers, "six seven four. Six seven four. Yes, here it is. A call placed at ten twenty-seven this morning."

"And it came from?" Ames asked.

"From three three five."

"And I assume you have a record of a name to go with that number?"

"Yes, of course. Thank you, Miss Robertson. If you all would just come back to my office—"

As he gave back the ledger to the operator, Ames saw her seize it as if it were some kind of prize, and he wondered if the women were paid according to how many calls they dealt with per hour. As he reached the door, he turned back to look at the room with its constantly ringing bells, its twin rows of women speaking into their contraptions, their hands flying as they plugged and unplugged the wires. They hardly looked human, he thought; they looked like machines themselves.

He'd heard that at first the telephone company had employed men as operators, but here in Boston the women had pushed their way in, insisting they could do the work as well as men and probably better. So now the position all over the country was thought of as one for females, and men wanted nothing to do with it. From the telephone company's point of view, the women had two advantages, at least: They were undoubtedly paid less than men for doing the same work, and they probably refrained from cursing into customers' ears as the men did when something went wrong.

Goodrich, back in his office, was thumbing through a file. As they waited, Crippen muttered to Ames, "The lady looks poorly."

Ames glanced at Mrs. Sidgwick. Edgeware was supporting her, gripping her elbow as he eased her onto a wooden chair. She was pressing her gloved hand to her mouth as if she stifled a sob.

"Courage, my dear," Edgeware murmured, bending to her. "In only a moment now, we will learn—"

"A Mrs. Williams," Goodrich said, looking up from his file.

"Address?" snapped Crippen.

"Four forty-three Columbus Avenue."

Mrs. Sidgwick uttered a small cry. "We must go there at once!" she exclaimed. But as she rose, she swayed as if she would faint, and Edgeware put his arm around her, heedless of the proprieties, and held her close to keep her from collapsing.

"Let Mr. Ames go, my dear," he said. He looked up at Ames. "You will do that—with the police?" he added, glancing at Crippen.

Crippen was already partway out the door. "Come on, then, Mr. Ames," he called over his shoulder. "I have my men outside. Let's find this fellow!"

CHAPTER
2 8

COLUMBUS AVENUE WAS A LONG, TREELESS EXPANSE LINED
with twin rows of redbrick swell-front houses, each with its tall
flight of granite steps like slanted ladders to the front doors, each
with its minuscule patch of greenery at the front behind a miniature iron fence. This district, part of the South End, had been intended to be as handsome—and expensive, and exclusive—as
the Back Bay. But it had rapidly fallen out of fashion, and its
present population was a largely transient one that lived in build-
ings originally meant to house single families, now cut up into
apartments or single rooms for rent by the week.

Ames was aware that the police wagon in which he and
MacKenzie traveled here with Crippen had attracted attention,
and he felt oddly conspicuous as passersby turned to stare.
Crippen, on the other hand, seemed not to notice. His ugly little
face was set in hard lines, in a kind of righteous anger. Ames,
glancing at him, thought: He sees himself as the power of the
state, making sure that justice is done. Crippen's attitude was

often offputting, but just now, when they were hastening to rescue Louisa Sidgwick, Ames felt the same anger himself toward
her captor.

Despicable man! Confidence man, carnival shill, swindler—
murderer. Yes, he could taste the triumph he would feel when at
last Crippen would put the fellow in irons once more—and keep
him there.

At number four forty-three they alighted and ran up the
steps. A cardboard sign in the bow window announced ROOMS
TO LET. Crippen pulled the bellpull, and after a moment the
door was opened by a middle-aged woman with a suspicious air
that turned to alarm as she saw the police wagon behind them in
the street.

Crippen produced his identification. "We're looking for a
certain man—and a girl with him," he announced, pushing his
way in so the woman needed to step back smartly to avoid being
knocked over.

"Who?" the woman demanded. "What's he done? I run a
proper house here, no trouble."

"Snell," Crippen snapped. He paused in the dimly lighted
front hall, not troubling to remove his bowler. "Which room?"

"Snell?" she replied dubiously. "I got no Snell here, Mister."

And why would we expect him to use that name? Ames
wondered, removing his own hat from long habit. "Slight
build," he offered. "Dark hair, mustache."

"Oh," the landlady said, her face clearing. "You mean Mr.
White."

"And a girl with him?"

"He said she was his daughter," the woman said. "Now, I
can't do no check on people who come here, and I have to make
up my mind on the spot if they're tellin' me the truth. But she
looked like him, an' so I figured it was all right. You can't get me
on disorderly house charges," she added, suddenly defiant of

Crippen's authority. "I run a decent place here, I never had no trouble—"

"Which room?" Crippen demanded, impatient.

"Top floor. Four oh six. But they've gone!" she called after them as they bounded up the stairs. "They cleared out not an hour ago!"

The room was at the top of the house at the back. It was a small, poorly furnished chamber with two single beds, a battered chiffonier, a small armoire, and a washstand with basin and ewer.

The water in the basin was bloodred. Ames stared at it, remembering Snell's grunt of pain as the blade went in. On the floor were several handkerchiefs and what looked like strips of torn sheeting. All of them were soaked with blood, some dark and stiff, hours old, others looking as if Snell had bled onto them only moments before.

But he'd left an hour ago, the landlady had said. Obviously she had not yet come to clean the room. The bedclothes were tumbled, the armoire door hanging wide, bureau drawers half open.

But nothing, except for those bloody cloths, to show who had lived here. Not a scrap of paper, not a stray shirt-stud, a buttonhook or a hair comb.

Crippen sniffed around like a small tracking dog.

"We've come up empty-handed, Mr. Ames," he said after a moment. He bent to peer under the beds. "Remarkably neat, they are, for folks on the run."

Ames grunted in assent even as he struggled with his disappointment. Once again Snell had outwitted them, had gone on the run—where? And what about the girl? Was she safe? Terrified? Conscious, even?

He stared at the nearer bed. Its sheets had dark stains: Snell's bed, then. He went to it, felt underneath the mattress. Nothing. He tried the other. Nothing there, either.

Crippen had been scrabbling in the armoire. After a moment he emerged holding a length of rope. "Looks as if he tied her up, don't it?"

Ames took it, examined it. It was perhaps three feet long, the ends hacked as if someone had cut it with a knife not properly sharpened.

"Yes," he said shortly, handing it back. Crippen folded it and stuffed it in his jacket pocket.

The landlady was waiting for them where they'd left her, in the front hall.

"Did Mr.—ah—White have any visitors?" Ames asked her.

"Just the one."

"And who was that?"

She stared at him, still defiant. "I don't know his name."

"Describe him."

"Tall, running to fat. Drunk, too."

"And what passed between them?"

She bridled at that. "I don't know!"

I'd wager you do, MacKenzie thought. This place depressed him, all the more because it was the kind of place he feared he'd have had to live in if he hadn't found the Ameses.

"When did he come?" Crippen asked.

"Two nights ago."

"And you heard nothing of what they said?"

She stared at him, sullen anger in her eyes. "They were shouting."

"So you did hear them?"

"I heard them shouting. I couldn't make out what they said."

"Not even a word or two?"

Her mouth worked. She seemed torn between the desire to gossip and the wish to remain, in their eyes, the respectable landlady who would not stoop to pry in her lodgers' affairs.

"It was just two words."

"Well?"

"Mary Lee."

Mary Lee. The name meant nothing to Ames, nor to Crippen, either, by the look of him.

"And you don't know who this Mary Lee is?" Crippen asked.

The landlady shrugged. "No."

A contact, Ames thought. A fellow carny? An old friend, ready to help in this emergency? A man like Chester Snell would have many friends, or many people afraid of him, perhaps, ready to spring to his aid, if only to get him safely out of town with no harm to themselves.

Mary Lee.

They could try the city directory, although relatively few women were listed there. Lee was an old, respected Boston name, nearly as old and respected as Ames. Surely none of the Lee family—some of whom he'd known all his life—could be in league with a man like Chester Snell?

Crippen was questioning the landlady further. "He made at least one telephone call, this morning about ten-thirty. Did you hear what he said?"

"It wasn't— No." Her mouth snapped shut into a sharp, angry line.

"Nothing? Nor what the girl said, either? We have information that she spoke, as well. Is that what you were going to tell me?"

The landlady drew herself up with a self-righteous air. "I told you, I don't eavesdrop. Or, leastways, not on folks who pay their way."

"And he did?" Ames asked.

"In advance."

"Anything extra for you?"

She stared at him. "No."

Yes, he thought, but he did not pursue it.

"He make any other calls?" Crippen asked.

"One, yes."

"At the same time?"

"Yes."

"And you didn't hear that, either?"

"No."

"We can trace that one, as well," Ames murmured at Crippen's ear.

"Right." The little policeman nodded, satisfied. "If you should hear from him," he added to the landlady, "I want to know about it at once."

She did not reply, but stared at them, hostile, as they went out to the waiting police wagon. The horses stood patiently in the warm spring sunshine, flicking their tails against the occasional fly; the driver, a red-faced young man in uniform, tensed as he saw Crippen approach.

"I'll be off, then," Crippen said before he climbed in. "What is it, Mr. Ames? You look like you've had an idea."

"I was just wondering, Inspector, where does a wounded animal go to die?"

"To his lair, I imagine."

"Yes. But where is that?"

"You think you got him so bad he's dying?"

"From the looks of the blood up in that room—yes. He must be in considerable pain, at least. Infection setting in, perhaps—yes, I have to believe that he is in rough shape. Your men haven't yet turned up anything at the hospitals, I assume?"

Crippen frowned, reluctant to admit it. "No."

"And, wounded as he is, he must deal with that girl, keep her confined, tied up." In his own world—the small, tidy world of Boston Society—men treated women with great delicacy, with punctilious manners and devoted deference. So he had been reared to do; so all his friends and acquaintances did. To manhandle a female, rough her up, tie her up—such behavior was anathema.

"Offer you a ride downtown, Mr. Ames?" Crippen asked, ignoring MacKenzie as usual.

"What? No—no thank you, Inspector. We'll walk a bit. You'll send a man to the telephone office about that second call?"

"Yes."

Ames watched the wagon as it set off, conscious that from behind the dingy curtains of the boardinghouse, the landlady was watching, too. She might well know something more than she'd revealed, but for the moment, he would not speak to her again. He had just remembered that they were in the neighborhood of someone who might be of more help. He couldn't recall the exact number of her place, but it was nearby, he knew. "Come on, Doctor," he said.

In a few moments they came to it: a tall, redbrick, bow-front building like all the others, with a small, discreet sign in the window announcing CLINIC HOURS. This was not one of those hours, but perhaps she'd be in all the same: Dr. Hannah Bigelow, a friend of Caroline's, who had opened this clinic to serve the poor.

"What do you say, Doctor?" he asked with a sidelong look at his companion. "Shall we visit Caroline's lady doctor friend?" MacKenzie, he knew, did not approve of lady doctors. "You haven't met her," he added unnecessarily. "You may find her quite charming."

MacKenzie winced. For some reason he didn't understand, he was in the wrong to disapprove of Dr. Hannah. He knew that Boston—and indeed all New England—was the home not only of conservative thought, but also some of the wildest radicalism and freethinking. The abolition struggle had started here, not to mention the Revolution itself.

Still. Abolition was one thing, lady doctors quite another. It offended his notion of the right and proper natural order of things that a woman should presume to take a medical degree. When he'd first heard of Dr. Hannah, he'd been unable to conceal his disapproval of her, and he'd had the sense that Caroline—and perhaps her brother, too—was laughing at him. For his provincialism, his old-fashioned ideas of woman's proper place? Well, he couldn't help his provincialism, and as for his old-fashioned ideas, they were the ideas he'd had all his life; it was too late to change them now.

"Certainly," he said in answer to Ames's question. As they mounted the steps, he felt as if he were being put to some kind of test. He hoped he wouldn't flunk it.

The waiting room was empty save for the secretary. When Ames spoke to her, she stared at him, every bit as suspicious as the landlady they had just left. "I'll see," she said.

Ames looked around while they waited. He knew Dr. Hannah hadn't come from the wealthiest of families, but still. She could have married well enough, had a comfortable life for herself. What had compelled her to give that up for this dreary, depressing suite of rooms where she spent her life ministering to the poor? The place smelled of garlic and unwashed bodies, overlaid by a faint medicinal odor. The walls were painted gray; the linoleum floor was bare, badly scuffed and worn. He was not a particularly charitable man, but now he thought he might donate a few bright posters, simply to liven up the place a little.

He caught MacKenzie's eye and shrugged. "You have to give the woman her due," he murmured.

Reluctantly, MacKenzie supposed he did.

Dr. Hannah received them in her small office, which was as

spare and drab as the waiting room. She rose when they entered (just as a man would have, MacKenzie thought) and shook hands with a firm grip that belied her delicate, even fragile appearance. She was a small, slight woman with gray hair pulled into a knot at her neck. Her fine-featured face was lined with fatigue, and it was only when one met her luminous gray eyes that one sensed her strength, her joy in fulfilling her mission.

"How pleasant to see you again, Mr. Ames," she said. "And Dr. MacKenzie, is it? I am glad to meet you at last. How is your knee?"

Over the winter, he had discovered to his consternation that his knee had become the topic of considerable gossip in Boston. But it had been some weeks since anyone had asked him about it, and so now he felt himself flush a little as he replied, "Fully healed, thank you."

She seemed to be smiling at him, savoring some secret joke at his expense. And yet she was hardly the Amazonian female he'd expected; with her modest gray dress overlaid by a white bib apron, her thoroughly unexceptional looks, she might have been anyone's maiden aunt instead of a female who brazenly trespassed into the jealously guarded male territory of medical knowledge. Women, MacKenzie believed, should not know the secret things about the human body that were taught in medical school. More, he believed that any woman who did know those things would, unavoidably, reveal that she had such knowledge by behaving in an unwomanly, domineering way, permanently unsexed. This woman was very different.

"How can I help you, Mr. Ames?" Dr. Hannah asked in a low, gentle voice as she resumed her seat behind her desk and motioned them to take the two Windsor chairs before it.

Ames settled his hat on his knees and studied her for a moment before he spoke. "It is a rather delicate matter," he began.

She inclined her head. "I understand. Your sister is well, I hope?"

"Quite well, thank you."

Dr. Hannah's lips twitched a little. "She has been so unfortunate as to have her name in the newspapers."

"Yes."

"It is an uncertain business, trying to contact the spirits of the dead."

"Very."

"Did she succeed?"

"Regrettably, no. And by being at that particular séance, she became—quite innocently—involved in a case that has turned out to be rather more complicated even than the death of Theophilus Clay."

In a few words, he told Dr. Hannah about Jones, about Louisa Sidgwick, about his midnight encounter at Crabbe's with Chester Snell.

Dr. Hannah's wide, luminous eyes widened farther. "This man, who you believe is a murderer, has now kidnapped his own daughter? But why would he do that?"

"For revenge. I don't know whether he was ever properly married to the mother—I think he was not, in fact—but in any case, he has a considerable grudge against her. I thought, wounded as he is, he might have come to you."

She frowned. "My patients' visits are confidential, Mr. Ames."

"But this is a criminal case—"

"Yes." She hesitated, sorting it out. Then: "He did not have the girl with him, so I can tell you nothing about her."

"So you have seen him?"

"Yes."

"But where was the girl?" MacKenzie wondered aloud.

"He may have an accomplice," Ames said. "Possibly that

Mary Lee we just learned about. When was he here, Dr. Hannah?"

"Two hours ago, perhaps."

"And his wound?"

"Bad. It was you who stabbed him?"

"In self-defense, I assure you."

"You fought with knives?" She only just managed to conceal her astonishment.

"Swords. He somehow managed to break into Crabbe's last night when I was there alone. Or thought I was," he added grimly. "I do not exaggerate when I tell you he had me in fear for my life. If he could have killed me, he would have. What did you do for him?"

"Not much. I cleaned the wound with hydrogen peroxide, dressed it, gave him opium for his pain, and warned him to get to a hospital."

"Infection?"

"Beginning, yes. I told him to soak in a hot tub to draw it out, but he seemed in too much of a hurry for that."

"Hmmm. Yes, I imagine he was. And besides, since he is on the run, I doubt he has a tub to soak in."

AT NO. 16½, WILLIAM JAMES HAD COME TO TEA, AND NOW he sat with them in the parlor as the afternoon darkened toward twilight. The lavender-glass bow windows were open, the familiar sounds and smells of the city wafting in on the breeze.

They had found neither Chester Snell nor Evangeline Sidgwick's daughter. The railway stations were being heavily patrolled, every livery stable in the city had been put on the alert with a full description of the pair, the telegraph had clattered busily between the major eastern cities, a hundred more posters had gone up.

The second telephone number that Snell had called, duly recorded at the offices of the telephone company, had led to a dead end: an elderly widow on Fairfield Street, alarmed and confused at the appearance of a tall, intense gentleman on her doorstep, demanding to know if she knew a man named Snell. When she denied it, he'd asked her butler if her telephone had rung that morning. Yes, the man said, but the caller asked for a man unknown to his mistress.

The telephone manager had explained to Ames that when a number went unused for a year, the company assigned it to someone else. This eminently respectable woman, all unsuspecting, had been the new assignee.

Half an hour ago, Harold Edgeware had come to No. 16½ to announce that he had doubled his reward—again. Ames, angry and frustrated, urged him to ask Mrs. Sidgwick to hold another séance.

"How can I do that?" Edgeware had protested. "She is nearly prostrate with worry."

Ames turned to the professor. "Sir? What do you think? You are a physician, you know Mrs. Sidgwick, you have worked with her these many years. Could she withstand the rigors of a séance tonight?"

A frown creased James's high, broad forehead. He set down his cup and saucer, cast a smile at Caroline as his frown eased, and after a moment's thought said, "I don't know."

"There you are," said Edgeware. "If even Professor James says he doesn't know—"

They heard the jangling of the telephone bell. It didn't seem so odd anymore, Ames thought. Was that good or bad?

They heard Margaret hurrying to answer, shouting as she dealt with the caller. After a moment she parted the pocket doors and looked in. "For you, Mr. Ames."

Ames shouted, too; he couldn't help it. Caroline and the others could tell, from hearing his side of the conversation, who had called: Evangeline Sidgwick.

"She wants to hold a séance," he announced as he came back into the room.

Chapter

29

AN HOUR LATER, THEY WERE GATHERED ONCE MORE around the medium's table. The room was dark and much too warm, and silent save for the sound of Evangeline Sidgwick's heavy, labored breathing. MacKenzie thought she sounded as if she were enduring some draining physical trial, and perhaps she was. But surely if William James thought she was not strong enough to endure this séance, he would advise her not to go through with it?

The medium sat between James and Edgeware. Next to James was Delahanty, then MacKenzie, then Caroline, then Ames completing the circle with Edgeware.

Suddenly Edgeware spoke, startlingly loud. "Roland?" he barked. "Are you there?"

No answer. Mrs. Sidgwick went on breathing in that heavy, labored way, so that MacKenzie thought her lungs must hurt her. Caroline's hand was gripping his tightly, and he could almost feel the intensity of her concentration.

Come on, Roland, thought Ames. And then he thought: Have I become a believer?

No. Even in this last desperate attempt to save Mrs. Sidgwick's child—an attempt he himself had urged—he could not believe. Despite William James's faith in her powers, despite the fact that so many people had made contact with their loved ones, or believed they had, he still did not—could not—believe that either Evangeline Sidgwick or her "control" could speak to the dead.

Still. Come on, Roland, he thought. Let us get this over with. He felt a trickle of perspiration run down his neck inside his starched collar, and he longed for a breath of cool air.

The medium gave a low moan, and he tensed. Was Roland about to speak?

"Roland!" Edgeware said again. "Can you hear us?"

No answer.

"Roland?"

Silence. But then, as if from very far away, came the eerie voice that was Evangeline Sidgwick's control: *"I am here."*

"Roland, we must speak to—him."

"Who?"

"You know. The man who has taken the child."

"Gone."

"He is gone? You mean, he has passed over?"

"Gonegonegonegone."

"Tell us where—where is *she?*"

Silence.

"Roland!" said William James sharply. "We have no time to lose! Where is the girl?"

Ames was appalled at what came next: a low laugh. Was Mrs. Sidgwick's control mocking them? Could a spirit control have a sense of humor, and a macabre sense of humor at that?

"Stop it!" cried Edgeware. "You are too cruel, Roland! Mrs.

Sidgwick has worked with you all these years, and now, when she so desperately needs your help, how can you laugh at her?"

"Not me," came the voice.

"What do you mean?"

"Not me. Him."

"Him? You mean—"

"In the water."

In the water. What did that mean? Ames wondered.

But Caroline didn't wonder. Sitting there in the dark, she could *see*: the ghastly white hand, the dark-clad body moving, undulating beneath the surface of the lagoon.

"It is Mr. Jones!" she said.

Ames heard someone's startled exclamation and realized that it was his own.

"Ask him," he muttered, to whom he was not sure.

"Is that Mr. Jones?" James asked then.

"Yesssss."

"And do you know who killed you?"

"Yesssss. He used me to take his revengerevengerevenge." The voice was whispery, sinister, filled with nearly palpable malevolence. *"Revenge,"* it said. *"He must have . . . revenge."*

Despite himself, Ames shivered. Snell had committed who knew how many murders before he'd come to Boston, he had undoubtedly killed Jonathan Dwight, had swindled Ames's father and caused his untimely death, had arranged for Jones to kill Theophilus Clay, had killed Jones himself, had kidnapped his own daughter. Who, then, was entitled to revenge? Not Snell, surely, but all the people he had harmed.

"Roland?" said Edgeware. "Are you there?"

"Yes."

"Well, make Mr. Jones speak to you! Make him tell us where to find Louisa!"

Silence. Then: *"He says he doesn't know."*

"Roland, you must! The child never harmed anyone, it is not her fault that her mother—"

"*Wait.*"

They waited. Ames felt slightly nauseated.

Then Roland spoke again: "*She is a bad woman, he says.*"

They heard the medium's sharp intake of breath, and then a low murmur from Edgeware as he tried to calm her, prevent her, perhaps, from voicing some insult in return.

I do *not* believe this, Ames thought. He wanted very much to let go Caroline's hand, and Edgeware's, and leave the room. But of course he could not do that; not now, when perhaps—perhaps—they might yet receive some hint of the girl's whereabouts.

"It does not matter if she is a bad woman," Edgeware said in what Ames thought was a remarkably level voice. "What matters, Roland, is that we find Louisa."

"Come on, Roland," said William James impatiently. "We need to know where the girl is. If her father has come over to you, it serves no purpose to—"

"*Water deep,*" said the voice.

"What?" James asked sharply.

"*Water deep.*"

"We don't understand you, Roland."

"*In the water deepdeepdeep.*"

The water in the Public Garden lagoon is not deep, Ames thought. Did this spirit—entity—whatever it was—refer to some different water?

"Mrs. Sidgwick is in trance," James said, "so I cannot speak to her directly, to ask her if she knows what you mean. You must be more precise."

Silence. Seconds dragged by with no further word from the spirit-control.

Then, startling them again: "*Six o'clock!*"

"What?" cried James. "Say that again!"

"Six o'clocksix o'clocksix o'clock."

"Roland! Give us more! We cannot possibly—"

"Mary."

Mary.

Ames felt a cold shudder run down his spine. Mary!

"Ask him if he means Mary Lee," he muttered to Edgeware.

Which Edgeware promptly did, but there was no answer. So after a moment, not able to contain his impatience, Ames blurted out, "Who is Mary? Is she Mary Lee?"

Silence.

He'd never felt so frustrated in his life. If he'd dared, he'd have lifted his edge of the table and tipped it over. That was what some mediums—fraudulent ones—were supposed to do. Well, this would be a genuine table-tilting, he thought grimly.

Then he tensed—tensed even more—as he heard a new sound. At first he thought it was some kind of weird lullaby, but after a heart-wrenching moment, he realized what it was.

"LouLouLouLou . . ."

"Oh, my God!" cried Edgeware. "Roland, what are you saying?"

And again came that eerie, otherworldly crooning—just the one syllable, and yet Caroline thought she'd never forget it. Softer and softer it came, fading until they could hear it no more:

"LouLouLouLou . . ."

"Roland!" called William James.

But there was no reply.

"Roland!" It was Edgeware's voice now, pleading. "Do not go! Please! Stay!"

They heard a sound like the rushing of the wind, and yet it could not be that, Ames thought, not in this small, confined, airless room. The rushing of the wind—the departure of a soul, perhaps? Swept up to the beyond on the wings of angels? But surely the soul of the man who had called himself Jones would not be taken by angels. Which did not, in any case, exist. He was sure they did not. Such things were the trappings of medieval superstition; they belonged to an earlier, more gullible age.

And now they heard Mrs. Sidgwick moan, and they sensed, even in the dark, that she was trembling, shuddering. From the release of tension? Ames wondered. From exhaustion?

Or from fear, perhaps. Perhaps, even still in trance, even coming out of trance, she understood that she had not succeeded, that her daughter's whereabouts were still unknown, and that the girl might even be—as Snell probably was—dead.

There was a commotion across the table where the medium sat, and then suddenly someone—Delahanty, Ames realized—left the circle to turn up the gas.

Mrs. Sidgwick had fainted. Edgeware was supporting her to keep her from sliding off her chair, gently patting her face with his free hand, and Delahanty was at the sideboard, pouring her a glass of water.

Her eyes fluttered, and she moaned again. Obediently she sipped from the glass that Edgeware held to her lips, and then she sat up straight and looked around. She seemed dazed, as if she did not know where she was.

"What—happened?" she said to William James.

"Not much," he replied tersely.

"He didn't—did Roland make contact?"

"Yes, but we didn't get much from him. He said something about someone named Mary. And water, and the hour of six o'clock. Does any of that mean anything to you?"

She blinked, obviously still not fully returned to them. "No."

"She must retire," Edgeware said. "Perhaps we can confer in the morning, but for now—"

"What else?" the medium said, as if she realized they hadn't told her everything.

Edgeware threw a warning glance at William James, who turned aside and said to the others, sotto voce, "Should we tell her?"

"I think we must," Ames murmured. "Lou" meant "Louisa," he understood, but whether the message was from her or about her was impossible to know.

James turned to Mrs. Sidgwick. "He said something—just a syllable, mind you—about 'Lou.' "

"But—that must have meant Louisa!" she said. Her hand clutched Edgeware's, and above the lace collar of her dress they could see the throbbing pulse in her neck.

Crippen's famous artery, Ames thought: the vulnerable place where swiftly, silently, one could be murdered.

"My child—my baby!" cried Mrs. Sidgwick. She had half risen, but now she fell back, sobbing. "And he didn't tell us if she has passed over! Oh, dear heaven, let it not be so! We must find her!"

"Hush, now," Edgeware said, encircling her shoulders with his free arm. "We will tend to it in the morning, I promise you. But for now—"

"Tell me again," she said to William James. "Mary, did you say? But I don't know any Mary. And a number?"

"Six o'clock, yes. Does that mean anything to you?"

She stared at him as if in his face she would learn the answer to his question. Then, in a voice flat with despair, she said, "No. Nothing at all."

AMES AND DELAHANTY WAITED AT CHARLES STREET TO see William James onto the electric cars for Cambridge. The professor was unwontedly subdued, obviously worried about his "white crow."

"It must have been hard for her to hold a sitting to learn the fate of her own child," he said. "And whether that emotional distress had some influence on what she was able to receive—I don't know."

They heard the bell in the Church of the Advent toll the half hour. A high white moon sailed over the black rooftops of Beacon Hill, and a cooling breeze blew up from the river. Ames ran his finger around the inside of his damp collar, longing to take it off. His arm was aching. He wanted to get home, to sit in his study and think.

The brightly lighted electric omnibus was approaching, rounding the corner at Beacon Street. It stopped and James bade them good night before he boarded. "Contact me tomorrow," he said. "My wife can send for me at once if I am at my laboratory."

Ames and Delahanty stood for a moment, watching as the omnibus pulled away. Caroline and MacKenzie had gone on earlier, while the others had stayed to confer with Harold Edgeware. Would they, also, be too restless to retire?

"Let us see if Caroline will give us something to drink," Ames said as they crossed Charles Street and started up the steep slope of Mt. Vernon.

"I don't want to intrude—" Delahanty began.

"If you'd be intruding, I wouldn't mention it," Ames said, and Delahanty heard the smile in his voice.

Louisburg Square was quiet, the lamplight gleaming on the trees, and at No. 16½ he saw a glimmer through the cracks in the shutters. Caroline was probably up, then. Good.

She and MacKenzie sat in the parlor, each with a small snifter of brandy. She looked rather tense, Ames thought, but she relaxed a little as he and Delahanty entered, and smiled to see them.

"Addington—Mr. Delahanty—I am so glad you've come. Dr. MacKenzie and I were just trying to make sense of what happened this evening. But we can't," she added as her smile faded.

"Yes, well, we weren't given much to go on," Ames said. "Will you drink, Desmond?"

"Thanks." The Irishman nodded and settled himself opposite Caroline. "So what do you think, Miss Ames?" he asked her. "Can we make any sense at all from what we heard?"

"I don't see how. And yet— Oh, it is so dreadful to think of that poor child alone with him!"

"Even worse, if she's with him and he's dead," Ames said, handing a snifter to Delahanty and sipping from his own.

"Much worse," MacKenzie said. "And if he has her bound—"

"Don't," Caroline said with a shudder. "I cannot bear to think of it."

The telephone rang. The harsh sound of the bell tore like a knife through the silent night. Caroline started badly, and MacKenzie nearly dropped his glass. Steady, he thought; this night is not over yet.

Ames went to answer. They heard him say "Yes?" and then, after a moment, he shouted, "What?"

Then: "You will notify Crippen? No, I think it best you stay there. How is she?" He thought he heard sobbing in the background, but the whines and whistles in the connection made it hard to tell.

When he came back to them, his face was set in grim lines, and Caroline noted that his hands were clenched. When he spoke, however, his voice was calm.

"That was Harold Edgeware," he said. "He has had another nibble at his reward."

"Someone with new information?" Delahanty asked.

"Yes. Let us hope this time it is accurate." He met MacKenzie's eyes. "Doctor, will you fetch your weapon?"

"Of course." MacKenzie rose at once and left the room.

"What is it, Addington? Where are you going?" Caroline's

heart had begun to beat very fast, and she was glad she was not standing because, even sitting, she felt suddenly light-headed.

Ames glanced at Delahanty, whose thin, ascetic face was pale against the red of his mustache. "Will you come, Desmond? We must get to the waterfront without delay. And even now we may be too late. Your friend Sweeney may be of help to us."

"Yes, of course I will come. But what is it? What did Edgeware tell you?"

"It was about the mysterious Mary Lee."

Caroline was near to bursting with curiosity. Oh, it was *not* fair that the men got to do all the most interesting things! And now they were going to leave, to meet heaven knew what danger—and excitement—and once again she was to be left out of it.

"Mary Lee?" she said. "Who is that, Addington? I know that Elizabeth Lee had a daughter a few years ago, but they named her Harriet, I believe."

He quirked an eyebrow. "This Mary Lee is not anyone's daughter, Caro."

"Oh, stop it!" she cried. "What *do* you mean?"

"I mean, my dear, that the *Mary Lee* is a sloop. Edgeware's informant said she was seen in Boston Harbor. We must get to her at once, before Snell escapes, for even though the informant did not say he was aboard, I am sure he is, and he is no doubt planning to depart as soon as he can. Perhaps that is what 'six o'clock' meant, as we heard just now at Mrs. Sidgwick's. I hope it meant tomorrow morning, and not tonight. Ah—Doctor, there you are. We are off, then. No, Caroline, I do not know when we will return."

And with that, they were gone, and she was left once again to worry and wait.

CHAPTER
3 0

AT THE GREEN HARP SALOON, THE ROOM FELL SILENT AS the regulars took stock of the two aliens and the one dubiously authentic Irishman who had just come in.

Wasting no time on pleasantries, Delahanty greeted Sweeney and told him what was needed: a man familiar with the harbor, who would be able to find, in the dozens of crafts anchored there, the *Mary Lee*. It was a matter of some urgency, Delahanty said, possibly even life and death.

Sweeney accepted it without question and surveyed the crowd. Then, although Ames did not see it, he must have given some signal, because a man detached himself from a group in one corner and made his way to the bar. He said nothing, but nodded at Sweeney and flicked a suspicious glance at the three newcomers.

"Would y'be wantin' to help my friends here a bit, Liam?" Sweeney said.

"What is it, then?"

"They need a man who knows the port. They're lookin' for a particular craft which name they will tell you. I'd be much obliged if you'd go with them. Won't take long—will it, Desmond?" he added, turning his gaze to Delahanty.

"With any luck—no," Delahanty replied.

"Be off, then," Sweeney said. "And good luck to you."

Outside, Atlantic Avenue was dark and deserted. They heard the slap-slap of water on the wharves, and the mournful clangor of bell buoys, and now and then a ship's bell. As their guide led them onto a pier, they saw a ferry, brightly lighted and tooting briskly, churning across the harbor to East Boston. The waxing white moon played a gleaming swath of silver across the rippling water.

Ames told Sweeney's man what they sought. "She is a sloop, we were told, called the *Mary Lee*, with the mast quite near the bow, and not neat enough looking to be a pleasure craft. She was seen moving along the piers not far from the bottom of State Street. I think, from his account, that our informant was describing not a sloop but a working catboat."

They were out onto India Wharf now. Sweeney's man surveyed the scene for a moment, the pale moonlight dimly illuminating the hundreds of craft that thronged the harbor, all at rest now until the dawn. "I have heard of the *Mary Lee* and her strange movements," he said, "within the hour. My guess is we should be lookin' among the smaller fishing boats along Commercial Wharf. Here at India, or at T Wharf, it's the larger craft mostly."

And before they could reply, he had turned and was making his way back to Atlantic Avenue and thence to Commercial Wharf. There, they moved along out onto the pier as their guide scanned the nested boats. Although each vessel tied up or at anchor carried sidelights and pilot lights, still, despite the moon, the night was too dark to make out the names painted on the hulls. So either this man had supernatural sight, Ames thought, or he already knew the craft they were searching for.

"Not here," the man said after a moment. But instead of returning to the street, he moved along to the head of the pier and stopped, staring silently into the night.

MacKenzie, his weapon heavy in his jacket pocket, shifted his weight from one leg to the other. As always when he was tense or worried, his knee was acting up. He hoped he wouldn't have to use his gun, or, if he did, that he wouldn't have to run anywhere to do so. They had seen no sign of a night watchman on this pier; with luck, there wouldn't be one.

"There she is," their guide said quietly, pointing to a place about two hundred feet out.

Ames peered into the darkness. He saw what looked like— yes—not a sloop but a large catboat, no light, its sail furled on the lower boom.

"You're sure?" he murmured. Voices carried across water, and he didn't want Snell—if indeed Snell was on that boat—to hear him.

"I'm sure," the man said. Like most of Sweeney's customers, he was grim and hard-faced, no nonsense about him. "But the harbormaster will hear of her and have her moved by morning."

MacKenzie saw what looked to him, a landlubber, like a boat adrift, but obviously that was not the case.

"She'll move out on her own long before morning," Ames muttered. "Is there a dinghy?" he added, moving to the edge of the pier to look.

Apparently not—and no guarantee of one at other piers, either.

All right, Ames thought, since time was of the essence, there was no help for it. He'd have to swim.

"See if you can find one and row it out," he said to their guide.

And, to MacKenzie, "Here, Doctor," as he removed his hat, his jacket, and vest, and handed them over along with his shoes, his cravat, his collar. He wasn't wearing longjohns, so he needed to keep his trousers, but these he rolled up to his knees. Then he was in the water, a freezing, numbing shock, as cold as he imagined Arctic water to be. The only way to survive it was to swim furiously.

He plowed through the water with strong, swift strokes. In moments he had reached the catboat, the name *Mary Lee* painted on the starboard bow. He drifted along her length—about twenty-five feet—to the stern. A careless skipper had left the rudder shipped, in place—or else was preparing to sail. Ames reached up and found a handhold, and at the same time rested one foot on top of the rudder. Then, in one quick movement, he was up and over the side, dripping wet and tumbling into the stern sheets.

He stood very still in the capacious cockpit, listening. Not a sound, no indication that anyone had heard him.

He reminded himself that corpses couldn't hear. When he began to look, what would he find?

Although the night wind cut through his soaking garments, making him colder than he'd been in the water, he hesitated a moment longer. Did his enemy—his prey—await him here?

Nothing. A bell clanged softly somewhere over the water. The boat creaked a little as she rocked in the wash of the East Boston ferry coming back.

Cautiously he moved forward toward the cabin door. He grasped the door handle, turned it, and pushed the door open. He heard its hinges squeak, and then, at last, he heard what he'd hoped for: a voice—a female voice, but muffled. He was sure she was not only tied but gagged. Still, she was here—and alive.

In the dim, wavering moonlight reflected from the water, he saw bunk beds on either side of the cabin. They were empty.

He heard the voice again.

There was a small door set in the forward bulkhead—locked. With the jack knife he'd brought, he prized it open.

It gave onto the sail locker—and a dark form, writhing at his feet, trying to cry out. She was tightly bound hand and foot, and he saw the whites of her eyes as she cast an imploring glance at him, not knowing, it was clear, whether he was friend or foe, rescuer or another man come to harm her.

"Miss Sidgwick!" he exclaimed softly. He was at her side now, and trying to untie the knot of the coarse cloth that gagged her. When he couldn't, he sawed at the gag with his knife until it came free.

"I am a friend," he said quickly to allay her fears. "And I must know—can you tell me where he is?"

He was cutting the ropes that bound her hands now, trying not to injure her.

She was sobbing, gasping, rubbing her aching jaw while he worked at the ropes that bound her knees and feet, trying not to damage her silk skirts. She'd been coming out of dancing class, he remembered, when she'd been abducted.

"Oh, please! Take me home!" she gasped, rather loudly, he thought, if Snell was still aboard. But he wasn't—or, if he was, he was dead, else by now he'd have made himself known.

"I will," he said. He knelt before her as she sat on the bunk and gripped her arms above the elbows. "I have someone coming with a dinghy, and you will be home before you know it. But I must know—can you tell me where your—where the man who took you has gone?"

She shook her head. "No. He was wounded."

"I know. It was I who wounded him."

"You did?" She stared at him openmouthed. In the moonlight shining through the small porthole, he could see the raw skin at the corners of her mouth where the gag had chafed her. Poor child, he thought.

"Yes. But I will tell you of that later, if you wish. For now, I need to know where he has gone. You have no idea?"

He heard a bump against the hull. He hoped it was Sweeney's man with a dinghy, and not Snell come back for one final encounter. Even wounded as he was, Chester Snell was a deadly, dangerous trickster.

Then he reminded himself that since he was asking Snell's whereabouts, he was looking for that encounter, after all— wanted it, in fact. Wanted to see, once and for all, his enemy dead.

"Miss Sidgwick?"

She seemed to be fainting. He couldn't allow her to do that—not until she'd told him what she knew.

She opened her eyes. Then, as if she hadn't heard what he'd asked, she pulled herself free of his grasp and held up her arm so that a shaft of moonlight fell on it.

"He did this," she whispered.

He looked. On the pale skin of her upper right arm, just above the elbow and marked in dark ink, was a cross-in-a-circle tattoo.

CHAPTER
31

CAREFULLY, AS GENTLY AS HE COULD, AMES HELPED HER into the dinghy while Sweeney's man steadied it against the wash of the ferry. She had stopped crying, but as Ames gripped her arms he felt her fine, steady trembling, as if she were suffering a fever.

She was stiff and awkward from her captivity, but otherwise, he thought, she was unharmed—physically, at least. She sat quietly, hugging herself and shivering in the chill night wind as Sweeney's man rowed them back to the wharf. Ames, too, was freezing in his soaking clothes, but it would be a while, he thought, before he'd get into dry ones.

Several men had joined Delahanty and MacKenzie awaiting them as they bumped against the pilings, and ready hands reached to help them up. Crippen's face peered down at Ames.

"Mr. Ames! Got her safe?"

"Yes."

"And Snell?"

"Gone."

Ames hauled himself up after the girl. "Edgeware notified you?"

"Yes. You were already out in the harbor when we arrived." Crippen waved a finger. "You shouldn't act on your own, Mr. Ames. What if he'd been there waiting for you?"

Ames shrugged. "I'd have dealt with him. Don't forget, Inspector, he's badly wounded."

"Hmmph." Crippen turned to one of his men. "You'll see the young lady to her home, Connors." And to Louisa, "You all right, Miss?"

She nodded.

"Any idea where he's got to?"

"No."

"Then give Connors your address, and we'll have you home in no time. I'll want to talk to you tomorrow."

As the girl disappeared down the wharf, Crippen muttered to Ames, "Flew the coop again, did he?"

"She gave me a name, Inspector. Frary."

"Aha. And who might that be?"

"He is the ringmaster at Barnum's circus."

"Is he, indeed? Well now, that's an interesting thing, because we traced that call made to Mr. Edgeware, and it came from the Barnum office. It was someone there who called Edgeware to give him this tip about the girl being on the boat. A temporary line, the telephone company said, but a solid trace—that's where the call came from, all right."

Ames's thoughts raced. "I spoke to Frary a few days ago, and he said he hadn't been in touch with Snell. But of course in the interim, he must have been, since Miss Sidgwick heard his name mentioned."

"And when he heard about the reward," Crippen said, "he snitched on Snell to get it. Nice folks we're dealing with here," he added with heavy sarcasm. "Honor among thieves and all that. Well, let's go. My men are there now, and with any luck they'll have this character Snell dead to rights."

"You think he went to Frary?" Ames asked.

"Where else? That's our best bet, Mr. Ames, and I can't stand here all night talking about it. You coming?"

Ames felt MacKenzie's touch on his arm, saw Delahanty's white, concerned face.

"You need to get into dry clothing," MacKenzie said.

"Yes, Doctor, I do. But even more, I want to find Snell. So the dry clothing will have to wait, I'm afraid. Will you come, both of you?"

"Wouldn't miss it," Delahanty declared.

Crippen looked none too happy at that, but he made no objection. His carriage, emblazoned with the words BOSTON PO-LICE, awaited them in the street, and in moments the driver had whipped up the horses and they were whirling through the deserted harbor district.

"There's something else," Crippen said as he put out a hand to steady himself against the door. "We had another tip tonight."

"Oh? From whom?" Ames asked.

"From a young lady as works at the telephone office, if you can believe it. Said she had information about the missing girl. It was the same information Mr. Edgeware got from your friend Frary, if it was Frary who called him from the circus."

"What? How did she—"

"She listened in to the call, y'see. You want to make sure you don't say anything on the telephone you don't want the world to know, Mr. Ames. No privacy there, and I'm damned if I won't have her in. She demanded the reward! Bold as brass, she was. No ladies down at the telephone office, that's for sure. I have a mind to arrest her."

"For what, Inspector?" Delahanty asked.

"Oh, I'll find something. Invasion of privacy—how's that?"

"Never heard of it," Delahanty replied, "but it sounds reasonable."

At the circus, the evening's performance was just reaching its climax, the band playing a rousing tune. As the four men went in, they saw a heavy show of police, and at once a plainclothesman came up to Crippen.

"Got him?" Crippen demanded.

"Not yet, sir. But we've surrounded the tent—"

They needed to speak loudly over the music.

"The office!" Crippen barked. "That's where the call came from, man!"

"Yes, sir. But I have to tell you—"

"What?" Crippen shouted. "What is it?"

"The ringmaster, sir. He's dead."

"God Almighty." Crippen's ugly little face seemed to contract into a mask of pinched, visceral anger. "And you have the man who did it?"

"Snell," said Ames. "Had to be."

"Right." Crippen rounded on his man. "And you say you let him slip?"

The detective looked ill. "We missed him, yes, sir. The office is out back. I saw him running away into the tent, but I didn't follow him because I was told to go to the office, and I didn't know I'd find the ringmaster dead, did I? I didn't see any blood, but he's dead, all right—and by the time I gave orders, the man running out had disappeared. We surrounded the tent when we came in, and nobody's left, so I wager he's still here."

"Still here." Crippen hesitated, glowering, his thoughts visibly churning through his brain. Then he barked a series of orders—men at every entrance if they weren't there already, men inside around the rings, try not to start a panic.

"I'm going to see what's what back there," he said to Ames, meaning in the office.

During this exchange, the performance had continued. In one of the two smaller rings, trick riders galloped in circles on the sawdusty earth; in the other, clowns cavorted with a zebra and several monkeys. In the big center ring, six tigers, magnificent orange-and-black-and-white beasts, were jumping through hoops on command, their handler cracking his whip with theatrical gestures. High overhead, several aerial artistes swung back and forth on their trapezes.

A ringmaster was in the center ring, but he wasn't Frary.

After Crippen left, Ames swept the crowded grandstands with his keen gaze, searching for his quarry. He saw a sea of faces glowing in the light from the flaring torches that illuminated the performers in the rings.

Was Snell's face among them?

Where are you, Snell? Show yourself, coward that you are, so that once and for all I can settle the business between us.

One of the tigers roared, slinking off its perch. Its handler yelled, made threatening gestures. At last, with exquisite grace, the big cat consented to resume its place on the little flat-topped wooden pyramid and with a yawn, settled itself while two others performed.

MacKenzie shook his head. A dangerous business, handling such wild beasts. Because no matter how well trained they were, you always knew that their wildness hadn't left them completely; it would be lurking inside them, waiting for a chance to break through.

He looked around. The big tent smelled of animals and sawdust and many human bodies packed tightly together. The musicians played energetically, very loud. The show was being well received, the crowd cheering and applauding. Clearly, the presence of all these police had not yet alarmed the audience; perhaps they thought it was routine to have so many police about.

Crippen was back. "Killed in the same way." He touched his throat. "Pressure to the carotid artery."

Snell must be badly weakened by now, Ames thought, and yet he still had strength enough to kill a man with his bare hands. Why had he done that?

Knowing that he was too wounded, too weak to make his escape by water, had he gone to Frary again for help, only to learn that the ringmaster had betrayed him?

"He won't get away," Crippen said grimly. "I thought of canceling the performance, but Barnum's men wouldn't have it, and in any case, I didn't want to cause a panic. People get trampled in a panic. Happened not too long ago in Worcester. So we're going to wait him out. He'll show himself soon enough. He's hiding up there, I wager—one face in the crowd, thinks we won't spot him."

The little police inspector peered up at the grandstands. "Bastard," he muttered. "Think you'll outwit me, do you?"

Ames started. "Look!" he exclaimed. He pointed to a spot high on the stands. A man was pushing his way along, trying to get out.

"It's Snell!" Ames cried, and at once he leapt onto the stands, bounding up the narrow opening between the seated spectators.

Snell saw him. Instead of trying to go down, he turned and ran up. When he reached the top riser, which was half empty, he ran along it, knocking people aside.

Ames was close on his heels, followed by Crippen and half a dozen police. MacKenzie and Delahanty stood where they were, peering into the half-dark upper regions of the grandstands. A shadowy figure darting along—yes, it was Snell, MacKenzie thought, and if Ames and Crippen weren't quick, he'd get away again.

As the crowd realized what was happening, a hush spread

CYNTHIA PEALE

over the huge tent. The musicians paused in mid-phrase, the conductor looking to see what was wrong. The trick riders and the clowns, after a moment of trying to keep on, stopped in place while the tigers' handler ordered his beasts back to their pyramids. He kept them still by virtue of his authority over them, MacKenzie thought—and the power of his whip. Instead, he should continue with his act in order to prevent a panic.

But people had lost interest in the tigers, the clowns and acrobats. They sat still, deathly quiet, as if they waited for some terrible thing to occur as they turned from the circus entertainment below to watch the more compelling performance on the highest tier of the seats—a man running, another man chasing him, and then, well behind, the police panting to catch up. In the silence, the air suddenly crackled with a tension that had nothing to do with the thrills presented by Barnum's circus, and MacKenzie heard Delahanty whisper, because a normal voice would have been too loud, "He can never escape now."

Oh, yes, he can, MacKenzie thought. Carnival trickster, charlatan, confidence man—Chester Snell was like a nightmare phantom, disappearing and reappearing at will, always just out of reach. Of course he can escape; he always has.

Snell had reached the place where the aerialists' rope ladder hung down along the side of the tent. Without hesitating, he scrambled up it.

Dear God, MacKenzie thought. Would Ames try to follow him?

But he didn't. He reached the ladder a moment too late, and now he stood in the gloom of the highest grandstand seats, watching along with everyone else as Snell rapidly mounted to the little platform from which the rope-dancers swung off.

MacKenzie saw one of the police aim his weapon, saw Crippen motion him to desist.

A trapeze swung close to the platform, its aerialist unable to halt it. Snell caught it—caught her, held the trapeze as he jumped on beside her. She wore pink tights; MacKenzie thought she was the girl they'd seen before, the one who had made that appalling leap into her catcher's grasp.

Snell pushed off, holding the trapeze with one hand and the girl with the other. She was his captive, MacKenzie thought—just as Louisa Sidgwick had been. They swung high above the center ring in a great swooping arc.

They are going to fall, he thought. He felt sick. Snell is going to lose his balance, and he will take her with him, and they will both come hurtling down to their death. He looked away, down to his worn boot-toes planted on the sawdust-covered ground. Dear God, he thought. Let it not happen.

Another aerialist, a man, had run up the ladder that Snell had climbed, and now he stood ready to grasp the trapeze as it came near. But it didn't come near enough, and he couldn't reach it.

The girl in pink tights seemed terrified, as well she might. They could see that she was trying to pull away from Snell while managing not to fall off the swing. Back and forth, back and forth—

"Jesus, Mary, and Joseph," Delahanty muttered. "D'you think he'll jump?"

"Let us hope not," MacKenzie replied. He swallowed hard, trying to quiet his queasy stomach.

Just then they heard someone calling to Ames. Amazingly, it was Chester Snell.

"Congratulations, Mr. Ames! You found me! But you haven't won yet!"

No, Ames thought, I haven't. Nor will I—not until you are cold in your grave.

Back and forth, back and forth— But not sure and steady like the rope-dancers, but wobbling and off course.

And now they saw that one of the other rope-dancers, perhaps the one who had partnered the girl the other day, had leapt onto a trapeze from the opposite platform and was swinging toward her and Snell.

But it is too late, MacKenzie thought. Snell would never let her go. Even if she could work up the necessary speed, even if she could manage to force an arc as wide as the one necessary to fling herself across the void, Snell would never allow her to do it. If he fell, he would take her with him.

They were struggling.

Ames's heart was in his throat as he watched the appalling spectacle high overhead. He glanced at MacKenzie far below. The doctor was standing with his head down, one hand over his mouth, the other braced against a wooden upright. Ames himself didn't feel sick at all. Rather, he felt a strange, horrid exultation. The man on the trapeze was the man who had killed his father, and he wanted to see him dead. Longed to see it— needed, for the sake of his own soul, to see it.

One of the tigers snarled and leapt off its perch, pouncing like a monstrous cat—on what? What had it seen? Or smelled?

The trainer yelled, cracked his whip. The tiger growled at him, but it slunk back into position.

Ames's gaze riveted on Snell. *Back* and forth, *back* and forth—the man was mad, obviously, to think he could escape now.

The catcher on the opposite swing was flat out, coming as near to Snell's trapeze as he could. The girl was making an effort both to control her swing and to free herself from Snell's grip. Would she try the leap, after all?

Someone in the crowd cried out: "Jump!"

Snell shouted. Impossible to make out what.

The girl screamed.

In the next arc, the two swings would be, so to speak, at perihelion—as close as they could be.

Now.

Instantly, seizing her chance, the girl wrenched her arm away from Snell's grasp and catapulted off the trapeze into the hands of her partner.

A triumphant cry went up from the crowd as he caught her, held her fast—she was safe.

The swing holding Snell soared back in a graceful arc, and then forward again.

In the next moment, Snell jumped.

The crowd gasped—a woman screamed—a man shouted—as Snell hurtled down.

He fell into the center ring, where the tigers were.

And now at last their thin veneer of circus training vanished completely. Maddened by the odor of Snell's bloody wound, they ignored the frantic cries of their trainer, the lash of his whip, and they roared and snarled as they leapt, lightning-fast, to attack Snell's prostrate body.

Neither MacKenzie nor Delahanty could watch what happened next, but Ames, with grim satisfaction, could—and did.

CHAPTER
32

HE'D CAUGHT A BAD COLD, AND CAROLINE PRAYED THAT was the end of it, prayed it wouldn't turn into pneumonia.

It was the next evening: a warm May twilight, the filmy white curtains billowing in the breeze, the lavender-tinted lights in the square just coming on as the lamplighter made his rounds—"l'heure bleu," her favorite time.

She'd given him and the doctor their tea, and now she sat back in her chair, exhausted—none of them had slept last night—and regarded her brother with a censorious eye. She knew she should simply be glad he was alive, and yet—

Well. She knew also he thought she sometimes ventured too far astray from the social code that governed their lives. Now, she thought, she could say the same of him: a sober, sensible Boston man, and what had he done? Quite aside from his involvement with Serena Vincent (which, Caroline hoped, was at an end, although she'd had no evidence that it was), his behavior last night had been far from sober and sensible. It had been, in fact, wildly irresponsible.

Jumping into Boston Harbor!

Swimming out to a boat that might have hidden his mortal enemy!

And then, soaked to the skin, pursuing Snell to the circus!

She sighed, shook her head, and caught Dr. MacKenzie's eye.

"More tea, Doctor?"

"Thank you." He rose to give her his cup. She would worry herself into a sickbed, he thought, if she didn't stop fretting about her brother.

He longed to end her worry, longed to care for her—for the rest of their lives, he hoped—but he didn't know how to begin. She was the loveliest, the sweetest, the kindest, most perfect woman in the world, and he adored her. But how could he find the courage to tell her that? And even if he did, why should she care? He wasn't much of a catch, he thought: a retired army man living on a tiny pension—what kind of prospect was that for a woman like Caroline Ames?

"He will be all right, you know," he said, not troubling to lower his voice. He didn't mind if Ames heard. He should hear—should realize what he'd put his sister through this past week.

Of course, in fairness one had to admit that she'd started it all with her surreptitious visit to Mrs. Sidgwick's, but still.

Ames sneezed.

"More tea, Addington?" she asked.

"No, thank you."

"How are you feeling?"

"I am feeling, Caroline, as if I have a cold. Which I do." He heard the irritation in his voice, and he paused to remove it. It was not her fault he'd caught cold, even if one could make the argument that if she hadn't disobeyed him in the first place by going to Mrs. Sidgwick's—

But then he might never have known in time that Chester Snell had been released from prison, and what might have been the consequences of that not-knowing?

They hadn't told her, or not exactly, what had happened to Snell in the end. Ames could see it now in his mind's eye—could not have rid himself of it if he'd wanted to: the tigers leaping to their bloody feast, their trainer screaming at them, lashing them with his whip but to no avail because all their ancient animal instincts had been aroused, and they were not to be deflected by a mere human with a whip. They would probably have gone after him, too, if Barnum's men hadn't come with their rifles and shot them.

But not before they'd eaten most of Snell. What little was left of him had been scraped into a canvas bag; Ames didn't know what had happened to it. Crippen would deal with it, he thought.

The newspapers lay on a low table. Of course the city's journalists had had a field day with the story. And of course Barnum's publicity men had tried to tone it down; it was hardly a good advertisement for them, after all, and in fact quite a few ladies and one or two children had been taken from the tent in a faint. Well, that wasn't surprising. He'd felt a little faint himself, and MacKenzie had been a virtual wreck.

They heard the door knocker, and then Margaret going to answer. Please let it not be Inspector Crippen, Caroline thought.

In a moment more, the pocket doors slid open and Margaret brought in the card tray and presented it to Ames.

"Excellent!" he said. "Send him in."

In the moment after that, William James appeared. He was his usual cheery self, Caroline was glad to see; it would have been awful if somehow, she didn't know how, he held Addington responsible for Snell's death. Did Professor James know the family's history with Snell? She hoped not.

Greetings dispensed with, he declined tea and settled himself in a tapestry chair. "I have just called on Mrs. Sidgwick," he said, "and having read today's papers, I couldn't pass up the chance to call on you as well. How are you?" he added, turning his intense blue gaze onto Ames.

"I'll do. A little head cold, nothing more."

"Hmmm. Well, the fellow met a terrible end, no doubt about it, but providence works its mysterious ways, and who are we to question it?" He turned to Caroline. "Almost more fantastic than one of Miss Strangeways' plots, wasn't it, Miss Ames?"

She smiled at him. When she'd first met him, she'd been intimidated by the fact that he was a world-famous scholar, a Harvard professor who might not want to talk to an ordinary person—and a female person, at that—like herself.

But he'd turned out to be quite different from what she'd feared, and his fondness for her favorite author had given him a permanent place in her affections, not to mention a handy retort to her brother whenever he denigrated the fabulous, the quite extraordinary Diana Strangeways.

"Perhaps you should write to her and tell her about it," she replied to James. "And if she used it, she could be forever in your debt."

He laughed. "I think she is quite capable of inventing her plots on her own, without my help," he said, but he said it kindly so it wasn't a reprimand. "I am just making the observation that life, from time to time, is so very strange, and sometimes even stranger than fiction. Even her fiction."

"Never more than when we deal with your white crow," Ames observed. "How did you find her?"

"Surprisingly tranquil, considering."

"And did you see her daughter?" asked MacKenzie. Like Caroline, he'd felt awkward with William James at first, but having gotten to know him a bit, having seen how little pretense James affected, he'd come to like him and, more, to feel comfortable addressing him.

"I did, yes. She has some superficial wounds, but nothing that won't heal soon."

"Superficial—on her body," said Ames. "But what about her mind? You, of all people, Professor, should be able to venture some kind of prognosis for the effect of her father's misdeeds on the poor girl's mental state."

James thought about it. "Hard to say," he ventured at last. "She is young—that is in her favor—but then again, she is her mother's daughter, and who knows what sensitivities she might have inherited? I mean, sensitivities that would make her more vulnerable to such an ordeal than an ordinary girl would be."

"Let us hope, if she did inherit, they are her mother's sensitivities and not her father's," Ames said.

"Yes. We can hope that, at least. But as for the long-term effects of the affair—I really can't say. Perhaps, this summer, I will be able to make a more detailed observation and analysis," he added. "I am making arrangements to take Mrs. Sidgwick—and her daughter, of course—to England for two months. I want Mrs. Sidgwick to meet the members of the Society for Psychical Research there—and, more important, I want them to meet her."

"You are going to show off her powers?" Ames asked.

It seemed a rather callous thing to do—to parade the woman like some exotic trophy from an expedition to an unknown land. Which, in this case, was the land of spiritualism, which Ames still did not—could not—believe in.

"They want very much to see her in action, so to speak," James replied, "and she agrees with me that the best thing would be to take her daughter away for a while. England is as good a place as any."

"Poor girl," Caroline said. "Her name was in the newspapers."

To have one's name in the newspapers, particularly in connection with a scandalous affair like this one, was a disaster not only for someone like herself, but also for any young lady hoping to make her entrance into Society. But then, she reminded herself, Louisa Sidgwick was not expecting to make her debut, or not in Boston, at any rate. Perhaps Harold Edgeware would manage to marry her off someplace else, possibly in England.

"So it was, Miss Ames. But we must hope that she will not be too badly besmirched by events that were, after all, none of her doing."

But life is so unfair, Professor, she thought but did not say. Girls are often besmirched for exactly such things.

He was asking her if they would summer at Nahant, as usual.

"Oh, yes. I always look forward to it," she replied, her thoughts effectively diverted from poor little Louisa Sidgwick. "The sea air is so healthy, and we get to see people we haven't seen all winter."

She glanced at MacKenzie. She'd invited him to accompany them, and he'd sounded as though he wanted to, but he hadn't definitely accepted. Perhaps he was shy (and he was a bit shy, she knew) about meeting some of the family members who would be there, cousins once and twice and three times removed, stray aunts and uncles, several older-generation in-laws. It was a big house, commodious enough to accommodate everyone; they always had a splendid time.

MacKenzie cleared his throat. He wanted very much not to be separated from her all summer; soon enough, he'd have to accept her invitation, possibly bringing it up on his own when he could find her by herself. He didn't think Ames would mind—hoped he wouldn't.

While Caroline chatted with the professor, Ames thought about William James taking Mrs. Sidgwick to England, and then he thought about someone else who was going away for the summer: Serena Vincent, who would be sailing the Mediterranean on Vandergrift's yacht. Who knew whom she'd meet there? Some unsuitable person, he was sure, some unsuitable *male* person who would do her no good.

He shifted uneasily in his chair, aware that while Caroline and William James were happily engaged in conversation, MacKenzie was watching him. The doctor seemed to know what he was thinking.

But I am powerless not to think it, Doctor. The vision of Mrs. Vincent surrounded—as she would be—by declassé men who wanted her favors and were willing to pay for them was a vision he was powerless to put from his mind.

Damnation!

He didn't think—he really didn't think—that he could endure a long, dull summer at Nahant. It would be, he knew, a summer like all the others he'd spent there since he was born: sea bathing, picnics, sailing, croquet, archery for the ladies, tea parties with elderly relatives wanting to know, yet again, why he'd never married.

No. Not this summer, when he'd have the vision of Serena Vincent in his mind every waking hour, and probably in his dreams as well.

Could he go to England with Professor James?

Probably, if he asked.

On the other hand, he didn't particularly want to do that, either. He'd only be a hindrance, seeing as how he was not a believer; they wouldn't want him along, throwing cold water on their party.

What, then?

He remembered that a few weeks ago, at the Somerset Club, someone had mentioned that Lawrence Eaton was going to Sicily to dig. I'll see if I can go with him, he thought. He was an experienced digger, had been on several expeditions with Harvard men, which Eaton was; Ames didn't know him well, but he seemed a reasonable enough fellow. Probably he'd be willing to let me come.

He closed his eyes. Sicily: He'd been there before, spoke passable Italian. Heat and light, and strange food for his Yankee palate. Still. It would be a busy summer, would take his mind off Serena Vincent, which was the point of the exercise.

On the other hand, he'd be in the Mediterranean, and if by chance the Vandergrift yacht happened to stop at, say, Messina . . .

He was aware that James was speaking to him.

"You have solved your mystery," he said.

"You mean, the mystery of who killed Theophilus Clay. Yes, I—we—have done that."

His unhappiness over Mrs. Vincent was somewhat assuaged by that fact. Not erased completely, but tempered a little.

But even more important, he had the satisfaction of knowing he'd avenged his father's death.

"And Mr. Jones," Caroline added. She forcibly put from her mind's eye the memory of Jones's hand protruding from the water of the lagoon. "We mustn't forget him. I will never be able to walk through the Public Garden again without seeing—what I saw."

MacKenzie uncrossed his legs. His knee felt better; perhaps he wouldn't have to see Dr. Warren after all. "You mustn't think of that, Miss Ames," he said.

And then, amazed at his own presumptuousness, he turned to William James. "There is a larger mystery that remains unsolved, however."

James nodded. "Yes, Doctor, indeed there is. You mean, the mystery of Mrs. Sidgwick's—ah—abilities."

"That's right."

James's bright blue eyes twinkled, and MacKenzie was glad to see he wasn't offended. "She is a mystery indeed, isn't she? Perhaps we will gain a little insight into her powers this summer in England, but I doubt it. What she does, she does from her own genius, and like all other forms of genius, it probably can't be rationally explained."

"But you believe it is genuine, at least some of the time," MacKenzie replied.

"I know it is—at least some of the time—yes. Proving it to the satisfaction of my brother scientists is another matter."

Caroline thought: Dear Mama. I won't try to contact you again. I think it's best that I don't. You are where you are, and I am here, and let us leave it at that.

She glanced at her brother. He looked very downcast, she thought, and why should that be, since he'd succeeded in vanquishing that awful man?

Mrs. Vincent. She felt a little surge of righteous anger at the thought of that seductress—Caroline was sure she was that, although she hated to think what that meant—and at the same time she tried to devise some way to distract his obviously gloomy thoughts.

"Well, Addington," she said brightly. "Do you believe in spiritualism, at last, after all this?"

He met her glance as if he had no idea what she was talking about.

But before he could fashion an answer, they heard the door knocker again, and then Margaret's delighted cry. At once the pocket doors flew open and there stood their young cousin Valentine Thorne, laughing at their surprise.

"Val!" Caroline exclaimed. She wouldn't have been more astonished if she'd seen a ghost.

But Val was most definitely not a ghost. She is more beautiful than ever, Caroline thought—dark hair shining, violet eyes gleaming, skin glowing with health and youth—oh, Valentine, how glad I am to see you again!

The men were getting to their feet as Val danced across the room to plant a kiss on Caroline's cheek. Caroline could hardly speak, but she managed to stammer, "But—but Euphemia said you were to arrive on Wednesday! She said she would telephone us when you came, to let us know at once. Aren't you a day early?"

"It is Wednesday, Caroline," Ames said dryly. "Hello, Valentine. How are you?"

"I'm fine!" Val exclaimed. "Never better! And bother the telephone! I wanted to see you immediately, not listen to your disembodied voices. People on the telephone never seem quite real, do they? They sound as if they are the voices of spirits speaking from the beyond. What's the matter, Caroline? You are looking at me as if I've come back from the dead!"

AUTHOR'S NOTE

IN SEPTEMBER 1910, WILLIAM JAMES DIED. HIS EXPATRI-
ate brother, Henry, at William's request, remained in Cambridge
over the winter, not only to console William's widow, but also to
be on hand in the event that William succeeded, as he had promised to try to do, in contacting them from beyond the grave.

William James spent a good part of his professional career
investigating the paranormal, particularly the question of
whether trance mediums could contact the dead. His prize ex-
hibit was a Boston housewife—and medium—Mrs. Lenore
Piper. James met her through his wife and his mother-in-law,
who had attended one of her séances. At their urging, he went
one evening to Mrs. Piper's Pinckney Street, Beacon Hill,
home—and came away astonished at what she was able to tell
him through her "control" while she was in trance.

That was in 1885. For the next twenty-five years, until his death,
James studied Mrs. Piper and tried to catch her out in a deception.
He never did. In that same year, 1885, he founded the American

branch of the British Society for Psychical Research, that very Victorian group of seekers who sought—who yearned—to make contact with those who had passed over. We can see them in our mind's eye now: earnest, bearded men and prim, corseted women sitting around the séance table in a darkened room, waiting for messages that, often enough to satisfy them, seemed to come through from the dead who, though dead, lived on in some other dimension.

Aside from her psychic powers, whatever they were, Mrs. Piper was the most ordinary of women; but those powers, of course, made her extraordinary in the extreme. When James was asked about his belief in her mediumistic abilities, he answered with the words I have given to him in this book: If you seek to prove that not all crows are black (or not all mediums are frauds), you need only one white crow, only one genuine medium.

I thought it remarkably fitting that at the same time the vogue for séances was reaching its first big peak (the second one came some years later, after the carnage of World War I), the telephone was coming into use. Of all the inventions and discoveries of the late Victorian age, the telephone, I think, must have been the most amazing. Certainly it was the one that most changed people's lives. Talking on the primitive instruments of the day must have seemed, at first, not only miraculous but so very *strange*—almost like talking to someone who had passed over and was speaking from the beyond. The voice coming at one from far, far away, perhaps even a mile or two away, fading in and out, occasionally distorted or crackling or blurred, sometimes drowned out by the whines and whistles along the line— all of it must have seemed terribly odd and weird.

As far as we know, William James, after he died, never did make contact with his wife or his brother or anyone else. Perhaps he—or they—simply never found the right connection.

—Cynthia Peale